The Scottish Boy

BY THE SAME AUTHOR

Bad Girls
Twisted Romance
Mayday
No Mercy
Semiautomagic
Grindhouse
Smoke/Ashes

The Scottish Boy

Alex de Campi

W S

First published by Unbound in 2020

This edition published by Wilton Square in 2026

Wilton Square Books
29 Wilton Square
London N1 3DW

www.wiltonsquarebooks.com

Text Design by Ellipsis, Glasgow

A CIP record for this book is available from the British Library

ISBN 978-1-80677-161-5 (paperback)
ISBN 978-1-78352-849-3 (ebook)

Printed and bound in Great Britain by CPI Group (UK) Ltd, Croydon CR0 4YY

1 3 5 7 9 8 6 4 2

MIX
Paper | Supporting responsible forestry
FSC® C013604

Our authorised representative is the EU for product safety is:
Logos Europe, 9 rue Nicolas Poussin, 17000, La Rochelle, France
contact@logoseurope.eu

Part One

Scotland and the North
SCOTLAND
Loch Ness
Aberdeen
Perth
Loch Lomond
Bannockburn
Edinburgh
Glasgow
R. Clyde
Halidon Hill
Berwick
R. Tweed
Roxburgh
The Marches
Loch Doon
Galloway
R. Esk
R. Tyne
Newcastle
Carlisle
Bishopric of Durham
Cumbria
ENGLAND
Kendal
York
Burstwick
R. Humber
R. Trent
County Palatinate of Chester
Nottingham

ONE

July 1333: Battles Without Honour and Humanity

Harry slows his horse as he reaches the marshalling field. He has pushed the little bay palfrey to her utmost, riding hard for a fortnight across the long spine of England to catch up with the King's forces. And now, at the edge of Edward's camp at Berwick, he finds he has missed the battle against the Scots by a single day. The only question that remains is whether he's missed the war.

It's a victory, at least. Harry can tell by the way cheerful men-at-arms lurch through camp well into their cups even though the sun has barely reached its midday apex. A tipsy longbowman, flushed red from the July heat, points out the knights' field to Harry and passes him a flask of something that smells like it could raise the dead.

Harry refuses. He doesn't feel like drinking. He's furious: at fate, at the summer crowds on the Great North Road, at having missed out on a chance to prove himself, again. And, much as he knows it's a craven and terrible thing to feel, he's angry at his mother for having died *then*. It was her illness that made Harry miss the marshalling of troops in Scotland. Instead of leaving with Sir Simon like a proper squire, he'd had to run home to Devon to attend to her last days. He knows it wasn't his mother's final act of protest against Harry following in his father's footsteps – training for knighthood, fighting the Scots – but it *feels* like it.

Harry knees Star, his palfrey, towards the bright pavilions of the knights' campground. He scans the sea of fluttering pennants, looking for a faded, frayed red flag with a white lion rampant, the Attwood coat of arms. Sir Simon will no doubt fill him in on what happened at Halidon Hill, and how he missed Edward of Windsor's first great victory against the Scots.

As Harry navigates his horse through the muddy field, past the canvas palaces of noblemen towards the smaller, shabbier tents of country knights at the far edge of the field, he lets his frustrations boil within him. He grew up listening to the stories of King Arthur, Gawain and the other great knights of history, while the real England writhed through a long winter of treason and infighting with Edward of Carnarvon, his French queen Isabella and her lover, Lord Mortimer. Now, finally, the country is reaching a sort of springtime, under the hand of the young Edward of Windsor, and Harry is nineteen years old, the perfect age for a squire to prove himself in battle.

Except, the battle was yesterday.

Perhaps there will be more fights against the Scots, but even to Harry's young eye, this doesn't look like an army that is getting ready to march anywhere but home to harvest.

Perhaps there will be war with France, in a few years. Its four-hundred-year-old Capet dynasty is fighting for life after Philip the Fair's three sons, sibling kings, have each died without a male heir. The French barons are discontented and mutinous, unhappy with the country cousin of Valois who has been placed on the throne. The other choice is Edward of Windsor himself, for his mother Isabella is a Capet princess, sister to kings. This has fired up a feeling in England of pride and hope, of daring glances across the Channel and a thought of *one day*. England has Gascony, sure, but once it had so much more. Once, and maybe again.

But first, King Edward has committed to restoring Balliol and the disinherited lords of Scotland to their rightful homes. On his long journey to Berwick, Harry had such daydreams about the feats of arms he would perform at Sir Simon's side: saving Baron Montagu's life. Saving the King's life. Capturing Archibald Douglas, the Guardian of Scotland. Enough for a squire to dazzle a baron, or a king. Enough to earn his knight's belt.

Harry reins up at Sir Simon's tent, at the most unfashionable edge of the field, and calls out for him as he slides off his palfrey.

There's no answer.

He looks around. One of Sir Simon's men-at-arms, Edgar, hustles over from where he's playing dice with a small group in front of another tent. Harry notices that Edgar looks shocked, but then Edgar isn't the brightest and always looks a bit stunned, so he doesn't think anything of it.

Until Edgar opens his mouth.

'*D'ye not know, Master Harry?*' Edgar says in English.

Harry swallows, his throat dry with road dust. No discussion ever ends well when it begins like that.

Edgar wipes his broad, spade-like hands down over his bony cheeks, pulling at the flesh there. '*They got 'im, they did. I'm . . . I'm sorry, lad.*' He shifts his weight from foot to foot, as he stutters out the story: Simon de Attwood has been slain on Halidon Hill. His old coat of mail was no match for a Scottish spear.

Harry nods his thanks at Edgar, ties up Star and, under the guise of loosening her girth, leans his forehead against her saddle. He loses time, leaning against the good little bay mare and listening to passing tales of valour, in noblemen's French, in commoners' English. If the camp chatter is to be believed, yesterday's battle was a massacre. A good third of the Scots' men-at-arms slain by the English longbowmen arrayed by Henry of Beaumont. Douglas is dead, along with a dozen other Scottish lords. English casualties were light, and Harry knows he shouldn't resent a drop of English blood against the tide of Scottish crimson spilt, but why Sir Simon? He hadn't even *wanted* to fight.

A terrible, crushing sense of culpability settles over Harry's shoulders. It's his fault. For urging Sir Simon to accept the King's summons, though he was old, and reluctant. For not being there to defend him. For wishing so hard and often to be out from under Sir Simon that God must have seen it as a prayer, and answered it with the terrible blind precision of the Almighty.

Now Harry stands, further north than he's ever been, by a shabby tent in a churned-up field on the Scottish borders, tears pricking at the corners of his eyes. His skin burns with shame and sorrow under its coating of dust from the road. Inside the tent, nothing has been touched. Spare swords, a change of clothes, a patched wool cloak. Sir Simon's little psalter lies open on the travelling chest to Psalm 23, his favourite. It is as if Sir Simon will walk back in at any moment, grumbling about the ache in his bones and passing off his shield to Harry.

But he won't.

He's gone.

Harry's mother is gone, too, falling to the wasting sickness just as Sir Simon was preparing to leave for Scotland. Harry feels torn in half, as if his life is nothing but a process of rushing from coffin to coffin, always a little too late to be any use. First his mother, then Sir Simon, as close to a father as Harry has ever known.

His real father, Sir Owen, is gone so long ago in the weeds of Bannockburn that his existence seems no more real than Sir Galahad's: a perfect shadow, and a set of ghostly footsteps for good young boys to follow.

And Harry stands alone in the midst of a camp seething in celebration of great victory, while he has only a pageant of ashes to share.

The first sign of trouble had been the day before they were set to leave for Scotland, when Annie's little cousin came clattering hellbent through the gates of Sir Simon's hall on the old plough-horse, crying for Harry to get back to Dartington as soon as possible, that his mother was dying.

The fields and hedgerows were lush with midsummer's rude vigour as Harry dashed down the lanes towards home. Every corner of the Devon landscape burst forth with life.

Every corner but one.

The apples bowed the gnarled branches of their trees, yet his mother could not eat. Honeysuckle lay heavy on the vine, its perfume almost stifling in the hot July air, and yet his mother could not smell. The gorse bloomed brash in the hedgerows, and the rose rambled wild down the lanes. And yet in the darkness of the solar, Joan de Lyon wasted away on her pallet, never to walk the lanes she loved again. She was a frail skeleton in summer, where she had been quick and strong through April's rains. And Harry fidgeted restlessly by her sickbed for five long days, praying to a God that had no answers for him.

He broke, finally, when his mother grabbed his hand in her trembling, birdlike fingers, looked at him with glassy blue eyes, and called him by his father's name.

'He's not here,' Harry whispered, kissing the sun-freckles that dotted the back of her hand. 'Try to rest,' he said. *He'll see you soon*, he didn't say.

And then Harry walked out into the stables to cry all his terror and loneliness and impotence into the flank of his palfrey. It was the first time he allowed himself to fall apart. To show weakness, even if it was to nobody else than a little bay mare.

Lady de Lyon, polite to the last, chose that moment to slip quietly from the bonds of this earth. *Mustn't cause a fuss.*

Harry knew his mother was no more as soon as he slunk back into the room. Her mouth and eyes were open, as if startled to finally receive welcome into the Hereafter after wandering its borders for so long. Her skin had faded to a strange yellow-grey. It was like some spirit, some fae, had stolen his mother away, taken this bright, witty, elegant ball of life, and left only sculpted tallow in her place.

It wasn't her.

And Harry didn't cry.

Her body was interred in the little Dartington churchyard next to the stone which marked only her husband's spirit, and their child rode north again, to catch up to the war.

When a man has had great wounds done to him, the urge to wound in return is an unbearable thing. Harry knew that blood and steel might not soothe the empty place in his heart, but he was sure as hell going to give it a try. Better the brash noise of battle than the quiet, pitying silences of Dartington Manor. The manor that was his now, its fate resting in Harry's shaking, too-young hands.

That, also, was why Harry spurred his horse towards the Great North Road: a reason that hid in every poor country noble's heart, if almost never on their lips. There was glory across the border in Scotland, and fortune to be won that would help his small manor survive. There was the chance of moving out from Sir Simon's shadow and becoming a knight on his own. Harry was young for it – only nineteen; they had been setting out north on his birthday, he and Sir Simon – but others had been knighted younger.

There was also the small matter of getting even against the Scottish barbarians for his father's death. Blood for blood, sorrow for sorrow.

And the manor's problems left for another day. He couldn't have missed the taut expressions of the household servants when he announced he'd be leaving straight after the funeral. Harry knew that riding off to war wasn't a form of cowardice, but it certainly felt like one.

Sir Owen de Lyon had died at Bannockburn a fortnight before Harry was born, another casualty of Scottish steel, and Harry had promised vengeance to his empty grave in Dartington Church every Easter. Lady Joan would shake her fair head and talk of Dartington Manor, of its seasons and its troubles, and of the gruesome poverty of manors with no lord to lead them. Owen had been Devon born, droll and easy and with a quiet wit (so Harry had been told). Joan was a Yorkshirewoman, sharp and practical, and though the great famine's touch on the West Country had been light, she remembered well the abandoned villages of Dartmoor, the reed-thin children, the death that reaped in midwinter what autumn's flood-rotten harvest had sowed.

But Harry could not be swayed. He *would* train to be a knight, like his father. He dreamed of coming home laden with favours from battle, bringing wealth and ease to his mother, to his manor and his name. More lands. Rich silks. Jewels and coin. Glory and honour. Lady Joan would kiss his forehead and whisper that his father had said the same thing, and then her eyes would grow distant and sad.

Harry was happy to take the gamble that knighthood offered. So was young Rabbie Ufford, just across the moor, who cheerfully announced on his eighth birthday that he was going into service with Baron Montagu, a powerful West Country lord. Rabbie's father had fallen right beside Harry's at the Scottish victory in 1314, and it seemed bitterly unfair to Harry that Rabbie, two years older than him and spoilt to boot, would be page to the great William Montagu. It seemed doubly unfair when Baron Montagu became the favourite of the young King.

Finally, Lady Joan acquiesced. There was no use fighting the delusions of youth, she said, there was only the hope that Harry would outlive them. But he went to no great landed household. Instead, Lady Joan had written to Sir Simon de Attwood, a modest but well-respected Wiltshire knight she had known in her days at court. Attwood was a man of great education and honour, but of little social cachet, and Harry at first resented the knight's small stone hall and meagre trappings on the unfashionable side of Salisbury.

But the knight had three books, which was more than Harry thought even the King might have, and he taught Harry to read from his psalter as he drilled him in the rules of chivalry and the ways of the broadsword. And when Harry half-closed his eyes, the high, lonely fields of Salisbury at the edge of Sir Simon's hall felt almost like the moors of home, too.

Once Harry was old enough to understand politics, he became profoundly grateful to be holed away in a minor hall while England writhed against itself. Edward of Carnarvon ignored Isabella, his French queen, spending his days with a chain of pretty young men: Gaveston, d'Amory, the younger Despenser. And much as the gossips chattered of the sins Edward committed with those favourites, it was not lust that undid them all in the end, but greed. The barons rose against the grasping favourites, the King sided with his lovers, and the country slid into civil war.

There were no tournaments in those years. The unpopular King was wary of encouraging too many armed nobles to assemble in one place.

He was right to worry. The furious barons rallied around Isabella, Edward's abandoned queen, and her lover Lord Mortimer, a powerful Marcher lord whose lands Edward's newest favourite had tried to steal. Isabella and Mortimer forced the King into abdication, imprisonment and death, while they ruled England in the name of Isabella's son, the young Edward of Windsor, a boy not much older than Harry himself.

England prayed for rest and a time to heal, but Mortimer proved as bad as Edward of Carnarvon's favourites, using his position to plunder lands and money from the noble families. And so, while Harry had been learning Latin and competing in the squires' sections of local tournaments, history repeated itself.

Baron Montagu and his squire Rabbie had broken into Nottingham Castle and arrested Mortimer, sending him on the road south to London and the gallows. The act made them England's heroes, and Edward of Windsor's right-hand men.

Edward took the throne in 1327. His mother, Queen Isabella, was cowed back into the shadows where she belonged. Glory returned to England, and tournaments, and chances for a young squire to make his name and fortune as Rabbie Ufford had.

And Harry, six feet tall by the time he was sixteen years old, could only writhe in his rural exile, never with the right people, never where events were happening. Sir Simon, who fought under the first Edward, would only shake his head at Harry's restlessness. 'The friendship of kings and princes is a double-edged blade,' the old country knight would sigh. 'Do you truly wish you were Baron Montagu's squire?'

Harry would not answer. It wasn't Baron Montagu and his coterie, so much, that Harry wanted to befriend. Baron Montagu was just a means to an end. It was the King.

He began to chafe under Sir Simon's tutelage, embarrassed by the man's cautious ways, ashamed to be seen next to Sir Simon's outdated suit of mail when the fashionable young knights and squires protected shins and joints with bright plate. He wanted more than anything else to prove himself in front of that golden crowd, to be accepted by them. When the summons came for the war against the Scots, Harry was sure it was finally his time. If only his mother hadn't—

—Harry blinks and shakes his head. Those thoughts are ones no good Christian could entertain. He rakes his hands through his dirty hair as he steps out of the tent's darkness into the bright midday light, and tries to figure out what to do next.

Pack up Sir Simon's things. Head back to the West Country, to manage his paltry estate. Leave Berwick and its triumphant throng as soon as possible. The bright glory here belongs to other people, not to him. Never to him.

Harry becomes aware that a voice is calling his name; has perhaps been calling him for a while. He turns, squinting into the sun. Rabbie is standing there, staring at him, as if seeing a ghost. A rough beard darkens his cheeks.

'It *is* you!' the squire booms out, striding forwards to clap Harry on the back. 'Harry! You missed out on all the fun.' Rabbie is a little shorter than Harry, with close-cropped dark curly hair, narrow, deep-set brown eyes and heavy cheekbones. He had always been an angular child, and as Rabbie grew up his sharp features hadn't filled out so much as they'd hardened.

Harry gives Rabbie a thin smile. He doesn't have much to say. 'You made it through without issue?' he manages at last.

Rabbie grins. 'Made it through? I cut down five of those bastard Scots. C'mon,' he says, slinging his arm across Harry's shoulders, 'there's dinner in the hall. I'll tell you all about it.' Harry fidgets, petty and diminished. Rabbie has a way of making him feel like a child, though Harry is only two years younger, nineteen to Rabbie's twenty-one.

Harry tags along silently as Rabbie brags about the battle on Halidon Hill, how the Scots turned tail under English arrows, how English knights cut the fleeing rebels down and sent them to Hell. He swallows down the bile that rises in his throat. This isn't valour. It doesn't sound like his daydreams, stabbing retreating knights in the back, even if they were Scottish. He can't bring himself to say that to Rabbie who, like him, has a father to avenge. He knows little of Bannockburn; maybe the Scots hadn't fought fair there. Maybe that's why they'd won.

He picks up the thread of Rabbie's story again, something about how the Scots are more like animals than people with their strange, grunting language, bare feet and long hair, and is about to comment when he realises where they're going.

It's a huge canvas tent; lords in bright, expensive clothes mill about its entrance. Above it flies the red-and-gold three lions pennant of England. Harry is in his drab travelling clothes, unwashed and dirty from the road, and Rabbie is taking him to eat in the King's hall.

Harry freezes. He is going to see the King. For the first time.

Rabbie looks up at him, concern softening the usually harsh line of his mouth. 'C'mon, Harry. You look like you're about to fall over. Come and get some food.'

And Harry doesn't want this, doesn't want Rabbie's *pity*, doesn't want to be the poor country cousin constantly in need of everyone's charity. He would wrench away but his stomach chooses that moment to let out a loud gurgle. So he allows himself to be towed into the hall and sat down on a bench with Baron Montagu's cheerful, rambunctious crew, all casually loud in the way of people used to being looked at, to being admired.

Harry doesn't see the King. For that he's thankful. He tears into the chicken, and bread and cheese, and the small beer, and mutters polite if terse responses to the condolences he gets from Montagu's crew.

He doesn't see the King until there's a hand on his shoulder.

And he looks up and it's *him*, tall and blond and in rich scarlet, with a gold circlet in his hair. King Edward is young, Rabbie's age, and slim, but the corners of his blue-grey eyes already crinkle with lines, from laughter or worry, Harry cannot guess. He has a small scar on the side of his chin, visible through the reddish hairs of his beard. While Harry knows that kings are human and of course they scar too, the small defect still surprises him. Harry realises he is staring. He stutters and blushes and mentally tries to work out the mechanics of extracting his too-large frame from the bench and bending to one knee.

The King smiles at him and pats his shoulder. 'Harry Lyon? Sir Simon's squire?' The other men around the table nod at the King, easy and familiar in his presence. 'We wanted to pass on our sympathies for your loss, for *both* your losses—'

God's teeth, Harry thinks, now even the *King* pities him.

'—and to ask you to come forwards to the front of the hall, with Rabbie.'

Harry blinks. *What?*

Then he notices Rabbie is already up front, in the no-man's-land near the King's own table, on one knee. Harry gulps, and nods, stumbling as he rises from the bench.

The King waits for him, like an indulgent older brother, and looks him up and down as he stands. Harry realises he's as tall as the King, maybe even a little taller, so he hunches his big shoulders slightly. The King notices and laughs, a ringing, beautiful sound. He shakes his head as he turns. 'You are the West Country personified, aren't you? We've seen haystacks smaller than you. Good thing you have to kneel for what's coming.'

It's only then that Harry understands what the King is doing. Harry's skin prickles with nerves as he takes his place next to Rabbie. He glances over, eyes wide and questioning, but the other boy won't meet his gaze. Rabbie looks forwards, solemn, as the King draws a sword and taps Rabbie three times on the shoulders. 'For your valour on Halidon Hill. Rise, Sir Robert Ufford.' And then the sword is touching Harry's shoulders, and Harry's heart is beating so fast he can't breathe, and through the ringing in his ears Harry can barely make out the King saying 'Rise, Sir Harry Lyon', and it's the moment Harry has been looking forward to since he first picked up a practice sword, the moment he was sure he would remember for the rest of his life, but even as it's happening it's running out between his fingers like water.

And then he's left standing there, next to Rabbie, as the King sheaths his sword and turns back to Queen Philippa. The moment is over. Rabbie claps him on the shoulder again, and Harry is dimly aware that the assembled knights are cheering and thumping their tables as they walk back to their bench.

He's a knight.

He is *a knight.*

And he's done nothing to deserve it.

Baron Montagu winks at him as he sits back down. 'Welcome to the family, *Sir Harry*. We put in a good word for you.'

Harry stutters out a thanks as someone – a finely dressed man at the tent's entrance – calls out towards the King, 'And when for France, milord?'

The King laughs again and raises his hands. 'I have no intentions towards my cousin of France, as long as he has no intentions towards Gascony.' He raises his cup in toast. 'Besides, my claim is through my mother, and France is not so keen on that.'

'Then we'll *make* 'em keen, like our Henry did!' another voice cries out.

Montagu smiles. Though he speaks softly, his voice carries across the entire tent. 'And what of the French forces in Scotland, Your Majesty?'

The King waves his hand in dismissal. 'Let us enjoy this victory, before planning more.' He places his hand on the arm of a weak-chinned, sandy-haired man sitting to his right. 'We must first attend to tomorrow's business, and restore our cousin of Balliol to his lands across the border.'

When Harry turns his gaze back to their table, he realises the man who had called out to the King about France has taken a seat next to Baron Montagu, and they are in whispered discussion. The man is older, and pinched-looking, something cruel about his tanned features. His hair is bristle-short, and the same colour as his skin. Harry can only hear bits and pieces of their discussion: an intercepted letter, and French spies, and the King.

His stare must be obvious, for Rabbie whispers in his ear, 'Baron de Percy. The new Constable of Berwick.'

Baron Montagu's gaze flicks up across the table to them, at that moment. His face is serious, now, compared with its previous open ease. 'So, *Sir Harry*, do you want to kill some Scots?'

Harry nods. More than anything, he does. To avenge his father. To avenge Sir Simon. To prove he's worthy of the knight's belt given to him out of charity.

Montagu smiles, and it's a nasty smile, but war is a nasty business. 'Good. Tomorrow we ride north with Balliol. There's something potentially troublesome we must retrieve.'

They leave at dawn, in light mail and plain surcoats, unmarked by heraldic insignia, choosing their palfreys for speed over their war-horses. Eleven of the brightest, most dashing knights in England, and Harry – *Sir Harry*, though the honorific feels false on his tongue, as if he is still playing crusaders and dragons with a wooden sword in the manor gardens. Montagu has promised that Harry's war-horse and belongings, along with Sir Simon's, will be packed up by Montagu's household servants and delivered back to Dartington.

Harry keeps reaching down to touch the heavy leather belt that sits just above his hips, the symbol of his knighthood. It had been Sir Simon's, and it's soft with age, moulding to him as if it were made for him. Its weight, and the sword on his left that it supports, is a constant reminder of what he has not yet earned.

Montagu's small party of knights is barely noticeable in the mob of exultant nobles flowing north, the disinherited English who had been given lands in Scotland by Edward Longshanks just to be thrown out again by Robert Bruce and Black Douglas. Percy stays behind at Berwick, his place in the group taken by the weak-chinned man who had dined next to the King: Edward Balliol, awarded land in Galloway for his loyalty to England. The man spends the entire first day trying to make conversation with Montagu, but thankfully Balliol soon falls behind, his progress hampered by the slow ox-carts of his household.

Over the next two days, they follow the lowland course of the river Tweed. The group grows smaller as the Disinherited break off to their various lands. Soon it's just the dozen of them, Montagu's raiders: Harry, Rabbie, a crass Yorkshire knight named Odo Waldegrave, Rabbie's best friend Colin Crocker, Guy d'Audley with the scar across his face, Thomas Howland, the two Billies (Shayler and Lang), Sebastian Sharp from Kent, Brendan le Rous and Roderick Griffith. And of course Montagu himself.

In another situation, the trip would be beautiful, but they are surrounded constantly by tiny flies and midges which are small enough to sneak through mail and bite the flesh beneath. They settle into a sort of grim determination, talking little, pressing forwards as fast as they can. The midges that flit senseless into their mouths when they talk are a reminder of the constant presence of the Scottish. This is a hostile land. Not a thing in it wishes them welcome. The glares of the peasants they pass on the road are enough for each knight to keep a hand near his weapons at all times.

By the fourth day, they are cutting north through Galloway Forest. Montagu still hasn't told them why they're here, what they're retrieving. Harry burns to ask, but his place in the group is too tenuous for such bold questioning. Instead he marvels at the forest, deep and dark.

They've hired a couple of Scots to guide them. The men are much as Rabbie described: stunted, twisted creatures, red of leg and bare of foot, in nothing but a leine and a cloak. They growl at each other in their incomprehensible, savage tongue. Harry wonders what sort of man can be so bought by gold to betray his own country, and he despises them for it even as he is thankful for their skill in navigating this endless ocean of trees.

Montagu stops them early in the afternoon, most of the way up a formidable hill. They make camp. The air is fresher here, the biting flies less prevalent. Harry can smell water nearby. He has absolutely no idea *where* they are – Galloway, Balliol had said, but the name means nothing to him. He just knows they're deep behind the Scottish border.

'We attack at midnight,' Montagu says as they swallow down a supper of stale biscuit and hard cheese. 'I need you to get as much rest as you can before then. Dress lightly. It will be close-quarters fighting.'

Harry is compelled to speak up. 'What are we retrieving, my lord?'

Montagu smiles, that cruel hawk's smile. 'I'll know when I see it,' he replies. 'You just make sure nobody gets through to me.'

Later, as they settle onto their cloaks in the forest floor to grab some sleep, Harry tugs at Rabbie's sleeve. 'Do you know?' he says. 'What we came here for?'

Rabbie smirks. 'Not what. *Who.*' Then he rolls over.

Harry stares up at the forest canopy, his mind restless. Montagu had been the man trusted to capture Lord Mortimer. Of *course* he'd be the one sent to capture a dangerous Scotsman. But who is it? What mighty lord wasn't present at Halidon Hill, but could threaten English supremacy? He realises then how little he knows of the Scottish. Devon, so far southwest, barely concerns itself with activities north of the Avon, much less the Tweed. He's only heard a handful of names: William Wallace; Robert the Bruce and his brother; Black Douglas. Is this man a relative of theirs?

Harry is seized with the realisation that this is *it*. He's not an outsider any more. He is with the right people, at the right time, about to do something important.

'Was it like this? At Nottingham Castle?' Harry asks Rabbie, soft in the night so as not to wake the others. 'When you took Mortimer?'

Rabbie mumbles sleepily, 'Mmhmm. Just follow Montagu. He knows what he's doing.' Then Rabbie kicks him. 'Go to bed, Harry. Work to do later.'

Finally, Harry thinks as sleep overtakes him, *finally* he's going to be where the action is.

The action is horrible.

They slip on their chainmail hauberks and chausses in silence, then follow their guides over the crest of the hill down to the edge of a vast lake. Three boats wait for them at the shoreline. They cast off under the moon's pale, reproachful gaze. The lake and the steep hills it nestles among are bathed in silver, silent and surreal. As they round a small headland, no sound but the clank and splish of oars, Harry startles. For, suddenly revealed, is their target: a small stone castle on an island, its foundations wrapped with evening mist like something out of legend. As if soon the boats would spirit them through some invisible barrier, into the land of the fae, to a hand coming out of the water with a sword.

Harry realises he is holding his breath as the boats' prows scuff onto the pebbled shore of the island, fearful of breaking the spell. The landscape is alien, savage, and more beautiful than his heart can hold.

Then they kick down the rotting door of the castle and slay every living thing inside.

They didn't need a dozen knights. Three could have done it. Harry stands agape, watching as Rabbie wields a torch in one hand and his mace in the other. Watches as he brains an old serving-woman who is trying to escape the massacre of half-asleep retainers in the hall. 'You know our targets. No witnesses, no survivors,' Montagu hisses as they rush up the bank, weapons drawn. Except Harry *doesn't* know. Nobody has told him.

In the flickering light of their torches and the glow of the hearth's embers, Harry has only impressions of the chaos in the hall, of women, their bodies thin and their clothes threadbare. A few very elderly men, their bones breaking like twigs under the boots and blades of the English.

Billy Shayler's long sword cleaves straight through an old man's spindly forearm, raised high against the blow, straight down to the skull beneath. Thomas Howland smashes his shield into the back of a thin redhead as she tries to flee past. She falls onto her face, cracking her head on the stone floor. Sir Thomas kicks her onto her back and sinks his sword into her heart.

And above it all, Lord Waldegrave is giggling.

Where are the men? Harry thinks, panicking. *Where are their men? Nobody is armed. This isn't fair.*

He realises the men must be away at war, as are the men of his own hall, and his stomach twists as he thinks of knights kicking down Dartington Manor's old door at night, wetting their swords with the blood of his dependants.

A beautiful woman of his mother's age stumbles down the stairs, her fine dress a faded turquoise velvet, the neckline marked and frayed where once-heavy ornamentation had been removed. She screams at them. Her black hair is shot with white and then, inevitably, red. Montagu swears at the knight that kills the woman – Colin Crocker, Harry thinks it's Crocker – back-handing him across the face.

Harry stands and holds his sword in trembling hands and prays they don't notice he hasn't killed anyone yet. The cries of the dying, their terror and the piss and shit that flows out of them, the stink of their intestines, it crashes against the hard stone walls of the castle's hall and over Harry like a suffocating blanket of evil.

Montagu is glaring around, looking for something, when Rabbie screams. There's a boy, and he's jumped on Rabbie's back and he's got his teeth locked on Rabbie's ear as he tries to shove a dull eating knife through Rabbie's mail coat. Montagu grabs the boy and pulls him off, and half Rabbie's right ear comes too and the boy spits it into Montagu's face and nobody knows what to do and Montagu is yelling 'Stay back! Stay back!' and the boy is thin and small and maybe sixteen years old but he is fighting like a hellcat, screaming at them in Gaelic and trying to rip Montagu's throat out with his bare hands and Montagu is punching him in the side of the head with a mailed fist, *shunk*, *shunk*, *shunk*, and finally the boy is still, his long dark hair falling over his face, soaking into a pool of Rabbie's blood and cartilage on the floor.

Harry turns around and vomits onto the flagstones.

Rabbie is keening, half in pain, half in fury, touching the ragged, bloody edge of what remains of his right ear. Montagu steps between him and the boy's limp form. 'Don't touch him,' Montagu growls. 'We need him alive.' Montagu turns towards Harry, and in the faltering torchlight Harry can see dark, bloody scratches down Montagu's cheek and neck from the boy. And something small and nasty in Harry thinks *good for you* to the Scottish boy. *Good for you.*

Montagu is suddenly in Harry's face. 'Got a problem?' he says, quiet and threatening.

'This . . . it's not chivalry,' Harry stutters, his hand sweeping to encompass the death and desecration of the hall.

Montagu snorts at him. 'You really think kingdoms are maintained by *chivalry*?' Then he points to the boy. 'Tie him up, gag him, and throw him in the boat.'

They're out of Galloway Forest by dawn, riding hard southeast, all of them exhausted when they reach the main road towards the border and can pull the horses up into a walk. The boy is thrown over a spare palfrey like a sack of oats, bound tightly under the horse's stomach so he can't escape. Harry can't help glancing back at him. He's so *thin*, his clothes almost rags on him. What of his face isn't pressed to the horse's side is covered by filthy, matted dark hair, and he either stays unconscious or fakes it, because he doesn't stir once.

Harry wants to see his face. Wants to understand this danger to England that they've ridden clear across the country to retrieve.

While he is staring, Montagu rides up next to him. Harry is too tired to school his expression into anything other than disapproval.

Montagu rolls his eyes and sighs. 'What do you think happened at Halidon Hill, Harry?'

Harry's brow furrows. 'I don't understand—'

'No, you don't,' Montagu says. 'Do you think we jousted sweetly with the Scots? Do you think it was like a mêlée?'

Harry blinks. War *was* like a mêlée. Wasn't it? That's why they had them to start off each tournament. Ten to twelve a side fake battles, blunt swords. So they could know what to do in real ones.

He's about to respond when Montagu cuts him off. 'We instructed our archers to shoot the nobles first. Set the longbows up on top of the hill where they could send arrows down like hail. We paid off Scottish lords to turn traitor, and tell us their order of battle. De Beaumont got himself a castle out of it. We had spies in their camp reporting to us.'

'That's horrible,' Harry says.

'And they had spies in ours.' Montagu smiles. 'Well, until I killed them.'

'I don't—'

'It's *war*, Harry. Pray it never comes to the West Country.' Montagu stretches, putting a hand to his lower back. 'The best thing you can do with war is win it as quickly and conclusively as possible. That is what we did.'

'Who is he?' Harry asks. He doesn't even need to specify who he's talking about. Montagu immediately glances over at the boy.

'He's insurance,' he responds carefully, after a moment. He glances back at Harry and takes in his look of hurt and confusion.

'But he's just a boy,' Harry says.

'As are you,' Montagu growls. 'Look at him. You can see his bones. They wouldn't have lasted the winter in that keep. They'd have *starved*. They suffered less with us. And the boy may even live to see a few more years.'

Harry thinks back to the woman's dress, finer than any his mother had ever owned. Of drops of blood on turquoise velvet. Of holes where cloth-of-gold embroidery and jewels might once have been.

'Who were they?' he asks.

'They're what happens when power moves on and leaves you behind, m'boy,' Montagu says. 'Never forget that.' Then the Baron nudges his horse into a trot, to resume his place at the head of their little party. As he passes Rabbie, bandaged and sullen, he squeezes the man's shoulder in reassurance.

The Scottish boy wakes up as the day grows hotter, a short while before they're due to rendezvous with Balliol and his wagons. He thrashes in his bonds, shouting as loudly as he can through the gag. It doesn't come out as anything more than unintelligible keening, but passers-by on the road begin to look at them.

Montagu draws his sword and the passers-by quickly find other things to stare at.

A few hours later, the boy has shouted himself out. His voice is shredded, nothing but angry growls and grunts coming from him, but he watches all of them as if cataloguing them for weaknesses he will exploit as soon as he can escape his bonds. His face through the lank hair is thin, wolfish, with fierce, pale eyes and sharp cheekbones.

When Balliol turns north to Galloway, towards his new lands, he takes their two Scottish guides but leaves a small horse-cart behind, its strange, boxy load covered in canvas. Montagu pulls their little group off the road behind a nearby copse. Then he nods to Crocker and Ufford. They cut the boy off the palfrey and manhandle him towards the cart. Though the boy must be exhausted, he still tries to fight, kicking his bound feet and trying to hit his captors with his head. Harry winces as he sees Rabbie drop the boy on the ground and boot him in the guts a few times.

Then Crocker throws the canvas off the thing on the cart.

Harry gasps.

It's *a cage*. A barred steel cage, the sort he's seen in Exeter Market transporting bears to the baiting pit. There are even shallow gouges in the metal bars, marks of claws or teeth or maybe both. Rabbie opens its door and they pick up the boy, still bound, and slam his face against the bars. He's dazed for a moment, blood already welling out of his nose, and then they shove the rest of him inside and lock the door.

Crocker pulls down the canvas again and the boy is out of sight. Would be out of mind entirely but for the low, animalistic hisses and growls that come from inside the cage; the dull ringing of the bars as the boy slams his body into them.

Montagu signals that they should break for dinner. The rest of them slide off their horses, glad of the rest.

There's little food other than hard biscuit and dried beef, but they'd all had the presence of mind to fill their skeins with the lake's cool water before they left. Harry catches Montagu's eye and nods towards the boy, holding up his skein and a bit of biscuit.

Montagu shakes his head.

'But—' Harry begins. The day is sweltering. The Scottish midges are back in full force as Montagu's dozen Galloway raiders wend their way south through the Lowlands, and it must be hotter than an oven under the thick canvas of the cage. 'I thought we were trying to keep him alive.'

Rabbie snorts. 'That rabid dog? He's too mean to die.'

Montagu gazes at him, serious. There's an air of disappointment in his eyes, as if he expected better of Harry. As if Harry should *understand*. 'You take that gag off, or untie him enough that he can get it off by himself, and he'll be howling in Scots that we're English knights who killed his family and took him prisoner. We're still a day's travel from English soil. You want to fight our entire way back?'

Harry looks down, ashamed. He hates what they've done, the ceaseless cruelty of it, but he can't fault Montagu's operational logic. He never can. Everything Montagu says makes perfect, terrible sense.

Harry falls in towards the rear of the group as they head back down the road. The cage sways in front of him, and along with the smell of horse and steel there's the sharp tang of human urine, and the stomach-churning scent of shit. *I'm sorry*, Harry whispers. He racks his brain for a way to give their young prisoner some dignity, but he can't think of anything that wouldn't compromise them all.

They stop for the night on the far side of a stand of trees, near a stream. There's been little traffic on the road. As word of Scotland's rout at Halidon Hill spreads, it's as if both kingdoms are holding their breath, waiting to see what will happen. These Lowlands have passed back and forth between Scottish and English rulership for years, and the people know to keep their heads down, to mind their business while borders shift around them.

Montagu decides they can risk a fire. The cart with its cage is drawn up at the edge of camp, close enough to be in the fire's light, but not its warmth. Rabbie has left the sheet over the cage. Harry can hear the occasional small scuffling sound from inside. It's easy to forget there's a human in there, a boy only a few years younger than Harry.

Seemingly, the rest of the men have. They're busy with the cask of beer Crocker bought from a passing merchant, and the chickens they're plucking to roast over the fire. They're giving less attention to the prisoner than they would a caged dog, Harry thinks. At least the dog would get tossed a bone or two.

Harry feels sick. He gets up, ostensibly to fetch his horse some water from the stream. The stench of piss is overwhelming as he approaches the cage. Trapped heat still radiates from under the canvas, fermenting the nauseating stink within. It must be unbearable inside.

Harry whispers an apology to his palfrey as he steals her water bucket and strides down to the stream. He fills it, and his skin, with the cool water.

When he approaches the cage again, he circles around it from the rear, away from the fire. He reaches up and flips the back of the canvas sheet over the top. He immediately has to cover his mouth and nose as the fetid smell assaults him. The boy had been near the bars; he scuttles away on his elbows and knees, his hands and ankles still bound, and turns to glare at him from the far side of the cage. All Harry can see in the dim shadows is a curtain of dark hair and pale wolf's eyes glinting in the dark.

Harry shivers, despite himself. The boy is every cautionary story he's been told of Scottish savagery, of Lowland bandits burning and raping their way over the border; of Highland tribes sweeping down like a barbarian tide to kill everything in their path.

But then, he thinks, what tales do the Scots tell of them? Pale monsters cased in steel who kill defenceless women and old men; who leave children to starve in their own filth.

Harry sticks his water skin through the bars. The Scottish boy flinches further back and hisses at him. '*Here,*' Harry says in English. '*I don't have the key, but I can give you water to drink through the gag. You need to come closer, though.*'

The boy glares at him uncomprehendingly, and Harry feels a hot blush of shame. He'd just switched automatically to the native, vulgar tongue, as if he were talking to a peasant at Dartington Manor. But they are a long way from Devon, and nobody speaks English here. Harry has not one word of Scots. For lack of anything better to try, he switches back into French, with no expectation of success.

But the boy is cocking his head at him, as if he understands.

'I swear it's not poisoned,' Harry says, waggling the skin.

The boy snorts, as if disappointed that Harry's offering won't finish the job.

But the boy inches closer.

'You understand French?' Harry asks.

The boy is still out of Harry's reach, but close enough for Harry to see his face now. So Harry gets a front-row view of how the Scottish boy eyerolls at him like he's the biggest idiot the boy has ever met.

Harry giggles, a little hysterical.

He tilts the skin so water begins to trickle out. The boy slowly, so slowly, puts his head under the trickle of water, tilting his gagged mouth so the stream goes into it. He drinks almost the whole skin. A lot goes down his face but enough makes it into his mouth that Harry feels like the boy may not die of dehydration. He realises how dirty the boy is when the rivulets of water leave clean marks down his face.

When the skin is empty the boy backs away again. There's no acknowledgement, no thanks, and at first Harry is put out by that. Until he remembers how he and his friends have just killed everyone the boy ever cared about.

So he holds up the bucket and offers to sluice down the cage floor. The boy glares at him, then nods once. He wriggles until he's sitting down on the floor, still out of Harry's reach, but close enough that the water will rinse his lower half too. Harry heaves the bucket of water through the bars; the cold stream-water splashes against the metal floor of the cage. The boy hisses as it washes over his thighs.

'What are you doing?' growls Rabbie, from behind Harry.

Harry turns away from the cage, leaving the canvas flap up for air circulation and hoping Rabbie doesn't notice. '*He stinks*,' he says, arranging his face into a look of disgust as he switches to English. '*Don't fancy riding behind a reeking cart full of piss and shit again tomorrow.*'

Rabbie grins at him. '*I wouldn't know*,' he winks. '*I ride up front, with Montagu.*'

Harry groans and bumps shoulders with Rabbie as they head back to the dying embers of the fire, back to their blankets. He thinks he's managed to snowball Rabbie, until Rabbie leans in and whispers, '*Don't go soft, Harry. You saw what the little savage did to me. He'll do it to you, and worse, with a smile on his face.*'

And the thing is, Harry doesn't doubt him at all.

They rise at dawn again and press on southwards. Dinner is hurried; they're only about six hours from the border and everyone is keen to be back on English soil. Harry is bolder this time, just looks Montagu in the eye and says, 'I'm going to give the prisoner some water.' He'd even filled a skin from the stream the previous night, to have on hand.

Montagu just shakes his head slightly in resignation. But the Baron's sharp grey eyes are on Harry as he flips up a corner of the canvas and beckons the boy over. He doesn't speak to the boy. Something in him doesn't want to let Montagu know that the boy speaks French.

It's different in daylight, the boy drinking. Harry can see the blood in his matted hair, the dirt and filth ingrained into his pores. How visible his bones are under his fair skin. And the boy looks back, his eyes not on the trickle of water from the skin but on Harry, watching him, assessing him. 'You must be hungry,' Harry whispers to the boy. 'I'll try to get permission to feed you, tonight.' The boy's eyes narrow. They're ringed in dark lashes, as long as a girl's, and it only serves to make his eyes look paler, more unnatural.

When the skin is empty again, Harry throws the canvas flap back down and turns to Montagu. 'When we cross into England, I'd like to get straw for the cage, and a bucket for him to piss in. They do as much for the bears,' he says, referring to the cage's original use.

Montagu raises an eyebrow, says, 'Hmm,' and mounts up on his horse. 'Ride with me,' he commands.

Harry mounts up and trots Star to Montagu's side. He can't resist a smirk at Rabbie. 'Guess you'll have to ride in the back for a bit, *Sir Robert*.'

Rabbie smirks back. 'We only let you up here so you understand how far away it is from where you belong, *Sir Harry*.' But then he peels his chestnut palfrey away and obediently takes a position in the rear.

Once Rabbie is gone, Baron Montagu smiles at Harry. There's surprise and amusement in his face. 'Making friends, are we?'

Harry blushes.

'Who is he?' Harry asks again. Because none of it adds up. A rural, poverty-stricken hall. A Scottish boy who looks like an urchin but speaks French as well as Gaelic. And who is so important to English politics that the great Baron Montagu himself crosses seventy miles of enemy territory to capture him.

Montagu looks forwards, his gaze growing distant, and begins to talk over Harry. 'Did you know we lose about a third of our noble families every hundred years?' the Baron says. 'New ones replace them, of course, but do you ever think about how the failing houses just . . . slip away? Where they go? Most don't fall very far, of course. But some do. Some fall very far indeed.'

Harry thinks of turquoise velvet and the frayed holes where embroidery used to be.

Montagu hums. 'How is Dartington Manor? Heavily indebted, last I heard.'

'We're making do,' Harry replies. 'Harvest looks good this year.'

The lie rolls smoothly off his lips. Dartington needs more than a good harvest. It needs Harry to come back from war laden with glory, with gifts from the King of land and jewels.

Except Harry missed the war, and his excursion with Montagu into Galloway has brought neither glory nor reward, just a hollow sense of shame.

This was the unspoken thing between his mother and Harry, the matter they never discussed. He wanted to make everything right, use steel and youth and muscle to pay off the carrion crows circling their home. And his mother, when she saw that determined look in his eye, would stroke his hair and say, 'You don't have to.' But he did. *He did.*

Montagu watches him, amusement tugging at the corners of his thin lips. 'Be careful of the path you tread, Harry. You walk it well, but it is narrow, and the rocks below it are deadly.' He flicks his reins, urging his horse on a bit faster, his dismissal of Harry clear. 'Feed your pet wolf tonight,' Montagu murmurs. 'Maybe he won't bite you.'

At camp that evening, barely three miles over the border into England, Harry stands at the bars to the cage and holds up one of the trout they've cooked over the fire. He tells the Scottish boy he's removing the gag. That he can't cry out. That if he's quiet, he can have the food.

The boy shuffles towards him and bends his head submissively, allowing Harry access to the knot at the back of the gag. The twisted muslin has tightened so much that Harry has to cut it off him, nicking the boy's jaw in the process.

The boy immediately launches himself at Harry.

He bites Harry's forearm so hard that Harry drops the knife. It clatters onto the floor of the cage. The boy howls bloody murder in Gaelic as his bound hands scrabble for the weapon.

Rabbie pushes past Harry, throws the cage open and clubs

the boy unconscious.

Harry gapes, aghast at how wrong everything has gone, how fast.

There's a trickle of blood making its way down the boy's forehead. His face looks so *young*, relaxed into unconsciousness. His lips are raw and cracked from the gag, but when his mouth isn't forced into the rictus caused by the tight fabric it's revealed to be strangely delicate. Everything about his features is refined, more an expensive, pedigreed hunting dog than a feral wolf.

Rabbie shoves him. The other knights are laughing; even Montagu is amused. 'This is what happens when you try to domesticate a wild animal,' Lord Waldegrave shouts. Rabbie shakes his head and mutters that they should just put all the Scots to the sword and resettle the whole damn country with sheep. Then he smacks Harry once on the side of the head as he struts back to the campfire. 'Dunno what that old knight taught you, but when we get back to Devon you're coming with us and learning how to fight properly,' Rabbie grumbles.

Harry rubs his sleeve. It wasn't his fault. The boy was *fast*. He glances down at the bloody teeth-marks on his sword arm and sends a quick prayer to God that it won't infect.

There's a shout from the edge of camp. 'Rider,' Billy Shayler echoes, backing slowly towards the fire and reaching for his shield.

They all look up as the clatter of hoofbeats grows louder. It's late, almost dark, and nobody good travels at night. Swords slide unbidden out of sheaths; bodies tense.

Montagu stands up. 'Johann?' he says, as the rider's face comes into view.

It's one of Montagu's men-at-arms, from the main body of

his retainers and chattels. The Baron's household is winding its way south with the King, now a good week ahead of them. The man dismounts and strides up to Montagu, taking a quick knee then leaning in to whisper in his ear. Montagu's expression turns stormy, and he swears under his breath.

'What is it?' Rabbie asks.

'The Earl of Arundel lies in wait for us at Carlisle, with *questions*,' Montagu hisses. Richard FitzAlan, Lord Arundel, is a latecomer to the King's graces. His father, Edmund FitzAlan, had sided with the King's father, Edward of Carnarvon, against Queen Isabella and Mortimer. For that, Mortimer had him executed with a blunt sword. They say it took twenty-two blows to separate the old Earl's head from his shoulders. Then Mortimer had seized the FitzAlan family lands – his aim all along, the gossips said.

But young Richard, rich as Croesus and twice as splendid, had convinced Edward of Windsor to restore him to his extensive holdings in Sussex and the Welsh marches. Harry knows there is no love lost between Montagu and Arundel, with Arundel's victories in Wales vying with Montagu's leadership against the Scots for who could do greater service to the crown.

Montagu stalks away from the fire, hissing and swearing like a wet cat. He returns a few moments later, a strange, mask-like calm over his features. Where Rabbie is easy to read, Harry feels like he never sees more of Montagu than exactly what the Baron wants him to see. Harry has no sense for the man himself, what he's like underneath the political machinations.

Perhaps there is nothing under the politics. Perhaps the game is all.

Montagu is smiling at him. That never ends well.

'You're a knight now,' Montagu says pleasantly, his fingers resting lightly on the old leather of Sir Simon's belt. His smile grows wider. 'You will need a squire.'

Harry stutters. 'I hadn't thought of that, sir.'

Montagu puts an arm around Harry, and walks him back towards the cart and cage. Montagu's voice is deceptively light, as if he were asking for Harry to help round up some costumes for a court masquerade. 'You will take the little wolf, and he will be your squire. Don't bring him anywhere public until he can behave. Don't harm him permanently. Try to get him on our side. Oh, and don't let him escape, whatever you do.'

'Do I have a choice in this?' Harry asks. He already knows the answer, he's just curious what Montagu will say.

Montagu purses his lips, feigning thoughtfulness. 'Well, if *you* don't want to look after him, I can ask Rabbie. Either way, we tuck the Scottish boy away in the West Country where nobody will look for him.'

'What if he escapes?' Harry says, running his thumb over the scabbing wound on his forearm.

'Ah, see, as soon as I return home to Salisbury I'm going to buy up all the debts of Dartington Manor,' Montagu replies, and Harry can feel a spectral silk cord tightening around his neck. 'Keep him alive and with you until his majority, and I'll forgive them. Lose him and, well, farewell to the House of Lyon.' Montagu raises an eyebrow at Harry.

Harry looks over to see Rabbie and Colin Crocker laughing as they whip stones through the cage at the unconscious boy.

'I'll do it,' Harry breathes.

TWO

August 1333: Stray Dog

The next morning, Montagu, Ufford and the rest of the Galloway Dozen break south, direct to Carlisle, leaving Harry at a small crossroads with Montagu's man-at-arms, a hired local guide and a boy in a cage. They're to take the long way around, bypassing the English nobles and their households streaming home down the main London road after the Scottish victory, avoiding questions about the prisoner.

Harry's little band head west, towards the Irish Sea. The guide tells them, in his odd, musical English dialect, that it will be two days along the Cumbrian coast until the old Roman road bends eastwards again through the forest and meets the London road at Kendal. Harry has always loved the ocean, and he feels as if a great weight is lifted from him now that he is out of the company of Rabbie and the other knights. He's almost calm. It's the most peaceful he's felt in months, and if he could get off his horse and kiss the English soil without his companions laughing at him, he would.

But as they sway in single file down the dirt track leading westwards, past dramatic hills dotted with curious sheep and wary peasants, Harry can't get his mind off the boy. He's still bound and gagged, his cage still covered by a sailcloth sheet. But he's awake.

An hour into the vast Cumbrian landscape with no witnesses but sheep, Harry makes a decision. He rides back and yanks the cover off the cage. This gets him a glare from Johann, Lord Montagu's bald, red-faced man-at-arms, but the boy is quiescent, huddled in a corner, glaring at them.

At midday, the hilltop road splits, a spur of it dipping down to a wide, sandy beach fed by a clear stream. They pull up by the stream to break their fast and water the horses. Their guide lopes off with some of Harry's coin to a nearby collection of hovels, looking for a peasant who can sell them anything other than salt beef and hard biscuit. He soon comes back with a brace of hare, and he and Johann set to skinning and cooking them.

Harry checks on their prisoner. He is all too aware the Scottish boy hasn't eaten in three days. The boy stares back at him, long hair now matted with dried blood, shirt stained with piss and filth. He looks exhausted but his eyes still burn with a pale, fevered fury, a determination Harry has never encountered before.

Harry can't find it in his heart to hate him, whatever Rabbie says about the Scots. The boy obviously had some upbringing, given that he could understand French. Harry thinks also of the boy's mother, and her velvet dress, finer than any his own mother ever had, fine as any of the great ladies at the King's table, even denuded of its embroidery.

Harry unlocks the cage and reaches in to pull the boy out. He flinches hard when Harry touches him, and Harry wants to strangle Rabbie in that moment. The Scottish boy shivers uncontrollably as Harry helps him out of the cart, shaking with hunger and exhaustion and some combination of fury and terror.

The boy's bare feet sink into the dark beach sand and there's a moment where he pokes it with his toes, digging in, feeling the wet grains. It's a strangely endearing, intimate gesture, so normal after days of blood and horror, and Harry has to glance away.

When he looks back, the boy is watching him again, waiting for whatever comes next.

'We're in England now,' Harry says. 'I'm cutting your gag. You can yell all you want. Please don't bite me again.'

The scent of roasting hare wafts over, causing Harry's stomach to clench in hunger. He can't even imagine what the boy is feeling.

Harry cuts the gag before he can second-guess himself. He steps back, holding the boy up but also at arm's length. The boy's wrists and ankles are still bound, but he does his best to stand tall, defiant, even if the shaking undermines it. Uncurled, he's not nearly as small as Harry thought, only a few inches shorter than him. But the boy is so *thin*. It's a thinness born of constant hunger, of *not enough*, for a prolonged period of time. Harry thinks back to Montagu's words, *they would have starved in that keep*, and realises their terrible truth.

The boy yells.

And yells and yells, in Gaelic.

At the sky. At Harry. At the hills.

Johann and their Cumbrian guide, Tom, jolt to their feet and reach for weapons but Harry stops them with a raised hand. After what seems like an eternity the boy falls down in the sand, shaking. No tears fall, but it looks like he's crying. His voice cracks and breaks, and the yells crumble away first into hoarse whispers, then nothing. He's just hitting his forehead against the sand, over and over, his lips moving soundlessly as if he's reciting a prayer, or a curse. The silence is startling after so much noise.

Harry squats down next to him. 'I'd like to wash you. Can you swim?'

The boy sits back onto his knees and turns his head to Harry. There's sand stuck to his forehead. Harry's hand twitches, the urge to brush it off stilled instantly by the *look* the boy is giving him. It's a narrow-eyed expression of complete and utter disdain.

Then, in the most beautiful French Harry has ever heard, the boy whispers, 'Of course I can fucking swim, you great Sassenach idiot. I grew up in a tower in the middle of a loch.'

Harry laughs, despite himself. 'Well, I'll have to leave your arms tied then.' He reaches forwards and cuts the rope binding the boy's ankles.

Harry helps the boy up. They walk towards the ocean, the boy shaky as a newborn foal, his thin legs barely holding him. The boy stumbles, and Harry should expect what happens next but he's still caught by surprise when the stumble becomes a sweep of leg that knocks Harry square on his arse.

The boy runs.

Harry shouts to Johann and Tom, and they give chase. The boy falls, skinning his knees, but pushes himself up rapidly and keeps running, blood coursing down his shins. He's not fast. He's too exhausted to be fast, and Harry catches up to him just as he gets to the stream at the top of the beach.

The boy glances back at the thunder of Harry's footsteps. Harry watches in horror as the boy's ankle turns on a stone and he starts to go down. With bound arms, there's no way he can break his fall.

Harry lunges and grabs the boy before he can hit the ground. They both end up in a heap on the marshy edge of the stream, the boy thrashing and keening his anger. But Harry has both height and strength on him, and just wraps his thickly muscled arms around the boy from behind. Harry still has to dodge the boy's attempts to break his nose with the back of his skull, and his shins get a bruising from the boy's heels, but they're both reasonably unscathed.

'C'mon,' Harry says, hauling the boy to his feet. 'Let's get you into the ocean.' Harry holds the boy by his upper arms, in front of him, and frog-marches him towards the slow roll of waves. The boy doesn't fight, and Harry can't tell if he's given up for the time being, or if he's just waiting for his opportunity.

The boy hisses as the cold salt water washes over his many cuts, over the irritated, broken skin at his wrists and ankles. But he obediently ducks under the water when Harry exerts a gentle pressure on his shoulder, letting the sea clean the filth and blood out of his hair. He dunks himself a few times and then stands up and shakes like a dog, managing to get a substantial amount of water on Harry.

Then the boy tips his head back and closes his eyes for a moment, the midday sun hitting his pale, elegant face and turning the drops of water in his raven-dark hair into something like jewels. His long linen shirt is translucent from the water, clinging to his slim body. His lips are rose-red from the abrasions of the gag and the irritation of the salt water.

Harry's throat goes dry. Who *is* he?

'Better?' Harry chokes out.

One pale eye opens, and a bowed red lip curls in a snarl. 'You honestly expect me to congratulate you on that being the least shit thing that's happened to me this week?' The boy spits, hitting Harry in the cheek. 'You killed my family. I will kill every one of you.'

Harry uses his free hand – the one that isn't gripping the boy's bicep against his next escape attempt – to wipe the saliva from his face. He sighs, and changes tack. 'I'm Harry. What's your name?'

The boy laughs, sharp and hollow. 'You killed them all and you don't even know my *name*. Fuck you. *Death*. That's my name.'

He turns his back to Harry. 'If you're done playing the Good Samaritan, I'd like to go back in my cage.'

They retie the boy's legs, but looser, so he can shuffle along in a slow walk, but not run. Harry has Johann and Tom hold him down while he cuts the boy's arms free, winds the wrists in a bit of worsted to protect the skin, then reties the arms in front of him so the boy can use his hands to eat. They don't gag him. They give him bread and cheese and half a roast hare, and water. He eats all of it.

Straw is acquired for the bottom of the cage in a small village on the forest's edge, as is a spare bucket for the boy's waste. That night, Harry unpacks his spare cloak and stuffs it through the bars. The boy glances at the worn woollen rectangle as it thumps onto the cage floor, then looks away. But by morning, Harry notices he's made himself a little nest in the centre of the cage, with the blanket and the straw.

The Cumbrian coast road is little-travelled enough that Harry can leave the cover off the cage. The few peasants they pass don't stare outright but Harry sees the corners of eyes sweep across the bars, and then to the men-at-arms, and then to Harry's knight's belt, before they inevitably decide the boy in the box is none of their business.

Trouble comes once they say goodbye to their Cumbrian guide at the London road. The first inkling is just south of Kendal: a friar on a donkey who stares a little too long. Johann, driving the cart, catches the man's eye and says, '*Scottish prisoner*,' and the man of God rides close enough to the cage to spit at the boy. The boy growls something back, and it almost sounds like Latin, but the friar just points at him and tells him he's going to Hell. Reluctantly, Harry covers the cage again. He folds the canvas so it doesn't quite reach the bottom of the cage, leaving about a foot of clear space for air circulation.

Knights and men-at-arms continue to trail southwards from the Scottish campaign, some with bandaged, still-weeping wounds, and Harry feels a pang of concern for his charge as he hears them curse the Scots and brag what they'll do next time they encounter one. And the further into peaceful England they go, the more obnoxiously curious people become. Hands grab at the cloth, tugging it up; faces peek under it. Harry is pushed into an exhausting hyper-vigilance, keeping himself and Star between the cart and the overly interested.

It's not just for the sake of their prisoner. Harry doesn't dare imagine what will happen if someone gets close enough for the Scottish boy to grab them.

The boy remains silent, even when asked direct questions. He eats enough for two men.

Harry teasingly calls the boy *Lord Death*, or *Your Majesty*. He gets no response.

At night, they stay at inns. Harry sleeps in the back of the cart, guarding the prisoner. Johann sleeps in the stables' hayloft with the other men-at-arms.

At an inn outside Shrewsbury, Harry's worst fear comes true. Johann cadges his pay and then drinks it all in the company of a quartet of Suffolk longbowmen. They're too drunk to realise that the lump of cloth in the front of the cart isn't bags, but Harry, awakened by their noise. The bowmen pull the cover off the cage and throw night soil and kitchen slops at the boy, insulting him in the crudest English terms.

The boy growls at them then turns to glare at Harry. 'Let me out,' he hisses.

One of the bowmen pulls out a long knife. '*He's not under King's guard. Fuck him*,' the man says in English, and stabs the knife through the bars of the cage. The boy lurches back as one of the other bowmen pokes his dagger in the space the boy moves into. The boy has to hop away, ungainly and off balance.

The two bowmen laugh, and the rest join in too, long knives clattering against cage bars, seeking pale, thin flesh. '*Dance! Dance, you savage!*'

The boy spins towards the slowest and drunkest of them and slices the ropes binding his arms on the man's dagger. But it leaves him open for a moment, and a knife darts in, nicking him deep on his thigh.

Harry stands up, drawing his broadsword in one smooth motion as he throws off the cloak he was sleeping under. They're drunk and he's not, and it's short work for him to knock some reticence into them with the flat of his sword. By the time three of them are on their arses in the gutter, Johann has vanished.

Harry turns to punish the fourth, just in time to see the boy grab the bowman's wrist, yank the man against the cage so hard his nose fountains blood, and then wrench the man's arm around until there is a sickening pop and a scream.

As the bowmen struggle to their feet and back away, Harry snarls, '*I am Sir Harry Lyon. The boy is under my protection. The next person who so much as* looks *at him will swallow my steel.*' He sheaths his sword with what he hopes is a dramatic enough flourish. '*Tell your friends,*' he says.

'*We weren't gonna kill him,*' the least-drunk bowman whines. '*We were just gonna rough 'im up a bit.*'

Harry grins. '*Well, he's a starving, unarmed boy in a cage and he still bested you. I'm sure your friends in the tavern would* love *to hear* that *tale.*'

The bowmen stutter their apologies to Harry – not to the boy, not to the actual person they harmed – and scuttle off into the night.

Harry sighs and sinks down onto the driver's bench of the cart. It creaks slightly under his weight. He needs Johann to drive the cart, but they are going to have a very serious talk in the morning. He looks over at the boy, his face barely visible in the moonlight. 'Are you well? Your leg—'

The boy grunts something noncommittal, and Harry can more hear than see him as he rustles in the straw, back underneath Harry's spare cloak. He curls up into a ball in the middle of the cage, as far from all the bars as he can.

Harry settles himself back down, his head pillowed on his rolled-up mail and surcoat, his good cloak over his legs, and stares up at the clouds scuttling across the stars.

He's almost asleep again when he hears a soft, rough whisper. 'Harry. Why did you do that for me?'

Harry rolls onto his side. 'Because I gave my word I'd take

care of you.' He snickers, because for some reason it's funny. 'Even if you are an absolute plague.'

The boy snorts, and then there's silence. Harry thinks it's the end of the discussion. But then, quietly, the boy says, 'I'm still going to kill you one of these days.'

'Well, until that day comes, sleep well, Lord Death,' Harry whispers.

There's a pause, and more rustling.

'Seonaidh mac Maíl Coluim,' the boy says, so softly it's almost inaudible.

'What?' Harry says, sitting up.

'My name,' the boy says grudgingly.

'Then, good night, Suh, uh, Shunay,' Harry says, his tongue stumbling over the strange name.

The boy sighs. He's lying on his back now, looking at the same stars as Harry. 'Iain. I was called Iain by my family.'

'Well. Good night, Iain,' Harry says. 'I'll be taking that bowman's dagger back off you in the morning.'

Harry goes to sleep full of a strange happiness, lulled into dream's embrace by the sounds of soft, emphatic Gaelic cursing.

Johann shows up shortly after the bells of Prime looking like he's been dragged through a hedge backwards. Harry gives him a very stern talking-to, the effect of which is moderated by the man-at-arms not remembering much of the previous night. The next day's travel is in unrelenting sunshine and by midday, Johann resembles nothing more than a very hungover beetroot.

Iain (and it's strange and thrilling for Harry to think of him as *Iain* rather than the Scottish boy) is reluctantly convinced to surrender the stolen knife in exchange for a half-dozen honey cakes, a few early apples and a flask of small beer. Harry is amused beyond measure that Iain has a sweet tooth, and tries thenceforth to pick up something for him at each market they pass through.

The rest of the ride south passes uneventfully. Johann doesn't drink his pay, and Harry doesn't retie Iain's hands, except at rivers and streams when they bring him out of the cage to wash.

They ride into Dartington Manor on a fine mid-August day almost a fortnight after leaving Shrewsbury. The manor's dozen servants are arrayed outside the small, wattle-and-daub hall to greet them, with Annie's strawberry-blonde head split by a grin nearly ear to ear. Annie has managed the day-to-day business of Dartington Manor for almost a decade. She's a dumpling of a woman, rosy and broad, country beautiful with her freckled cheeks and easy smile.

She throws her arms around Harry almost as soon as his feet touch the ground, chattering in broad West Country English her thanks to God for his safe delivery, and then shrieking in delight when she spies the knight's belt sitting at his hips. She demands he tell her *everything*, but before he can answer she pulls him into a triumphant little jig, right there in the courtyard, in front of everyone. Harry would be mortified, but the servants had known him his whole life and they've seen worse. So much worse.

Then the cart comes through the gates, and sound stops coming out of Annie's mouth. Her brows furrow, and she looks at Harry. '*A cage?*' she mouths.

Harry rolls his eyes, a gesture that he realises he's picked up from Iain. '*It's a long story, Annie, but he's . . . he's a Scottish prisoner. And my new squire.*'

Annie marches over to Iain and chatters pleasantly to him in English, asking him his name, where he's from, and so forth, while Peter the stable-boy unhitches the cart-horse and Johann's palfrey that was tied behind the cart, and Harry directs Katie the kitchen apprentice to pull Johann into the hall for some food.

Iain just cocks his head at Annie, watching her, as she watches him, waiting for him to answer.

Harry realises what's going on once the initial bustle of their arrival settles, and calls out to Annie. '*Annie, he only speaks French and, uh, the Scottish language. He hasn't understood a word you said.*' And he prays that Annie won't react badly to Iain being Scottish. She doesn't seem the sort, but he's learned on the road back from Berwick that people can surprise you in odd and uncomfortable ways.

Annie, bless her, merely clucks in annoyance and waggles her finger at Iain. '*We'll have to teach you English, m'boy! Scots ain't much use 'round these parts.*' Harry turns and snorts into his sleeve at Iain's somewhat cross-eyed expression of shock.

Then Annie rounds on Harry, and it's Iain who splutters with laughter as Annie braces her hands on her hips and scolds, '*He's too thin, Harry! Looks like he could barely lift a sword, much less swing one. You know you have to* feed *them, right?*'

Harry shakes his head. '*Annie, he has eaten every damn bit of food England can provide, from the border to here. I swear he puts away more than Ralf does.*'

A delighted, if somewhat manic, glint appears in Annie's eye.

Harry turns to Iain, his expression forbearing. 'Annie's a

feeder. She's eyeing you up like a Christmas goose, Iain. You and your appetite are about to become her favourite people.'

Iain raises an eyebrow, looking hilariously nonplussed.

Annie elbows Harry so he translates for her. As Harry talks, Annie just folds her arms and nods at Iain, a slightly unhinged smile on her face. She then pats Harry's shoulder. '*We'll get him settled in soon enough and then he'll never want to leave*,' she says. '*All the prayers I've said to find you a friend your own age, looks like the Blessed Virgin was listening after all.*'

Harry's smile goes tight. '*You know I was knighted by the King himself, Annie?*' he says. She squeals in delight and grabs his arm, and all talk of the horrifying events in the North is forgotten for now.

The kerfuffle their arrival causes dissipates within an hour as Annie smacks people about the head and sends them back to their tasks. Harry sends for Ralf, the blacksmith, and they have a hurried conversation in English about Iain's . . . *proclivities*. Harry at first tries to be subtle, out of a reflexive shame for what they did in Galloway and his part in it, but when Ralf's brown eyes cloud with confusion Harry finally huffs, throws up his arms, and explains that Iain tries to run away at every opportunity.

'*Then why is he your squire, if all he wants is to run away?*' Ralf asks.

Harry grumbles that it's a complicated situation and it's best for everyone if Iain stays around for a while.

Ralf frowns, glancing from Harry to Iain, who is sitting cross-legged in the cage watching them, then back to Harry again. Thankfully, Iain has been on best behaviour since arriving at Dartington. Harry can't help but worry that he's planning something.

Ralf returns to his forge and comes back towards the end of the day in a cart containing a pyramid-shaped lump of iron with a chain and a cuff attached to a loop at its top. He also brings a set of leg manacles, loose enough to allow walking, but heavy enough that they'll significantly hamper any attempt to run.

Harry and Annie decide it would be best if Iain slept in the solar, with Harry – the one person who can communicate with him – rather than in the hall with the servants. Annie catches something in Harry's tone, a hesitation, and she narrows her eyes at him. '*You want me to make up a pallet?*' she asks.

'*That might be best,*' Harry sighs. '*He threatens to kill me on a regular basis.*'

Annie hums, and gives him a look, and that look says, *we will discuss all of this later*. Then she marches off to make sure Katie has supper under control and Blond Peter (who they've all nicknamed Piers so he doesn't get confused with Brown Peter, the stable-boy) is actually making up bedding and not just sitting on a fence woolgathering.

It takes both Ralf and Harry straining together to carry the pyramid of iron up the stairs from the hall to the solar. They put it near a window, a good fifteen feet from the family bed.

Harry stands and wipes the sweat beading on his brow with his forearm, looking around the room that should contain a whole family, but now holds only him . . . and his prisoner.

There's the big bed, a horsehair mattress on a heavy wood frame. Given the summer heat, the curtains are off the bed, and only feather pillows and light wool blankets atop it. The shuttered windows are wide open, to let as much air through as possible. The main carved chest sits snug against the far wall, under a row of pegs for clothes. Smaller chests line the bed. Next to the bed is a little desk, with a polished silver mirror, a washbasin, and a bone comb on it, and a bench tucked underneath it. The chamber pot is beside it too, for Dartington Manor is old enough not to have a dedicated garderobe.

He realises this is the first time he's been back in the solar since his mother died. Her personal effects are gone, or perhaps just put in the chest against the far wall, but it's still a room Harry associates overwhelmingly with *her*.

The room even still smells of her, somehow. The way she *should* smell, of fresh-cut grass and baked apples and just-washed linen. Not the way she was at the end.

Ralf grabs Harry's arm and only then does he realise that he's stumbled. That his cheeks are wet.

'*I— I'm sorry*,' he stutters, swabbing at his face with his sleeve. '*We should get the boy.*'

The scabbard of his broadsword bangs against his leg on the way down the steps, and it's a reminder to Harry of how everything has changed. He runs Dartington Manor now. It stands or falls by his decisions. He's nineteen, an age where boys his class are normally riding from tournament to tournament, following the court's progress around England the way flowers follow the sun. But instead he's responsible for all these people, for whether they flourish or starve. All of them looking to him, to *him*, who accidentally wished a man dead, for wisdom and guidance.

Except for the one person who wants to kill him, of course.

Harry feels like he can't breathe. All he wants is to sit down on the stone steps and not do anything, not decide anything. But there's a boy in a cage outside, and a dozen people downstairs in the hall who think of him as their lord, and they're all depending on him.

Harry clears his throat, tugs down his tunic and steps into the hall. He thanks Ralf, who pats his back a little too hard with his spark-scarred hands and says, '*Anytime*,' and they both go outside.

Harry squints against the late-afternoon sun.

Iain is lying on his back in his cage, hands folded under his head, one ankle thrown over a knee, as if he doesn't have a care in the world. He lazily rolls into a sitting position when he hears Harry fumbling at the lock.

'I don't want to have to tie your arms in front of everyone,' mumbles Harry, when he feels those pale eyes on him.

Iain grins, wolfish.

Harry groans. Of *course* the boy is going to be a little shit about it. He grabs the length of extra rope from the front of the cart. 'Give me your wrists,' he says.

'No,' Iain replies.

'Then you'll stay out here all night without supper, instead of sleeping on a nice pallet indoors with a stomach full of—' and Harry sniffs over his shoulder— 'roast mutton, and damson pie.'

Iain shrugs, and lies back down again. 'Eh, I'm fine here.' Then he smiles again. 'Your vassals give me a lot of funny looks, Harry. Guess you don't get people in cages very often in this backwater of yours.'

Harry flicks the lock on the cage, opens the door and deliberately turns his back, walking a few steps away. When he speaks, it's barbed, deliberately so. 'My people are concerned about me. But then again, I make sure they have plenty of food and clothing. You may not remember what that's like, but I can assure you that a *well-run* manor—'

—And then ten stone of concentrated Scottish rage slams into him.

Harry is expecting the hit, so he twists with it and ends up sitting on top of a flailing, furious Iain, who's yelling at him hysterically in a nonsensical mix of Gaelic and French in between trying to bite him and claw his eyes out.

Both the Peters come running out of the hall at the noise, and they sit on more of Iain, and after a frantic few moments of wrestling they manage to tie his arms and hobble his legs. Iain gets a split lip and opens one of the cuts on his head again. Peter gets a nasty scratch on his face, Piers is bitten on his leg, and Harry gets kneed in the balls, but the job's done. He thanks the Peters and tells them to go back inside. As his gaze travels to the entrance to the hall, he can see Annie standing there, watching them.

Iain snarls at them, sprawled in the dust.

And Harry has had enough.

He gets up, grabs Iain's shoulders hard enough to bruise, and hauls him to standing. Then he marches the boy at arm's length into the hall. Harry can feel the population in the hall staring – and it's *everyone*, word has got around that their lord is back, knighted and with a prisoner. Dozens of new faces, eyes burning with curiosity, tongues blooming with gossip.

Harry keeps his head down and concentrates on getting Iain up to the solar without the boy wrenching free again.

When they're finally upstairs, Harry can't resist shoving Iain so hard he topples to his knees. Iain twists so his shoulder takes the rest of the fall, rather than his face.

'Sorry,' Harry says reflexively, as he attaches the leg iron to Iain and snaps its padlock shut. Then he cuts the ropes and steps away before Iain can take a swing at him.

Harry sits down on the good chest, the one with the carving, and puts his head in his hands. What has he got himself into?

Distantly, he hears Iain exploring the range of motion the chain allows him. There's even straining and muffled swearing that suggest the boy is trying to shift the giant chunk of iron at the end of his tether. Harry can't even muster the interest to look.

He should have said no. He should have told Montagu to go to Hell. He can't do this.

Johann is due to leave tomorrow to head back to Salisbury. He can carry a letter to Montagu, Harry thinks. Tell him the deal's off. Tell him that Dartington Manor can't hold Iain. It's too small. It's not meant for keeping prisoners.

Montagu won't have had time to buy up the manor's debts. Iain can go somewhere else.

Just . . . not here. Anywhere but here.

It's quiet in the room.

Harry rakes his hands through his hair and looks up, suddenly filled with dread.

Iain's sitting on the floor, half turned away from Harry. His fingers absentmindedly trail over the iron cuff around his bony ankle as he stares off into space.

Harry follows the direction of Iain's gaze: he's staring at the bed, and the desk next to it with Lady Joan's mirror and comb.

And he's crying, completely silently.

Three

August–September 1333: Youth of the Beast

Annie works out that Harry and Iain aren't coming down to the hall for supper that evening. She and Katie come up to the solar an hour later with trays of food, to find two sullen boys sitting at opposite ends of the room staring moodily at the floor, the sun nearly down, the hearth nearly out, and not a single candle lit in the room.

But even in the half-light she can see the puffy redness around both boys' eyes.

Annie clucks to herself and motions Katie to put down her tray near Harry. It's mutton and crusty bread and pie with clotted cream, and the smell of it – hearty and so much of *home* – breaks Harry out of his reverie.

Katie sets herself to lighting candles and stirring the embers of the hearth into life again, so as the room begins to flicker with light Annie's shape becomes clearer as she bustles towards the boy sitting on the ground.

'*What's his name, Harry?*' she asks.

'Uh,' Harry says, glancing down at his tray. At the eating knife lying on it, glinting dully in what little light is left. He stands up so fast he feels dizzy. '*Annie, wait!*'

He strides over to her quickly. '*It's Iain. He's called Iain.*' Then he plucks the utensil off the boy's tray. '*And no knives.*'

Annie frowns at him. '*What did he do, Harry? That he has to be chained like this.*'

Something twists inside Harry. '*Nothing. It's . . . he did nothing.*' The dizziness of earlier is rapidly morphing into a headache. '*I'll tell you later. I'm too tired right now, Annie.*'

Annie hums her disapproval and puts the tray down on the floor in front of Iain. Harry idly notes that it has almost twice as much food as his own. And that Iain is glaring up through his curtain of dark hair at Annie.

She grins at Iain, oblivious.

And then she reaches out and *pinches his cheek*.

Harry gazes in horror as it happens. He remembers a tournament in Cheltenham where he watched a knight break his neck. It had seemed to take forever for the man to hit the hard-packed ground once he'd fallen free of his horse. Harry feels now exactly as he did then: that something inescapably terrible is coming. His mind pushes back against it, slowing time, trying to keep the moment from arriving by any means possible. And Harry thinks, *so help me if Iain lays a finger on Annie I'll—*

—'*get some weight on you before the harvest! You eat up, m'boy, and if you want more we have plenty. I thought I'd make blackberry crumble tomorrow.*'

She's ruffling his hair.

Iain's hands aren't bound and Harry knows how snake-fast the boy is when he's out to do damage. Harry's heart skitters in his chest; every muscle in his body is tight with stress. 'If you even *think* of harming her, Iain,' Harry hisses.

'I don't believe in hurting women,' Iain snarls back out of the corner of his mouth. 'Unlike *some*.'

Annie canters on, her good cheer almost a physical force.

She's pointing to herself, repeating loudly and slowly, '*AN-NIE.*'

And Iain brushes his hair out of his face, inclines his head and smiles at her. The complete, utter little shit.

Harry is seized with the urge to strangle him as Iain murmurs, in his beautifully accented, courtly French, 'Thank you so much, milady Anne. For your kitchen's fine cooking and your generosity in sharing it with a prisoner like me.'

'*Coo-er*,' Katie calls admiringly from where she's poking the hearth. '*He's a proper young lord, isn't he?*'

'*What did he say, Harry?*' Annie asks, turning to him.

Harry sighs and folds his arms. 'Iain, if you want to thank her you can do it in English. *Thank you.*'

Iain switches to Gaelic, because he can, and says something to Annie that sounds pleasant but could be *I hope you get fucked by a syphilitic donkey* for all any of them know.

Harry nudges Iain's tray out of his reach. He raises an eyebrow at the boy. '*Thank you*,' he repeats.

Iain rolls his eyes and groans, then turns to Annie and puts that smile back on his face. '*Fank you*,' he says to her, bowing as much as he can from a sitting position.

'*Aww, you're welcome, duck*,' Annie says and reaches in to pat Iain's cheek again.

Harry winces. She could lose a finger that way.

As she and Katie leave, Annie whispers to Harry, '*He seems sweet. Are you* sure *he needs to be chained up like that? He won't run, will he?*'

'*He fucking will*,' groans Harry. Then, once they are in the stairs and away from Iain's view, Harry puts his hand on Annie's arm. '*Annie, don't let Iain's innocent act fool you. He's not safe. He's not getting used to us. He's just* waiting.'

'*Hmph*,' Annie grunts, poking Harry in his stomach. '*There's good in that boy. You know I have the sense for these things and I can tell just by looking at him, Harry Lyon. He'll surprise you.*'

'*And the thought of that keeps me awake at night*,' Harry says wearily. '*In the meantime, make sure he can't get his hands on any sharp objects, please?*'

Harry sits down on the chest and tucks into the cooling mutton and bread. Iain is, as usual, all but inhaling his portion. The meat and loaf is already gone, and he's making short work of the pie, damson juice and clotted cream trickling down his fingers.

And he's staring at Harry.

Harry feels his cheeks redden, and ducks his eyes down to his tray.

He's just finished his own meal when Iain asks, 'Where are your parents?' His voice is carefully neutral.

Harry sighs. 'My father died just before I was born, at Bannockburn. My mother died last month, of the wasting sickness.' And it's still— there's still a hollow ache in his chest when he thinks of her, as if it's some sort of error that she's gone. That something's gone amiss with the world because she won't be striding through the door, needlework tucked under her arm, a bouquet of flowers in her other hand. Some small part of his mind still thinks that soon he'll wake up and she'll be there like always, on the other side of the family bed, embroidery frame propped on her knee, and everything will be right again.

Iain looks down at his empty tray, swabbing up a few pastry crumbs with a finger. 'My father died of that three winters ago.'

Harry crosses to the bed and strips out of his dusty travelling clothes, tossing the breeches and the tunic to be cleaned later, until he's down to his braies. 'I'm sorry,' he says, sitting heavily on the bed. His headache is still throbbing in the front of his head, and he shuts his eyes. 'I'm sorry about everything.'

Iain shrugs.

'I'm . . .' Harry gestures around the solar. 'This is us. It's not very much. I was apprenticed at ten to a Wiltshire knight who had retired from service to the King and I always wondered why he would leave.' Harry sighs. 'And now I know. There's no honour in fighting, is there?'

Iain won't meet his eyes. He's looking at Harry, but not at his face.

'I don't know why I thought war would be like a tournament . . . but what we did with you, that wasn't even war. That was just . . . slaughter. I don't understand why. Do you know?' Harry asks. His voice has stretched to a reedy, desperate thinness by the end, out of energy.

Iain nods, but says nothing. He crawls onto the pallet made up for him, the straw rustling under his weight, and arranges his tattered wool cloak over himself. 'That makes you nineteen, doesn't it? If you were born the year of Bannockburn.'

'It does,' Harry says, snuffing out the candles near the bed. 'How old are you?'

'Seventeen,' Iain mumbles.

'Who were they, your people?' Harry presses, his voice soft in the darkness. 'Why . . .'

He doesn't have the courage, in the end, to say *why did it happen? Help me understand. Give me a reason for the evil we did*. He just lets his voice trail off into a whisper in the night. 'Why?'

'It's better you don't know, Harry,' Iain replies, his voice a tired rasp.

There's more rustling as Iain gets comfortable in his pallet, about ten feet away from the end of Harry's bed. Then Iain's hoarse whisper comes through the darkness again. 'I remember you standing there, in the hall of my castle. You were taller than the others. I don't remember much from that night, not much I want to recall, but I remember you. Your sword was clean.'

Harry shuts his eyes and buries his face into his pillow, tries to stem the flood of tears threatening to burst out of him. He doesn't understand why it means so much to him that Iain *knows*, that Iain realises he didn't participate in the slaughter, but it does. It does.

Johann leaves the next morning for Salisbury. He's hungover again, flushed with it, bleary from too much of Annie's frankly lethal cider. But he remembers to ask Harry if there's any message for Baron Montagu.

Harry freezes.

He looks out at the hall, at his people, who he's sworn to protect. His eyes travel up to the windows of the solar. Iain's still up there, still chained. Harry had left him with a washbasin and a cloth, and the chamber pot, and told Annie to send up a tray of breakfast for him.

He closes his eyes.

'*No. No message*,' Harry says at last. '*Not at the moment.*'

'*You sure?*' Johann says, clumsily mounting his palfrey. '*The Baron'll send Rabbie round to check, otherwise. He probably will anyway, an' all.*'

Harry wipes a hand down his face. The ghost of yesterday's headache still haunts him, and he's suddenly aware he needs to phrase his message just right. '*Tell the Baron that the Scottish boy is being appropriately contained and isn't causing any trouble.*'

Johann snorts. '*Appropriate containment for that little savage is a wooden box, six feet under a priest.*' He flicks the horse's reins and she perks to life, twitching her flank and beginning to turn. '*Dunno why the Baron wants him around,*' the man mutters. '*Only good Scot's a dead 'un.*'

Harry opens his hands in a gesture of powerlessness. '*And yet, we both have our orders.*'

'*That we do,*' Johann sighs.

Harry slaps the palfrey's rump. '*Safe travels, Johann. Thanks for your help on the trip.*'

Johann raises an arm in farewell and kicks his horse into a trot. The groan he gives once she hits her stride suggests he hasn't fully taken into account the effect it'll have on the cider still washing about in his skull.

Harry silently prays Johann throws up over himself further down the road.

The rest of the day passes quickly. There's much for Harry to catch up on around the estate. He straps on his knight's belt and saddles up Star, apologising to the faithful bay for the lack of rest. He sets out to ride the bounds, greeting his vassal farmers. Harry doesn't miss how the farmers' gaze lingers at the leather belt on his hips, the sword hanging down his left side. How they now address him as *Sir Harry*.

He chats to them about the harvest; how it looks like it's

coming late this year. It's the middle of August already, but they don't expect to bring in the wheat until the first week in September, and the beans thereafter. It'll be a push to get everything in and processed by Michaelmas, and Harry is glad he's back to help out.

It's strange, though, riding the narrow, hedge-walled lanes and stopping by the patchworks of fields, accepting and returning the waves of the men and women in front of their dwellings. He knows his vassal families, mostly, but he's been away at Sir Simon's most of the past nine years with only short stints back at Dartington for high holy days and harvests. Time, distance and more pressing concerns have rendered his memory vague, and on top of that there seem to be so many *new* people on the estate. Or were they always there, and Harry just hadn't been paying attention?

He never really needed to know the farmers' names; his mother was the expert there. *That's Rufus, he knocked up the dark-haired scullery maid, you know, Mariah, the one who always puts too much pepper on everything? They're marrying in the spring, we'll send her fabric for a dress. Oh, and you remember Old Donald, if he ever has a nice word to say about anything you know it's the End Times. Good with chickens, though. Hens'll lay for him like nobody else.*

His mother could also explain the relationship of everyone to everyone else in the village, the way a horse breeder could sketch the interconnecting lineage of his best nags for generations. *Aelfred's mother's first husband, the one we all think she poisoned – nasty man had it coming, if you ask me, he beat her – his family were none too pleased she kept his fields, and Eleanor from down moor is going around with one of those cousins, they all work for Ufford now, so if you catch any of them hanging around believe you me they're here for no good. And don't give Eleanor a job, whatever sob story she tells you.*

Harry knows the older faces, in a sort of dull, familiar way, and makes pleasant conversation with them, but he barely knows a single name. He feels a fraud. A fake lord, making fake gestures, to people who can probably see right through him.

At the far end of the manor's lands, at the foot of Dartmoor itself, there's a forest, tangled and ancient, that by tacit agreement nobody touches. It's for the deer and the wild boar and the partridges, not for the humans.

Well, not for *most* humans.

A lonely boy began sneaking away to the pond hidden in its wooded depths almost as soon as he could ride, after a particularly cussed little pony ran off with him and didn't halt until they were at the water's edge. The boy had come back to the pond as often as he could afterwards. His most magical days of childhood were spent there, imagining faerie queens and silver knights holding a forest court, cloaked in robes of state made of spider silk and blossoms from the gnarled apple trees that line the bank.

And now the man returns, lonely still.

It is Harry's most cherished place, completely private during times when he feels nobody will ever leave him alone, nearly silent when he feels surrounded by noise. He loops Star's reins around a birch sapling and walks carefully out onto the flat, mossy boulder that extends into the water.

He lies down in the sunbeam that always seems to reside there, as he has done hundreds of times before, and lets himself be mesmerised by the light filtering through the leaves of the mighty oak and birch trees that surround him.

When Harry was a child, and thought as a child, he would dream wild adventures here. He would be a knight then, as he is now, but all in gold, and he would defeat the dark knight who guards the bridge but not kill him, and that knight would become his staunchest friend. They would ride out together and slay giants and dragons and go home to Harry's fine castle in time for supper. And they would laugh and make merry and swear eternal brotherhood.

Harry was born in a famine year. There were no children of his age or social status nearby. Nobody but Rabbie, and he wanted nothing to do with little Harry. Two years' age difference means nothing now, but it's *everything* when you are eight.

Harry closes his eyes in the warmth of the mid-morning sun and thinks of how he used to pray for God to grant him a knighthood, and a brother-in-arms.

And God . . .

Tears well up in Harry's eyes.

. . . God listened.

God gave him everything he prayed for, and only took the two people he loved most in the world in payment.

And he can't complain, for he had never thought to ask the cost of his dreams.

He is a knight, made so by a king who pitied him in his youth and loss. And he has a squire. A feral, murderous squire of nigh-insufferable temperament.

Harry lies there and tries to glimpse the divine reason for Sir Simon's death. For his mother's. Because the alternative thought

– that God *doesn't* have a plan, that all this random pain and cruelty is merely the purposeless lurching of the human animal as it comes howling into the world and then goes screaming out of it – is *unbearable*.

Perhaps Iain is a test. Perhaps Harry has been too complacent, and God wants to remind him of all he takes for granted.

Iain is someone from whom everything has been taken: family, land, status, country. Who has nothing but the shirt on his back and a ratty wool cloak besides. And Harry was going to send him back to the very man who planned the premeditated murder of his family, because Iain is *difficult*. Because Harry doesn't want to be embarrassed in front of the servants.

Harry's lips form the words of Sir Simon's favourite passage from Luke: *Verumtamen diligite inimicos vestros et benefacite et mutuum date nihil desperantes … Estote ergo misericordes sicut et Pater vester misericors est.*

He opens his eyes, gets on his knees and folds his hands in prayer. He begs God's forgiveness for his weakness, his unworthiness, his impatience, and he promises to try harder. He knows that for too long he has placed faith in worldly men above faith in God, and for that he has been sent these trials.

He will not fail God.

More importantly, he will not fail Iain.

Tomorrow, he will begin again.

Harry stops by the village church on the ride home and says hello to Father Gilbert, the redheaded parish priest, who hugs him fiercely and tells him that they've been saying Masses for his safe return every day. Harry's grip falters a little then, and he asks if instead they could say Masses for Sir Simon's soul, as his body remains in Scotland. Father Gilbert grips his shoulder with a firm hand and gives him his solemn word that he'll do so.

He embraces Father Gilbert again on the way out, and promises to be at Mass on Sunday.

Next, he returns to the manor to go over the accounts with Annie. Things aren't great, and he shakes his head at her when Katie pops into the kitchen to say that Ralf and Piers are butchering a trio of calves for a welcome-home feast later in the week.

'*We can't spare three calves, Annie*,' Harry complains. Their annual payment to the lenders is due on Michaelmas and selling those calves at market would inch them closer to being able to make it. Or, at least, a part of it.

'*Nonsense*,' Annie snips. '*We've lost too much. The village needs to celebrate. You can't keep people working if you don't give 'em something happy every so often, Harry. Life's about more than chores and duty.*'

Harry frowns, but she has a point. At least as far as the vassals are concerned.

'*And besides*,' she continues, '*we don't want the little Scottish lord to think we don't have any manners.*'

Harry groans, dropping his head onto his forearms on the table. He's been ignoring Iain all day, trying to catch up on all his other duties. Trying to get back on an even keel, before Iain goes and knocks him off balance again. '*How is he this morning?*' Harry asks.

'*He's lovely! Ate half a roast chicken for dinner, and a goodly portion of roast parsnips and carrots. I think Katie's sweet on him*,' Annie chirps.

'*God help us all*,' Harry moans.

'*Oh, and he asked about a bath. I said I'd talk to you*.'

Harry nods, his brain already cataloguing everything used in the bathing process, and the likelihood of Iain repurposing it as a deadly weapon. There can't be much trouble he'd be able to get into with lye soap and a rag . . . could he?

'*Tomorrow afternoon, before supper. I need a bath too. You think you can draw enough warm water for both of us?*' Harry says.

Annie grins. '*I can even manage enough to wash both your clothes, too*.'

'*Good. He can have one of my old shirts until his dries. And he'll be coming down to the hall for dinner tomorrow, and every meal after, as long as he behaves. But it would be best if nobody sits too close to him*,' Harry says.

'*Other than you?*' Annie says.

'*Other than me*.' Harry sighs.

Harry stays down in the hall through supper, listening to the quiet gossip of the people of Dartington, *his people*, and solving small grievances where he can. The children ask him for stories of the war, as do a few of the newer servants he doesn't recognise. He just shakes his head, and instead tells them of their bright young king.

When he finally goes up to the solar it's after dark. A few candles have been lit; Annie must have done it when she collected Iain's supper tray. Iain is awake, sitting on his pallet, and Harry can feel cold, silver eyes watching him as he strips off his clothes.

'I'm sorry about today,' Harry says. 'A lot to catch up on around the manor.'

'You don't have to apologise to me, Harry,' Iain murmurs. 'I'm your *prisoner*.'

'You're supposed to be my squire,' Harry says, trying to put some levity into the gulf between them.

'Because I had so much say in that,' Iain hisses.

Harry sits on his bed and hits his hands against his thighs in frustration. 'I had about as much say in it as you did, Iain. This is neither of our first choice—'

The boy on the pallet snorts derisively.

'—but the alternative is a lot worse, and for heavens' sake, Iain, I'm *tired*. Can we just try to make the best of this?'

There's no answer.

Harry blows out the candles and says his prayers under his breath, adding an extra plea to the Virgin for patience.

Harry wakes at dawn. Iain has kicked his cloak off himself in the night and is splayed out on his pallet on his stomach, head pillowed on an arm, his long hair covering his face. His ribs are still visible under his pale skin, and dark bruises blossom over far too much of him. The sores at his wrists and ankles from the ropes are healing – red, angry, crusty, but not infected, thank God. The brutality visited on the Scottish boy's body by Montagu's men sickens Harry, and he's seized with the urge to brush the ratty hair out of Iain's eyes and tell him he'll never be hurt like that again.

The boy would probably tear his hand off if he tried.

Harry can't tell if Iain's still asleep or not. The boy doesn't move as Harry potters around the solar, slipping on his clothes from yesterday and grabbing a few things out of the chests, but he swears he can feel Iain's eyes on him.

'We're going out today,' Harry says, as he pulls the last item he needs out of a chest near the bed. He tosses a pair of his old woollen chausses at Iain's head, along with braies and a breech belt. 'Here. You'll need these.'

'Why?' Iain frowns at the bundle in his hands. 'I distrust immediately any endeavour that requires *hose*.'

After a day of listening to the simple chatter of servants and farmers, something in Harry's heart leaps at Iain's casual eloquence. But he doesn't say anything. Iain's not his friend, and probably never will be. He just holds up his right hand. In it is a two-foot length of iron chain, with heavy, lockable rings at either end. He can tell the moment Iain's expression changes in understanding: *leg manacles*. 'You still have sores on your ankles from Montagu's ropes,' Harry explains. 'These will let you walk around, but unless you put on these chausses and let me wrap over them with some strips of hide to protect those sores, you'll be in agony before we even leave the hall.'

Iain glares at him, but shoves his free leg into the chausses. They're a little big on him – they're an old pair of Harry's for riding, mended at the knee until they couldn't be mended any more – but they'll do. Iain then looks at his other leg, chained to the weight by his pallet, and looks up at Harry, pointedly.

Harry kneels down over Iain's clothed leg and wraps his ankle and lower leg with soft leather. Then he latches one of the manacles over the dressed leg, and detaches the cuff on the other. He looks at Iain expectantly.

'I could bash you over the head with that,' Iain says, tilting his cleft chin towards the other, unlatched end of the leg manacle.

'Indeed, but then you wouldn't see what I have planned for today,' Harry says, grinning. 'Also, the Peters and Ralf are at the bottom of the stairs with clubs, if you try to make a run for it. And trust me, you *never* want to get hit by Ralf.'

Iain narrows his eyes and yanks the hose up his other leg. He sighs in frustration at how loose they are at the top, and sets himself to trying to tie them up as tightly as possible to his breech belt.

'All Annie can talk about is how much you eat, so no doubt we'll have that problem solved soon enough,' says Harry as he wraps and manacles Iain's other leg.

He steps back and offers Iain a hand up.

Iain ignores it, and stands up under his own power. He takes a few experimental steps, his eyes cutting over towards Harry, working out distances to windows and stairs. Figuring out how fast he can move. Calculating.

Harry stands in front of the stairs, arms folded, smiling his mildest smile.

Iain's hands ball into fists and the boy exhales in angry frustration as he realises the manacles' chain is too short and too heavy to allow him to do anything more than shuffle. He looks up, his jaw tight. 'So. What do you have planned for today,' he says, his voice expressionless, 'Harry.'

'Thought we'd get some of that pent-up aggression out,' Harry says, turning and going down the stairs like it was the most natural thing in the world. 'Coming?'

Iain follows, stomping and clanking with every step.

Harry leads him through the hall, stopping to grab a bag filled with bread, cheese and apples on his way past from Annie.

Once outside, they head around the back of the manor to a small, disused paddock near the home barn.

Brown-haired Peter follows them, carrying a bundle that, to Iain's surprise, reveals itself to be wooden practice swords, quilted jackets and padded metal helmets.

Harry tosses Iain a protective jacket and helmet. 'Squire training. Day one,' Harry says. 'I need to see how well you can use a sword.'

Iain picks up one of the wooden swords and gives it a look like it's personally insulted his family. Then he holds it up and raises an eyebrow at Harry. 'I'm not a *child*, Harry,' he grumbles.

Harry checks the ties on his jacket and picks up the other sword. 'If you think I'm letting you anywhere near proper weapons at this moment, you're out of your mind,' he says.

Iain smirks at that. 'I can never decide if you're soft or not.'

'Don't mistake being soft as treating someone with a modicum of human decency,' Harry says, loosening up his shoulder with a few practice swings. 'That's all I'm trying to do.'

'It would be easier if you didn't,' Iain mutters, putting his helmet on.

Blond Piers and Ralf wander up and join Brown Peter sitting on the paddock fence. Ostensibly, they're just casual observers, and so they will remain, unless Iain tries to murder Harry. Which Harry estimates as having about even odds of happening. Ostensibly, that's a walking stick Ralf has, not a shillelagh.

Harry assumes a *garde* position and beckons Iain. 'Come on, then. Rabbie says the Scottish can't fight.'

He barely gets the last word out before Iain is on him.

Now, Harry is very good with a sword, and he knows it. He's spent the past nine years practising every day. He's won or placed highly in every squires' competition he's entered since King Edward started up tournaments again.

But what Iain lacks in technique, he makes up for in ferocity and speed.

Very few swordsmen actually *want* to hit the person they're fighting. It's something Harry's learned in countless tournaments. They shut their eyes at the last moment, aim for the sword rather than the man, or wait too long for their opening.

Iain has no such qualms. It's *exciting*. Every swing, he's aiming to kill. Harry's sword is just an inconvenience to be batted away so he can continue to move his blade towards Harry's body. Iain doesn't have full mobility because of the leg irons, but it simply means he can't advance as fast as he wants. Retreat doesn't occur to him as a possibility.

Iain lays on another full-strength blow, and Harry dances a step backwards, leaving Iain to swing at nothing but air.

'Stop,' Harry commands. 'You have no pacing. There's no point going full strength on a blow you know is going to be parried. You'll just tire yourself out. And you're parrying too far. It's a waste of energy.'

'Won't matter if I'm tired, when you're dead,' Iain pants through his wolf's smile.

'Look,' Harry says, walking back towards Iain and gently nudging at the boy's sword with his own. 'What do you think you're accomplishing by parrying this far—' and Harry pushes Iain's blade about eighteen inches away from his body— 'versus *this* far?' Harry taps aside Iain's blade just enough that it will miss his body by an inch or two.

Iain wrinkles his nose. 'It gives me more time if I've hit your sword way over there.'

'But then *your* sword's way over there too,' Harry says mildly. 'And if you commit that hard to the parry, I can do *this*.' He motions for Iain to parry his swing. Just as Iain commits, Harry flicks his wrist, sending the tip of his sword on a sweet little disengage under Iain's blade. Then he extends and pokes Iain in the stomach. 'See? You left yourself completely open.'

Iain stares at him, head cocked, mouth slightly open. 'Do that again,' he says.

Harry swings, Iain parries, and Harry dips his blade around Iain's again, this time tapping him on the helmet.

Iain mutters to himself in Gaelic, then squares up. 'Again,' he says in French.

Harry holds up a finger. 'Let me show you one refinement that works better in real-world situations. Go slowly, so you can see this.'

Harry swings, Iain parries, Harry disengages again and brings his blade under and around to the inside of Iain's, then rides his blade up the edge of the boy's sword, keeping it locked up to the side where it can't damage him as Harry's own sword-point pokes into Iain's shoulder.

'And honestly,' Harry says, 'going for the shoulder or the chest or the head is all very tempting but their forearm is closer and if you stab it good, they'll drop the sword. Nobody recovers from losing their weapon. Other squires will try to be heroes, waiting for a clean shot at your head or chest. Just nail 'em in the hand or arm, Iain. Then finish 'em.'

Iain's gone still. Harry can't tell what the boy is feeling. His expression is distant, as if he's performing calculations in his head. The boy's shoulders are slumped, his sword hanging listlessly at his side.

Harry bites his lip. Maybe he's being too hard on him for a first day.

'Iain, listen,' he says. 'You're good. You're a natural, and you've clearly had some training. You could be great, though. And I'm selfish.'

That makes Iain look up.

Harry grins. 'Think how Montagu's gang will feel when my Scottish squire wipes the floor with all of their English squires at the first tournament we roll up to.'

Iain doesn't smile but his eyes glitter. He raises his sword up to a *garde*.

And when, about half an hour later, he manages a perfect disengage and stabs Harry hard enough in the bicep to make him yelp, Harry swears that Iain grins under his helmet.

When the church bells ring Sext, the manor's dinner hour, both Harry and Iain are soaked with sweat. Harry peels off his practice jacket and helmet, and staggers over to stick his head in the horse trough near the paddock gate. As he slicks his wet hair out of his eyes, he smiles at Iain. 'Feels good to get the blood moving, eh?'

Iain unlaces his shirt collar and pushes the baggy linen garment down around his waist as he shuffles up to the trough. His face is back to its impassive, sullen mask. He doesn't say anything as he dunks his head, then splashes the cool water on his bare chest.

Harry frowns. He'd hoped for more, somehow. He thought that the sparring had broken the ice between them. But Iain turns away from him and shuffles towards the hall, silent again.

Harry can't understand where he went wrong. He sets off after Iain, afraid of letting him out of sight.

Harry hears Ralf stride up beside him, and glances up at the big blacksmith. '*Thanks for standing by today.*'

'*My pleasure,*' Ralf says, his eyes on Iain's back. His next words are a whisper. '*He's determined to hate you.*'

'*I know,*' Harry breathes.

'*And he's furious with himself that he's failing,*' the blacksmith continues.

Harry looks at Ralf in amazement. Ralf smiles and pats him on the back. '*I must get back to my forge. Keep trying, Harry. The best steel is strong and takes much effort to shape, but with patience, it can become something beautiful.*'

Harry catches up with Iain, his head dizzy from Ralf's parting words.

Iain instinctively turns right, towards the stairs to the solar, but Harry takes his arm and brings him to the short table at the head of the hall. He pulls the bench out and settles down, indicating for Iain to sit next to him.

Iain takes his place and gazes out at the hall, at the couple of dozen servants and farmers and visitors who have assembled for the big midday meal. They'd all stopped talking when Iain came in, the clanking of his leg irons echoing loud in the spreading silence, drowning all conversation. Now, most of the hall stares at the boy, either directly or covertly.

'If you don't mind, I'd prefer to eat upstairs,' Iain mutters, ducking his head so his wet hair falls forwards to cover his face.

Harry sighs and stands up. '*Everyone, this is my new squire, Iain. He's from away and doesn't speak English. I'm sure you will all join me in trying to make his adjustment to life here in the West Country as easy as possible.*' He continues standing, stretching to his full height of six feet two inches as he tucks his thumbs into his knight's belt, and glaring at the people treating Iain like a zoo animal. Slowly, they get the message and turn back to their food. The swell of conversation in the hall rises again.

'What did you say?' Iain asks when Harry sits down.

'I'd say you need to learn English,' Harry says, digging into the pottage and roast trout and bread in front of him.

'I'm going to kill you one day,' Iain sighs, digging into his own food.

'Well, if you could wait until the end of next tournament season I'd appreciate it,' says Harry.

'Unlikely,' mutters Iain around a mouthful of stew.

Annie brings out summer pudding for dessert, with huge portions for Harry (it's his favourite) and Iain (because his appetite remains a thing of joy and wonder to her). She sits down next to Harry and starts in on her own plate. Once the consumption of England's greatest seasonal dessert has been given its due attention, Harry gets to talking to Annie about what day they'll have the feast. They're midway through deciding they should postpone it to Saturday rather than Friday, when Annie nudges him and jerks her chin towards Iain.

Harry glances over.

Iain is asleep, his head pillowed in his forearms, his lips messy and dark with berry juice.

'*Poor lamb must be exhausted*,' Annie whispers.

Harry looks down at Iain, at how peaceful he looks in sleep, long lashes fanned down over sharp cheekbones, and realises he's exhausted too. He hasn't stopped since . . . since before his mother died. Two months of unimaginable stress and misery, and constant travel. And then watching death ride in on wings made of English steel to a mist-shrouded Scottish loch. Harry shakes his head, trying to get rid of those thoughts before they overwhelm him again.

'*I'll take him up*,' Harry says. '*I think I'm going to rest too. The travelling's finally caught up with me.*'

'*Good*,' Annie says, gathering their plates. '*You need it. There's more to life than duty, Harry.*'

Harry doesn't answer her, because he's not sure what to say. *Not for me*, is what he thinks. *Not for me*. Instead he says, '*Definitely postpone the feast to Saturday.*'

He scoops Iain up – the boy weighs so little – and freezes when he stirs. But Iain just mumbles sleepily in Gaelic, tucking his head into the crook of Harry's neck and slinging an arm around his shoulders.

Harry wrinkles his nose as he gets a whiff of Iain. '*And we'll both need those baths tomorrow.*'

Iain sits bolt upright at dawn, his breath coming in ragged, terrified gasps, his eyes darting around the room without recognition.

The clank of his leg chain sends Harry hurtling into wakefulness, his sleep too light, lying as it is on a bed of fear that Iain will somehow escape in the night. 'You're fine, Iain,' Harry says, rubbing his eyes. 'You're safe.'

Iain curls in on himself, hiding his face behind his hair. 'How did I get here?' he murmurs.

Harry smiles. 'You fell asleep after eating almost an entire summer pudding by yourself. Right on the table.'

The look of affront on Iain's face is somehow the most adorable thing Harry has ever seen. 'I . . . would *never*,' the boy chokes.

'You did,' Harry grins. He can't help the warmth that creeps into his voice.

Iain moans something in Gaelic and rubs his face. Then he switches back to French. 'If we hear howling, that's my mother's unquiet spirit come back to haunt me for a horrific lapse in table manners.'

Harry giggles. 'Your mother would really come back to haunt you and not Montagu?'

'Without a doubt,' Iain snorts. 'In our family, murder and betrayal are commonplace. But lapses in etiquette? *Unforgivable.*'

'Sounds like you have an interesting family,' Harry says, hoping he can prise some information out of the Scottish boy about his background.

'Yes. They were,' Iain says quietly, idly rubbing one of the flaking scabs on his wrist with a thumb.

Silence hangs awkwardly between them after that, and Harry gets up to clean his face and hands in the washbasin. When he finishes, he looks over at Iain again. 'Can you ride?'

Iain wrinkles his nose and makes a *so-so* motion with one hand. 'We, uh. We had to sell our horses. After Father died.' A blush colours his high cheeks. 'We wrote to my mother's family for aid but I think the letters were intercepted. Or they didn't want to help us.'

Harry thinks back to Percy and Montagu, and the conversation he half-overheard in Berwick. 'At least one was intercepted. That's how Montagu found you.'

Iain hums, a resigned, hopeless sound.

'Well,' Harry says, forcing himself into a cheerfulness he doesn't feel, 'if you're going to squire for me, you have to know how to ride.'

Iain glares at him, and for a moment Harry is fiercely happy to have that back, to see the fight in Iain's eyes return. 'You're *serious* about this, aren't you?' Iain says.

'What else am I going to do?' Harry replies. 'It's either that or chain you up in here all the time, and Iain—' Harry gestures out the window to the brilliant August sunshine— 'it's too nice outside for that.'

Iain grumbles briefly to himself, but is quiescent as Harry attaches the leg manacles and leads him down and across the hall to raid the kitchen. Harry steals a couple of carrots for the horses and shoves a hunk of cheese and sausage into his mouth. Iain gets his cheeks pinched by Annie and his pockets stuffed with honey cakes by Katie and nearly manages to palm a knife before Harry hustles him out to the stables.

Harry exhales as the smells of straw, sweet hay, leather and horse manure envelop him. He loves the stables, and he can more than understand why Peter chose it as his life.

Iain, on the other hand, is looking around as if he is in a strange, alien land.

Harry goes up to his everyday horse, who sticks her bay

head over her stall and whickers to him. As he scratches her bristly nose, he says, 'You know my palfrey, Star.'

'Well, not *personally*,' Iain says.

Harry pulls a face and gestures to the mare. 'Then come and meet her.'

Star flicks an ear.

Iain pulls a face back at him. 'I'll pass, thanks.'

'C'mon, give her a carrot,' Harry says. Star is a great horse, sweet and mild but fast when she wants to be, and friendly with all strangers. Even strangers who don't seem to be thrilled with the whole concept of horses.

'She's your horse. Give her a carrot yourself,' Iain mutters.

Harry sighs, then indicates the empty stall next to Star. 'My destrier, Nomad, normally lives here but he's still on his way back from the North with Montagu's household.' Then he walks down to the end stall. 'This'll be your horse.'

Harry looks over the half-door into the stall, and groans. 'Get up, you fustilugs.'

He can feel Iain peering over his shoulder as there's a disgruntled whuffle from the stall, and the horse inside stands up.

And up.

And *up*.

Iain gasps as the horse's massive, strawberry-roan head looms over the stall door. 'Jesus, Harry. That's not a destrier, that's an *elephant*.'

Harry steps away from the stall door with a grin. 'His name is Numbles. I'll let you two get to know each other.'

Numbles glances between the two of them, works out that neither will be offering him treats, and sticks his big nose into his hay net.

Iain's face is aghast. He gestures at Numbles. 'Are you having me on? Harry. That's a plough-horse. Look at him. He misses the plough. Don't do this to either of us.'

Numbles looks up, hay falling out of his mouth, and grunts like he's been insulted.

Iain flails angrily. 'And he only has *one eye*.'

Numbles retaliates by butting his head into Iain's chest, smearing his shirt and neck with copious amounts of green, hay-filled saliva.

'Och, you horrible creature!' Iain screams, brushing at the slimy green mess. His panicked ministrations only make it worse.

Harry can't help it. The ice that's gripped his chest since his mother died suddenly cracks open, happiness bursting through him. Before he knows it he's fallen over into the pile of clean straw, clutching his sides as he overflows with laughter.

'Oh, fine, laugh it up,' Iain pouts.

Numbles blows his lips at Iain.

Iain frowns at him. 'Not you too. It's a conspiracy. You're all conspiring against me and my dignity.'

Numbles coughs, spraying small flakes of hay all over Iain's hair and face.

'Plough-horse,' Iain hisses. Then he turns to Harry, who is red-faced and gasping with mirth. 'Harry. *Why?*'

Harry wipes the tears from his eyes. 'He's Nomad's idiot brother. Nobody wanted a one-eyed war-horse who's too lazy to gallop. They were going to sell him for meat, so I said I'd take him. Nomad loves him, and they're great paddock mates. Plus, he's a perfect learner horse.'

Iain folds his arms and glares at Harry. 'I am not going to ride this monstrosity.'

Unfortunately, Iain turns his back on Numbles.

Which is something Harry probably should have warned him about.

Numbles stretches his neck over the stable door and pulls his lips back, then bites Iain hard on the shoulder.

Iain *screams*, then turns around and smacks Numbles on the nose, cursing him in Gaelic.

Harry should feel sorry for Iain but instead he starts howling with mirth again. He gestures helplessly between horse and boy. 'Look, Iain,' he chokes out between ragged gasps of laughter, 'you're *meant* to be together. He's a bitey bastard, too!'

Iain's face does something complicated, going through shock and surprise and then it's like something in him gives way, too. A grin lights up his face, and then he's cackling as well, clutching his stomach and stepping away from Numbles. He trips over his leg chains, overbalances, and lands in the straw next to Harry, the pair of them helpless, shaking with laughter.

It's not even that funny, Harry thinks, but somehow that just makes him laugh more.

Harry looks over at Iain and suddenly understands why Annie calls him *the little lord*; his face is transformed in happiness, eyes crinkling, dimples appearing in his cheeks. He's incredibly, stunningly aristocratic when he's not scowling or hiding behind his hair. Like how Harry pictured Sir Lancelot when he'd play King Arthur all alone down by the pond: his imaginary best friend, the exotic, dark-haired knight of the lake.

Harry coughs as he swallows a breath.

Then Iain makes a profoundly inelegant snort-laugh, punching Harry gently in the side, and the spell is broken.

Peter comes running in a moment later. '*What happened? Is anything the matter?*' he gasps, panting heavily.

He's presented with Iain and Harry lying almost on top of each other in a pile of straw, giggling their heads off. '*He turned his back on Numbles,*' Harry says, gesturing at the bite-mark on Iain's shoulder.

'I hate you all,' hiccups Iain, tears of mirth in his eyes.

FOUR

September 1333: Rusty Knife

Harry isn't really surprised when Iain shuts down again after their morning in the stable, but it still aches. He wants Iain to be happy. He wonders if it's just his guilt talking, his complicity in the massacre of Iain's people, but he doesn't think so. Iain has turned out to be funny, smart and surprisingly athletic, and Harry is surprised to discover that not only can he endure Iain's company, he would seek it out. Yet Iain persists in shutting down Harry's every gesture of friendship. For Harry, starved so long of companionship his own age, the rejection feels especially sharp.

But he has no choice, so he presses on.

He doesn't know if it's his imagination or not, but Iain does seem less combative over the next few weeks. He behaves at the feast on Saturday, and even parrots back a few words of English that various villagers try to teach him.

Harry drags him to Mass on Sunday and is forced to endure Iain sitting in the front pew with him and eye-rolling his way through Father Gilbert's Latin. (It's one of the few times Harry has been grateful for Father Gilbert's poor vision.) 'It's not that bad,' Harry whispers to Iain.

'It bloody well is,' he hisses back.

'Because you're a Latin scholar on top of everything else,' Harry replies.

Iain crosses his arms and slumps in the pew. 'Of course I understand Latin, Harry. Do I *look* like I was raised in a barn?'

Harry raises a judgemental eyebrow at the threadbare Scottish leine Iain still wears, and his messy long hair. Iain has steadfastly refused to don English clothing, beyond borrowing Harry's old pair of chausses for riding. (Harry notices they're not quite so loose as before; Iain's ribs and hip points are no longer standing out so sharply, and when he prays he asks God to bless Annie and her family.)

The days fill up with the estate's business for Harry, as a newly minted lord at nineteen. The first sign is a vassal from the upper bean fields, clutching his hat one morning in the hall and accusing his neighbour of stealing turnips out of his garden. That opens the floodgates of a summer's worth of unresolved disputes and simmering feuds around the manor, all of which Harry must settle by Michaelmas. He wonders how his mother did it all, how she managed to be so sure and confident in her decisions. For him, it feels most of the time that the judgement he metes out is arbitrary, a blind guess as to which vassal is telling the truth and which is lying. If, indeed, either of them is telling any truth at all.

Iain starts spending mornings in the kitchen while Harry is out mending fences both physical and metaphorical. He charms Annie and Katie into teaching him English phrases, and eats everything within reach. They become used to his presence, and turn their backs on him.

He steals a knife.

Harry doesn't find out about it until the blade is pressed to his stomach, Iain plastered against his back and grabbing for the key to his leg irons that hangs on a cord around Harry's neck.

Hot rage blazes in Harry's chest, a fury born of betrayal, and he twists, getting inside Iain's reach and throwing the boy over his shoulder onto the stone floor. Harry is much broader and stronger than Iain and he uses every bit of the power in his massive frame when he takes Iain down. He doesn't even feel bad when the leg chain snaps tight, yanking cruelly at Iain's ankle.

Iain hits the flagstones hard, cracking an elbow, splitting a lip. The knife clatters out of his grip across the floor.

Harry picks up the knife and looks over at Iain, still sprawled on the floor. Iain glares up through his hair at Harry, insolently licking the blood off his lip. And Harry thinks about what Iain said that morning they first went riding: *in my family, murder and betrayal are commonplace.*

Harry realises how little he really knows about the boy. And how masterfully Iain is manipulating him and everyone else at Dartington. He was a fool to think he could befriend someone like Iain. Harry grinds his teeth and walks out of the solar without a word.

He leaves Iain there for the rest of the day.

Piers waves at him cheerfully as he stalks across the hall towards the kitchens and calls out, '*You and Iain going to spar today?*'

Harry whirls at him, muscles tensed and a string of curses on the tip of his tongue. Piers blanches, eyes widening. He is slight and so fair as to seem under-cooked, a good eight inches shorter than Harry. Harry realises he's looming over the boy, fists balled. He backs off, ducking his head in apology and raising his hand. The hand that still has the knife in it. '*I'm sorry, Piers. It's nothing. Not today. Iain's not feeling well.*'

'*Oh. You want me to go and keep him company?*' Piers asks.

'*No. It. Uh,*' Harry stutters. '*It might be catching.*'

He turns tail and stalks towards the kitchen, avoiding everyone else's gaze. Then he slaps the knife down on the kitchen table and tells Katie and Annie in no uncertain terms how close their lapse in attention came to fetching him a blade between the ribs.

That night, Harry is pretty sure Iain is only faking sleep, his eyes shut and his body still. Well after midnight, he's proved correct. From the pallet come quiet sounds of exertion, and the muffled chink of a chain wrapped in a ratty old cloak so it won't make a noise.

Harry squints into the gloom. Iain is trying to move the weight at the end of his chain. Harry's lip twitches. *He* can barely lift that weight. There's no chance of Iain, skinny and small as he is, shifting it.

In the coming days, Harry continues to spar with Iain, more for his own sake than the boy's. His life seems to be an endless grind of frustration at the moment, full of squabbling vassals, mounting debts and a Scottish serpent in his home. It feels *good* to hit things.

He doesn't force Iain to fight. Every morning he offers Iain a choice, and Iain never refuses. The boy is getting better, too. He's a fast learner, and turns out to have a patience and tactical cunning that matches his ferocity. He's still nowhere near an even match for Harry, and still doesn't understand the concept of retreat, but Harry finds himself having to work for his wins a little more each day.

He also has Ralf forge a set of manacles with a longer chain that Iain can wear on horseback, the chain looped behind him on the saddle. Harry had originally hoped he could unchain Iain while riding. Star can easily outpace both Numbles and Iain, but Harry is growing to respect the Scottish boy as an opponent and decides not to hand him an easy opportunity for escape.

Numbles and Iain come to a grudging understanding, and Iain stops insulting Numbles to his face after the horse 'accidentally' steps on Iain's foot. (Harry thinks that perhaps Numbles understands Gaelic.) Harry still can't tell if Iain enjoys their rides but, like the sparring, he's always offered a choice, and he never says no.

Harry also notices the carrots and apples that Iain sneaks Numbles when the boy thinks nobody is watching.

A week later, the afternoon before the start of harvest, while the kitchen is overloaded preparing bread and pies to eat in the fields the next day, Iain steals another knife.

Harry isn't so easily fooled this time. He notices the shifty way Iain acts that evening, his right hand lurking near his back as he watches Harry.

Harry makes him give the knife back.

'Go to sleep,' Harry growls, placing the knife under his own pillow. 'You're going to spend the next week working sun-up to sun-down in the fields like everyone else, and if you stay up half the night trying to lift that hunk of iron, you'll have only yourself to blame when you drop dead on your feet by afternoon.'

Iain mutters darkly in Gaelic but, for once, does what he's told.

At Lauds, the sun just breaking over the horizon, Harry drags a half-asleep Iain to the home fields and shoves a scythe into his arms. Iain's eyes take in the nimble, wickedly hooked sickle tucked into Harry's belt, and travel along the crowd of similarly equipped vassals at the edge of the field. He frowns, hefting the heavy, clumsy implement in his hands. 'Why do I get this?' he grumbles.

Harry shakes his head. 'You know why, Iain.' Then he notices that Iain is still looking at the scythe in confusion. 'You *have* harvested before, haven't you?' Harry asks.

Iain blushes, and bites his lip.

Harry sighs, and hands his sickle to Annie's cousin Kit to hold. He takes the scythe back from Iain. 'Watch and learn, Your Majesty.'

Kit snorts with laughter. Iain crosses his arms and pouts disdainfully.

Harry steps forwards and swings the scythe in a low arc. It's the official beginning of the harvest, the lord of the manor taking first cut, and a cheer rings out across the fields as everyone else begins. The wheat falls with a *whush-shush* sound that's like a lullaby to Harry's soul, a song of the turning seasons that he's known as long as he can remember.

'You want to aim as close to the ground as you can,' he explains, breathless with effort. 'After we thresh the wheat, we'll use the stalks as winter straw. Keep going straight and even to the end of the field; I'll be working to your left, and the women will follow behind and gather.' He hands the scythe back to Iain. 'Try to use your hips and legs and shoulders, not your lower back, or you'll regret it tomorrow.'

He indicates for Iain to begin. Iain narrows his eyes at him and shuffles forwards. Harry's left him in the longer leg irons, the riding ones, since he'll need more mobility for swinging the scythe.

The sun is barely up and it's already hot. As Harry unlaces his shirt and pushes it down to his waist, he feels mildly guilty that he's given Iain the heaviest harvest tool they have, when he already has to walk in leg irons. But an exhausted Iain is an Iain less likely to murder anyone. Given what a hectic time the harvest is, Harry has no qualms about playing dirty if it helps them all survive the week.

It takes eight days in the end, just for the wheat, and they're all nut-brown and bone-sore by the end of it. Iain turns out to be the sort who gets freckles in the sun, and Harry watches them bloom over his shoulders and back as he works, first constellations of them, then galaxies, his skin getting not so much tanned as all his freckles merging together. Copper highlights appear in his dark hair, which Annie ties back for him in a twist so it stays out of his eyes as he works.

Iain never complains, never refuses, even though the work is back-breakingly hard. Every night they return to the hall at sunset, asleep on their feet. Iain is out as soon as his head touches the pallet, and Harry is never far behind.

They sleep through the Sabbath, and then the following day everyone who didn't cut wheat moves on to the bean fields and the threshing. On Tuesday afternoon there's a feast to celebrate the successful harvest. They're a week shy of Michaelmas and everything is in safely. There will be food for the winter and extra for the market, and the villages and manor breathe a collective sigh of relief.

Annie brings out a new batch of cloudy cider and they roast mutton over pits and there's special bread, made with the very wheat they've just harvested, the first ears to fall, gathered specially and threshed first and ground.

Harry explains this to Iain as he breaks the braided loaf that Annie had put in front of them. 'This is made from the wheat of the home field, the wheat that you and I cut on the first day. It's good luck.'

Iain looks at the ragged-edged half-loaf that Harry extends to him, and then takes it in his hands, examining it. The boy's eyes are curiously bright, and Harry can't tell what he is feeling. 'It's, uh, good.' Iain mumbles at last, tearing off a piece and cramming it into his mouth.

'Yes,' Harry says. 'Annie makes good bread.'

Iain is silent for the rest of the meal. Harry respects that, even though he's not sure what Iain's latest mood is or how it's been brought on.

Vassal farmers come up to Harry's table to thank him for his help with the harvest. It's tradition in their area for the lord to cut the first wheat, if he's around, but not every lord stays to help with the real work. Harry's learning their names, slowly. Rufus, Eddie, Gawain. Walter. John. They thank Iain too, which surprises Harry, and even more so when Iain looks up and quietly responds, in heavily accented English, '*You're welcome.*'

The problem is that everyone wants to toast their health when they stop by, so Harry consumes a little more of Annie's cider than he intends. Maybe a lot more, he thinks muzzily, as he gets up at the end of the meal only to find his legs unsteady beneath him.

Iain is staring glazedly off into space, blinking occasionally and swaying slightly in his seat, and Harry reckons that Iain's been drinking along with the farmers' toasts too. Ugh. They're both going to feel like a cow shat in their head tomorrow, Harry thinks. 'C'mon, Iain,' he says, slinging an arm around the boy's chest and helping him to his feet. 'Let's go sleep it off.'

'What *is* that stuff?' Iain slurs.

'Scrumpy,' Harry hiccups. 'Issa West Country speciality.'

'Och,' Iain moans.

They sway against each other, shoulders bumping, arms slung around each other's waists as they make their way up to the solar. It's only just gone dusk, the low sun filling the sky with streaks of rose and gold, but both of them crash down onto Iain's pallet. Iain sticks his legs out and grins at Harry. He has a really nice smile, Harry's fuzzy brain thinks. 'Do the honours?' Iain murmurs, gesturing at his leg irons.

Harry nods, and unlocks the manacles. 'Wish we didn't have to do this, Iain,' he says, his voice coming out thick. He reaches for the single cuff that will keep Iain tethered to the weight for the night, but Iain chooses that moment to flop bonelessly against him, tucking his head into Harry's collarbone. The boy hums, and slings a warm, solid arm around Harry's waist.

'Iain, what are you doing?' Harry frowns. He's had *way* too much to drink. All he wants is to lie back and go to sleep, with Iain curled up against his chest. There's an alarm dimly ringing in the back of his mind telling him that would be a terrible idea. But Iain's hair, now that it's washed regularly, is so soft. He runs his hand through it, and then makes the mistake of looking down.

Iain turns so he's sitting in Harry's lap, his legs straddled around Harry's waist, and gazes up at him. Harry feels pinned by those pale-grey eyes, glowing in the last of the summer sun.

Iain licks his lips and—

His mouth.

It's so *beautiful.*

Something low in Harry's belly sparks into flame, and Harry shifts uncomfortably, his brain going *no no this is wrong* but he can't get his body to respond with anything but *yes* as Iain reaches up and strokes Harry's cheek. 'You're so nice to me,' Iain mumbles. 'Nobody's ever been as nice to me as you are, Harry.' There's something akin to regret in his voice, and Harry's too drunk to figure out why. Then Iain's thumb passes over Harry's lower lip.

Harry leans forwards, a moth to a flame, drawn in by pale fire and red lips. His eyes fall shut.

And the iron cuff crashes into the side of his head.

Harry jerks back to consciousness in the middle of the night, face-down on Iain's pallet, his hair sticky with blood.

Iain is nowhere to be seen.

Harry lurches to his feet, his head pounding with a mixture of cider hangover and blunt force trauma. As he shuts his eyes to steady the spinning room, he remembers something from the feast that he'd dismissed as unimportant at the time: Iain's mug of cider had been full when they left. Harry remembers thinking *waste of good scrumpy* as they passed it.

Iain's mug had always been full. He mustn't have drunk a drop, no matter how many times he put it to his lips.

It's a clear night with a full moon, nearly as bright as day. Iain could be halfway to Exeter by now.

Harry staggers downstairs and wakes the hall. The Peters, Kit, Adam the shepherd's apprentice, Wat the pig-boy and the other men of the hall quickly rise from their pallets and light torches in the embers of the fire. Harry's already halfway to the stables, barefoot and furious, when there's a clattering of hooves at the gates of the manor.

He looks up, clutching his torch, as Rabbie Ufford canters in with a crew of his bully boys. Rabbie reins up hard, only a few feet from Harry.

And he realises Rabbie is pulling something behind his horse.

'Sir Harry,' Rabbie sneers.

'Sir Robert,' Harry returns, as politely and tonelessly as possible. 'What brings you to Dartington so late?'

'You know Montagu made me Sheriff of Devon on the way home from Carlisle?' Rabbie says, his voice haughty. 'Or maybe you didn't, seeing as you weren't with us.' Then he yanks the rope anchored to the pommel of the saddle. 'Found some livestock of yours running loose on the moor.'

Iain stumbles forwards. His hands are bound and the rope is around his chest.

And he's been *dragged*.

His knees and shoulders are a mess of dirt, blood and shredded clothing, but he is somehow still standing, glaring at all of them like a wet cat. Harry is sure the only thing keeping Iain on his feet right now is pure spite and suddenly he's fiercely proud of this boy.

He steps forwards to take the rope from Rabbie.

'Ah-ah!' Rabbie says, lifting it away. 'Lyon, part of my duty as sheriff is to put down any stray dogs that get reported to me. You need to keep your animals in pens, where they belong.'

Behind Rabbie, Iain spits in the dirt. His saliva is red with blood.

Harry desperately wants to make a comment about how that stray dog managed to all but bite off Rabbie's ear, but he knows there is only one way he'll get the rope back without further violence on Rabbie's part. So he closes his eyes and recites, 'I'm very sorry, Rabbie. We'll keep better control of him next time. Thank you for bringing him back.'

He holds out his hand again for the rope. Rabbie leans down and whispers into Harry's ear as he hands over the length of hemp. 'Use your head, Harry. Who do you think will take over Dartington if Montagu closes on your debts? I get your Scottish dog and your hall if you keep fucking up. So do better, because I honestly don't want to add this fleapit of yours to my lands. It doesn't make enough money.' Then he sits back up on his horse and gives Harry a mocking salute. 'Nighty-night, Harry! Don't let the bedbugs bite.'

They watch Ufford and his boys ride back out of the manor and turn onto the north road through the moor. Everyone is still hungover, half-asleep, and frozen in confusion at what they've just witnessed.

Iain is the first to move.

As soon as Rabbie and his men are out of sight, he collapses. He sinks down to the ground in stages, first the knees, then the hips, then the arms, like a puppet with his strings cut.

Harry wants to run to the boy, wants to gather him up, but he refuses to get played for a fool again.

Iain convulses in the dirt, shaking uncontrollably.

Harry hears Annie's sleep-fogged voice behind him. '*What in the name of Jesus—*' Then she sees Iain and she shoves Harry aside, her tone sharpening into one of command. '*God's blood! Adam, well water. Kit, Harry, carry him inside. Peter, draw a bath. Wat, fetch me a jug of vinegar and a handful of mint. Piers, get my scissors from the kitchen, we need to cut his clothes off him.*'

Everyone jumps to her orders. Harry picks up Iain in his arms and carries him into the kitchen, as Peter rolls out the big wooden, cloth-lined tub Harry's family use for bathing. They put him straight into the tub as it's clearest, and begin the process of separating fabric from torn flesh. Iain hisses and flinches into wakefulness after a particularly ground-in strip of wool is peeled off his knee, and he glares round at them with the eyes of a wounded and cornered animal.

Annie motions for Peter to hold off pouring water for a moment.

Harry leans in so Iain sees him, and smooths the hair out of Iain's face. 'Ssh, all is well, you're safe,' he says as soothingly as he can. 'You're back at Dartington. You're with us.'

Iain shivers uncontrollably again and squeezes his eyes shut, fat tears dripping down his dirty cheeks. 'I hate you,' he whimpers, his voice reedy with pain.

Harry keeps brushing through his hair. 'I know,' he replies. He gently untangles twigs and bits of hedge from the boy's locks, watching how their copper highlights glitter in the hearth-light.

'Why can't you just hate me?' Iain sobs under his breath. 'It would be so much easier.'

'Save your energy,' Harry says. 'We can fight tomorrow. Right now we have to rinse those scrapes out with vinegar before they fester. You've brought half the moor home with you.'

Iain lifts a shaking hand out of the water and slowly reaches out to tap the crusted blood on Harry's temple. He frowns.

'Yes,' Harry says softly. 'We'll clean me up too, don't worry.'

Iain spends the next day recovering up in the solar, newly kitted out in a threadbare, hand-me-down shirt of Harry's that's still like a dress on him. The servants take shifts to watch over him.

Harry passes the morning on his knees in church, praying for guidance. Because he'd . . . he'd *wanted* things that no man should want from another man. Father Gilbert asks him three times if he wants to go to confession, and on the third time Harry relents and says yes.

He's furiously ashamed, though. He doesn't confess fully. Instead he tells Father Gilbert he'd got drunk at the harvest feast (which he's sure qualifies as gluttony) and almost acted on lustful thoughts. He just leaves out that those thoughts were about a *man*, and that the only reason he didn't act on them was the man knocking him on the head with a length of iron chain.

Father Gilbert smiles at him through the screen. '*If only all confessions were like yours, Harry, Devon would be considerably closer to God than it already is.*'

Harry makes a low noise in his throat because *no*, he wants to be punished for this. He *needs* to be punished.

Father Gilbert shakes his head. '*Harry, you don't make a habit of being drunk, do you?*'

'*No, Father*,' Harry replies. This was the first time he'd been inebriated in *years*. Not since he'd won a squires' competition at sixteen, up in Newmarket against much older competition, and everyone from Sir Simon on down had stood him drinks all night. Harry distinctly remembers throwing up on a hedgerow, then falling headfirst into said hedgerow, and waking up there the next morning feeling like Nomad had kicked him in the noggin. He hadn't been much of a one for drunkenness since.

'*Drink makes a man do strange and stupid things that he would never consider sober. Have you had lustful thoughts towards this woman before or since?*'

Man, Harry mentally corrects, cringeing inwardly. But his mouth says '*No.*' Because it's true, isn't it? He furrows his brow and thinks back over all his interactions with Iain. It breaks down to wanting to strangle the boy half the time and wanting to be his friend the other half. '*No*,' he repeats, more certain.

'*That's what I thought. I'd like you to say two Ave Marias and stay away from Annie's cider. I think the homily this Sunday will be on temperance, as well, so we'll pick some good passages from the Bible to discuss.*'

'*Thank you, Father*,' Harry says.

'*And perhaps it's time for you to start looking for a wife*,' Father Gilbert smiles. '*How old are you now? Twenty?*'

'*Nineteen, Father*,' Harry says.

He rides out to his forest pond afterwards and confesses fully to God, kneeling on the rock, begging for forgiveness.

And as he looks over the still, quiet waters of the pond, he thinks perhaps Father Gilbert is right. Perhaps the companion his heart cries out for is a wife, not a brother.

Then he lies back on the rock in the sunshine and does the *other* thing he comes to the pond for. The second reason he needs a private place, beyond the solar he shared with his mother and a rotating bevy of female servants. Because, he thinks, as he unlaces the front of his breeches, Ave Marias are all very well, but they don't ease the frustration that's been simmering under his skin since he got back from Scotland.

He pulls out his cock and begins to stroke himself, closing his eyes and imagining the curvy, coiffed women of the King's court slipping out of their dresses, beckoning to him. His cock fattens into hardness surprisingly quickly, and it's not long until he is arched off the rock, sucking his breath in through gritted teeth and trying to stifle his moans as he fucks up into his own hand. The fantasy of courtly beauties in his mind shatters into confused fragments: his hands fisted in dark hair; wet, ferocious open-mouthed kisses; and strong legs wrapped around his waist. Harry comes hard, grunting his release, the orgasm almost painful in its intensity. He keeps his eyes shut until the waves of pleasure shudder to a stop and he lies panting on the mossy rock, his head feeling clearer than it has in weeks.

Iain tries again a few days later.

They're on their horses. Iain wears the longer manacles on his legs, the chain tucked over Numbles' back behind the saddle. Harry unconsciously leads them north through dale and lane, until he realises they're heading towards the pond, to the secret place he's never even considered showing another person. He pulls up, surprised at himself, and waves for Iain to stop too so he can decide whether he's truly ready to share with Iain something so . . . *private*.

But Iain doesn't stop. Instead he digs his heels in and Numbles lurches into a canter. Harry is momentarily amazed that Iain managed to coax Numbles out of a trot, when Iain kicks the big horse into a gallop and reins him sharply east towards the Exeter road.

Harry swears, spurring Star to follow. Star flattens her ears and neck and darts forwards into her fast, ground-eating gallop and then both of them are racing down a narrow, hedge-lined lane, the big lumbering roan and the quicksilver bay palfrey.

Harry is gaining on Iain and yells at him to stop, that he'll never outrun them. Iain glares briefly back at Harry, his face a mask of savage determination. But Harry isn't a fool; he gave Numbles to Iain for a reason, and the reason is that Numbles is possibly the laziest horse in the county. Numbles is galloping, after a fashion, but it's slower than Star can canter, and Star is rapidly catching up.

Harry's already planning how he's going to lean out and grab Numbles' reins (and possibly smack Iain on the back of the head on the way past) when Iain pulls an eating knife out of his clothes and stabs Star in her shoulder. The palfrey shies hard, skittering sideways into the hedgerow. Harry stays in the saddle but reins her up so she doesn't injure herself further. He looks down. The knife is embedded in Star's shoulder a couple of inches, blood sluggishly welling around the blade. Harry has never been so furious.

And Iain has a brief, glorious few moments of freedom, grinning back at Harry, fiercely proud of his own cleverness, before Numbles decides to investigate a tasty-looking tuft of grass he's glimpsed. The horse plants his big hooves, and Iain goes flying over his head into a drainage ditch.

Harry dismounts, shaking with anger. He straddles the ditch and pulls Iain out by his hair until they're face to face. Iain visibly blanches at Harry's expression of fury.

'Do. Not. Ever. Stab. My. Horse. Again,' Harry growls, glaring at the wet, muddy boy. 'I don't mind you trying to escape, but think up better plans.' Then he hauls Iain by the upper arm over to Numbles, throws him over the roan's back like a sack of oats, and they limp back to Dartington Manor. They make swift progress, if only because Numbles always moves faster towards his stall than away from it. Star hobbles along as best she can, each painful step causing Harry's stomach to churn in rage.

Halfway back, Harry stops Numbles.

'What,' Iain says, his voice flat.

'I just want you to know that I'm giving up on you,' Harry hisses. 'I'm tired of trying to get somewhere with you. You just *use* us. You use me and you use Annie, and we're not even people to you, are we? We're just things to manipulate so you get what you want.'

Iain squirms uncomfortably, trying to avert his face, but Harry grabs his chin and forces the boy to look at him. 'I'm *done*,' Harry says. 'Congratulations. I hope that's what you wanted.'

When they arrive back at Dartington, Harry doesn't even chain Iain up to the weight in the solar himself. He has Kit and Piers do it while he and Brown Peter clean Star's wound. It's a straight cut into the muscle, neither long nor deep, the sort of thing he's seen destriers come back from perfectly all the time. But Star isn't a destrier, and hasn't been trained to the noise or pain of battle. Harry feels horrible that she's been made to face it. He throws his arms around her neck in a wordless apology, and Star whickers, nuzzling at his hair, reassuring him.

Annie gives Harry a questioning look in the hall at supper, her eyes going to the empty place at his left where Iain normally sits. When he visibly sags under her gaze she grabs him and pulls him towards the kitchen to talk. Harry assumes she'll stop there, but she keeps going, tugging him past the ovens and out the back door.

Once they're outside, Harry shoots her a puzzled look.

'*I'm not too sure about some of the new kitchen help*,' Annie sighs. '*Best they don't know your business*.' She puts a hand on Harry's arm. '*Peter told me what happened*.'

Harry leans against the stone wall of the manor and shakes his head. Tears are trying to force their way out of him, and he presses his lips together. He *won't* cry. Not over this.

He mulls over what to say to Annie for a long time. '*I thought he could be my friend*,' is all he manages in the end.

Annie doesn't reply; there's really not much to say. Iain isn't their friend. Rabbie was right. He's the kind of stray dog that will bite you as soon as you're done feeding it. Instead she just opens her arms and Harry steps in for a hug. '*Some people you can't fix*,' she whispers to him, '*no matter how much you want to*.'

Behind them, the kitchen door creaks. Harry looks up, but not in time to see who had been listening in on them.

The silence is mutual now.

Harry leaves Iain chained to the weight in the solar through the Michaelmas celebrations. He handles the affairs of Dartington, goes to church, and has the servants take food up to their Scottish prisoner.

And when Rabbie Ufford's new squire, a boy called Mark, rides up with an invitation for some sparring at Ordlington Hall, Harry grabs his practice kit and Numbles and rides off across the moor to Ufford's. When Harry arrives by himself, Rabbie asks, 'Where's your dog?'

'On his chain,' Harry replies, which gets a big smile from

Rabbie and an arm slung around his shoulder. He manages to bear it for about three breaths before stepping away with an apologetic smile.

Harry comes back to Dartington a few days later, tired, sore, and content in the way that only a good, hard fight can provide. He still doesn't like Rabbie or his cronies, but you don't have to like a man to swing a blunted sword at him.

Peter waits at the gate with news. Star's wound became infected from the rusty knife, and she has sickened. They don't expect her to survive.

Harry goes into her stall. She's lying down on her good side. She can barely lift her head to greet him, offering only a weak whicker when she sees him. Her bad shoulder is inflamed, oozing a stinking green pus which runs in crusted rivulets down her leg. They've lanced it, and bled her, but the pus keeps coming.

Harry stays with her, putting her head on his lap and stroking her cheek, until she falls asleep. Then, finally, he returns to the hall, his mood as black as Hell's paving stones.

He goes up to the solar to change. He doesn't even look at Iain as he walks past. Just goes to the bed and starts to strip off his travelling clothes. His knight's belt comes off first; leather, sword and scabbard hitting the mattress with a dull thunk. Then, as he's about to pull his shirt over his head, he hears Iain muttering something behind him.

'What?' he says, not bothering to turn around.

'I'm sorry,' Iain repeats, a little louder. It seems like there is genuine regret in his voice, but Harry is finished with having his own decency used as a weapon against him.

He whirls around, fists balled, and yells at Iain. 'No! No

you're not. You're just saying that to get in my good graces so I'll let you go again.'

Iain's eyes are wide with shock, but then they narrow and a hollow, nasty grin spreads across his face. 'You got me,' he hisses.

'You killed Star, Iain. She's going to die, probably by tomorrow night.' Harry takes a step forwards. 'Who are you going to hurt next? Annie? Peter? You going to finish off poor stupid Numbles like the knackers wanted to do when he was a colt? Club him on his blind side? You're only here because the other choice was for you to go to Ufford and he was the sort of boy who'd pull the legs off kittens just to watch them die. But apparently you two deserve each other. Because all you do is hurt people.'

Iain tries to speak, his lips shaping the beginnings of words, but no sound comes out.

Harry waves a hand at Iain in dismissal, strips off the rest of his clothes slightly more violently than necessary, and crawls into bed. 'Go to hell, Iain,' he says as he blows out the bedside candle.

Harry's belongings finally arrive back from the North the next morning. It's Johann who brings them. Harry is strangely happy to see the man, but not as happy as he is to see Nomad, his big blue roan destrier. Nomad looks more like a pack-horse now, and Harry raises a quizzical eyebrow at Johann. He's sure that Nomad is carrying more things south than he'd brought north. Especially as he'd only packed a change of clothes, spare hauberk and sword, and his tent.

'*Sir Simon 'parently left you some things in his will,*' Johann explains. '*It's what's taken so long. We've been stuck in Salisbury waiting for the lawyers.*'

'*Do you know what?*' Harry asks.

'*His armour and swords, and his books.*' Johann shrugs. '*Nothing important.*'

Harry tries to quiet the racing in his chest. He owns books. *Books*. He thanks Johann profusely, presses some coins into the man's hand, and has Annie pack him the finest provisions she can manage.

Johann grins as Annie comes out with a sack. '*This lady's pies is why I offered to come back here. An' her cider,*' he says with a wink.

Annie elbows him. '*Got a full skin of the new batch in your bag. Go easy on it, it's got a kick like a stung mule.*'

They make small talk for a while, Harry's eyes continually wandering over to the packages Peter is unloading from Numbles, and finally Johann gets the hint.

'*Baron Montagu asks about the boy?*' Johann says as he mounts back up on his palfrey.

Harry groans.

'*That good, eh?*' Johann commiserates.

Harry is so bloody tired of pretending everything is fine. He looks up at Johann and says, '*Honestly, at this point if I could back out of my deal with Montagu and send the boy to Rabbie instead, I'd do it in a heartbeat. I don't want him here.*'

Johann frowns. '*You* really *want me to tell his lordship that?*'

Harry sags. '*Yes, Johann. Let's tell him the truth for once. Maybe he'll forgive me out of its sheer novelty value.*'

Johann laughs. '*He just might, an' all*,' the man says, as he touches his fingers to his cap and spurs his horse down the road.

They move the books up to the solar. Harry clears the table for them, placing his mother's comb and mirror away in a chest, as Piers carries the volumes up one by one. Harry runs his finger reverently down their leather spines. There's the Gospels, a psalter and the *Historia caroli magni*. The psalter and the *Historia* are older books that had come down to Sir Simon from his father, and their pages are faded and torn in parts. Harry has read them all at Sir Simon's, but can barely wait to look through them again. He still can't believe that he owns books, *plural*. *Multiple* books. Even one book, he would never be able to afford given the poor state of Dartington. But *three*. Three is unimaginable luxury.

Iain watches them, his eyes wide behind his ragged curtain of dark hair. But neither Piers nor Harry speak to him, and he remains as silent as ever.

Harry leaves soon after to open Sir Simon's other gifts. Piers follows him, as curious as Harry about his new possessions. As they walk through the hall, Piers looks over it and says, '*Room for one more down here, y'know*.'

Harry nods. '*Good point. Next time Ralf's about, we'll move Iain downstairs*.'

They have dinner, then go out to examine Sir Simon's armour and weaponry. The mail coat is small on Harry, but finely made, and it never hurts to have another set in case his first becomes damaged in battle. And, surprisingly, there's plate too, simple and unadorned, to protect shins, knees and elbows.

There's a pair of swords, and Harry unwraps them from the

waxed cloth one at a time. The first is old and well notched, its blade almost concave from sharpening. Harry knows it well; it was Sir Simon's favourite sword, the one that came with him to every battle England fought for a score of years. The other sword is longer and heavier, and brand new: blade, hilt, belt and scabbard in perfect condition. The sword doesn't seem as if it's ever been drawn.

Harry looks at it, and loss clutches at his heart as he realises what it is.

Sir Simon had a sword made.

For Harry.

For the day Harry would become a knight.

He sits down heavily on a stool, and covers his mouth. The sword is finely made, but plain – a weapon of war, not a courtier's decoration. It's beautiful, and it's perfect for Harry.

The moment is interrupted by Annie running in. '*Harry! I— it's Iain*,' she says, her voice tremulous with worry.

'*What?*' Harry says, springing to his feet. '*What's he done now?*'

'*Just . . . come with me. You need to see for yourself*,' she says.

Something in him eases at that. For one horrible moment, he was afraid the boy had killed himself. He chases at Annie's heels as they cut through the yard, the hall, and then up the stairs to the solar.

Annie points and makes a *what are we going to do with him* gesture.

Because Iain has somehow moved the giant, heavy pyramid of iron over, so he can sit comfortably at Harry's mother's table.

Where he is calmly leafing through Sir Simon's psalter.

'Get away from those!' Harry yells. 'If you harm them in any way, so help me—'

Iain cowers, flinching in on himself, and it's enough for Harry to leave his threat unfinished.

'I was just . . . reading them,' Iain says, his voice rough with disuse. 'I miss them,' he frowns. 'We, we had my mother's Book of Hours. It's all she was able to bring with her when she fled to Scotland. Well,' he snuffles. 'That and me.'

Harry puts his hand on his forehead and exhales, tired. 'Go to your pallet,' he says.

Iain curls a lip and barks at Harry, apparently deciding that if he's going to be ordered around like a dog, he'll respond like a dog. Then he rolls his shoulders, grabs the weight and waddles it back to where it belongs.

Harry sleeps in Star's stall that night, curled up against the horse's neck, trying to soothe her, to let her know as she passes from this earth that she is loved, that she won't die alone. She survives the night, but she's in such distress the next morning that he and Peter take the decision to end her suffering.

The first thing Harry kills with his new sword is his own horse.

He spends the rest of the day getting good and drunk, and staying away from Iain. By evening Peter and Piers have to carry him up to the solar, not that either of them are much better off, and they all crash to sleep on Harry's bed.

'*Tomorrow*,' Harry mumbles to Piers shortly before he passes out, '*tomorrow when we're sober, we'll move Iain downstairs to live in the hall.*'

When they wake, Iain is gone.

Harry should have expected it, but he can't bring himself to care.

Iain had hauled the weight over while they were asleep and stolen its key from where it hung around Harry's neck. The pyramid of iron sits next to the bed, the manacle open, the key still in the lock.

Harry sighs as he rubs his eyes. At least Iain didn't stab him in his sleep. He supposes he should be thankful for small mercies. He staggers downstairs and wakes Annie, has her count the knives in the kitchen. She comes back, shaking her head and cursing. Two long carving knives gone. And bread and cheese and dried meat.

Harry saddles up Nomad and sets to organising the search. He figures Iain will head north, back to Scotland. The easiest route would be through Exeter, but the fastest would be to strike out across Dartmoor. He dispatches Peter to Ordlington Hall to warn Rabbie. As High Sheriff, Rabbie can whip up a search force to cover the far side of the moor. Meanwhile, Harry warns the people of Dartington Manor that Iain is armed, and will fight, and they don't have to participate in the search for him if they don't want to. The servants still all set out, on foot, on donkey and on horseback. This isn't the frantic haste of the first time Iain ran. They spread out slowly, methodically, apathetically, searching down lanes, checking in barns. Harry and Kit and Piers ride the main roads, stopping at each inn to let the keeper know that there'll be silver for Iain's capture and safe delivery back to Dartington. Harry doesn't hold out much hope, though. Not a single person recognises Iain's description.

The search goes on all day. There's no sign of the Scottish boy.

He's gone.

As the bells of Vespers sound across the valley and the shadows of the hedgerows lengthen across the lanes, Harry gives up on the peasants he'd been questioning on the Exeter road and turns Nomad towards home. They'll have supper, and Iain will turn up or he won't, and Montagu will take over Dartington or he won't. In any case, the awful unease and frustration of the past month will be over and Harry can get on with his life.

But halfway home there's a shout. Little Wat, the pig-boy, canters up on an extremely unhappy Numbles, waving his arms. 'He's on the Plymouth road! They got him cornered, trying to steal a horse.'

Harry swears, and spurs Nomad south. 'Get Rabbie!' he shouts to Kit. 'Tell him to come to Dartington for the boy.'

The bells of Compline ring as he and Piers reach the dingy little inn where Iain is holed up in the stable. A few travellers and villagers block the exits, weapons drawn. A short distance away, two big men-at-arms nurse deep gashes to their forearms. Something flickers in Harry's gut when he sees that, a pride at Iain's growing skill with a sword. He tamps it down. Now isn't the time.

He dismounts Nomad and draws his own sword as he approaches the stable. 'Iain,' he calls out.

There's no answer but silence, and Harry takes another step towards the stable doors.

There's a blood-curdling yell as the doors explode open and Iain gallops out on a skinny chestnut palfrey. The horse is wall-eyed with fear as it charges towards Harry. Iain has the reins in one hand and a carving knife in the other and his knuckles are white around both. He barely has control of the palfrey, its bridle is too loose, the bit already in its teeth. Harry can hear the villagers behind him scattering as he tenses his jaw and turns his blade.

The first thing Sir Simon had taught him was how to fight on foot against a mounted opponent.

Harry steps aside when the palfrey is almost on top of him, and swings his sword high and hard. Iain flinches away, but not far enough, and the flat knocks him across the hand and stomach. He lets go of the reins, lurching so far to the left that he's completely off balance, barely on the horse's back at all. There's a moment where it looks like he may be able to cling on, throwing the knife aside and scrabbling for a hold on the horse's mane, but the palfrey hops sideways and bucks and it's over.

Iain lands with a thump in the dirt, howling his fury and disappointment. The horse puts its head down and bolts across the road into a field, its high whinnies of fear gradually easing to annoyed snuffles.

Harry sheaths his sword, sighs, and yanks Iain to his feet. 'Piers, get the rope,' he says.

Iain is tense under his hands, all hard muscle and spite, his head down, face hidden. 'Let me *go*,' he hisses.

'I can't do that,' Harry replies, as he pushes Iain against the stable wall so Piers and Wat can tie his arms.

'Why not?' Iain whispers.

Because I'll lose my home, Harry thinks. 'Because it's my duty,' is what he says.

Numbles seems almost happy to see Iain, whickering cheerfully as the boy is again tossed over his back. They trudge home to Dartington in the moonlight. It takes almost an hour, not helped by Iain trying to writhe his way free the entire time. He succeeds, once, and only manages to dump himself onto the ground again. He doesn't even make it to his feet before Harry and Kit slide off their mounts and tackle him. By the time the manor is in sight even Numbles is fed up, arching his head back to nip at Iain.

Annie's got torches burning and as Harry rides into the courtyard he can see four strange horses tied up by the stables. Rabbie's horses, no doubt. Peter lurks by them, wringing his hands.

Harry shuts his eyes and thinks for a moment before he slides off Nomad. Just tries to figure out what he can do, to lessen his burden but keep his estate. Annie pushes the hall door open; Harry can see the fire inside roaring, and everyone still awake inside, restless at what the night still holds.

He drags Iain inside. The boy's pale blue eyes burn with hatred, and he's tense under Harry's hands, a coiled snake waiting to strike. Harry looks around his hall and thinks of how his people had welcomed Iain into their home, fed him and taught him English, and tried to be kind to him.

He's about to rebuke Iain, under his breath, but then he sees what Iain is glaring at. And it's not the hall. It's Rabbie, sitting by the hearth, his feet propped up on Harry's table, his mace on the bench beside him.

Rabbie shakes his head and clucks at Harry like a disappointed parent as he brings Iain further into the hall. The firelight illuminates the ragged edge of Rabbie's ear and the sharp planes of his face. 'Still got a problem with your dog running stray, Lyon,' he says.

'I do,' Harry admits. He swallows his pride and confesses the one thing he'd hoped never to have to say to Rabbie. 'I need help. With him. I can't— we're not— I just need two weeks. To prepare. Please. Can you hold him at Ordlington? Just for . . . a fortnight.'

Iain jerks savagely then, out of Harry's exhausted hands, and Kit and Piers dash forwards to grab him. The boy is hissing with fury, glaring at Harry like he's betrayed him.

And Rabbie must be able to see the weariness in Harry, the way his shoulders slope in defeat, because he looks almost sorry for a moment. Hope swells in Harry's breast, and then Rabbie says, 'Bad luck, Harry. I can't.' He grins, thrusting his chin forwards. 'I'm due at court.'

Harry's mind churns as he stares beyond Iain and Rabbie, into the blurry, dancing flames of the hearth. He thinks of the cage, banished to a corner of the home barn to be a perching place for hens. He considers moving Iain's iron weight and manacles to the hall, where more eyes can watch over him . . . and where Iain could hurt more innocent people.

He comes back to himself to hear Rabbie calling his name. The fire snaps into focus, and then Harry looks over at the dark-haired, rough-hewn knight as he rises to his feet. Rabbie jerks his head in Iain's direction, his eyes never leaving Harry's. 'I can solve that problem for you, if you want.'

Yes, Harry thinks. Please. Let Iain become someone else's problem. Anything to bring an end to all this confusing, stressful, heartbreaking turmoil. Then he can sleep. Then he can know his people and his horses are safe.

And all he has to do is nod at Rabbie.

His head twitches downwards. The act is done.

Rabbie grins and picks his mace up off the bench.

I'm sorry, Iain, Harry thinks, staring down at his feet. *I tried. I tried so hard.*

Then Rabbie calls out, 'Mark! Hold him down,' and Harry looks up in confusion. They aren't leaving. They aren't taking Iain away.

Rabbie's squire hauls Iain roughly away from Kit and throws him onto the ground. Iain snarls at him in Scots, the strange, alien language vibrating through the hall, and attempts to kick the squire. Mark visibly flinches back, but one of Rabbie's men-at-arms steps in and pins Iain's ankles. The whole time, Rabbie strides towards the boy, swinging the nasty big mace in his hand. When he reaches him, Rabbie looks at Harry expectantly. 'Got a preference? Right leg or left?'

Harry's brain stutters. His mouth opens and closes like a fish seeking air.

He's about to lift his hand to tell him to stop, when Rabbie gets bored of waiting. 'Fuck it. Left leg,' he says, and swings the mace down onto Iain's shin.

There's the horrible, wet-twig snap of bone cracking in half, and Iain goes white with pain. The lower half of his shin is . . . wrong now. The angle is *wrong*.

Iain doesn't scream. He just grunts high in his throat, and it tails off into a whine.

Ufford spits in Iain's face as he cleans blood and gobbets of Iain's flesh off the mace with his thumb. 'Where were you going to run, you stupid cur?' Rabbie says. 'Balliol rules Scotland now, sitting pretty in Galloway. You manage to get north of the border, you're only going to find English and our allies. Balliol's got an army of retainers. You going to kill every one of them with your kitchen knife?' he taunts.

Iain snarls silently, blood welling up from his curled lip where he's bitten it.

Rabbie points his mace at Harry next. 'And you. Do better, Lyon. If you weren't so soft with him, this never would have happened. *Riding lessons*. Jesus' blood, it's like you *want* him to escape.'

Harry gapes. 'How do you—' he begins.

'I know everything that goes on in this hall,' Rabbie calls over his shoulder as he swaggers towards the door, his men falling in behind him. '*Everything*.'

Harry sinks to his knees and cuts the bindings on Iain's wrists, taking the boy's hands (cold, too cold, and shaking) in his own and trying to rub some warmth back into them. He doesn't even look up as the hall door slams shut. He just presses Iain's bruised knuckles to his lips and mumbles *I'm sorry* like a litany.

Dimly in the background he can hear Annie clapping her hands, calling for hot water, and wood for splints, and linen to bind. She sends Piers, the fastest runner, to fetch Ralf. The big blacksmith is as good at setting bones as the butcher, and closer.

They're working by lamplight as Ralf arrives. By then, they've eased Iain onto his back, and he's biting a strip of bridle leather against the pain as Ralf hops off his horse to examine him. The blacksmith shakes his head at the wound, his expression grim. Harry can do nothing but hold Iain's hand and try not to look at the mess of his leg as it's set. He thinks perhaps Iain doesn't want him, doesn't want the contact, but when he tries to pull his hand away Iain whines and grips his fingers so tight his knuckles go white. *Don't go. Don't let go.*

Harry feels completely lost. Everything around him is this cavalcade of cruelty, and no matter what he does he can't seem to stop it. He tries to act with chivalry and honour and it doesn't matter a damn bit.

Ralf carries Iain up to his pallet. Harry turns to leave.

'*Where are you going?*' says Annie, picking up wet cloths stained pink with blood and tossing them into a bucket.

'*To the chapel,*' Harry says. '*I need to pray. I need guidance.*'

Annie puts her hands on her hips. '*God can wait, or you can talk to Him from right here. You need to be with your* friend.'

'*Iain's not my friend,*' sighs Harry. '*He's made that abundantly clear.*'

Annie looks up at the heavens beseechingly as she exhales in frustration. '*He's in tremendous pain, Harry, much as the little bastard's too mean to show it. You're the closest thing to a friend he has. Don't leave him alone right now.*'

Harry nods and goes up to the solar. Ralf is arranging Iain on the pallet, trying to make him comfortable. Iain's eyes are wet with unshed tears and he's shaking, slipping into shock from pain and exhaustion.

'*He should sleep in my bed,*' Harry says to Ralf. '*It's more comfortable.*'

'*No, Harry,*' Ralf says. '*This is not the time to confuse the boy with something new. We'll stick with what he's used to. But if we could put some of your pillows under his leg . . . ?*'

Harry lurches to the bed and grabs as many pillows as he can carry, and he and Ralf tuck them under and around the splinted leg.

Harry goes to bed but sleep doesn't come, just the nightmare sound of snapping bone echoing again and again in his memory as he combs over everything he could have done differently, every way that if he'd tried a little bit harder, they wouldn't have arrived at this point.

Iain cries out in the night, whimpers of terror rising to a full scream of pain as he moves his leg. Harry catapults out of bed and fumbles for a candle. He crawls over to Iain's pallet and touches the boy. 'Are you well?' he whispers.

He feels more than sees Iain shaking his head.

'Here,' he says, lying onto his side and moving backwards so his back touches Iain's shoulder. 'I'm here. I won't let anything else bad happen to you, Iain. Not tonight.'

The night crawls by slowly for both of them. Harry's brain is still stuck in a morass of self-blame and regret, and Iain still flinches in terror every hour or two. But he doesn't scream again, and Harry finally drifts off into an exhausted sleep shortly before dawn.

They don't talk about it in the morning, and they don't repeat it the next night.

Iain is catatonic. He barely eats. He won't speak. He doesn't want to move from his pallet. Harry goes about his days in a kind of sleepwalk himself, off balance, his thoughts spiralling over how many of his retainers could be earning an extra penny from Rabbie, and how little Harry can do about it. It's a secondary concern, though, compared to the dark-haired boy huddled in the corner.

Not a boy, Harry corrects himself. Not for long. Iain's only two years younger than Harry. In March, he'll be eighteen.

Harry is used to Iain's silences, but before they'd always burned with quiet fury, or a fierce, calculating intelligence. Now, it's as if something has died within Iain. He's just . . . blank. Staring into space out the window, all day and night.

After four days of fasting, Iain at least begins to eat, mechanically, what Annie puts in front of him. But he still won't speak.

Harry can't stand this oppressive misery. Can't stand to think that Iain's ferocious spirit has finally been broken. He never wanted that. All he wanted was less stabbing, and no more running away.

So Harry starts filling the silences, each night.

He reads aloud from Sir Simon's books. He asks if Iain wants to take a turn. He wilfully mispronounces some of the Latin, which before would have got at least a groan from the boy, and now provokes no reaction at all.

When that fails, Harry moves on to telling stories of his squireship in Wiltshire with Sir Simon de Attwood. He lies on his bed in the dark and talks of his life growing up in Dartington. Of his mother, who raised him, and ran the entire manor herself. The time he fell out of a tree. The time he learned to swim, by falling out of a boat. All the times he fell off horses. And he hopes maybe there'll be a quiet, rough, sarcastic voice whispering back through the night, teasing him for falling off so many things.

But there's just more silence.

Then it begins to rain. They have three nights of it, and the patter of the downpour on the thatch is better than silence. Downstairs at dinner they sing. Iain shows no reaction when Harry asks if he wants to be carried down for it, just as he shows no reaction to Annie changing his bandages.

Harry is babbling away to the ceiling on the third night, some idiotic story about his first tournament as Attwood's squire that isn't interesting at all, about how he'd cried behind a tent because he was homesick, because he missed his mother so much. He's just saying words to fill the void Iain has left inside him, and—

Iain says something. It's drowned in the rain.

Harry just about falls off the bed. 'What did you say, Iain?'

'Her name was Marguerite,' Iain whispers, his voice raspy and faint.

'Your mother?' Harry says, scooting onto the floor and sitting near him.

Iain nods, tears rolling down his face, as ugly sobs emerge from his mouth. Harry realises it's the first time he's seen him cry, *really* cry out loud.

Harry flaps his arms awkwardly. 'Please don't stab me,' he says. Then he reaches in, very slowly, and hugs Iain.

He tenses for a moment, then sags into Harry's arms, letting the older boy take his weight.

Harry whispers in his ear, 'Do you want a Mass said for her?'

Iain nods into Harry's shoulder, trying to stifle his sobs.

Harry smiles, and rubs circles on Iain's back. 'It's raining so loud, nobody can hear you cry,' he says.

'You can,' Iain snuffles.

'Iain, I saw Numbles drop you into a drainage ditch like you were yesterday's night soil,' Harry smiles. 'Your dignity is long gone with me.'

Iain's arms come up tentatively around Harry's back, but then he is hugging him fiercely, pressing himself into Harry's broad, warm chest like it's the only safe harbour he knows. And he sobs for what feels like hours, great wracking sobs, finally mourning everything he has lost.

Sometime when the sky begins to lighten, the rain still pattering against the roof, Iain confesses, 'I was going to run to France. She was French.'

'Do you know anybody in France?' Harry asks. 'Or were you just going to run to her people?'

'I . . . no. I don't remember France. I was very young when we left. And . . . she has no people. She was disgraced. My father was not the husband they chose for her.' Iain shuts his eyes. 'There was a scandal. She had petitioned the new King, but . . . it's complicated. She could have returned long ago, if not for me.'

'I'm so sorry, Iain,' Harry says.

'It was a stupid plan,' Iain sighs.

'So is that why your French is so good?'

'No,' he says, poking Harry in the ribs. 'It's because in Scotland we believe in education, you great Sassenach idiot.'

Harry barks out a surprised laugh. 'I missed you,' he says, and the words are out of his mouth before he can think about them.

Iain hums, and snuggles his face into Harry's neck. 'I'm sorry I'm so much trouble.'

That Sunday, and every Sunday afterwards, a Mass is said for Lady Marguerite mac Maíl Coluim in Dartington Church. And occasional sighs are heard from the Lyon family pew as Sir Harry's squire takes issue with matters of Latin pronunciation.

Part Two

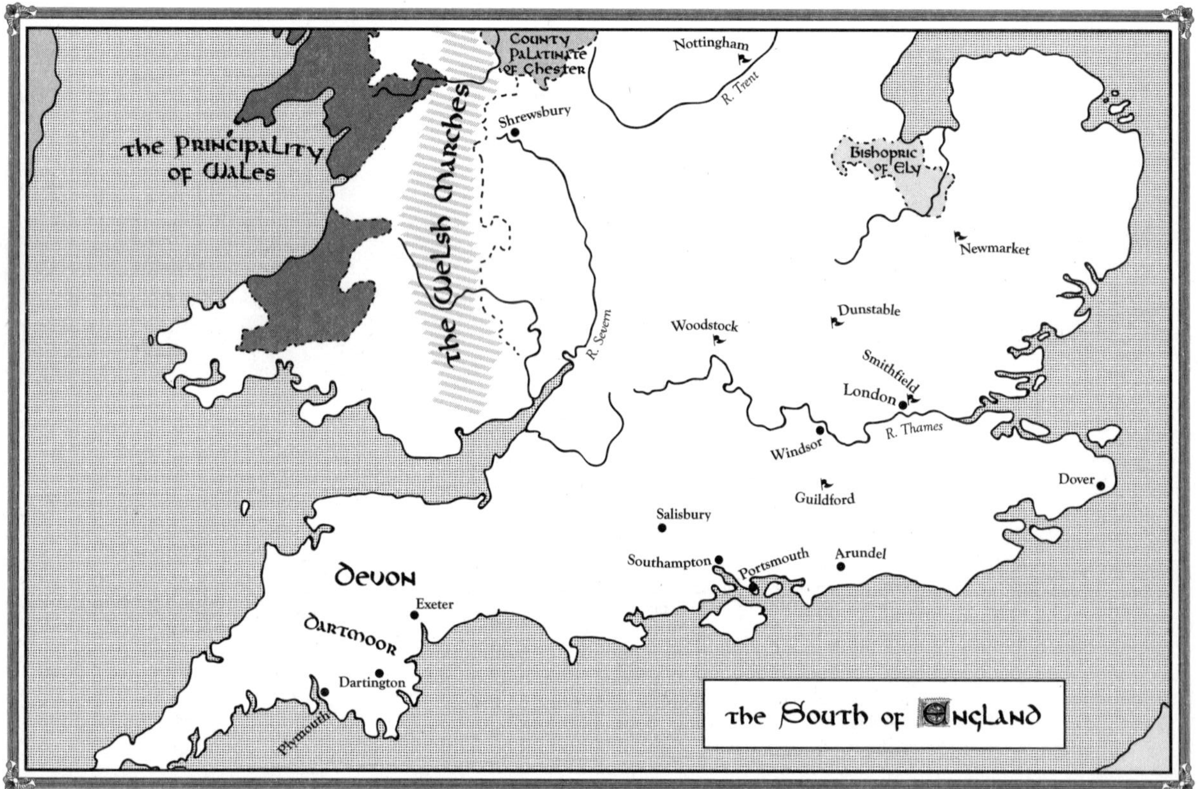
the South of England
the Principality of Wales
the Welsh Marches
County Palatinate of Chester
Bishopric of Ely
Nottingham
R. Trent
Shrewsbury
R. Severn
Newmarket
Dunstable
Woodstock
Smithfield
London
R. Thames
Windsor
Guildford
Dover
Salisbury
Southampton
Portsmouth
Arundel
Devon
Exeter
Dartmoor
Dartington
Plymouth

FIVE

November 1333: Pale Flower

Iain's leg heals slowly. He's bed-bound for a good few weeks, through the rest of October. The entire hall breathes a sigh of relief when Ralf brings Iain a crutch, because the boy is a mass of frustrated, pent-up energy, bored out of his mind and making everybody's life difficult.

When Ralf leaves, he takes away with him the weight and the sets of leg manacles, hopefully forever. Harry never wants to see them again.

Iain's appetite is still a thing of joy to Annie, and she makes it her mission to pack on him the weight he'd lost through his difficult, rebellious September.

He adapts to the crutch quickly, and takes to hobbling around after Harry like a dark, murderous duckling as Harry goes about the business of the manor. He's still restless, and finally Annie grabs him by the ear, hauls him into the kitchen, and presses a knife into his hand.

Iain blinks at it, surprised.

Annie narrows her eyes and points to a bushel of onions on the kitchen table. '*Cut*,' she says.

'*But*—' says Iain, gesturing with the knife.

Annie picks up a heavy iron pan and raises an eyebrow.

Iain sits down on the bench and cuts the onions.

As soon as he's done, Annie removes the knife from his

hands and gives him the first of several bowls of dough to knead. The work is tough – the manor goes through a *lot* of bread – and Iain limps out to sit next to Harry at dinner with aching shoulders and a quiet mind.

'Peter needs some help with the horses this afternoon, if you're up for it,' Harry says, smiling at Iain.

Iain nods, and so finds himself in the stables, currying horses and fetching hay and raking manure, as Peter uses a combination of simple words and demonstration to teach him what to do. Harry wants to stay and watch but he's due to inspect the winter stores in the north barn, so he grabs Nomad and sets off.

Late in the afternoon, his business done, Harry goes to check on Iain. The Scottish boy is sitting on the old, cracked milking stool, his shirt shoved down to his hips, lost in the task of cleaning tack. Harry just stands there, leaning against the stable door, watching him.

Iain has a look of concentration on his face, the tip of his tongue peeking through his lips as he rubs dirt off the old leather of a bridle with a rag dipped in oil. His hair hangs down in messy waves over his face, and there's a play of lean muscle across his shoulders and forearms as he performs the delicate actions of the task. His tan has faded, but galaxies of freckles still remain, coating his shoulders and back and trailing down his arms.

Perhaps Harry is deceiving himself, but he thinks Iain looks more relaxed than he has previously at Dartington, like he's no longer bent under the weight of a burden only he can see.

Harry scuffs his feet against the dirt floor of the stable and says, 'Are you well enough?'

Iain glances up at him and smiles, his face full of a soft warmth. He says, 'I am,' and the smile stays as he looks back down at the dirty bridle in his hands.

Iain continues to work for the next week at whatever chores the hall and stables can find for him, his English improving by leaps and bounds as he's forced to communicate with the servants. By early November, Ralf prods his leg, watches him walk, and declares him fit to ride. The blacksmith cautions Iain should ride bareback, as the pressure of a stirrup on the healing leg might cause problems with its mending.

But Iain's already looking up at Harry, a pleading expression on his face. 'Ri-ding less-ons,' he parrots, in a good approximation of Rabbie's nasal sneer.

Harry laughs, and promises his friend they can go out tomorrow. They'll pack their dinner and make a day of it, go up to the forest at the north end of the manor's lands. Then Harry looks over at Ralf. 'Could he swim?' Harry asks.

Ralf shrugs. 'If he wishes.'

Iain just about drags Harry out of bed the next morning and propels him to the stables. Half-asleep though he is, Harry can't help but feel a thrill of delight as he watches Iain get both Nomad and Numbles ready for a ride, the boy's hands swift and sure.

Because his left leg still can't bear his weight, Iain has to mount Numbles from the wrong side, which is also his blind side. Horse and boy are both deeply uncomfortable, Numbles trying to sidestep away from the mounting block and Iain hesitant to throw his wounded leg over the huge horse's back when the horse won't stop fidgeting.

Finally Harry sighs, returns Nomad to his stall, and swings nimbly up on Numbles' back from the left side. He holds a hand out to Iain.

'Oh no. I can do this myself. I'm not some damsel to ride *pillion*,' Iain declares.

'I don't know, Iain,' Harry grins, glancing down at the boy in his baggy, hand-me-down shirt and the pair of loose linen breeches they'd found to fit over the brace. 'That long hair of yours, all we'd have to do is put you in a dress and you could sit on my lap. Whole county'd think I'd got myself a wife.'

Where did that come from? Harry thinks. He needs to wake up. Or at least his brain does. Because his loins woke up quick at the thought of a woman's body nestling against his own, on the horse.

Iain narrows his eyes. 'I'll stab you, don't think I won't,' he says.

'Seriously, Iain,' Harry sighs. 'This is your first ride since your leg was broken, and you're not that great on a horse anyway – no, don't make that face – and if you ride in front of me I can keep you from falling if you lose your balance. A spill off Numbles would set your leg back by months, you contrary idiot.'

'Ugh. Fine,' Iain groans.

'It wouldn't kill you to accept help, you know,' says Harry, extending his hand. 'You don't have to go through everything by yourself, like some great daft Scottish martyr.'

Iain swings up onto Numbles' back, settling in front of Harry, his arse tucked against Harry's thighs. 'French,' he says.

'Hm?' says Harry, taking the reins in one hand and settling his other one awkwardly around Iain's waist.

'I'm French, Harry,' Iain corrects, softly. 'The world cares about me because I'm French, not Scottish. But don't . . .' Iain sighs, and leans into Harry's chest with his back. 'Don't tell anyone. It'll just bring down danger upon you. And I don't want to see what happened at Loch Doon repeated down here. Once is enough,' he breathes. 'Once was too much.'

Harry hugs Iain with the arm around his waist, and presses a brotherly kiss into his hair as a fierce feeling of protectiveness washes over him. 'I won't tell. I promise,' Harry whispers into Iain's hair. Then he smiles. 'I'll even trade you. I have a secret of my own to show you.'

Harry nudges Numbles into motion and they spend the morning winding gently, unhurriedly northwards through the lands of Dartington until they reach the forest. It's a cool morning, the kind where Harry can feel winter waiting in the shadows, and it's pleasant to have the big horse under his legs and Iain's warm body against his chest. Iain sings softly, Gaelic work songs and old French melodies in time with Numbles' hoof steps, and Harry rests his chin on Iain's shoulder, profoundly content.

He holds Iain a little tighter as they make their way through the thick undergrowth of the woods and down the slope that leads to the hidden pond. It's still early enough that a low mist sits on the water, cold silver lapping the roots of white birches. Harry can tell the moment Iain sees it: the boy gasps, the muscles in his torso growing taut under Harry's hand.

'This is where I go when I want to be alone,' Harry says, speaking quietly so as not to disturb the peace of the morning. 'I've never shown it to anyone.'

Iain half-turns to look at Harry, his expression awestruck. 'Thank you,' he breathes. 'It's . . .'

'Yes,' Harry says, looking into Iain's pale eyes, profoundly moved by how much he understands, how he appreciates what this means to Harry. 'I know.'

Harry realises that at some point he's started rubbing little circles with his thumb against the silky, firm skin of Iain's hip, and the other boy exhales and leans into him, shutting his eyes as their foreheads touch. They stay like that for one beautiful, suspended moment, breathing in sync, one with each other and the idyll around them, until a fat trout splashes out of the water and Iain startles, then giggles.

'Here, get off first,' Iain says, shoving at Harry.

Harry laughs too and slides off Numbles' back, holding his hands out for Iain to come next. Iain hisses slightly as he hits the soft ground, and then limps over to look at the pond. 'Next time we come here, let's bring a hunting bow,' he says, glancing back at Harry as he ties Numbles' reins to a low branch. Iain's mouth takes on a devilish smirk. 'I grew up on a loch. I can catch our supper.'

Harry holds up the bag he'd slung over his shoulder. 'Today, Annie has provided.'

They spread out their picnic on the great, flat, mossy rock that sticks out into the pond. The two of them fall into easy conversation as they break fast, Harry telling Iain of his childhood games of King Arthur and the Faerie Queen on this very rock, and Iain telling Harry of running through Galloway Forest playing Cú Chulainn and the Wild Hunt, of rowing and swimming in the loch.

'Wasn't the water cold?' Harry asks.

'Mm,' Iain hums, around a leg of chicken. 'But so clear, you could stand there with the water up to your chest, and watch your toes turn blue.'

Harry snorts with laughter and admits, 'The water here's not much better. Not as clear, though.'

They have a vague plan to swim, but first they stretch out on the rock after their meal, not for long, just for a few moments. Then full bellies and fresh air pull them both under the tides of sleep.

Harry wakes first. He and Iain have tangled together in sleep, both seeking warmth in the crisp morning. Iain is curled up against his chest, his forehead tucked under Harry's ear. Harry's arm is over Iain's back, his leg over Iain's hip, and his hand is entwined in Iain's long hair, cradling the nape of his neck.

And he's so hard he could pound nails.

Dammit, Harry thinks. Damn his ingrained response to lying out on the rock. He grits his teeth and contemplates how he can shift away from Iain without waking him. He had told Iain about his imaginary adventures at the pond and he'd told Iain about the praying, but he hadn't mentioned *all the masturbating.*

Because that's not really something you tell your friend. *Oh, by the way, Iain, the moss grows so well on the rock because it's regularly fertilised by my seed.*

It's at that moment Harry realises that twin slivers of grey-blue are watching him from under dark lashes.

'Um,' Iain says, his voice thick with embarrassment.

'Yes. Uh. Sorry,' Harry coughs, scooting away from Iain and curling in on himself.

Iain sits up quickly and turns from Harry, his own shoulders hunching. 'I had a dream. I didn't, uh. I'm not. Um,' he murmurs, and there's the unmistakeable motions of a man readjusting himself.

Harry barks out a laugh, then, causing Iain to look at him in surprise.

'I had a dream too,' Harry says, relaxing. 'I thought you were, uh, because you saw that I was, you know.'

Iain turns back towards Harry, and his eyes rake down Harry's body to his very erect cock. Harry squirms as Iain's pale gaze leaves a trail of fiery embarrassment in its wake. There's a blush high on Iain's cheeks, and his own breeches are still tented, a hand half-covering his shame.

And. Uh.

It's a *lot* of shame.

'Jesus, Iain,' Harry says, staring.

'Sorry,' Iain whispers, drawing his good leg up to hide himself.

Harry presses his palm against his cock because it aches so badly, he thinks he's going to go out of his mind. 'It's fine,' he says, biting his lip. 'I also pleasure myself here, please don't judge me,' he babbles, squeezing his eyes shut.

Iain snorts, his face creasing up in amusement, and he bashes his forehead against Harry's shoulder. 'My spot was up on top of the main tower of our castle. You could bolt the door from outside.'

Harry can feel him shift. 'Fuck, I need it,' Iain breathes. 'I haven't felt any urge since, *you know*, and now it's like four months of not defiling myself has hit me all at once.'

And then the Devil climbs into Harry's mouth and makes him say, 'We could, you know.'

And Iain ruts against him and says, 'Please,' his voice husky, his cheeks still flushed.

Harry had meant *maybe we can lie next to each other and rub ourselves off*, but then Iain is unlacing his breeches and taking Harry's hand and putting it around that big cock of his, and Iain's other hand is finding its way around Harry's dick, and Iain whispers in his ear, 'Have you ever had someone else do it to you?'

Harry's heartbeat is racing. He's dizzy with terror and arousal and he wants to pull away from Iain and he wants to get closer too and boys in the hall do this with each other all the time, he's *seen* it, sneaking downstairs at night to the kitchens, but *he* never has, and he's not sure—

And then Iain moves his hand.

Harry nearly blows his load right there and then.

Because.

Iain's right. It's like.

Nothing. It's never.

Been. Like this.

Oh. *God.*

He moans, as his body goes taut like a bowstring, and he starts moving his own hand over Iain's cock, and they're leaning against each other, cheek to cheek, both going at each other furiously, panting and groaning and at some point their faces turn that final inch towards each other and they're moaning into each other's mouths, it's not kissing, but it's not *not* kissing either, and he never realised lips could be so sensitive, could feel so *good*, and then Iain reaches his other hand into Harry's braies and cups his balls, and Harry shoves his mouth against Iain's as his orgasm slams through him, the world dissolving into a sparking bonfire, and he pulls Iain off faster, and Iain takes a hand out of Harry's braies and fists it in his hair and yes now they're *definitely* kissing as Iain fucks his cock up into Harry's hand and his tongue into Harry's mouth then he's coming too and Harry can feel his eyes squeeze shut as Iain moans his release down Harry's throat, hot ropes of come painting Harry's hand and forearm, and they slump against each other, blissful and spent.

Iain leans back first, pulling one hand out of Harry's braies and the other out of his hair. Harry looks down at Iain's hand, covered in his seed, and his eyes widen as Iain raises that hand to his lips and licks Harry's release off his fingers. Harry's cock twitches again, fattening.

Iain smiles around his fingers. 'I got come in your hair. Sorry.' He pulls his thumb out of his mouth. 'But it is *your* come, so, no regrets.'

'We. Uh,' Harry stutters. 'That. Was.'

'Yes,' Iain says, looking up at him through his ridiculous long lashes, his chest still rising and falling with the aftermath of their exertions.

Then Iain looks away, embarrassed. 'We should swim. Clean off.' He starts to shimmy out of his shirt.

'It's cold,' Harry warns.

'Good,' Iain says, sliding off the rock, still in his half-laced breeches, and splashing into the pond.

They both swim around in the water, playing tag and ducking each other, then haul themselves out to dry on the rock before setting home. The silence between them is strained thereafter, with an exquisitely painful consciousness of exactly how much space is between them at any given moment, how it's both too much and not enough.

Then, Harry realises, they have to ride home. On one horse.

With Iain's taut, muscular arse swaying against his crotch on every step. With his hand on Iain's stomach, his fingers rubbing against the waistband of Iain's breeches. Occasionally, accidentally, dipping underneath.

He's going to *die*.

Because he's just had the single best orgasm of his life and rather than calming down the fire under his skin, it's stirred it hotter. His body just wants to do it again, and *more*. And sure, helping your friend out when you're both hard is probably fine, but reaching into his breeches and grabbing his dick and rutting yourself against him while riding down a lane where anyone could see you? No, that's . . . definitely not acceptable.

God's blood, but he can picture it. His nipples get so sensitive when he's aroused, and he could rub them against Iain's back, the rough linen of their shirts trapped between his chest and the lean, hard muscles of Iain's shoulders, and he could bite Iain's neck to stifle his own moans and—

He coughs. 'Um, you want to try riding by yourself for a bit? See if you can manage?' Harry says, digging his nails into the palms of his hand because he needs to stop thinking about this *right now*.

'Yes,' Iain says, his voice a little strained. 'You'll walk?'

'Mm-hm,' Harry grunts, untying Numbles' reins.

When they return to Dartington, there's a letter with a fancy wax seal for Harry, and a dozen servants milling excitedly, waiting for Harry to read it to them.

It's from the King. Harry's been invited to Windsor for the first two weeks of the court's Advent celebrations. Counting up the travel time to the outskirts of London and back, he'd be gone a full month.

He nearly falls on his knees right there in the courtyard and thanks the Almighty.

Annie squeals when she hears the news. The entire household of Dartington flies into a panic to get Harry ready to depart. He has four days to prepare. It's nowhere near enough. There's everything to tie up around the manor, instructions to leave for Annie and the other senior staff, decisions about what and who to take, and through it all Annie panicking about what Harry can wear in front of potential future wives at court and, most importantly, the King. *The King!*

Harry has one good outfit.

There's no time and, more importantly, no decent fabric, to make another.

Annie eventually relents upon strong pressure from Harry and surprisingly persuasive arguments from Iain that Harry translates. *Tell her the King won't care; he knows you are a country knight and he won't be expecting you dressed up in fancy things. The only people who care are second-rate courtiers, because they have no confidence in their own status and find it only in putting others down. So wear your simple clothes, and be a country knight, and the people who are rude to you are people you don't want to know. Plus, it's near enough to Christmas that the King will lavish gifts on those in attendance on him. You'll get a new set of clothes from him; if you're lucky, a lot more.*

Harry doesn't ask Iain how he knows these things, just as he doesn't ask Iain if he wants to come. Given the hints he's dropped about his background, Harry figures that taking him to the centre of English political machinations would be the worst of all possible choices. He explains this to Iain, not wanting the boy's feelings to be hurt, and Iain nods in agreement.

It's the first real conversation they've had since the afternoon at the pond, and it's still a meagre thing, half-sentences and glancing looks as they sit side by side at supper. They've stopped touching each other, and Harry never realised how tactile their friendship was until it ceased. He misses it. Harry catches Iain watching him out of the corner of his eyes, though. It's as if he's waiting for Harry, but Harry has absolutely no clue what to do. He's never thought about men that way. He's barely even thought of women that way, not that he's had much opportunity to be around any of his age and status. Now he can't *stop* thinking about it, and he finds himself getting aroused by the most ridiculous things—

'Will the Queen Mother be there?' Iain asks.

Harry shakes his head, trying to clear it, and shoots Iain a confused glance.

'At court,' Iain says. 'Do you think she'll be there?'

'Oh,' Harry says. Then he shrugs. Isabella, King Edward's French mother, leaves her small castle but rarely since her son wrested control of the crown from her and her lover six years ago. Harry heard rumours of a rapprochement in Berwick, but he knows nothing of the court's current intrigues and he'd like to keep it that way. 'I have no idea. I don't even know if Rabbie will be there, or Baron Montagu, though I suspect they have more chance of being in attendance than Isabella.'

Iain gets a faraway look in his eyes and says, 'If you meet her, tell me what she's like.'

Harry promises, and gets back to packing. Peter will go with him, and Kit. And Harry realises as the day approaches that, while he's worried about a lot of things, Iain isn't one of them.

Harry looks at his friend as they go out for their now-daily morning ride (not to the pond, they haven't been back there since the first time). Their horses walk side by side down towards the western fields, and Iain seems at ease here in Devon, accepting it as his home. But something still gnaws at Harry, an unwillingness to lose Iain again. It would be horrible to come back from court and find him gone. He finally says, 'You won't do anything while I'm away, will you?'

Iain looks down at his still-braced leg, then raises an eyebrow at Harry. 'Rabbie will presumably be at Windsor too?'

Harry nods.

Iain hums. 'Then if killing Rabbie is off the table as far as entertaining myself while you're gone is concerned, I promise I'll be a good boy and return your manor to you in the same condition you left it.' Then he smirks. 'Maybe even better condition.'

Harry snorts and punches him in the shoulder, and just like that, the lingering strangeness between them is broken. Iain grabs at the ticklish part of Harry's side and Harry yelps, whacking him in the head. Iain swears, drops Numbles' reins and makes a grab for Harry's hair.

A short while later, Ralf is driving his cart down the lane from forge to manor when he turns a corner and is presented with a most unusual sight. The young lord of the manor has his dark-haired friend in a headlock as they ride down the lane abreast on two huge roan horses, Harry howling with laughter and squirming as the Scottish boy tickles him and tries to writhe out of his grasp, cursing him out as a great Sassenach idiot.

Both pause their high jinks to wave and smile at Ralf as they pass, and the blacksmith just shakes his head fondly, his big shoulders quivering in amusement. '*Harry, don't you dare pull that boy off his horse and injure his leg again*,' Ralf calls out to them.

'*Thank you*,' yells Iain, exasperated and somewhat breathless. Then there's a squawk and an '*och, ye bastard, I'll get you for that*'.

As the days count down to his departure, Harry watches the Windsor Cart (as it becomes known) grow higher and higher with packages. His armour and Sir Simon's plate, surcoat and sword and shield, in case there's a tournament. Changes of clothes. Extra food for the journey. His one court-acceptable outfit. Peter's things. Kit's things. And then finally it's the night before he's due to set off.

He's never been so nervous. Iain will take over the stables while Peter's gone – easy enough, there'll only be Numbles and a couple of ponies to look after – and continue to help out Annie whenever she needs it. Annie keeps reassuring him everything will be fine; they coped when he was in Scotland and they'll cope now. Harry can't help but fret.

And now instead of sleeping ahead of their dawn start, he's stalking back and forth in the solar after supper, wearing a hole in the floorboards, trying to work out what he's forgotten.

'If you don't stop that pacing,' Iain finally snaps from his pallet, 'I am going to tackle you and tie you to the bed.' Iain is ready for sleep: stripped down to his braies, sprawled on his back, head pillowed on an arm.

Harry stops and stares at Iain. 'You should sleep in my bed while I'm gone,' he says.

'What?' Iain says, sitting up.

'It's much more comfortable than your pallet. And bigger. It'll be better for your leg, and someone might as well sleep in it,' Harry says.

'Ugh. No,' Iain says, flapping a hand and lying back down.

'Because you enjoy discomfort?' Harry says.

'No,' Iain sighs.

'Why, then? It's a good bed,' Harry huffs.

'Because *I said so*,' Iain grumbles.

'That's not a reason,' Harry says, crossing his arms. 'Why not?'

Iain snorts and squeezes his eyes shut. 'Because, Harry, if you absolutely need to know, I feel like a cat in heat right now and as soon as you leave I'm going to defile myself every single night and probably go and fertilise the moss on your stone too, and spilling all over your nice bed is *definitely* bad manners.'

'Iain, you're disgusting,' Harry frowns.

Iain opens one eye and glares at him. 'And you do not know when to drop a subject, Harry.'

Harry sits down on the edge of his bed. Then something occurs to him. 'Wait, have you not been pleasuring yourself because I've been in the room?'

'Uh, yes?' Iain says, and even in the candlelight Harry can see the blush colouring his cheeks.

'You're such an idiot,' Harry says, shaking his head. 'Iain, I don't care. Have at it.'

Iain shifts nervously. 'It's just . . . I never hear you doing it, so I didn't think I should . . .'

'Yes. Well,' Harry says, staring at his feet. 'For a long while I was too worried about someone *stabbing me in my sleep* to think about getting off.'

'And now?' Iain whispers.

Harry closes his eyes and tips his head back. 'If I don't find a girl to mess around with up at Windsor I think I'm going to die.'

Iain makes a sound like a low moan. 'You ever done it? All the way?' he asks, his voice soft in the night.

'No,' Harry says. 'Not much chance. There was a serving-girl at Sir Simon's and I thought we might, I mean, we were going to, but . . .' Harry gestures, not wanting to talk aloud about July, and the loved ones it harvested from him. 'Have you?' he asks.

'I've messed around with village girls up in Scotland, but I've never done everything. Getting one pregnant would be, um, very bad,' Iain says, tracing a finger up and down his own thigh. 'But boys. I've been . . . all the way. With. Uh. Boys,' he whispers.

'Isn't that a sin?' Harry whispers back.

'Yes,' Iain breathes.

He looks up at Harry, pale and beautiful in the moonlight. And Harry shifts because his braies are getting uncomfortable. In fact, this entire conversation isn't helping with his libido problem.

Harry unlaces his braies and shimmies out of them. And puts a hand around his cock, which is well on its way to hard. He swallows, and looks over at Iain, and can see he's similarly affected.

'Harry,' Iain says, licking his lips, 'you have to understand. I'm not going to live to my majority. I'll be killed. My very existence is . . . enormously inconvenient. I didn't want to die without knowing what pleasure was.'

'Tell me,' Harry says. 'What it's like.'

'With a girl?' Iain asks.

'With a boy,' Harry says. 'What *you* like.'

'Jesus, Lyon,' Iain groans, his head flopping back. 'I'm trying to last until you leave.'

'And I said you didn't have to,' Harry replies, slowly starting to move his hand over his cock.

Iain notices the motion and his lips open in a little 'o' of surprise. He swallows, and moves his own hand down to his dick. 'Uh, there's a lot, there's a lot that's the same. I like . . . I like messing people up so bad they can't even speak. Some girls, and some boys, you can make 'em come just from playing with their nipples, sucking on them, biting them, blowing on them. Pin their arms above their head and use your mouth on 'em – for a boy moving down and sucking his dick, Harry, the first time a boy or girl takes your dick in their mouth, you'll swear you've found paradise, *Jesus*, you have no idea how good it is.'

Harry groans, and moves his hand faster. 'Don't stop,' he gasps, between strokes.

'Me . . . God's breath, Harry, are you sure you want to hear this?'

'Yes,' Harry says, his voice thick.

Iain exhales, nervous and long. 'I like to be fucked. I love it when a boy takes me in his mouth, and then sticks his tongue in my arse, and opens me up for his cock, and then just pounds into me, Harry, you wouldn't believe how hard I come, it's like

I die for a moment, it feels so incredible if he's doing it right, he doesn't even need to touch my cock . . .'

'Nngh,' Harry says. He can't take his eyes off Iain, who's arched up off his pallet, staring back at Harry, the moonlight lining his lean form with silver as he strokes himself and babbles the filthiest things Harry has ever heard. It's taking all Harry's self-control not to crash into Iain and finish him off himself.

' . . . And if he's decent sized, you feel it all the next day, this little soreness, these sparks of pleasure that last long after the act. There's this spot, up there inside you, and Harry if you've never found it you need to, because once you do you'll come like a fucking beast, I swear . . . Jesus, Harry, I'm aching for it so bad, talking about it is killing me, wanna be fucked . . .'

And then Iain pushes out of his braies and sticks two fingers in his mouth and trails them down the side of his chest, past the hand stroking that big cock of his, and further still, until he sticks them up inside himself. Iain's face is almost religious in its ecstasy then. Those fingers start thrusting back and forth inside of him and Harry has to swallow hard and grab on to his own cock because it is the single most erotic thing he has ever seen.

'Keep talking,' Harry says, his own brain so muzzy with pleasure he can barely think to form the words.

Iain moans, ragged and wanton. 'You enjoying the show, Harry?'

'God yes,' Harry whispers.

'Is that your pleasure?' Iain murmurs. 'Do you like to watch? Tell me what—*nngh, oh God*—tell me what you like, Harry. Get me off on your words.'

Harry's brain goes sideways. He's had no experience beyond his own hand and a couple of fumbled kisses with that serving-girl, feeling her breasts and between her legs. And Iain's naked in the moonlight, looking like some sort of faerie prince, and Harry can't decide what turns him on more, watching those fingers go in and out of Iain, or the expression on his face—

'I . . . I want to fuck you,' Harry stutters.

'Then get over here,' Iain growls.

Harry gets up, trips over the breeches pooled around his ankles, falls onto his knees, kicks the fabric off him, and then since he's on the ground already he decides to crawl over to Iain. Iain has stopped stroking himself, stopped everything, and is just kneeling and watching Harry come towards him with amazed desire on his face. When Harry gets close enough, Iain whines and grabs him by the back of the hair, crashing their lips together.

The kiss is over far too soon, and Harry moans his disappointment. Which turns into almost a scream as Iain sucks one of Harry's nipples into his mouth. Harry has to stick his fist in his own mouth, because he's already on the edge of coming, so turned on by the filth spilling out of Iain's lips, and now Iain's using those lips on one nipple while the other nub is being pinched and rolled between his fingers. Harry jerks like he's having a seizure, grabbing Iain's hair and yanking, which earns him a *fuck, yes* from Iain.

Then Iain continues his way down Harry's stomach, and Harry has a moment to realise what's about to happen before Iain puts his mouth over Harry's cock and sinks down, slowly, until his lips bump against the base.

At this point, Harry doesn't even know what he's saying.

Just that.

Iain wasn't kidding.

About paradise.

He squeezes his eyes shut and tries not to come. 'Iain,' he moans. 'Please, I need to fuck you.'

Iain pulls off his cock, and says, 'Ssh, *a sheòid*, I need you in me so bad I can't even tell you. I just have to get you good and wet first.' His voice is husky and Harry thinks: fuck his nipples, he could probably get off on Iain's dirty talk alone. Hell, he almost already did.

Iain gets Harry's cock coated with saliva and then shifts back, throwing his good leg over Harry's shoulder and pulling Harry down on top of him. He guides Harry's cock towards his entrance and presses it there. And he's looking up, right into Harry's eyes as he does this.

Harry pushes into him.

And looks into Iain's eyes as his cock is enveloped in Iain's tight heat, and it's *so* tight, right on the border of pain and pleasure, and Iain whispers *keep going* and Harry braces himself over Iain and pushes all the way in.

They stay there for a moment, both getting used to the overwhelming sensation, and Harry dips down and kisses Iain, because his lips are right there, and because every time they kiss Harry thinks about it afterwards and doubts himself, it couldn't have felt *that* good, so he has to do it again to check, and the answer is always *yes*, it *was* that good, it *is*.

Iain runs his fingers up Harry's sides, and scrapes his short nails down them. 'Do you have any idea how beautiful you are?' he whispers, running his thumb over Harry's cheekbone.

'And kind. I wasn't lying, that night when I said nobody has ever been as nice to me as you are. And you were my *enemy*.'

Something in Harry's heart cracks then, overflows, and he can't handle it, so he rolls his hips and Iain arches and moans, *yes, yes, move*, and Harry plants one arm near Iain's head and supports Iain's arse with his other hand, and thrusts. And.

He's not. This is.

Holy God.

This must be why. It's a sin.

Because nothing. Should feel this good.

Iain urges Harry on, *harder, faster*, and Harry is pounding into him, raking his nails down Iain's hip and over the round, muscular curve of his buttocks, mesmerised by Iain's cock as it bounces between their stomachs. Iain's so hard it looks painful, solid and purple-red and smearing precome over both their abs.

And Harry has to get his hand on it again. He lets go of Iain's hip and wraps his fingers around Iain's cock and strokes it, twisting at the head and smearing up into the slit with his thumb and snapping his hips up into Iain, and Iain all but shouts as he comes suddenly, his whole body seizing, his cock pumping come, and Harry can feel it under his hand, and feel how Iain's body clenches down on him as he thrusts and then he can't hold it any longer, he falls apart too, shooting his load into that hot, tight channel, and he keeps thrusting and keeps coming, and he's mumbling Iain's name over and over again and Iain is *glowing*, there's no other word for it, he looks like a damn angel, and as Harry slowly drifts downwards from the heights of his orgasm he settles into the pallet next to Iain, still inside him, and pulls the boy into his chest. Iain hums contentedly and wiggles against him, getting comfortable.

Then Iain brings Harry's hand to his lips. 'Are you well?' he murmurs over kisses to Harry's knuckles.

'Gluh,' Harry says. Then, as his brain resumes functioning, 'I can't believe I lost my virginity to you. You bit me.'

Harry can feel Iain's smirk, even in the dark. 'If you ask me nicely enough, I'll bite you again.'

Then Iain stills, and his voice grows serious. '*Bon courage* at Windsor, Harry. Don't . . . don't trust anyone there. Especially if they try to be your friend too quickly. There are no friends at court, only advantages.' He squeezes Harry's hand. 'And don't tell *anyone* about me.'

Harry squeezes the boy's hand back. 'I promise, Iain.'

SIX

November 1333: High and Low

Harry slips out of Dartington in the pre-dawn light, leaving Iain still sprawled in sleep. Tiptoeing past the waking forms of his servants in the hall below, he's reminded of the responsibilities he ignored to an almost criminal extent when he lay with Iain. He saddles up Nomad, consumed by fear at what he and Iain have done, and by horror about how much he wants to do it again. Harry is pathetically grateful for the distractions of the early departure, wrangling Peter and Kit and the Windsor Cart out the gates, Annie with their food, the goodbyes. Cruel daylight has brought with it crushing regret, and Harry wants anything but to be alone with his thoughts.

He becomes lost around Iain. It's like the boy bewitches him. There are no boundaries; everything is possible, everything is permitted.

Even sin.

He knows boys experiment with each other. Heaven knows he's stumbled across Peter and the pig-boy Wat with their hands down each other's breeches often enough; half the county has. But what he and Iain did last night went far beyond harmless boyish fumbles. He lay with Iain as a man lies with a woman.

Harry shuts his eyes as a thrill runs down his spine. As he

remembers Iain's face as he came; the feeling of Iain's body around him. His—

Harry shudders.

'*Cold, sir?*' says Kit, from the seat of the cart, behind him. '*Your cloak's in here if you want—*'

'*No need. I'm fine,*' Harry mumbles.

He will go to Windsor.

He will set aside this unnatural infatuation with his . . . his *prisoner*.

With prayer, discipline and self-control, he will regain his composure, and refocus on his duty as lord of Dartington Manor.

He will begin the search for a wife.

Before he is condemned to Hell, and his estates fall to ruin as the King's father, Edward of Carnarvon, almost ruined England.

Because this is the iron rule of their life, especially for a minor nobleman such as Harry: provide an heir. Better yet, provide several heirs, because sickness, accident and death are birth's constant companions. Harry has no siblings, so Dartington's future rests completely on his shoulders. If he fails to provide for adequate succession of the manor, he endangers the lives of all his servants and vassals. Everything his family has built over the past century can crumble in one careless, childless generation, and this cold tomorrow is an ever-present spectre haunting his actions. *Hurry*, it whispers. *Hurry*.

Harry is not yet late to wife, but it will be expected of him in the next couple of years. He must not disappoint his people; he will not fail them.

He looks beside him, to Kit's shaggy blond head and wide smile. Then back, to dark, sharp little Peter, riding the fat little pony they all call Goblin because she isn't nice for anyone other than him.

Both are attractive men, in their way. Harry can admit that. He can also admit he feels nothing for them, other than a vague kinship.

Harry exhales in relief. He's not . . . he's not a sodomite.

He remembers riding through Salisbury Market a year ago with Sir Simon, and there was a man being hung for sodomy. When the body stopped jerking, the executioner had cut his genitals off, and then they had quartered him. The crowd had cheered at the butchery.

Harry realises he's faded away, lulled into a trance-like contemplation by the steady rhythm of Nomad's hooves on the road, when Kit's voice snaps him back to the present. '*Sir Harry? We stopping at Exeter Market?*'

Harry blinks. The villages are getting closer together and larger as they approach the port city; Harry can already make out the stone roof of Exeter Cathedral looming over the thatch and tile of meaner buildings. The soaring grey stone calls out to him, promising peace, and guidance.

'*Yes, we'll stop and get dinner in the market,*' Harry says. They've been on the road for six hours, and Nomad isn't a long-haul kind of horse. '*Kit, you stay with the cart and horses. Peter, I have something to take care of, but after we eat I want you to go to the horse-sellers and pick out a couple of possibilities for my new palfrey. I'll come and make a final decision after my business is done.*'

Peter's face is awestruck at the responsibility he is being

given. '*Uh . . . yes, sir!*' the boy babbles. '*Any preferences? Mare or gelding? Colour?*'

'*Just a good horse that's strong enough to carry me over distances*,' Harry says. He's tall and solidly built, with the broad shoulders and muscular chest of a man who swings a longsword for a living. Star had been big for a palfrey, at sixteen hands, but she'd been nimble.

He misses Star still. He can feel the weight of her head on his lap, her last night in the stall. The look in her once-bright eye when he raised his sword, as if to say, *I know this must be done, and I forgive you.*

Harry sighs. He supposes they're lucky, that the only casualty of Iain's first months had been a horse. But everything now seems to come at the cost of a life. His mother's, for the chance to go to war. Sir Simon's, for becoming a knight. And Star's, in exchange for gaining a friend.

For gaining *Iain*. Mysterious, lost, wild Iain.

Liquid fire courses through Harry's veins as his mind throws up sounds of flesh on flesh, long dark hair and pale eyes half-lidded in pleasure, plush lips spit-slick and kiss-bitten—

Harry chews the inside of his cheek until he can taste blood. He spurs Nomad on faster; the big horse tossing his head in annoyance at the increase in pace. '*I'm riding on ahead*,' he calls back to a perplexed Kit and Peter. '*I'll meet you at the market.*'

Harry rides straight to the cathedral. The huge stone palace of God terrifies and thrills him. He has made the journey dozens of times into its cool interior, past the crowds milling on the sunlit steps. Yet each time, its size and splendour shock him anew. His heart shivers as his eyes take in the long, soaring vaults of the ceiling and the great explosions of colour and image from immense stained-glass windows. The midday sun sends beams of dappled light filtering through forms of martyrs and kings onto the huge flagstones of the central aisle. Further up, rosy light from the nave's great window glints off the dark wood of the bishop's throne, fifty feet tall, taller than Dartington Manor itself.

The very first time Harry had seen window glass had been in Exeter Cathedral, one Easter Mass with his mother. Neither Dartington nor any of the surrounding manors had glass. Not even Rabbie's. Shutters and a hearth and heavy curtains round the bed kept them mostly warm in winter, and open windows caught what breeze there was in summer.

Only the Church and the greatest of lords have the incomes to build these soaring, arching confections of stone and inlay their windows with mosaics of coloured glass. The great cathedral is a testament both to the forbidding majesty of God and the serenity which He could bestow.

A serenity Harry desperately craves.

He ducks to the right, pacing past the side chapels until he finds the confessionals. There's a short wait until a booth becomes free, so Harry leans against one of the tall stone pillars supporting the roof, breathing in the cool, incense-tinged air as he organises his thoughts.

An older man, a merchant by the looks of him, exits the endmost confessional. The heavy curtain doesn't stop moving before Harry pushes it aside and sits down in the little wooden enclosure. He doesn't look at the priest through the metal screen; he doesn't want to know the man's face. It would make what he has to do harder.

'In nomine Patris et Filii et Spiritus Sanctii, Amen,' says an older, tired voice from the other side of the screen.

'Bless me, Father, for I have sinned,' Harry begins. And in this smallest of chambers in the greatest of churches, in the dark, seen by nobody but God and His agent on earth, Harry's guilt tumbles out of him. In the strict format of church confession, the description of his sin feels to him like an iceberg, barely hinting at the vastness of his transgression under water: 'It has been three weeks since my last confession. I have committed the sin of masturbation once and the sin of sodomy once. I have also committed the sin of lust several times. For these and all the sins of my past life, I ask pardon from God, penance and absolution from you, Father.'

'Do you intend to keep committing the sin of sodomy with this individual?' says the priest.

'Uh . . . no,' Harry says, clenching his jaw. 'No. I do not.'

Black hair fanning across the pillow, pale eyes and a lean body, and that thick cock—

'No!' Harry says, the sharp word bouncing off the hard wooden surfaces of the confessional.

'Very well,' the priest says. 'An indulgence is two shillings. You can come back for another in one month's time if you commit the sin again.'

Harry opens his mouth to argue, to *deny*, when it hits him: he'd done the entire confession in French. The priest knew he was noble born.

Only the Church and the greatest of lords have the income for glass in their windows.

Harry bites his tongue. Idly, he wonders if the merchant who had confessed before him had been charged more or less for his forgiveness.

'I'm sorry, Father,' Harry says at last. 'I don't intend to commit those sins again. I would prefer a penance.'

'Suit yourself,' the priest sighs.

Harry says his act of contrition and is given his list of prayers to say and psalms to study. '*Ego te absolvo*.' He feels absolved of nothing as he steps back out into the soft light of the cathedral.

His stomach grumbles as he makes his way through the great doors to the midday brightness beyond, and it gives him an idea: he will fast, and hold night vigil at the altar of whatever quiet, out-of-the-way chapel he can find in Windsor. If the priest will not give him a proper penance for his sins, he will find one himself.

By the time Harry makes his way to the main market square of the city, it's creeping towards early afternoon and the livestock traders are packing up. Peter waves to him excitedly, his body vibrating with delight. Harry grins and strides over to him, following eagerly as Peter shows him three different horses. He ultimately decides on a grey mare named Libertine, a little taller than Star but with strong conformation. Libertine has the tip of one ear cut off and a few scars on her flank despite her youth (Peter reckons she's about four), and for that reason she's going cheaper than she's worth.

They saddle up and resume the ride northeast. Libertine very quickly becomes 'Libby', and she turns out to be a good palfrey, with a long, easy trot and plenty of stamina. Plus, Nomad seems to have a crush on her, as he arches his neck and picks up his big fluffy feet a little more nimbly when she's next to him.

Harry's little group arrives at Windsor from the town side six days later. All three of them are struck to silence by the huge, low, sprawling castle on the hill: the squat, great Round Tower in the centre; the Lower Ward to the left, still damaged from the great fire thirty years previous; the Upper Ward to the right.

Harry gives his *bona fides* to the gatekeepers and they are ushered inside. Servants descend on them in a swarm, taking the horses and the cart, unloading, and showing them down to the Lower Ward where the lesser nobles will pitch their tents for the next week. The area within the five-foot-thick outer walls is immense, an entire city in and of itself. Harry has seen other castles, mostly from the outside during tournaments, but he is as speechless as Kit and Peter as they struggle to comprehend the sheer size and wealth of this, favourite among the King's dozens of castles.

They set their small pavilion, unroll the pallet they will share, and then go to gawk shamelessly at the other guests. Households are still arriving – the *ludi*, the games that begin the courtly entertainment, are not set to begin until the Feast of Saint Martin on the following day. On the town side, a queue is forming of carts and horsemen. Beyond the castle on its other side, in a gentle slope stretching seemingly to the horizon, are gardens, parklands and hunting grounds. The Upper Ward, adjacent to the King's hall, is filled with a half-dozen huge marquee pavilions, temporary palaces of canvas for the greatest lords.

Harry recognises the pennants of Montagu and Arundel. His stomach twists. Of *course* Montagu is here. Rabbie probably will be too, and others of the dozen knights who had massacred Iain's family in Galloway. Harry doesn't see Ufford's pennant, a gold cross on black, which means if he hurries, he may be able to speak to Montagu before Rabbie twists his ear about Iain's escape attempts.

Harry groans inwardly at the need to confront the Baron. There's probably an hour until supper and the light is already fading, but enough sun fills the indifferent late-autumn sky that he can find his way to Montagu's grand tent. After a week of riding, he is unused to walking, and his sword in its scabbard bangs against his left leg with every step, as if to remind him how this whole blasted adventure began.

Few take note of him as he cuts between the great pavilions of the Upper Ward; but for the knight's belt at his waist, Harry would pass for a poor man-at-arms in his unfashionably loose-fitting tunic and cloak. The wealthier nobles are already resplendent in their best scarlets, damask and velvets, their tunics tight to their bodies with low waists and topped with a small, decorative cloak with jagged edges and a liripipe, an absurdly long-tailed hood that serves little purpose other than to display status. He sees portly old Lord Waldegrave, one of Montagu's Galloway Dozen, in a gold-stamped tunic that probably cost more than Harry's entire little estate makes in a month. And Harry has to catch himself, *Hey Iain, look at him* on his lips. *What do you think of that?*

When Harry reaches Montagu's pavilion, the man himself is nowhere to be found. He doesn't recognise any of the Baron's servants but he gives them his name anyway, and asks them to tell Lord William that he'd stopped by. He is just turning to leave when the Baron himself comes striding through the tent's opening, resplendent in a peacock-blue silk pourpoint jacket over a scarlet fitted tunic.

The Baron's tanned face breaks into a grin. 'Harry,' he exclaims, leading the young knight to a table and beckoning for beer. 'What news of the boy?' he asks, sitting on the opposite bench and leaning forwards. 'I heard there have been . . . *difficulties.*' His face takes on a pitying mien at those words, at the same time appearing both sorry for Harry's troubles and unimpressed that he got himself into them.

Harry coughs, but meets Montagu's small blue eyes. 'There was some trouble,' he says, 'but Rabbie helped me sort it out. The boy is . . . he's fine, now. There won't be any further problems.'

'My man said you didn't want him there any more?' Montagu says, so mild that it immediately makes the hackles rise on Harry's back.

'No!' Harry says, startling the young serving-boy pouring their beer. 'No, I was just . . . I was tired, and spoke out of turn. He has been, uh.' Harry takes a deep breath and schools himself to look collected. 'He's been brought to heel.' *The wet snap of bone; the quiet whimper of a boy too proud to let the English know how much he hurt.*

Montagu grins. 'Good man. I knew you were one of us. Perhaps we'll ride down and visit the both of you for Christmas. It would be nice to see how our little prisoner is getting along.' The Baron leans over to pat Harry on the shoulder. 'And of course our newest investment. The money-lenders were quite glad to sell me Dartington's debts. Even gave me a nice discount.'

The serving-boy puts a plate of fine bread, cheeses and sausage between them, but Harry finds his appetite has vanished completely.

'Our hall is. Very small,' he stutters. 'I'm afraid we couldn't provide hospitality of the standard to which you're accustomed.'

'You underestimate—' Montagu begins, but the rest of his sentence is cut off by a commotion from the pavilion's entrance and the Baron's name being shouted out.

By Rabbie. *Sir Robert.*

Upholder of such knightly virtues as murder, torture and casual cruelty.

Montagu greets the brash, strong-boned young knight with a jovial shout and a hug. Harry realises the situation, unpleasant as it is, has handed him a tactical advantage. 'Hello, Rabbie!' Harry says, plastering a big smile on his face. 'The Baron was just saying how he wanted to come down to Dartington for Christmas! Perhaps you'd be able to stop by as well.'

Rabbie's face wrinkles in distaste. He turns to Montagu, exclaiming, 'Have you *seen* their estate? Your dovecote in Wiltshire's bigger than his whole hall. My lord, stay with us instead at Ordlington. You can go for an afternoon's ride down to see Lyon and his threadbare patch of land, and at least you can stay in comfort while you do it.' Montagu glances at Harry and tilts his head, assessing, but then Rabbie throws an arm around the slightly shorter Baron and says, 'I insist.'

Montagu raises his hands in mock defeat and pouts at Harry.

Harry shoots Rabbie an angry look then sags, defeated, exactly as he had planned. 'Well, we'd love to see you, if you do manage to come down our way,' he mumbles, staring at his thumbs like a truculent child.

Rabbie leans over and stage-whispers into Montagu's ear, 'I can't remember if he actually has a barn, or he just keeps his farm animals in the hall.' Then, louder, so Harry can definitely hear, 'Not that he can keep his animals under control.'

'The boy?' Montagu says.

'That fuckin' little savage,' Rabbie groans, throwing a leg over the bench and settling across from Harry. He reaches for the bread and sausage and stuffs a chunk of each in his mouth. ''Nother reason you don't want to stay in that shithole,' Rabbie slurs around the food. His hand goes unconsciously to touch the ragged remains of his right ear. 'Little bastard's likely to try to kill you in your sleep.'

Montagu looks at Harry, sharp and curious.

Harry sighs, slouching. 'He's settled down with us, but I can't guarantee his behaviour with any of the people he saw murder his mother. I'm working on it.' Then he looks up, a smile tugging at one corner of his lips. 'He's actually a surprisingly good squire.'

Rabbie laughs so hard he spits breadcrumbs all over the table.

The King's games, the *ludi*, start at dinner the next day. Over a hundred lords and ladies assemble in the Upper Ward's great hall, the jewel colours of their tunics and dresses resplendent in the candlelight. There is a play: twelve men in costume, among them Montagu and Percy and (recognisable from his girth) Waldegrave, pantomiming the story of the Green Knight coming to offer a bargain to King Arthur's knights: that one behead him, and in a year's time the Green Knight can return to behead a knight of his choosing.

From his distant table, Harry watches as the bargain is accepted, and a painted wooden sword is raised by a knight dressed as Sir Gawain. The papier-mâché head of the Green Knight comes off to raucous laughter, and bounces down the central aisle, revealing a slim, middle-aged lord with merry eyes and a close-trimmed dark beard. Gawain is, of course, King Edward himself.

Harry stands with the other nobles to applaud the play, as the King unmasks himself and declares that, an adventure being had, the feast may begin.

When Harry sits back down, there is a woman sitting across from him.

She is his age, if not slightly younger, and her slim, dark red overdress in fine Bruges wool hints at a fashionably curvy figure. The equally fine embroidery on the sleeves of her cobalt-blue underdress hints at great income. Her dark hair is loose, free of gorget and wimple: the prerogative of an unmarried maiden, or a queen. Her face has a fierce intelligence to it, and brown eyes sweep assessingly over Harry.

'Milady,' Harry says, inclining his head. 'Harry Lyon, a poor knight of Devon. I am afraid you are several tables below where you belong.'

Full, bowed lips quirk in amusement. 'Adelaide de Morton, of the Lancashire Mortons. Call me Alys. And, Sir Harry, I am exactly where I wish to be.'

Harry raises an eyebrow.

Alys leans forwards, conspiratorial. 'They sat me next to this Ufford character and if he tries to put his hand on my backside one more time, I'm going to nail it to the bench with my eating knife,' she hisses. 'So rather than cause an incident, I thought I'd discover whether *all* you West Country knights are such rude lumps, or he's an exception.'

'He's definitely an exception,' Harry says.

'Thank goodness,' Alys smiles, leaning back. 'You're a little too handsome to stab. I'd have no qualms about maiming him, though, especially seeing as someone's already started the job.' Alys touches the tip of her ear, to mark the place where Rabbie's own is missing.

'Did he tell you how he got that?' Harry asks. He can't help but smirk. This is going to be good.

'Strangely not,' Alys says, crossing her arms and tilting her head. 'Which is curious. Knights are usually so *dull* about their battle wounds, blathering on about them at the slightest opportunity.'

'That's because he got it when he was jumped by an unarmed boy, who knocked his helmet away and damn near bit his ear clean off. Rabbie was in full armour at the time.'

Alys guffaws into her sleeve. 'I must remember to ask him about it the next time he gets grabby.'

'Please do,' Harry says.

'And tell me he didn't kill the boy,' Alys says, her face growing serious.

'No, despite his best efforts,' Harry says. 'The boy—'

And then he recalls what that very boy had said before he departed, about trusting too quickly at court. He also remembers glancing over earlier to see where Rabbie had been seated, out of a petty desire to quantify the social gulf between them. There had been no scarlet-clad lady next to him.

'—I don't actually know what happened to the boy,' he finishes. 'I think he ran away.' He smiles mildly at this lovely, witty woman, several levels above his status, who has sat with him on the flimsiest of pretences.

Alys shifts and smiles back at him. 'A shame. I'd like to find the boy and congratulate him.'

'Alas,' Harry says.

Alys presses her lips together, and appears about to say something else, when servants begin placing a variety of fancy meats along their table.

'Have you ever had swan?' Alys asks, as a pair of the roast birds, necks entwined in a decorative heart shape, is placed on the table in front of them.

Harry shakes his head. 'I thought only the King could serve them? And,' he blushes, 'this is my first time at a royal feast.'

Alys rolls her eyes. 'They're beastly things. Unpleasant alive, virtually inedible dead. Thank heavens the royal kitchen hires Moorish cooks – if it weren't for their skill with spices we'd all be in for a miserable meal.'

They eat in peace after that, Harry fending off casual questions from Alys that seek to turn the conversation towards the recent Scottish campaign, his relationship with Baron Montagu, and what his journey home from Berwick had been like. It's by far the most charming and stealthy interrogation to which Harry has ever been subjected, and something in him regrets that this bright beauty will leave him for good as soon as she has exhausted her questioning.

But beautiful as Lady de Morton may be, he will not betray Iain's existence to her. Iain has nobody left but him.

There's dancing, after dinner. Fancy caroles and saltarellos that Harry doesn't know. Alys tries to coax him to the floor a few times, but finally gives up and returns to the lord with the beard and the merry eyes who had played the Green Knight. They chat animatedly in a corner, clearly friends of old acquaintance. The man glances at Harry, his brown eyes narrowing. Harry wonders if he is the source of Alys's clever questions, this interest in Iain. He wishes he could ask Montagu, but he fears getting more enmeshed in this spider's web than he already is.

He slips away early through the still-bustling castle grounds, and eventually finds a quiet chapel dedicated to Saint George. The simple, rough stone of the little church is somehow reassuring after the overwhelming splendour of King Edward's court. It's also empty but for a friar who looks in on Harry's kneeling form and, nodding, leaves him to be alone with his faith.

Harry spends the rest of the day and evening praying to the saint for help vanquishing his own dragons: the serpents in scarlet finery that prowl at court, keen for fresh meat, and the scaly dark thing that writhes within him, whispering of sins of the flesh.

The next day is a hunt. Peter saddles up Libby for Harry, who pulls on the same decent green-blue wool tunic he wore the day before. There are only about thirty lords assembled with the huntsmen at the park entrance to the castle. Thirty lords and three ladies. One is the Queen, Philippa, who rides pillion behind a man-at-arms dressed in an aketon in Edward's colours: scarlet, with gold lions. Harry doesn't recognise the second lady. The third is Alys, and she rides alone.

Harry hangs around awkwardly at the edges of Montagu's set, who are boisterous, passing around flasks of cherry brandy to ward off the early-morning chill. He's not sure who are louder, the Baron's coterie of knights (each trying to perform having the *most* fun, being the *most* amused), or the pack of deerhounds, braying for the blood of the stag.

He smirks, and imagines what Iain would say. Iain would pull Numbles over close to him and murmur about how Waldegrave is already as red as his coat, that garment straining at its seams like an overstuffed sausage casing. How Thomas Howland's horse looks like it was cobbled together from the spare parts of other, unrelated horses. Whether Colin Crocker, swaying in his saddle, would pass out from his hangover before or after the hunting horn sounded.

And then Iain's lips would brush Harry's ear and he'd say *we can out-ride them all, c'mon, Harry, first one to the stag gets a forfeit*. And then he'd ride like the Devil himself, because Iain mac Maíl Coluim never understood the concept of retreat.

'. . . Harry?'

He looks up. Montagu is watching him, a furrow of dismay on his once-handsome brow.

'I'm sorry. Miles away,' Harry says. 'Thinking about home.'

The Master of the Hunt sounds the off then, the blast of the horn cutting down further conversation, and the dogs are loosed into the woods. Harry canters into the perfect, fairy-tale forest, marvelling at the complete absence of undergrowth and low-hanging branches. He wonders if there is an entire gardening staff devoted to keeping it that way. His mind can't comprehend the scale of wealth necessary to accomplish this; it passes into the realm of the fantastic. Perhaps that's the sort of thing Iain might know, Harry thinks. He'd been eerily well informed about court life for a boy slowly starving to death in a remote Scottish keep.

He pushes these thoughts of Iain out of his head. It's a beautiful morning, a low mist still hugging the mossy earth, and the physical exercise feels good: the rhythm of Libby's hooves; the shifts of posture Harry makes to communicate with her and to retain correct balance. Harry pushes Libby faster; she's a tall horse and fleet of foot, and soon he finds himself passing the main body of the hunt. Alys gives him a wink as he speeds past, and he salutes her in turn. Then, before he knows it, he's in the vanguard, and reining back lest he overtake the King. (He must remember to praise Peter, loudly and publicly, for his choice of horse.)

The King looks over his shoulder and grins when he sees Harry gaining on him. 'Sir Harry,' he calls out. 'Well ridden!' He motions for Harry to ride next to him. They're at an easy canter; the dogs have slowed, crossing back and forth around them, trying to pick up the scent again.

Edward seems so *young* to him then. The King is only two years older than Harry himself, yet he bears the weight of a fractious kingdom on his shoulders with ease. It's this that makes Harry's breath catch in the King's presence. This effortless grace of true royalty, managing all of England while Harry struggles with a few hundred muddy acres in Devon.

He swallows his thoughts as he remembers his manners. 'Thank you for inviting me,' he stutters. 'This is my first time at Windsor, or at court at all. It's an honour.'

'It won't be your last,' says the King. 'We've a celebratory tournament coming up in the New Year in Dunstable. We expect you to be there, and show all the promise in the main competition you showed as a squire.'

Harry is momentarily speechless. That the King would take notice of him, of his progress in tournaments – it was his boyhood dream come true. And yet, a sarcastic part of him whispers, *who's left to die for this one?*

Then the King's eyes narrow. 'Are you simply exceptionally fond of that colour, or do you only have one set of clothes?'

'Er,' Harry says, glancing down in embarrassment. 'It's a very comfortable tunic.'

The King throws his head back and laughs.

Out of the corner of his eye, Harry can see Rabbie riding up on the King's other side, and he realises his time with Edward is about to end. 'I'm sorry,' Harry whispers.

The King waves off his apology. 'No, all is well. We'd far rather our knights out-ride us than out-dress us.'

Harry's eyes widen, and before he can stop himself he says, 'Is that a dare, Your Majesty?'

That warm grin splits the King's face again. 'Yes,' he says. 'Get to the stag first and we'll give you all the clothes you can carry.' The King spurs his horse into a gallop.

Harry leans forwards and urges Libby on, and they both tear away from Rabbie, who is cantering up behind them, calling out and asking if His Majesty has heard the new joke going round.

When they corner the stag, Harry's horse is half a head in front of the King's. Harry reins back at the last moment, allowing Edward to make the kill.

He doesn't think more of it but at None, shortly after dinner, a tailor and three apprentices arrive at his little pavilion. The apprentices bear bolts of fabric: costly sky-blue linen and fine Bruges wool in several colours; a heavier winter-weight wool for cloaks; soft leather, and furs for trimming. Shiny ribbons and threads for embroidery. The tailor brings two mostly completed suits of clothes, tunics and pourpoints, an aketon for under his armour, tight woollen hose to replace his looser breeches, and fine, slim linen undershirts. He makes Harry put on each piece of clothing inside-out, then cuts the seams and re-marks them for better fit. Then he disappears again with the clothes. The bolts of fabric stay, apparently a gift. There's enough for each person at Dartington Manor to get a new tunic or cloak and thus, with one offhand action, the King has bought their little Devon estate the best Christmas it has had in Harry's memory.

Kit pulls out a deep purple heavy wool and is stroking it, staring at the colour. It's a shade that neither he nor Harry has ever seen in a fabric before.

The tailor arrives the next morning with the completed clothes. He's accompanied by a palace servant who explains that Harry is to perform in the game at dinner, and must come immediately to practise. Harry slips into the outfit indicated for him and follows, immediately tangling the long liripipe tail of his hood in his legs. The courtier rolls his eyes and shows Harry how to wrap the ridiculous thing over his shoulders in the proper way.

Harry fidgets as he walks. Court clothes are tight. And stiff. And *short*. And the damn hood tail keeps unwrapping itself off his shoulders, like the garment knows it doesn't belong on him and seeks to make its escape. As beautifully crafted as the clothes are, they make Harry painfully aware of the fact that he's wearing them, with their subtle but definite restrictions on his movements.

The game turns out to be a tableau of the hunt, with the twelve most eligible bachelors at court portraying beasts of the forest. Each is given a tabard of emerald damask gilded with leaves and vines to wear over their tunics, and a visor to wear over their heads. The King is Lionel, the lion, of course. Harry is the stag. Rabbie is a boar, and it feels sharply appropriate for his brusque manners and blocky features.

While they wait their turn, their papier-mâché beast heads in their hands, Rabbie offers Harry double what he paid for Libby. Harry remembers the gashes from the spurs on Rabbie's palfrey after the hunt and politely declines.

Rabbie offers him triple.

Harry points out that they aren't likely to go hunting again this week as the King seems to value variety over habit.

Rabbie grumbles and moves to sit closer to the King.

The performance goes well, and afterwards each of the 'beasts' is paired off with one of the eligible ladies at court, for a dance. Harry is chosen by Alys de Morton, who is as elegant as she was the first day, this time in a forest-green overdress with a saffron underdress.

'I'm sorry,' Harry whispers. 'I don't know how to dance.'

'Just follow,' she whispers back. 'It's quite simple, really. And it's I who must apologise, about dinner the other day. I do enjoy your company and I fear you think that is not so.'

Harry inclines his head. He has been avoiding her; easier to do than face the inevitable disappointment as she passes him over for someone closer to her rank. 'But there are so much better for you to spend your time with,' he says as they spin around the hall in a complicated formation.

'In pocket, yes, but not in spirit,' Alys replies. 'And I have enough lands of my own that I need not be impressed by theirs.'

Harry relaxes slightly. 'Well, that's good, for I have only a tiny corner of Devon.'

'I've heard Devonshire is pretty. Is your corner such?' she asks, her brown eyes warm and her smile wicked.

'It's the most beautiful place on earth,' he says, smiling back.

The dance draws to a close and they face each other for the final steps. 'I would like to see it one day,' Alys says as she releases his hand and flows into a curtsey.

'I would like that, too, milady,' Harry replies as he bows to her. And he finds he's not simply being polite – he really *would* like to walk around Dartington with Alys and hear her quick, clever take on things. Annie would love her. Iain would . . . Iain would hate her. At first.

He stops again at the chapel after supper and prays until late into the night. Again, it's empty but for a friar or two from the nearby cloisters. It seems everyone at court is too busy this week with matters temporal to bother with the sacred.

For the first time, however, Harry feels he is as he wishes to be. He only thought of Iain once that day, and without the hot curl of lust that usually waylays his mind. He thinks of Alys more often now, but even that is appropriate: courtly admiration, rather than base, sinful desire.

The next morning is Sunday. No games are planned. Instead, the court is expected to go to Mass with the King at noon, but their time is their own before that. Harry rises with the bells of Prime to find both Lower and Upper Wards still sleeping off the previous night's amusements. He decides to explore the royal gardens, which are spectral in the late-autumn morning fog. Burlap shrouds protect the more delicate bushes, and the skeletons of perennials still reach their withered stalks heavenwards. The distant lamentations of peacocks echo like the cries of lost souls.

Harry assumes he's alone, until he rounds a corner and finds himself not twenty feet away from a white lion. His hand drifts to his sword-hilt, but the beast merely blinks red eyes at him and shakes its mane, then turns to go. Its huge feet are soundless on the frosty ground. The lion fades back into the mist, white on white, and Harry is left wondering whether it had existed at all, or had been some strange vision.

'It's an albino,' says a voice behind him. 'Gift from the Doge of Venice.'

Harry turns. Nearby, on a bench under a rose bower, sits the Green Knight, the lord with the trimmed beard and the merry eyes. Alys's friend. The man sees the confusion on his face and bows slightly. 'Richard FitzAlan, Earl of Arundel, at your service.' Then he pats the open space next to him on the bench. 'Come. Sit with me.'

Harry introduces himself, though he feels Arundel knows exactly who he is already, and begs to remain standing.

Arundel shoots him a *suit yourself* look, then asks, 'What do you know of French politics, Harry?'

'I know little, and care less,' Harry replies, as he begins to trace connections between Alys's interrogation of him and the Lord Arundel whose presence in Carlisle caused Iain to be thrust into Harry's care in the first place.

He still doesn't know the reason for the game between Montagu and Arundel, nor where he or Iain fits on their chessboard. But to admit that, Harry feels, would be fatal. So he must continue to play, though he knows neither the rules nor the stakes.

Arundel raises an eyebrow at Harry's blasé answer. 'You *should* care. There's going to be war.'

'Now that we've solved Scotland?' Harry says.

Arundel snorts. '*Please*. We'll never solve Scotland, not as long as the Scots are in it. That moron Balliol can't even hold a candle without spilling wax; he's never going to hold the North.' Then Arundel favours him with a cockeyed smirk. 'But I hear you're aware of the tenaciousness of the Scottish, firsthand?'

Harry glances over his shoulder at the position of the sun. Even it is choosing to be unhelpful, hidden behind a screen of featureless grey cloud. 'I'm sorry, milord, I must go. I have an appointment.'

Arundel reaches out and seizes Harry's sleeve, pulling him closer. Those dark eyes now are steely, and his voice drops to a near-whisper. His words turn Harry's blood to ice: 'There is a rumour, Harry. Of an inconvenient boy. Do you know how Edward is going to justify war with France? Get the barons to cross the Channel for him, when they wouldn't for his grandfather?'

'I . . .' Harry stutters. He has no idea.

Arundel's lip curls. 'His mother, Isabella, is a daughter of Philip the Fair. Which makes our king a direct successor to the House of Capet, who have ruled France since time immemorial. In England you can succeed down the female line, Henry FitzEmpress proved that. In France, you can't. Not yet. But thanks to Isabella's scheming, there are no other Capet heirs. Our Edward is it. Or should I say, there are no other *known* Capet heirs.' He lets go of Harry's sleeve, and pats his hand instead. 'Just rumours.'

They stare at each other for a moment, before Arundel smirks again and says with a shrug, 'French politics, Harry. Fascinating stuff.'

'And what's your angle?' Harry asks.

'I'm your friend, Harry,' Arundel says, his eyes wide in mock affront.

Harry smiles thinly. 'There are no friends at court, only advantages,' he replies.

Arundel looks at him with a curious respect, and a little smile plays on his face. 'Those are awfully astute words for someone on his maiden visit to Windsor.'

Harry glances down at his feet. 'I'm an astute man.'

Arundel makes a face. 'No you're not. You're a hedgerow knight half a generation off tilling your fields yourself. Don't lie to me, Harry. You're not good enough at it. Who coached you? Not Montagu; he wouldn't help his own mother unless there was profit in it.'

'I'm not lying,' says Harry, as evenly as he can.

'Dammit, boy, you are,' Arundel hisses, leaning forwards. 'Those are the words of someone who's lost at court and lost *badly*. That's the only way you learn that lesson. I know because my father was executed by Roger Mortimer. We lost everything, Harry. *Everything*. That's how I know there are no friends at court. But what burns me up with curiosity, *farm boy*, is how *you* learned this lesson. Or who learned it for you.'

'Sir Simon told me,' Harry replies, as mildly as possible.

'Do not lie to me, Harry,' Arundel growls.

'Don't try to play me, *Richard*,' Harry counters, tensing for a fight.

But then Arundel slumps back, the exaggerated poses and tension slipping off him like water. 'I'm actually not,' he says simply. 'My ward, Lady de Morton, *likes* you. And I hate to see a good man caught up in something he doesn't understand.'

Arundel looks up at Harry, expectant.

Harry says nothing. He can't incriminate himself, or Iain, if he stays silent.

Finally Arundel gets up and pats him on the shoulder as he goes. 'When you want a primer on French politics, come and see me. Knowledge is power, Harry.'

The end of the fortnight comes both too soon and not soon enough, and thankfully without anyone else trying to pigeonhole Harry into uncomfortable conversations about politics he doesn't understand. He spends more time with Alys, and they agree to write to each other. Her address is Arundel Castle. She tells him that Lord Mortimer killed her parents for their lands, and she has been under the protection of the Earl of Arundel since she was eight. When she marries or reaches her majority, whichever comes first, her family lands revert to her from the crown – so King Edward has promised.

They receive more gifts from the King. At the final breakfast, he hands out a bag of coins for each of the nobles in the Lower Ward. Harry stares at the heavy purse in his hands as he walks back to his tent. It takes an angry shout from a cart-driver for him to look up. When he does, he realises that the Lower Ward is in chaos. Pavilions are being taken down and packed onto carts. Merchants from the town and beyond squeeze into every available space, exhibiting their wares and helping the nobles spend the money they have just received. Harry waves them all away until an African perfume-seller comes past. The woman is dark-skinned and honey-eyed, slipping charmingly between English, French and several other languages as she explains each scent and where its ingredients come from. It's fascinating, and Harry loses himself smelling Arabian sandalwood and oud, French jasmine and lavender, roses from the Bulgarian Empire, limes from Portugal, myrrh from Egypt.

He is buying a small vial of perfume for Annie (it's the sort of luxury she'd never dream of buying herself) when his attention is caught by a bottle hidden slightly behind the others. 'What's that one?' he asks, expecting to be told it's a larger container of one of the scents he's already smelled.

But the woman flashes a bright grin at him and leans forwards, lowering her voice. 'Rose oil,' she whispers. 'For the bedroom.'

Harry says, 'What—' then blushes furiously as he remembers his last night with Iain. *Get you good and wet.*

The woman winks at him, and wraps the bottle up in waxed cloth. 'Just one more of those nice silver coins,' she says, passing the little package to him.

Harry hands over the groat.

His brain starts to function again a short while later as he stares down at the bundle in his hands. He's too embarrassed to run back to the woman and return it, so instead he tucks it into his saddlebag. The perfume is for Annie. The . . . *other*, he'll lay aside for his wedding night.

Harry's little party rides down the dear, familiar lanes into Dartington a week later, their cart groaning with gifts and the air pregnant with snow. Piers spots them near the upper pastures and, shouting, tears ahead on foot, their harbinger. When they turn in to the gates of the manor, the entire population of the hall is waiting in the courtyard to welcome their lord home.

In all the sea of smiling faces, Harry searches restlessly for only one.

But it's not there.

Harry slides off Libby and hands her reins to Peter just in time for Annie to envelop him in a hug. Harry lifts her up and swings her round and she squeals in delight like a little girl. '*I'm so happy to be home*,' he says. '*Everything went well while I was gone?*'

Given everyone's abundant good cheer, Harry guesses that Iain hasn't killed anyone and/or run away. But it's always good to check.

'*No disasters*,' Annie smiles, patting his cheek.

Harry lowers his voice. '*How was he . . . ?*'

Annie's smile widens and her eyes take on a mischievous twinkle. '*Ask him yourself*,' she says, putting her hands on his shoulders and turning him towards the stables.

Iain is prowling towards him with the half-limp, half-strut he's developed since his leg was broken. In Harry's absence, he's reverted to his Scottish habits: despite the early winter weather he is barefoot, wearing only a long, baggy shirt, belted low on his hips. He's looking down, raking a dirty hand through his hair to dislodge the pieces of straw from it. His shirt is a mess, almost translucent with wear and badly torn at the shoulder. Then he looks up, and grins as he sees Harry.

Harry's breath fails him.

Iain's hair has been cut. His face is exposed to view, no longer hidden behind dark, matted locks.

Harry's heart fails him next, skittering strangely in his chest.

Iain is the most beautiful thing he has ever seen.

He knows he's grinning like a fool, unable to take his eyes off his friend, overcome with what feels like not just butterflies in his stomach but the whole damn aviary. In between one breath and the other they're hugging, crushing each other to their breasts, Iain warm and hard with muscle and smelling of the stables. Harry whispers to him, 'I missed you.'

'How was it?' Iain says, separating them enough to look into Harry's eyes, checking to make sure he's survived the month away.

'I don't really know,' Harry sighs. 'I both hated it and loved it at the same time.' Then he remembers the gifts, and switches from French to English to call out, '*Annie! The cart is full of things for the manor. Gifts from the King!*'

Annie squeals again and gets the boys to unload the cart before shooing everyone into the hall, complaining about the cold. Iain slings an arm around Harry's waist and they go inside, Harry unable to stop the smile constantly tugging at his lips.

The fine fabrics, trim and clothes have all been arranged on one of the long dining tables, and the inhabitants of the manor are already looking over them, exclaiming over the colours and the weaves. Harry sees the linen undertunic from one of his court outfits and grabs it from the pile. It's far too narrow on him to wear in the country, but Iain is small and slim, so it would serve as a good everyday shirt for him.

He passes it over to his friend. 'For you,' he says.

Iain fingers the fine linen and the careful stitching and looks up at him, questioning. 'Are you sure?' he says softly.

'I'm not going to wear it, Iain. It'll fit you better. Besides,' he says, plucking at Iain's frayed sleeve, 'this shirt's about to fall off you. Here, try it on.'

Iain snorts, then undoes his belt, bends to doff his old shirt, and pulls Harry's court shirt on.

And.

Harry tries to make words happen, but they catch in his throat.

The shirt is even tighter on Iain than it was on Harry, stretched taut across shoulders tanned and bulky from work, a waist thickly corded with muscle. The hem barely comes to the tops of his thighs, and Harry has to force his glance to stay at Iain's chest, rather than look down to see if he can catch a glimpse of Iain's manhood. He can see the small shifts in every muscle under the shirt as Iain fidgets, uncomfortable in the tight linen. There is . . . There is nowhere safe to look.

'*Iain! There are children here*,' Annie yells good-naturedly from the other side of the table as she playfully covers Katie's eyes. Katie swears at Annie and tries to duck underneath her hand.

Iain groans, turns away, and wriggles out of the shirt, putting on his old, torn one with visible relief.

'*Sorry*,' Harry says.

Iain shrugs and hands him back the shirt. And Harry realises they're almost eye to eye, that Iain is no more than a scant inch shorter than him now.

'*When did you get so big?*' Harry says, putting a hand on Iain's shoulder, his brain not comprehending how the skinny Scottish boy of midsummer has bulked up into the man in front of him. But yes, that is . . . a lot of muscle under his hand.

(The assorted flying creatures in Harry's stomach move lower, and begin to cause disturbances *there*, too.)

Iain smirks. '*Had to take care of some Sassenach idiot's manor while he was off gallivanting around with his king. And his steward's trying to fatten me up to be the Christmas goose.*'

'*I try my best*,' Annie groans melodramatically, '*but the boy only puts on muscle, not fat*.'

Harry smiles as he realises all this has been said in English. He's so overwhelmingly proud of Iain, for holding down the estate in his absence, for adapting so well to their home. Iain still has an accent, but his English has improved immeasurably in the month Harry has been away. He looks over to congratulate Iain, but his eyes dip low and catch on Iain's nipples, erect in the chill of the hall, the thin linen draping over the hard nubs. He forces his gaze upwards, to Iain's face, to those dark lashes and pale eyes, the dusting of freckles across his cheeks.

Iain licks his lips.

And in the space between breaths, all Harry's plans of fortitude and chastity burn to ash.

He realises he's leaning forwards, desperate to feel those lips against his own. He steps away, shaking himself, then hands the linen shirt to Annie. '*Maybe this will fit Piers*,' he says.

Annie tucks the shirt under her arm. '*Not to worry, I'll sew Iain a new shirt from some of this nice blue linen*,' she says. '*It'll bring out his eyes*.'

God, no, Harry thinks.

'*You remember my old shirt?*' Iain says, leaning against the table to speak to Annie. '*Can you make it like that?*'

Annie frowns. '*You're in England. You should wear English clothes*.'

'*No*,' Iain says, sticking out his lower lip in a pout. Harry wants to bite it.

'*Any of the court ladies catch your eye?*' Annie says, elbowing Harry.

Katie groans.

'*What?*' Annie grumbles. '*I want children to spoil. It's about time.*'

'*There was one,*' Harry says, ducking his head shyly. '*A very highborn lady from Lancashire. I don't think she'd ever settle for me, though.*'

'*Nonsense,*' Annie says. '*She'd be lucky to have you. Let me tell you, Harry, there is nothing worse than the prison of a bad marriage. The heart of a good man is worth untold acres of lands and manors.*'

Harry sneaks a glance at Iain and grits his teeth as the castles of his contrition collapse within him, their foundations worthless sand.

He is not a good man.

Iain's face betrays no expression, but he quietly excuses himself to go up to the solar.

Annie sees Harry's distant gaze and mistakes it for exhaustion. '*You must be bone-tired from the journey, Harry.*' She turns to her young assistant cook. '*Katie, grab him some bread and apples and cheese from the kitchen, and some of that roast chicken.*'

Harry goes upstairs not much later, excuses made, and laden with a basket of food and a jug of cider.

Iain is naked, bent over the washbasin, cleaning the dirt of the day off his neck and shoulders with a wet rag.

Harry sinks onto his bed and just watches.

Iain wrings out the rag then starts on his armpits, and stomach, and down between his legs. He pauses when he feels Harry's eyes on him.

'I'm sorry,' Harry breathes. 'You got even more beautiful while I was gone. I didn't think that was possible.'

Iain snorts and throws the rag at Harry's head. He catches it with a bark of laughter and flings it right back at Iain.

'Didn't mess around with your girl at Windsor?' Iain rumbles, turning back to his ablutions.

'She wasn't that kind of girl,' Harry says.

'And I'm that kind of boy,' Iain says, something mournful fraying the edges of his voice.

'Iain, no,' Harry says, walking over to his friend. 'Somewhere you became my best friend, and at court . . . I kept turning around to tell you things, imagining what you'd say, and . . . I wanted you there. With me. All the time. Alys is beautiful and perfect and brilliant, but you're *you*, and nobody will ever replace you. What you mean to me.'

Iain still has his back to him, and Harry puts his hands on Iain's shoulders, leans his forehead down so it touches the base of Iain's neck. 'I don't know what we're doing. I don't know what this is. I prayed so hard, throughout my time away from here, that I could . . . be your friend. W-without sin. I thought I had succeeded. And I come back, and with one look from you I am ablaze again.'

Iain turns, a wild look in his eye. He steps into Harry's space, his bare chest pressed against Harry's tunic. 'Does she make you feel like this?' he growls, his broad, calloused hand moving to cup Harry's burgeoning erection.

'N-no,' Harry stutters, shutting his eyes against the wave of lust that slams through him.

Iain leans in closer still, and traces his lips along the shell of Harry's ear. Harry is shaking: exhausted, overwhelmed, and so, so turned on, that he barely hears what Iain whispers: '*Da mihi castitatem et continentiam, sed noli modo.*'

He palms Harry's erection again and Harry moans. 'What do you want, Harry?' Iain says, tracing his lips along his cheekbone. 'Do you want me to stop? Or do you want to go to bed?'

Harry slams his lips against Iain's, forcing his tongue into the man's mouth. Iain shudders and lets out his own low groan as Harry's hand comes around the back of his neck to hold him there. All Harry wants is to plunder this man, ruin him, learn every swell and cut of his new, work-broadened body until his fingers can recall each muscle perfectly. As his other hand grips Iain's arse, pulling their hips together, he can feel the man's thick erection pressing against him.

When they break apart, breathless, Iain wipes the saliva from his glistening lips and says, 'Take your clothes off now, or I will take them off, violently.'

Harry nods and backs up until his knees hit the edge of the bed, and then he sits down and begins fiddling with the new and confusing buttons of his clothes. Iain watches him, lazily stroking himself, a predatory look on his face.

Harry kicks his fine clothes into a pile on the floor and opens his knees, staring his own challenge back at Iain. And then Iain is between his legs, licking a wet stripe up his palm and reaching down to—

'Wait,' Harry says.

'I swear to God, Harry, if you're telling me we have to stop now—' Iain begins, but Harry silences him with a kiss.

'Just wait,' he whispers, and glances around the room. One of the servants has already brought up his saddlebags; they're on the carved chest near the door. Harry slides off the bed and walks over, one hand on his erection to hold it against his stomach. He pulls out the waxcloth-wrapped package and brings it back to bed.

The cloth falls away in Iain's hands, revealing the bottle of scented oil. 'I want—' Harry begins.

Iain looks up at him, and the naked wonder and adoration in his face is enough to shatter something within Harry, another wall, another barrier between them. 'What do you want, Harry?' he murmurs.

Harry feels the blush climbing to his cheeks. 'I want you to show me the place inside me. The place that feels good.'

Iain's mouth opens in surprise, and then he kisses Harry very gently on the forehead, then his eyes, then his cheekbones, then down to his mouth. As he does this, Iain uses his bulk to push Harry gradually further onto the bed, on his back. 'Yes,' Iain breathes with each kiss.

When Harry is lying down in the middle of the bed, Iain reclines on his side and drags one hand all the way down Harry, reverently. 'You're like an angel, you know,' Iain whispers. 'My golden angel.' Then he untwists the stopper on the bottle of oil. 'This feels strange at first,' he says, his voice more serious. 'But trust me.'

Harry nods. 'I do,' he whispers, watching Iain spread oil over two of his fingers.

Iain ghosts his fingers down over Harry's cock, and Harry hisses and bucks his hips into the stimulation. Then he's running his fingers down over Harry's balls, and back further, to where the hair grows sparser.

Harry gasps as he feels Iain's index finger pressing against his hole. Iain uses his other hand to shift Harry onto his side, against him, so they're almost chest to chest. Their cocks bump against each other, both silky and solid at the same time, and that makes Harry's breath hitch as well.

He groans as Iain's finger begins to press inside him. Iain breathes soft shushing noises at him, as if Harry were a horse he was trying to calm. Harry writhes under the pressure. As he shifts, his cock rubs up against Iain's, and it sparks up every nerve in his body.

Iain pulls out of him to put some more oil on his fingers, spreading it around his hole, and Harry finds he misses the intrusion. It hadn't been pleasant, but it is incredibly intimate. When Iain replaces his fingers, Harry presses down on them, and grits his teeth. Now there are two, pushing in.

Iain kisses the furrow between his brows, making Harry aware of it. Harry tries to relax. Then Iain presses those fingers in even further, and turns them, and—

—Harry arches, gasping in surprise.

He can only see half of Iain's face, but the man's pale eyes glint mischievously and he's smirking at Harry. 'Mmm?' Iain hums.

'*Fuck*,' Harry breathes, pushing back on Iain's fingers. 'Do that again.'

Iain stares right into his eyes, pulls his fingers out about half an inch, and shoves them in harder. He hits the exact same place as before.

Harry tries to hold Iain's gaze but his eyes roll back in his head as a wanton moan rips through him. Then Iain loosely circles their cocks with his free hand, pushing them together, letting the movement of his fingers in Harry's bottom and his reaction to it rub them off against each other. He's finger-fucking Harry mercilessly now, rubbing the spot within him that's sending wave after wave of dizzying sensation through Harry, who can't do anything but shut his eyes and hang on for the ride.

'Oh God,' Harry moans. 'I see why you love this. *Nngh*.'

And Iain is whispering to him, 'That's it, *a sheòid*, let yourself go, you look so good, you're taking it so well,' and Harry could come from the stimulation on his cock or the stimulation in his arse alone, but both is so much, and yet not enough.

Harry opens his eyes. 'I want you,' he says, his voice rough and sex-wrecked as his body falls out of his control, quivering on the hits of pleasure rolling through it.

'You have me,' says Iain.

'No,' mumbles Harry, shaking his head. Words are *hard*. 'I want you *in* me.'

Iain slows his assault on Harry's arse, as doubt crosses his face. 'Harry, I'm not really the man for your first time. I'm—'

'Huge, I know,' Harry growls. 'Now stop acting like I'm delicate, and fuck me.'

Iain glares at him, and without warning shoves three fingers into him.

Harry arches, gasping, overfull. 'Are you *sure*?' Iain asks, drawing those fingers all the way out and then ramming them in again. 'Because it's even more than this.'

'Yes,' Harry says through gritted teeth, shoving himself back onto Iain's hand. '*Yes*.'

'Christ's blood,' Iain says. 'You're unbelievable.' Then he's tilting his head up to kiss Harry's mouth, down his neck, biting and sucking at his nipples, all the while fucking Harry on his fingers. Harry is writhing, wanting to pull himself away from that mouth and thrust himself into it at the same time, until he feels his orgasm building inside him and he pushes himself away from Iain before it gets out of what little control he has left.

'Now,' he orders.

'As you desire,' Iain says, his eyes shining. 'Get on your hands and knees. It's easier that way.' He helps arrange Harry, keeping a hand on him at all times, gently rubbing his flank, up his back, down his thigh. 'I don't get to do this a lot,' he murmurs from behind Harry, as he spreads more of the oil on his cock and on Harry's hole. 'Casual fucks behind a stable don't usually . . . they take one look and they say, *no way*.'

Harry can feel a warm, rough hand on his hip.

And then Iain is pressing into him.

It's more pain than anything else at first and Harry feels tears come to his eyes, his breath coming short. The hand on his hips begins to caress, soothing, and the first tendrils of pleasure begin to lick up Harry's body.

'I missed you so much,' Iain breathes. 'Defiled myself so many times thinking of you, dreaming of sucking your cock, of you fucking me, of lying on that rock and touching you for the first time.' He brushes his lips along the peaks of Harry's spine. 'I never imagined you'd let me do this.'

And Harry just wants Iain to get to that spot, less talking, more fucking, and he rams himself back on Iain's cock. And Jesus Christ, it's *so much*, so much more than Iain's fingers and Harry curls his back and all but screams into the pillow. Iain's hands are on his hips and gripping him so tightly Harry knows it's going to bruise.

'Are you. Trying. To kill me,' Iain hisses, wrecked, barely able to speak.

'Yes,' Harry growls.

Iain moves his right hand from Harry's hip to his shoulder, and snarls, low and dangerous.

Harry has a moment to realise how much trouble he's got himself into before Iain all but pulls out of him and then rams back in. 'Is this what you want?' Iain says, grinding his hips, pushing in even deeper, then withdrawing.

'Yes,' Harry says again. It comes out as a whine.

There's a pleased sound from Iain and then he thrusts forwards again. Harry angles himself so Iain is hitting the spot with every thrust. Iain's also muttering the most filthy things about Harry's face, his tits, his arse, and it's brutal and perfect and all Harry can do is hang on and let Iain punch waves of crashing pleasure through him. His cock is bobbing underneath him, rock hard and flushed purple, dripping all over the sheets.

And then Iain's hand slips off his shoulder and grabs Harry's hair instead, yanking hard, and that sends Harry over the edge, his entire body bowing back and clenching as he comes untouched, his cock spilling hot all over the bedspread.

As he gasps and shudders through his release, Iain is still hammering into him, his rhythm messy, and the torrent of filthy talk coming out of his mouth slurring into nonsense, and then Iain is coming inside him, filling him up even further and his cock twitches again at that, dribbling out more come.

They both rest against each other as they come down, breathing hard, Iain draped over his back but not making him take his weight, gently nosing kisses into the damp sweat of his hairline. Finally by a sort of mutual agreement Iain throws an arm over Harry and they both fall down onto their sides, curled up in each other, Iain still inside Harry. When he slips out, Harry can feel the pout Iain makes against his back.

Then Iain pulls at Harry's shoulder, turning him around so they face each other. Their noses are almost touching. 'Are you well?' he asks. He strokes Harry's cheek, at the stubble there. 'We, uh, that was a lot.'

Harry nods, then leans forwards to kiss Iain, gently, softly. He glides a hand down the solid muscles of Iain's chest and side, until he can rest it on his hip. 'I don't like other men,' Harry says. 'Only you.'

Iain hums, absently combing his fingers through Harry's hair, petting him. 'Lucky you,' he says.

Harry snuggles further into Iain's arms, the two of them curled together against the early-winter cold that descends mercilessly with the setting of the sun. He's finally back in his own bed, safe and sound, and blissful from release. Sleep is not long in coming.

Harry wakes at dawn to find himself still tangled up in Iain. His head is pillowed on Iain's chest. His leg is thrown over Iain's thighs . . . and his erection is pressing into Iain's hip.

He shifts in embarrassment, and one silver eye opens to look at him. Iain smiles and presses a kiss into his hair with a mumbled 'Good morning'. Then he stretches, catlike, and Harry's breath catches at just how *much* of Iain there is now, at the way his muscles stretch under his tanned skin. At the fact that Iain's hard too, his thick cock arching out of the tangle of dark hair towards his belly.

Iain noses at him. 'I have to go and start chores soon, but fancy a tumble first?'

Harry was going to say no.

He was going to explain how he was still reconciling how he

felt about Iain, how *right* everything was with him, with how *wrong* the Church says it is. They are committing a mortal sin.

He was. Going. To say. No.

But then Iain is sliding down his body, scraping his stubble along Harry's chest, kissing his way down his stomach, kissing his cock good morning, wet and sloppy.

And then *no* was somehow a distant concept, a thing to be dealt with later. After breakfast, perhaps. Or maybe tomorrow.

Iain takes Harry's balls in his mouth, rolling them about in the wet heat, then gently releases them. Naughty pale eyes look up to Harry. 'Just going to check I didn't hurt you,' he says, then sinks deeper still between Harry's legs.

Strong hands slip under his rear, raising him up, and then Iain is kissing his hole, running his tongue around Harry's puffy, abused rim. There's a low growl from the man between his legs, and then Harry feels Iain's tongue in him, lips sucking on his rim.

Harry begins to pant, his head tossing back and forth on the pillow. 'Iain—' he moans.

Iain presses one more kiss to his hole and levers himself back up over Harry. 'You're still all loose and sloppy from last night,' he murmurs, his lips and chin glistening. 'I can taste myself in you.' Iain shifts his hips so his cock lies heavy on Harry's, and both of them start lazily grinding against each other. 'I bet I could slip right back in there, no preparation, just a little oil.' He presses a kiss to Harry's lips. 'Would you like that? Or do you want to fuck me?' he breathes into Harry's mouth.

Harry doesn't answer with words. He just spreads his legs.

The side of Iain's mouth twists into a smile. That's all the warning Harry has before he feels Iain's muscles bunch, then Iain rolls them so he's on his back with Harry lying on him. He reaches for the oil that's sitting on one of the bed-boards, in the gap between it and the wall, and slicks himself up. 'Here,' he says, positioning Harry over him, 'you have more control this way.'

Harry nods and reaches behind him, lining up on Iain's cock and lowering himself down slowly, so slowly, as his still half-asleep body sparks alive in erotic bliss. He has to admit, it's a wonderful way to wake up. He starts rolling his hips, lazily, watching Iain's face as his lover bites his lip and arches his broad chest, eyes closing in happiness.

Iain reaches between them and grabs Harry's cock, fisting him in time with the increasingly energetic rolls of Harry's hips. 'That's it, *a sheòid*,' he murmurs. 'Ride me.' He twists his hand, his thumb rubbing over the slit of Harry's cock and Harry gasps, pulling up off Iain and then sitting down on him hard. Iain thrusts up to meet him, squeezing his eyes shut and cursing in a mix of Gaelic and French.

'Good morning,' Harry grins, and then sits hard on Iain again. Iain curses more in Gaelic, and Harry can feel Iain's knees draw up behind him, as he braces his feet against the bed to push back against Harry. And Harry begins to ride Iain properly, establishing a rhythm and then speeding it up as he bites his own lip, runs his hands over his own nipples, and Iain is watching him, mouth open, lips wet with desire, moaning 'Yes, play with yourself,' when there's the unmistakeable sound of feet on the stairs.

Iain twists, sending them both onto their side, Harry closer to the door, and then he pulls out, lying on his belly and trying to look inconspicuous. Harry yanks the blankets over both of them.

His face is still flushed and he's breathless as Annie and Katie tumble cheerily in with breakfast.

Annie spots the two of them in Harry's bed and smiles. '*Ah, 'twas a cold one last night, wasn't it?*'

There is nothing abnormal in sharing beds. In fact, it's abnormal to sleep alone, testimony to how dangerously diminished Harry's family is. Harry shared the bed with his mother until he left to go to Sir Simon's, and then whenever he returned to Dartington. The servants sleep in pallets in the hall and kitchen, four or five or six people cuddled together on the same stuffed straw mattress. Hell, he and Kit and Peter had curled up on the same pallet together in their pavilion up at Windsor.

But there is something greatly abnormal about what he and Iain had been doing in the bed, and Harry feels like the mark of his crime is written clearly across his face.

Thankfully, Annie's concerns rotate more around the sin of gluttony than lust. She clucks in surprise at the full basket of food abandoned by the bed. '*But you two didn't touch your supper! Are you feeling unwell?*'

'*Harry was tired from the travelling,*' Iain says, leaning his chin on his elbows. '*He fell asleep as soon as his head hit the pillow. I was going to sneak out and eat, but then his snoring put me to sleep, too.*'

'*I do* not *snore!*' Harry says, indignant.

Iain makes a face, and Harry elbows him. Then Iain's on him, trying to pin his arms while tickling him, teasing him about how loudly he snores. Harry looks out at Annie and Katie as he tries to shove Iain away, and says, '*Don't worry about breakfast, we'll make do with what's left over from last night.*'

'*We bloody won't,*' says Iain, trying and failing to get Harry into a headlock. '*I can smell honey cakes and scones from here and if you let Annie take them away again I will show no pity.*' He switches tactics and pinches Harry's sides, where he's really ticklish, and Harry squawks.

'*Leave the honey cakes!*' Harry yells, breathless with laughter, grabbing Iain's wrists and wrestling them away from his sides. '*Ow! No kicking!*'

Annie rolls her eyes. '*Boys*,' she chides merrily, dropping off a tray of breakfast cakes on a nearby chest while Katie changes the water in the washing pitcher and grabs the chamber pot.

The two women leave, Katie looking back over her shoulder as the door swings shut to see Harry sitting on Iain, twisting one of his arms behind his back, as Iain tries to dislodge him. Both boys are red-faced with laughter. As Katie descends the stairs, she hears a nearly simultaneous yell and thud, suggesting Iain has managed to throw Harry.

Harry flings himself on Iain again, but their play-wrestling, now that they're alone, feels dangerous, the veneer of boyish japes stripped away. Now when Harry grabs at Iain's arms to pin him, he grinds down on him too. Iain grinds back, pressing his mouth to Harry's and kissing him, long and dirty. When they pause to catch their breath, Iain fingers the shiny pink-and-white scars on Harry's forearm, the scars he made. Then he kisses the mark, gently, apologetically.

'No,' Harry says, pulling his arm away. 'I love this scar. The first . . . the first thing I knew about you was *this*, that you were so fierce, that nothing could break you. I thought, what I would give to be that strong.'

Iain traces a finger over Harry's lips. 'The first thing I knew about you is that you were kind, and you did not want to be there. I wanted so desperately to use that softness against you. To win my freedom.'

'And yet you are still my prisoner,' Harry says.

'Am I? Would you not let me go, if I asked?' Iain says.

'No,' Harry breathes. 'I cannot.' He kisses Iain, and to his surprise Iain doesn't pull away. His lips open for Harry, his tongue caresses Harry's own. 'Would you stay with me here, if I let you go?' Harry asks, pulling away.

Iain looks at him, and those pale eyes widen as a long moment passes.

'I belong elsewhere,' Iain says at last, softly. 'This is not my country, and I have only enemies here.' He presses his lips into Harry's neck, beneath his ear, and mumbles, 'and my Sassenach idiot.' His arms circle Harry, and hold him close. 'I know that nobody *here* is my enemy. But I'm the blackest sort of bad luck, Harry. And I don't want to bring that to your door.'

'Please stay,' Harry says. 'Play at the charade of being my squire. Let me do my best to protect you. If you truly want to go, give me time to find a way.'

Iain's eyes narrow. They're tangled around each other again, faces close, staring into each other's eyes. 'They have something on you, don't they.' It's not a question.

Harry exhales. 'They have Dartington. If you vanish, I lose all of this.'

Iain goes limp against him. 'And if I stay, you have no idea of the trouble I could bring here.'

Harry thinks of his strange conversation at Windsor with the Earl of Arundel. He leans his cheek against Iain's.

'I do,' Harry sighs. 'It's already started.'

SEVEN

December 1333: Intimidation

The day starts out peacefully enough, once they drag themselves out of bed to face it. Peter is nowhere to be found, so Iain sets in on the stable chores while Harry catches up with the business of the manor.

It all goes to hell, though, shortly after dinner.

Peter comes tearing into the courtyard on his pony, hysterical, eyes streaked with tears. '*They're, they're gonna burn Wat, on Dunwich Common*,' he gasps.

'*What?*' Harry says. Wat is their pig-boy. Not the brightest spark, but possibly the most cheerful boy in the county, and closer to Peter than any brother.

Peter collapses off the pony, and Harry catches him when his legs don't. '*Talk to me, Peter. What's going on? Who's trying to burn Wat?*'

Peter blushes and wipes his nose with his shirtsleeve, strings of snot going everywhere.

Harry shakes him. '*Talk to me*,' he hisses. Over Peter's shoulder he can see Iain watching them from the doorway of the stables. He's close enough to hear, and he's standing like he knows there's going to be a fight.

Peter's lip quivers, and then a torrent of words come spilling out, interspersed with great, wet sobs.

'*His ma got that priest* – snkkkkt – *you know that awful one from Ordlington— to exorcise him but he said it's no use, Wat has to burn, as an example,*' Peter chokes out.

'*Exorcise him?*' Annie says, striding out of the kitchen. '*For what? Being possessed by a particularly soap-shy demon? Because the only sin that boy's ever committed is slovenliness.*'

Peter's shaking his head, tears and snot scattering everywhere, and mumbles his answer so quietly as to be unintelligible.

'*What is it, Peter? Speak up,*' Harry says.

'*W-witchcraft,*' Peter mumbles a little louder. '*And sodomy.*'

'*Oh.*' Harry's eyes widen as he realises what Peter isn't saying. '*You and he—*'

Peter nods. '*His ma wants him to* – sob – *marry and kept introducin' him to girls while I was away, and then I came back and she caught us together and she and Wat had this big fight and* – snukk – *he said she couldn't make him, and he wanted to stay with me, and then his ma called the priest, and Wat doesn't have anyone to speak for him and he's just the pig-boy and nobody* cares—'

'*He has us,*' Iain declares, as he marches back into the stable and begins saddling the war-horses, Nomad and Numbles.

'*Wait here,*' Harry says to Peter, pulling him in for a hug. '*We're going to fix this.*'

Kit and Piers come running out of the hall. Kit has his bow and Piers has a spear. '*We're coming too,*' Kit says.

'*Gonna need more horses,*' Peter sniffles, and shambles into the stables to help Iain.

Harry runs up to the solar and pulls his mail hauberk out of his travelling bags, yanking it over his head. He grabs his sword belt off the chest and his shield off the wall. There's no time for the chausses, and probably no need. The point is a show of armed force.

After a second's hesitation, he grabs his old broadsword and belt for Iain, and his spare coat of mail.

He runs out of the hall towards the stables. Five horses are lined up, four with riders: Kit, Piers, Peter and Iain. Iain is astride Numbles, and holds Nomad's reins. Harry takes them and then tucks his left foot into Nomad's stirrup, swinging up easily.

He passes the spare hauberk and weapons to Iain, who quickly wriggles into the mail and straps on the sword. Iain nods at Harry.

'*We're ready, Peter. Take us to Wat,*' Harry says.

Peter spurs his pony and they ride off, out of Dartington, down the lanes and across the stream that marks the end of Harry's estates, towards where the land gets low and miserable, and the hovels of those who couldn't find work on decent land, or have been cast off it, are clustered. It's a half-hour canter and a world away from Dartington proper.

In the middle of the scrubby common, there's a pillar, and a slim figure writhing against the ropes that bind him to it. A few dozen villagers heap dry brush against its base. The crowd's shouts and jeers echo across the heath to Harry and his men.

It's late afternoon in December, when the colour leaches out of everything, even the sky. There is no green here, only browns and greys. Even the first lick of flame in the brush is colourless: a brightness, nothing more.

Harry spurs Nomad into a gallop, and soon reins up at the edge of the crowd. A figure in black strides towards him. It's the priest from Ordlington, Father Francis, a narrow man with shaven blond hair, a hooked nose and the small, bright eyes of the fanatic.

Harry unsheaths his sword, but lets his arm hang by his side. '*This man belongs to Dartington. Release him.*'

The crowd boos, and a rotten cabbage flies near Harry's head. He hears the low, steely hiss of Iain's sword leaving its scabbard; out of the corner of his eye he can see the flames begin to catch in the heap of brush. The boy, Wat, is skinny and small like Peter, but with huge eyes, and ears that stick out like jug handles through indifferent, sandy-coloured curls. He looks like he's been crying for a long time, and his eyes now are fixed not upon Harry, but past him, to Peter. The dry hawthorn and ash branches lay around him in a pyramid, almost to his shoulders. The fire is spreading fast.

Father Francis cocks his head. '*On whose authority are you here? Dartington ends at yon stream, as you well know, Sir Harry.*'

'*This man is ours and his crimes will be tried by us,*' Harry says, his voice firm with command. '*On whose authority are you here?*'

'*On* God's,' yells Father Francis. He points accusingly at Wat, who is sweating, wincing at the heat around him. A hawthorn branch crackles and pops in the sudden silence. Wat flinches hard. '*This boy is a sodomite, who refuses to marry his betrothed, and instead lies with men!*'

The crowd jeers and hisses at this, and pelts Wat with stones and clods of earth. One sharp rock hits his cheek, opening up a gash almost to the bone.

'*All the same, he is our vassal and he will be tried by us*,' Harry says.

Father Francis stalks towards him, arms wide in theatrical disbelief, his robes flapping like the wings of a carrion crow. '*And you would stand in the way of the Bible? Because you are a better judge than the Word of God?*'

There's more jeering now, this time directed at Harry. The priest is a weasel, but he knows his audience – and the seething crowd loves nothing more than seeing nobility laid low.

'*Answer me!*' Father Francis shouts. '*Are you above God?*'

'Fuck this,' Iain mutters.

And that's all the warning Harry has before pandemonium breaks loose.

Numbles, for all that Dartington knows he is a lazy, mischievous beast, is still a giant of a horse, huge and intimidating with his scarred-over right eye. And Iain in a coat of slightly too small mail, with the same murderous feral look on his face he'd had in the cage in Scotland, is damn near terrifying. When the crowd doesn't part for him, he just rides through them, swatting a few across the head with the flat of his sword for good measure. Someone tries to grab Numbles' reins and the horse bites them, hard. The resulting howl of pain causes the crowd, finally, to skitter back.

'*Stop him!*' screams Father Francis as Iain approaches the fire, Numbles tossing his head in unhappiness at the flames' proximity.

Harry sheathes his sword and folds his arms. '*Why don't* you *stop him? Seeing as my authority ends at the stream*,' he counters. '*Or maybe you could ask God to do it.*'

Kit and Peter follow Iain, Kit's bow trained on anyone who

tries to get close. The crowd backs off, their anger blanched by their fear. Harry feels more than he sees Piers ride up next to him, fingering his spear.

Iain swings his broadsword and Harry can hear the blade hacking into the post, cutting the ropes binding Wat.

Too weak to stand, the boy falls face-first into the fire.

Peter shouts and slips off his pony, running to his friend. He drags Wat out and Wat is on fire, hair alight, pigshit-covered clothes burning.

'*Roll him!*' yells Kit, but Peter is frozen in terror, staring at the flames dancing around his friend's head.

Harry dismounts, shouldering Peter aside and all but throwing himself on Wat. He pats out the flames, pressing wet dirt to his head, and then turns him over to make sure no part of him remains alight. Wat's skin in patches is black and red, burned like overcooked meat. But his fingers close weakly over Peter's, and a hint of his former irrepressible smile pulls at the corner of his cracked lips.

'We need to get him out of here,' Iain says, in French, so only Harry can understand. 'Both of them need to leave and never come back.' He's still on his horse, keeping guard in front of them, glaring at the remaining crowd and Father Francis as if daring them to step forwards.

The crowd doesn't.

They're angry, and they're beyond poor, but they're not stupid.

Father Francis has his foot in the stirrup of a fat chestnut pony. He glares at them as he mounts up. '*I know the Sheriff. Soon it will be you tied to that post,* Sir Harry,' Father Francis sneers, his voice dripping with contempt. '*You will feel the fire of God's judgement. You* and *your Scottish savage.*'

The Scottish savage spurs his huge horse forwards a few steps, curls his lips into a snarl, and barks at the priest.

Father Francis's eyes go wide, and he kicks his chubby horse until she's skittering down the path. He turns back every so often to glare at them.

Harry is riven with terror. He is aware, logically, that Father Francis can't possibly know about what he and Iain have done, what they were doing *that very morning*, but part of him is sure that the priest has stared into his soul and seen the black stain of mortal sin spreading across it.

Peter's snuffle and a low moan of pain from Wat shake him from his thoughts. There are, thankfully, more important things to focus on right now.

Harry picks Wat up in his arms like a child and sets him on Nomad's saddle, gently wrapping his sticky, burned fingers around the pommel. '*Wat, you need to hang on, just for a moment.*' The boy clings on obediently, weaving slightly, drunk on pain. Harry swings up behind him and holds him with one arm around his waist. '*I know you'd prefer Peter,*' he says, '*but I'm stronger and if you start to fall, Peter won't be able to keep you on the horse.*'

Wat nods his understanding.

'*Come on, then,*' Harry says. '*We have some riding to do.*'

He lays out his plan to them once they're back within the borders of Dartington. There's every chance Father Francis will send for the High Sheriff immediately. And the High Sheriff is Rabbie Ufford. So, running home to the manor, even to treat Wat's extensive burns, would be a tactical mistake. Instead they'll ride for Plymouth port, where many of the big trading ships come in from the Bay of Biscay, Spain and North Africa.

Harry still has some of the King's coin in his pockets, and he can buy the boys passage to anywhere.

Peter stutters his thanks, saying they're not worth it, just leave them off, they'll make their own way, but Iain swats him and tells him to shut up and enjoy seeing the world. And Harry tells the story of his talk with the perfume-seller (leaving out the part about the oil, of course), of how many languages she spoke, of her tales of scented desert trees and fields upon fields of roses, of all the wonders of the world beyond their tiny emerald corner.

The ride will take them deep into December's early night. Thankfully, the sky is clear and lit to near daylight by a full moon, so the way is easy to navigate. While riding by starlight isn't exactly safe, not many highwaymen would be foolish enough to risk taking on an armoured party of a knight, his squire and three retainers for no visible reward.

When they reach Plymouth docks at midnight, there is still a surprising amount of activity on the waterfront. Harry stops a man, a sailor by the looks of him, in baggy breeches and no shirt with tattoos covering his dark skin, and asks what's going on. The man gawps at him like he's an idiot, but then schools his expression to something more polite. '*'Tis the tide, o'course. Been low all day. Can't get out of the river mouth with a big ship unless it's nigh-on high. Our clock is the sea, m'lord.*'

'*Do you know any ships short of crew?*' Iain says, staring down at the blue sea serpent tattooed across the man's chest and his slanted, Asiatic eyes, both a startling contrast to his sea-bleached mop of reddish-orange hair.

The sailor's eyes skate over them, and Iain indicates Peter

and Wat. He narrows his brown eyes at Peter. '*You got any experience on a boat, pup?*'

'*N-no, sir,*' Peter stutters.

'*How old are ye?*'

Peter fidgets, nervously. '*Sixteen, sir. Wat's seventeen.*'

Harry can't help but glance between Wat, still so clearly a boy in build and manner, and Iain, who stopped being a child long ago. Something in him mourns for both of them, both seventeen, both forced to grow up too fast without homes or parents.

The sailor runs a hand through his thatch of copper hair. '*Can ye climb?*'

Peter nods. '*I can get all the way to the top of an eighty-foot oak,*' he says.

The man grunts and turns away. '*I'm called Davey. Follow me.*'

They leave Kit with the horses and follow the sailor as he weaves his way down the docks, past men shouldering burdens of English wool and Devon slate to load on the outgoing ships. Davey leads them out onto one dock, where a small group of men are loading up a long rowing boat. '*'At's the* Halygast,' Davey says, pointing out towards the sea, to a large ship anchored in deeper water at the river mouth. Then Davey points at a light-skinned African man with an easy smile and an air of natural authority. '*'At's her boss. Captain Wekesa.*'

The man turns at his name, nodding a greeting at Davey. Davey indicates Peter and Wat. '*Ye still need a topgallant man, cap'n?*'

'*I see* two *men, Davey. Although one of them might be a side of salt beef from the looks of him. You been drinking again?*'

the captain teases. One of his top front teeth is golden; it glints in the moonlight.

'*They must stay together*,' Harry says. '*Peter can climb anything, and Wat, once he heals up, well, he used to be our pig-boy and the more disgusting the task you find him, the happier he is.*' Harry pauses, worrying he's overstepped. '*If indeed you have room for them. We, we can pay for their initial passage until they learn the ropes*,' he adds.

Captain Wekesa's eyebrows rise. '*And what have they done, to be scouring Plymouth docks for passage at midnight?*'

Iain looks pointedly at Wat and Peter, at the way they're draped around each other, and then at Captain Wekesa, and snorts.

And the captain grins at him. '*Fair point*,' he laughs. '*Nothing more than that?*'

'*That's enough, around here*,' Harry sighs.

Captain Wekesa and the other sailors gather close around Peter and Wat, inspecting them as if they're horses at market. Then Wekesa and the copper-haired sailor exchange a look.

'*A man goes to sea for many a reason*,' Davey says to Peter. '*A profound love of boats usually isn't among them. Your past is your own, if your future is ours.*' Then he indicates the rowing boat.

Peter looks like he's going to cry from gratitude. He hugs everyone and then he actually does start crying, and then hugs Wat, and cries some more. '*You'll tell my nan what happened? That we're safe?*' Peter asks Harry.

Harry nods. '*Of course.*' Then he turns to Captain Wekesa. '*What do we owe you?*' he asks, reaching for his purse. '*For their training.*'

Captain Wekesa waves his hand, and responds in French. It's not Norman French, but the softer, sibilant lilt of Parisian French, similar to the unique accents and phrasing of Iain's speech. 'A trade, if you will,' he says.

Harry raises an eyebrow.

Captain Wekesa sighs. 'Not all men adjust to life on a sailing ship. I have a cousin, Jed, crewing with me at the moment. The sea and his stomach refuse to come to an understanding. He was a herdsman, in his past life.'

'What did he do?' Harry asks.

'Murdered a man,' Captain Wekesa replies, evenly.

'Did he deserve it? The man?' Iain says.

'Yes,' the captain says, firmly and without hesitation. 'But the man had powerful friends, and our home, Zanzibar, is a small island.' Then he turns. 'Jed,' he calls out.

A large black man, his skin several shades darker than Wekesa's, climbs up the ladder from the rowing boat. 'Yes, Captain,' he says.

'Does he speak English?' Harry asks.

'No,' Jed replies directly. 'French and Arabic and our own language. There's not much use for English at sea. And the cows don't care what language a man speaks.'

Iain suppresses a laugh. Harry glares at him, then steps forwards, extending his hand to Jed. 'Harry Lyon, lord of Dartington Manor. We have sheep, pigs, cows, goats and various fowl. The crops are mostly wheat and beans, though we've an apple orchard too.'

The man's hand is strong and firm in Harry's as he shakes it. 'Jelani Wekesa. They call me Jed on the boat. Sheep are new to me, but I grew up looking after the rest.'

'You'll have to learn English. The only other French speaker on the estate is this one,' Harry says, indicating Iain.

'I apologise in advance. English is a cursed and confusing tongue,' Iain says to Jed. 'Its only use is swearing.'

'Well, to a speaker of High Court French, of course everything else sounds terrible,' grins Captain Wekesa. 'Don't they strip away your title if you admit otherwise, milord . . . ?'

Iain salutes. 'Iain mac Maíl Coluim. His *squire*.'

Captain Wekesa catches the wry twist to Iain's words and makes a face that rests somewhere between amusement and shock. 'Whoa, there's some history there, and would you look at the tide. We must be off. Jed? Would you stay?'

Jed's brown eyes sweep over their small group, lingering on Harry and Iain. He nods, slowly. 'If they'll have me.'

'Grab your things,' Harry says.

Wat's rescue is the gossip of the surrounding area for the next few days. As Harry gets Jed settled in with the livestock, he begins to hope the event will pass without recriminations.

It does not.

Three days after the *Halygast* slips out to sea, a harbinger arrives at Dartington at mid-morning, announcing the impending arrival of the Bishop of Exeter, the High Sheriff of Devon and Father Francis Osgood for an overnight visit.

The terrors return. Harry is convinced, in his heart, that they have come to arrest him, and punish him for the very crime that Wat had committed. Someone in the hall has seen them, and told Rabbie for a pocketful of silver.

Iain takes one look at the way Harry is avoiding him, and quietly moves his pallet into the stables' hayloft.

'I'm sorry,' Harry mumbles later at dinner.

Iain inclines his head and goes to sit with Kit and Jed, who have become fast friends despite having only a few shards of English in common.

The guests arrive as Annie is placing big pots of mutton frumenty on the table, thick with carrots and parsnips. The Bishop is a rough-hewn bantam of a man in his late twenties, richly dressed, and he looks down his sharp nose on their humble hall as if it's soiled his shoes. The bishopric is often a political appointment, though it must be approved by the Pope in Avignon, and Harry guesses by the man's youth that he probably hasn't risen up through the Church by holy merit.

The political bishops go one of two ways. Some are content with their status as a figurehead, enjoying their temporal rewards while they leave the Church's extensive administration to attend to sacred matters in peace. Others are plagued by a certain inadequacy, and resolve to show the lumbering, gilded leviathan of the Church that they *deserve* their position, and its respect. The Church, which in its thousand years has seen men like this come and go, slumbers on, no more bothered than an elephant by a flea. Yet the common people of the parish, with their three score years or less, they suffer.

Harry knows immediately what sort of man this bishop will be.

Rabbie strides in behind the Bishop, and Harry notices a certain resemblance in the sharp angles of their faces. He remembers then that the Bishop is a cousin of Rabbie's. Father Francis stalks in too, grinning in triumph.

Harry slips into his role as lord of the manor easily, smiling a welcome he doesn't feel and bringing the noble visitors up to his table at the top of the hall.

He doesn't miss how Rabbie's eyes widen when they alight on Iain, rising up from his place at that top table, or how Iain glares at the man in tightly controlled fury as he stalks past them to see to their horses.

'You sure it's such a good idea to keep your monsters that well fed?' Rabbie murmurs to Harry, under his breath.

'I do indeed,' Harry smiles mildly, waiting as the Bishop arranges his gold-embroidered robes in preparation for sitting. 'Makes them all the more effective when I let them off their chains.'

'What?' the Bishop says, his brow furrowing at the exchange.

'My squire is Scottish,' Harry says, taking his own seat and gesturing between Rabbie and himself. 'Both Sir Robert and I have lost fathers and friends to the Scottish campaigns. They are . . . savage fighters.'

'And yet you let this wolf in your house?' the Bishop says, his voice climbing in surprise.

'Fate makes fools of us all,' says Harry. He switches to English at Father Francis's angry stare. '*And to what does our modest hall owe the honour of your visit, Your Excellency?*'

'*Your standing in the way of God's judgement*,' hisses Father Francis.

'*Ah, there was a misunderstanding*,' Harry says mildly, offering the men small beer from the pitcher on the table. '*A vassal of ours was off-estate, visiting his mother, when he was seized and accused of crimes. We prefer to mete out our own judgement on our people. We collected the vassal, and have taken care of him, swiftly and irrevocably.*'

'*You've hidden the man here*,' says Father Francis.

'*Are you accusing me of being a liar?*' Harry asks. '*You are welcome to search every corner of Dartington. The man and the stable-boy he corrupted have both been rendered unto the Holy Ghost. We are an orderly estate, and believe in squaring our accounts with both God and man.*'

Katie leans over the table, then, putting down fresh, steaming loaves of bread and pots of butter made that morning. Harry's stomach recoils at how the Bishop's eyes follow her small breasts.

Katie is fourteen.

'*Sodomy is a mortal sin*,' the Bishop intones. '*One which I intend to stamp out in my counties as quickly and effectively as possible.*'

I'm sure the Church administration won't hinder that at all, Harry thinks, uncharitably.

The Bishop continues, tearing off a hunk of bread and sopping his stew with it. '*My cousin the Sheriff will take on all cases of accused sodomy from now on, and the guilty will be hung, drawn and quartered in Exeter Market.*'

'*We're all eager for our first example*,' Rabbie leers. '*Nothing like a good hanging; the people go mad for it.*'

There is nothing Harry can say. '*A most noble initiative, Your Excellency, and we are thankful for your efforts to bring Devon closer to God.*'

The Bishop beams.

'*Flattery and falsehoods*,' hisses Father Francis. '*Where are the bodies of the men you judged?*'

'*We fed 'em to the pigs*,' Kit calls out. '*You're welcome to look through the manure in the sty for their teeth, if you'd like further proof.*'

Even Rabbie wrinkles his nose at that.

Harry closes his eyes. '*And how would you like to spend your afternoon? Your harbinger said you'd be staying overnight. Would you like a tour of the estate?*'

'*Heavens, no,*' the Bishop groans. '*One field looks much like any other. I wish to be* amused. *Have you dancers? Musicians? A fool?*'

Harry looks around his hall. There's often singing, but it's tavern songs, not the sort of thing a nobly born bishop would consider worthwhile. '*Kit can play the lute, and a few of the men know work songs . . .*'

'*Ronald,*' Rabbie whispers to his cousin. '*Fuck this. Let's go back to Ordlington.*'

Before the Bishop can answer, Father Francis cuts across him. '*No,*' the priest hisses, loud enough that Harry can hear it. He's not sure whether the priest is careless or deliberate. '*They're hiding something. I want to stay.*'

'*Please do,*' Harry smiles, his tactical brain working overtime. '*It's not often we get such distinguished guests. I'll see what I can manage.*' If he handles the situation correctly, and remains calm, then with luck the Bishop will begin to tire of Father Francis's accusations and a rift between the two men can be opened. The trick will be feeding Father Francis's suspicions, while making him look increasingly foolish in front of the Bishop.

Alcohol always helps.

He gets up from his seat and strolls into the kitchen, outlining his plan to Annie, and warning her to keep Katie away from the Bishop. Annie nods, and heads to the root cellar to grab jugs of scrumpy and the cherry brandy. Then he cuts out the back of the kitchen and around to the stables, where Iain is lurking.

Harry outlines the plan to him. Iain grumbles, but promises to behave and do his part. Yet the problem remains: how to discredit the priest beyond simple (and forgivable) drunkenness.

As little Piers sticks his head out the door, signalling to Harry that his guests are restless, Iain looks at Harry, and a slow grin spreads across their faces.

Harry motions Piers over.

A few moments later, Harry walks back in the hall with Iain and Piers behind him. He slaps his hand on the nearest table for everyone's attention. '*Some songs, for His Excellency!*'

Kit immediately begins to howl a tavern favourite called 'Four and Twenty Virgins', and both Jed and Piers smack him.

'*Some* civilised *songs*,' Harry clarifies with a sigh, and raises a brow at Iain.

Iain shuffles nervously, and takes a deep breath. His rich baritone fills the hall, hesitantly at first, and then more confidently. He sings a French ballad of Fair Roland, of simple melody but complex rhyme and wordplay. After a verse or two, Kit's lute can be heard, joining in, harmonising.

Harry returns to his seat, noticing with happiness that his guests are deep into the cider. Rabbie looks confused, unable to reconcile the beautiful French coming out of Iain's mouth with what he knows of the Scottish boy. The Bishop's mouth hangs open, but his gold-ringed fingers are tapping along with the rhythm.

When Iain finishes, to much stamping and applause from the hall, the Bishop says, '*I thought you said he was Scottish?*'

Harry grins and calls over to Iain, '*Sing something in Scottish!*'

Iain grins back, and begins beating a rhythm on the table. The song is faster now, the kind of song to stir men's blood, and Iain sings it with an almost feral look on his face. Soon the whole hall is clapping along, and attempting to shout the refrain, though not one of them other than Iain can speak the language.

'*What's the song about?*' the Bishop whispers across the table.

'*Beats me,*' Harry shrugs. '*Knowing him, it's probably about murdering your enemies and burning their castles to the ground. More cider, Your Excellency?*'

'Mm,' says the Bishop, going a little pale.

'*Don't worry,*' Harry smiles. '*We keep him locked up in the stables at night, with the dogs and the war-horses.*'

When Iain is done, Annie and Katie shove him aside and sing a simple roundelay about the flowers of springtime, their voices mingling prettily with each other's and with Mariah, the gardener's wife.

Harry refills everyone's glasses again, and winks at Piers, who disappears out the back. The sun is setting; by Vespers bells the night is already creeping across the sky.

Iain steps up and grabs Katie, spinning her, as her song finishes. She squeals, and he takes her hands, very formal, and bows to her. She curtseys in return, giggling.

Father Francis gets up, unsteady. Harry points towards the hall's back door. '*Out there, about ten feet in front of you and then to the right,*' he says, giving the directions to the privy.

The priest sneers at him, then toddles towards the door, walking like a man at sea.

Iain begins singing again, a French dancing song. He walks Katie through the steps at half-time. Harry recognises some of them; they're very similar to those of his dance with Alys at Windsor. As Katie becomes more sure-footed, Iain takes her through the steps faster, until they're dancing in time with the song, Katie laughing all the while. He then passes her off to Kit, and grabs Annie, who shouts and squirms to get out of his hold, loudly complaining that she is *not* the dancing kind.

The Bishop's eyes are keen as he leans forwards, watching the motley dancers. There's a flicker of sadness in his face, of something very dear laid aside out of necessity.

'A bishop does not dance?' Harry guesses.

'I used to love the carolle,' the Bishop sighs. Then, after a moment, 'Your man dances it well.'

'I wouldn't know,' Harry says. 'The only dancing I do involves a broadsword.'

There's the most almighty shout and bang from outside the hall, and all noise inside ceases.

The next sound they hear is Father Francis's triumphant cry: '*I have him! I have the criminal! I knew they were lying!*'

Both Rabbie's and the Bishop's heads whip round to look at Harry. Harry raises his hands, helpless. '*I have no idea what he's talking about—*'

Just then, Father Francis comes in, robes open, hose around his ankles, his holy acorn bobbing for everyone to see (Annie places her hand over Katie's eyes). He's clutching a struggling, furious Piers in his arms. Piers is wearing a raggedy, rust-coloured shirt such as Wat would wear, and has helpfully rolled around in the dirt to approximate Wat's usual state of cleanliness.

'*Can't a man take a shit in peace?*' yells Piers.

Kit is biting his fist to keep from laughing.

'*If you're going to drag me off the jakes you could at least wipe me arse for me first!*' Piers howls at Father Francis.

Kit loses the fight. He tips his head back and roars with amusement, banging his hand on the table.

Harry exhales. '*Father Francis, would you mind letting go of my messenger boy, Piers?*'

Piers's father, a tall farmer named Jasper, stands up. '*Boy, what have you done with that priest?*' he growls.

'*Nothing, Pa! I was just sittin' there having a crap and he sticks his head in an' starts yellin' at me about fuckin' other men and God's judgement!*' Piers yells back, gesturing.

Father Francis squints down at Piers, then realises he's looking at the boy's bare arse, blushes, and dumps him on the ground.

'Ow,' Piers says.

'*You're not the pig-boy,*' mumbles Father Francis.

Jasper turns his hawklike stare on the priest. '*If you laid a hand on my boy, priest or no, I'll skin you alive, sure as they skinned Saint Bartholomew.*'

'*He's drunk!*' yells Kit, helping Piers to his feet and seeing the way Father Francis's eyes can barely focus. '*Bloody grockle can't handle his cider.*'

'*S' no excuse,*' snarls Jasper.

'Uh,' Harry says, turning to Rabbie and the Bishop, and waving his arm in Father Francis's general direction. Rabbie looks furious, while the Bishop has a high, patchy blush colouring his cheeks. Harry can't decide if it's rage, or embarrassment, or both. 'Perhaps that's enough amusement for tonight. It looks like we did find a fool, after all.'

'Sober him up,' the Bishop says, his voice steely.

'Iain? Jed?' Harry calls.

'Horse trough?' Jed says. Iain nods. They pick up the struggling priest and carry him out. A short while later there's a loud splash and a howl of agony.

'Ooh,' Harry says, feigning concern. 'Hope the top of that trough wasn't frozen over.' He indicates the stairs. 'Shall we go up to bed?'

The Bishop sighs, and nods. Rabbie narrows his eyes at Harry.

'I'm sure you'll find someone to hang, Rabbie,' Harry commiserates.

He spends an uncomfortable night sharing his bed with the Bishop and Rabbie, both of whom really do snore, while Father Francis sleeps off Annie's scrumpy downstairs in the hall with the servants.

The holy visitors are up and out of their hair by shortly after dawn.

Harry doesn't see Iain for the next few days. It's barely a week until Christmas, and there's plenty to do around the manor ahead of the holiday feast. It's just a busy time, he tells himself. It's safer this way, he also tells himself, still afraid that they've made it onto some list, that one of the many relatives and friends streaming into the hall for the holidays is reporting back on him to Rabbie. That Father Francis has more fanatics like him, watching from hedgerows and through keyholes, bigots who believe that the climb to heaven is best achieved by stepping on the backs of fellow sinners.

The rational part of him knows it's paranoia. That nobody has ever seen him and Iain together like that. But he feels like the whole world can read in his face what he wants from Iain, if they just look. It's so overwhelming, he can't believe it doesn't shine out of him like some terrible beacon of sin. How his hands ache to run down Iain's sides, to grasp his hips, feel the smooth curve of his backside. How his lips tingle, hungry for a kiss. How other parts of him want even more forbidden things.

The simple lust Harry feels is not the worst of it. The fire that Iain ignites in him is unbearable up close, but it dies down with distance, as an iron's attraction to a magnet waxes then wanes. No. The worst is how much he misses his friend.

He'd forgotten how lonely it is in the solar at night, by himself.

He'd forgotten what it's like to be surrounded by crowds of people during the day, but none of them an equal. None that could read his mind with a look, lighten his mood with a comment, relax his worries with a touch.

Three days before Christmas, Iain is late for dinner.

Everyone but him is tucked up warm in the hall, the heavy doors shut against the cold. Kit offers to go and fetch Iain, but Harry raises a hand, bidding Kit to stay. He'll go. He signals for Annie to begin serving the big midday meal.

Harry slips out into the courtyard, his soft boots crunching over the frosty ground.

He finds Iain, as he expects, in the stables. Iain is stripped down to the waist, pitchfork in hand, tossing hay up into the eaves for storage. A sheen of sweat covers his chest, and his thick muscles ripple as he throws the heavy loads overhead.

Harry chokes on his next breath. It's a sight to tempt a saint.

Iain hears it and turns, cold eyes through those sinfully long lashes sweeping over Harry as he rests the pitchfork against the wall. 'What time is it?' he murmurs. 'Did I work through dinner?'

Harry shivers. He'd thought the fire in his loins had been quenched by fear and distance, that as simple an act as fetching Iain to the hall couldn't possibly reignite it.

He thought wrong.

The embers of his attraction have apparently been smouldering all this time, like peat, deep under the grassy earth of his composure, waiting for the merest breath of oxygen to burst into flame again.

Harry groans, and gets in Iain's space, gets his hands on his bare chest, shoving him back towards the tack room. Once they're inside, Harry kicks the door shut and latches it.

Iain is sprawled back against a saddle, chest arched and shoulders and biceps flexed, and he raises an eyebrow at Harry.

'*Fuck*,' Harry breathes.

The side of Iain's mouth twists into a smile.

Harry isn't even conscious of advancing on Iain. One moment he's looking at the broad expanse of sweat-shined flesh and muscle on display for him, and the next he's got his hands on Iain's waist and his tongue in Iain's mouth.

Iain moans and kisses him back just as hungrily.

'I'm going mad without you,' Harry pants, unlacing his breeches so he has fewer layers between himself and Iain.

Iain just growls into his mouth and palms Harry's dick. 'You're not the only one,' he says, his voice husky with desire.

'Fuck,' Harry murmurs again as he runs his hands down Iain. 'They're waiting for us, in the hall.' He rolls one of Iain's nipples between his fingers, and is rewarded with Iain arching towards him further, biting his lip to stifle a moan.

'Then skip the damn foreplay, Lyon,' Iain hisses.

Harry growls and grabs Iain's hips, turning him around and shoving him over the saddle. Iain gasps his surprise, and it turns into a low moan as Harry tucks the tail of Iain's shirt up into his belt, exposing his backside.

Iain's already hard, and Harry has a perfect view of exactly what he wants, of how Iain's skin darkens slightly as the cleft of his rear leads down to his hole. He grabs Iain's cheeks in his hands and spreads them to get an even better look, and that's not enough either, so he runs his dripping cock up and down the cleft, hissing at the sensation.

Iain whines, needy, and pushes his backside towards Harry. And God, Iain's arse looks amazing, draped over the saddle, the cords of muscle on his thighs standing out as he spreads his legs.

Harry grabs a bottle of leather oil from the shelf next to him and pours some over his cock. Then he's got one hand on Iain's belt and the other hand on his backside, and he's pushing into Iain, his mind empty of anything other than the overwhelming need to fuck him raw, right there in the tack room among the saddles and bridles and combs and blankets, the horses shifting and snorting in their stalls on the other side of the wall.

It's still.

It's heaven. It's.

Like drowning. But. In light.

When Harry bottoms out, he puts a hand on Iain's back, leaning on him, breathing hard.

'Christ's blood,' Iain moans. 'Harry, please,' he says, and rolls his hips.

Harry bites out his own curse as hot sparks of sensation course through him, and he pulls out and snaps his hips back in.

The leather of the saddle creaks as Iain is forced against it, and he arches his back and whimpers. 'More,' he says, his voice a wrecked whisper. It speaks to the thing in Harry, the vicious, primal beast that only comes out around Iain.

Harry lets go completely. They're due at dinner; any minute now someone will come out looking for them and Harry's not going to let this end unfinished, it's too much, too good, so he starts pounding into Iain, hard and fast, and his hand slips off Iain's back and down to the shelf where Iain is bracing himself with one hand, and he covers it with his hand and their fingers interlink, and *that*, that is somehow more intimate than anything they've ever done, and Harry squeezes Iain's hand as his orgasm builds within him, this liquid fire unspooling from his groin throughout his entire body as he keeps slamming into Iain over the saddle, and he reaches his other hand down where Iain's cock is trapped between his stomach and the leather of the saddle, and he can't really stroke it hard so he makes do with rubbing his thumb over the top of it, under the head, on the slit, and he starts biting at Iain's neck and shoulder because it's not *enough*, he needs every part of him to touch every part of Iain, because touching him is like reaching paradise, and he wants to revel in it as much as he can, worship it as often as he can, because like all men he knows that paradise exists only to be taken away.

Iain throws his head back as Harry bites into the muscles at the back of his neck. His eyes are shut and his mouth hangs open in a sort of erotic disbelief, and he whispers, 'Harry—' as his body begins to shake and clench. Harry thrusts into him as far as he can, and holds him, against everything, against all the people coming for them, wraps him in his arms and drags his lips up his neck and thrusts shallowly into him, trying to stave off his own orgasm so he can watch the beauty of Iain falling over the edge, until Iain's body contracts just right around him and Harry falls too, without a sound.

Iain comes back to his senses first, and eases himself around so he can sling his arms about Harry's waist and stand, kissing him gently, stroking his face, as if marvelling in his very existence. He smiles against Harry's cheek. 'Making extra work for me, cleaning tack,' he murmurs playfully.

Harry pinches his hip. Then he frames Iain's face with his hands. 'Come back to the solar,' Harry begs. 'Stay with me.'

'On the pallet, like a good squire?' Iain says, and Harry can hear the sarcasm in his voice.

'Yes,' Harry says, kissing the tender spot under Iain's ear in apology. 'For now. I can't shake the feeling we're being watched. That there are spies in the hall.'

Nobody notices, or nobody comments, when Harry comes in midway through dinner, saying that Iain still isn't done putting away the new hay and wants to finish before he eats.

Iain is back with Harry at supper that evening, and again in the solar afterwards, on his pallet, the two of them quietly talking about everything and nothing late into the night.

There's snow the next morning, stealing across the moor silently in the low hours before dawn and cloaking the rolling fields of Dartington in white. The estate explodes into holiday spirit. Everyone is in a cheerful bustle of decorating and cooking and making last-minute gifts.

Harry checks at least once a day that his present for Iain is still where he hid it. The perfume-seller wasn't the only merchant to get his coin at Windsor.

He hasn't touched Iain since the day in the stables, not as lovers touch, barely as friends do. It's difficult, not to press in closer, to reach towards Iain's warmth. Even at night they remain chaste. Iain hasn't said anything. Harry knows he owes him an explanation and he's going to give one, as soon as he can formulate anything beyond *I'm scared*.

A little part of Harry thought that because what they had between them blazed so hot and sudden, if they just indulged it a little bit, it would gutter out by itself. Yet the flame only increases as the days pass, and Harry fears it will burn him up until nothing is left.

He's profoundly thankful that it's Christmas, when there's more than enough seasonal distractions to ignore the problem until the New Year. And then there's the list of royal tournaments in January, starting in Dunstable on the 16th and then carrying on solidly through March. He needs to *practise*, and he needs to finish training Iain up as his squire.

They start sparring again. It helps.

They drink too much at supper on Christmas Eve when the whole estate staggers tipsy down the lanes to Dartington Church, bellowing carols in English and other languages, to listen to Father Gilbert give Midnight Mass.

They drink too much again at Christmas Dinner and Harry hands out the gifts. For most of the estate, warm tunics and cloaks, courtesy of the King's largesse. For Annie, a new dress, and the bottle of perfume. Annie in return gives Iain a shirt she's made him, a dead copy of his Scottish one, but in the King's pale blue linen with red embroidery, and a cloak in the Scottish style made from the dark purple wool that Kit had so admired.

Iain puts on the shirt and cloak and, before he can react, Annie snatches up his old tattered shirt and throws it in the fire. He cries out his dismay, though falls quiet when Harry hands him a package bound in soft leather.

Iain unwraps it, and his eyes widen.

Harry has given him a long dagger, of finest quality steel. It's plain, a working weapon, not a showpiece, with a simple metal guard and a cord-wrapped handle.

Iain snorts with laughter, shaking his head. '*Well, that's one way to get me to leave the kitchen knives alone.*'

Harry puts his hand on Iain's shoulder and says, '*We trust you, Iain. And I want you to be able to defend yourself if anything happens.*'

Iain's face grows sad. '*I have nothing for you,*' he says, looking down at the fine clothes on his body, the wicked dagger in his hands, then back up at Harry.

'*You don't have to give me anything,*' Harry smiles, unbearably fond of him in that moment.

'*I do,*' Iain says, serious.

Harry has a moment to think about how mulishly stubborn Iain is, when he—

When Iain—

—He gets down on one knee.

He is down on one knee and bowing his head before Harry like the graven image of a crusader knight swearing fealty to the cross, and softly he says, '*I give you myself. I have never knelt for any man, nor did I ever think I would.*' He looks up. '*This is all I have to give. Please accept it.*'

There's silence in the hall. Harry doesn't know what to say. He reaches down and tugs on Iain's hand to make him stand up, and says, '*I don't think I'm worth it. I'm just—*'

Iain rises to his feet with a catlike grace, and says, '*That is my decision, not yours.*'

Harry's mouth opens, then closes, then opens again. '*I, I will try to be worthy of this honour,*' he says finally.

Iain inclines his head in acceptance.

There's more alcohol at Christmas Supper, even though most of the manor hasn't sobered up since dinner.

The meal is cold leftovers and stories round the fire of King Arthur and his knights, spun until jugs are empty and eyes are unfocused. Harry and Iain stagger upstairs and pass out in their fine new clothes.

The estate sleeps in the following day, the embers cold in the kitchen hearth and not a care to be had in the whole manor. The day dawns unseasonably warm, and the *drip drip drip* of melting snow out the window rouses Harry somewhere around mid-morning. He can smell wet dirt in the air, and wonders if the snowdrops will already be poking their sharp little noses through the soil.

He pisses in the chamber pot and splashes cold water on his face from the washbasin and goes in search of something to eat.

He pads quietly around Iain's pallet, towards the door. Iain is still asleep, on his back, head pillowed on an arm, shirt rucked up around his thighs. He's kicked his cloak off in the night.

Harry pauses and picks up the cloak to throw it back over Iain. But then he looks down at his friend. At his body. It's very much not the body of the thin little wolf-boy that had come from Scotland in a cage. Harry wonders how underfed Iain had been, for how long. Because this wasn't just farm labour that put on all that muscle. His body was clearly meant to have this sort of build, but it had been held back, starved to the point of underdevelopment, until Iain came to Dartington, and blossomed into the man lying in front of him.

His eyes skim lower. Iain is hard, his cock peeking out from under the hem of his shirt, the head thick and purple and glistening. He shifts in his sleep, his free hand moving down to rest on his stiff cock, fingers smearing the liquid pearling at its tip as his hand moves down to circle the base of it. Another pearl bubbles up almost immediately.

Harry feels his throat go completely dry, and he's seized with the almost visceral need to know what those pearls would taste like on his tongue. His own cock twitches, thickening.

He figures it's only fair to kneel for Iain, too.

Harry lowers his lips down on the silky-hard head of Iain's cock. He touches the tip of his tongue to Iain's slit. It tastes salty, a little bitter, and thick, and Harry hums a quiet moan of delight. He pulls off and licks his lips, then sinks down lower until he has the entire head in his mouth. His lips are tender, and running them back and forth over the ridge of Iain's cockhead is more erotic, more pleasurable, than he ever imagined possible.

He reaches down and pulls his own cock out of his braies, stroking himself slowly.

Then he gently moves Iain's hand away, replaces it with his own, and sees how much of Iain's cock he can take in his mouth.

He gets halfway down, sucking Iain gently, running his tongue along the man's thick shaft. Harry can feel more warm, salt-bitter liquid at the back of his throat. He never thought doing this would turn him on so much; he'd assumed it was all for the person getting sucked, but he's wound up so tight he'd go over the edge with the slightest touch.

Then Iain writhes under him, making sleepy little moans of pleasure, and Harry wants him to do that *again*. He forces himself to take more of Iain's stupidly thick cock in his mouth, until it's hitting the back of his throat, and he speeds up his pace, pulling almost all the way off until his lips brush over the ridge of Iain's head, and back down again until he's gagging, and saliva is flowing out of his mouth. He's so hard himself, his hips are twitching, desperate for more than his hand is giving him.

Iain cries out in his sleep, jerking his hips up, shoving his entire cock into Harry's mouth, choking him. But Harry feels some sort of perverse victory in getting his lips all the way down to the dark hairs at the root of Iain's shaft. He puts a hand on Iain's hips to still them and bobs his head up, running his tongue up and around the sides of Iain's dick, and then sinking all the way down until he's choking once more.

He feels a hand grab the back of his head, pushing him down still impossibly further, then a sleepy grunt. Then a muttered 'Holy Christ', and Iain shifts beneath him, rising up on his elbows.

Harry sucks up and down Iain's cock again then glances up at him. He knows he must look a wreck, lips and eyes red, saliva all over his mouth and dripping down his chin, but he doesn't care. Iain is staring down at him in stunned amazement as Harry kisses the head of his cock, licking it and playing over it with his lips as if it were Iain's mouth. Then Harry growls and takes Iain's cock down his throat again. Iain shuts his eyes and tilts his head back, hissing. His hips start pushing up against Harry's hand.

Harry pushes his pace still faster, harder, and from the volume of precome in his mouth and the completely wrecked expression on Iain's face, he knows Iain is close. He's moaning himself now, hand between his own legs, fisting himself, unbelievably turned on by the act of worshipping Iain's cock with his mouth.

Iain tries to say something, puts his hand on Harry's head to push him back, but Harry growls and bats his hand away and sucks as hard as he can and he can *feel* Iain's orgasm moving up his cock, the hot come being pumped into his mouth, down his throat, down his chin. And when Iain's done, when he can feel Iain's cock softening, Harry drags his lips up it one last time and then sits back on his own haunches to take care of himself. He can feel come and saliva dripping off his chin onto his stomach as he stares at Iain, his own orgasm incredibly close, and then he squeezes his eyes shut and he's coming, so hard everything goes black for a moment, and he bites his lip to hold his scream inside.

Harry feels like jelly afterwards. He's kneeling there, legs shaking, hand on his sticky, softening dick, dizzy, staring at Iain, who's lying sprawled like a startled satyr, and he's still soaring, floating, unable to say anything.

Iain moves first, tossing off his new shirt and, naked, reaching down to help Harry up. Harry goes with him, pliant as a newborn lamb, and just works on remaining standing as Iain divests him of his shirt and braies.

'C'mon,' Iain says, pressing a kiss to Harry's forehead as he leads him over to the washbasin. 'Let's get you cleaned up.'

Once there, he leans Harry against him, so they are chest to chest, their soft cocks nestling against each other. Iain drapes an arm around the small of Harry's back, resting it right on the swell of Harry's arse. It's comforting. That's all Harry can figure out to say about it. It's casual and gentle and makes him feel good.

Iain soaks the cleaning rag in water with his free hand then tilts Harry's chin up. He blushes, wanting to apologise for what a mess he is, but Iain just smiles at him softly and leans forwards and kisses him. They've kissed so many ways, even in their short time as lovers: hungry, furious, demanding, apologetic, chaste. But this is new. There's no hurry, no purpose to the kisses. It's just sharing warmth, just exploring. Iain will occasionally draw back and wipe a little of Harry's chin or neck with the damp cloth, but he always leans back in to kiss some more.

Harry moves his own arms to the top of Iain's backside. Not pulling him close, not grinding. Just creating another point of connection. It feels right, to have his hands there. Like they belong on that firm, silken swell of skin.

Iain moves down to cleaning Harry's chest and stomach, and then their cocks, and every time Harry thinks *that's it, this is as intimate as I can get with another person*, something simple happens, like his lover softly cleaning his spent cock while taking breaks for kisses, and another part of him is broken open, revealed to the sunshine that Iain pours into him.

At this point he's not sure how he isn't leaking light out of every pore, so enraptured is he with existing at this moment, with this person.

Iain tosses the cloth aside, finished, and they stand there for what seems a lifetime, loosely holding each other, bodies resting together, lost in a slow conversation of kisses.

Harry avoids Iain for the next day or two. He can't help it. He has built his life around discipline, control and duty; it is the heavy shield he holds against the world.

And Iain can strip him defenceless with a look.

Harry feels like he's lost control of himself. Since the infinite tenderness of their morning after Christmas, his limbs seem to want to move without his permission. His fingers itch to tangle in Iain's hair. His body seeks to find its home against Iain's. His lips seek his, always. His heart, *his heart* wants to float straight out of his chest to where it belongs, in Iain's strong hands.

The problem is that he no longer trusts himself in front of others. He knows he'll slip up, touching Iain in a way that will shout to the world, *this is my lover*. So he solves the problem by not allowing himself to be near Iain at all.

It is the worst sort of penance.

Annie corners Harry outside the kitchens the next morning. '*Heard from your Lancastrian lass?*' she chirps.

'*Not yet*,' Harry says. '*I expect I'll see her in Dunstable, at the tournament coming up*.'

Annie puts her hand on Harry's arm and leans in close. '*You need to find a wife, Harry*,' she says, under her breath.

'*I intend to*,' Harry says and blinks at her. '*Annie, where did this come from?*'

She just gives him a look, and then her eyes flick upwards, towards the windows of the solar. '*Be careful, Harry*,' she whispers, turning to head back to the kitchen. '*Lot of new folk about.*'

For the rest of the day, Harry smiles and talks and goes through all the motions of being lord of the manor, but it's as if he's an automaton, a clockwork knight with nothing beneath its armour but hollow fear.

He rides up to Ordlington, checking with Rabbie's squire, Mark, about practising before Dunstable. Much as he and Rabbie aren't fond of each other, they can vastly improve their chances in the tournament by breaking a few lances together. He can't practise jousting at Dartington, not yet, not until Iain learns how to hold a lance.

When Harry returns Libby to the stables, it's just before supper, and nobody's there but Iain. Iain in his damned new shirt that brings out the ice in his eyes and the warmth in his skin.

Harry takes a moment to gather himself, to say what needs to be said. He's surprised to feel tears pricking at the corners of his eyes. He looks up at Iain and opens his mouth.

Before he can speak, Iain turns away, his proud posture faltering.

'Don't say it,' Iain whispers. 'Whatever excuse you're going to make, *don't*.'

Harry steps forwards, and Iain flinches away, as if burned.

'I know you're torn up about the sins you commit with me. I know it keeps you awake,' Iain says, his voice hoarse with barely controlled emotion. 'Have you ever thought how it makes me feel?'

Harry stutters.

'It's destroying me,' Iain mumbles, staring at his feet.

He paces in a futile little circle, cornered, and then grips the top of a stall door so hard the hinges squeak. 'One moment you want me with a hunger that's overwhelming. The next you won't even speak to me, won't touch me. Like I'm *diseased*.' He shakes his head, then looks up at Harry, his eyes blindingly beautiful and raw with hurt. 'I want you *all the time*, Harry. This isn't an experiment for me. It's how I am. I like boys. I'm a filthy pervert who likes boys. I can't just go and find a wife and move on. I don't have that choice.'

Iain makes a choking sound that's half rueful laugh, and half the beginning of tears. When he continues, it's in a whisper. 'And the worst of it is, I feel like the foulest, most ungrateful bastard on earth.'

'No, you're not—' Harry begins.

Iain's head is tilted back, and Harry watches as a tear tracks down his cheek. 'And the most hypocritical,' Iain says, his voice going high with the struggle not to cry. 'Because if all I get are crumbs, if I get less than the gnawed bones you toss to the dogs, I'll take them.' He sucks in a great ragged breath. '*I'll take them.* Because it's better than nothing, and I know too well what nothing tastes like.'

The pain in his face is like a spear piercing Harry's heart. It feels as if the order of nature itself has been overturned. *Iain* is the strong one. He should never look like this. He should never hurt. And Harry has injured him, perhaps mortally, perhaps in a way that can never heal again.

Harry reaches out to him, his instincts overwhelming him with the need to wrap Iain up in his arms and keep him safe.

But Iain jerks away, his lips twisting. 'No,' he says, sharp and final. 'Have enough respect to make it a clean kill. Don't touch me. Don't ever touch me again.'

He stalks out into the winter night without another word.

Harry can only stare after him, the fear of being discovered replaced by terror at what he has broken.

Part Three

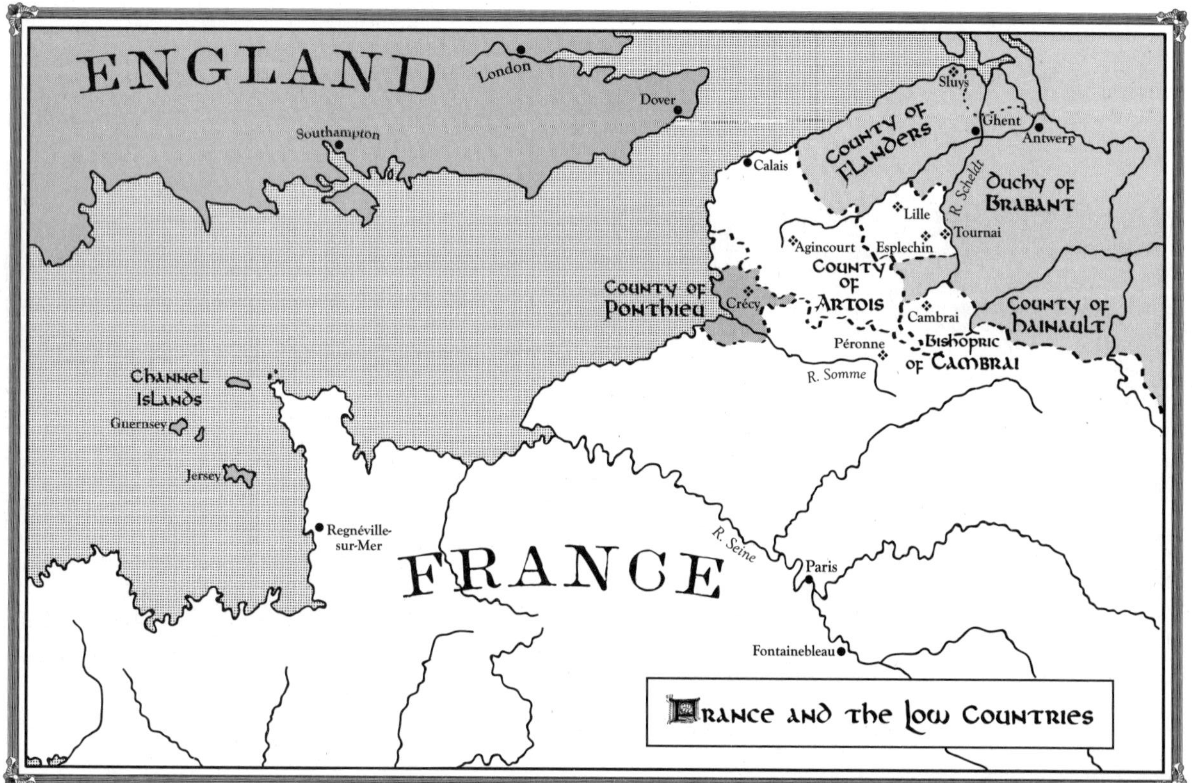
France and the Low Countries
ENGLAND
London
Dover
Southampton
County of Flanders
Sluys
Ghent
Antwerp
Calais
R. Scheldt
Duchy of Brabant
Lille
Tournai
Agincourt
Esplechin
County of Artois
County of Ponthieu
Crécy
Cambrai
County of Hainault
Péronne
Bishopric of Cambrai
R. Somme
Channel Islands
Guernsey
Jersey
Regnéville-sur-Mer
FRANCE
R. Seine
Paris
Fontainebleau

EIGHT

January–February 1334: Drunken Angel

The tournament at Dunstable is two weeks away, and directly on the heels of Dunstable are competitions at Woodstock and Newmarket. With travel, Harry will be away from Dartington for over a month. He loves his lands, but the hall has begun to feel like a prison, a boiling cauldron about to blow its lid.

It will take a week to ride to Dunstable. For the week before that they'll stay at Ordlington to practise with Rabbie and a couple of other West Country knights, shaking off the winter cobwebs and sharpening their steel against each other.

Iain was to come with him.

Harry thinks about leaving Iain behind, but the truth is, he needs a squire. He can't handle preparing, packing and competing in three tournaments in a row without help. Someone has to put up the tent; take care of the horses. Someone has to pass him a new lance or a new sword if his breaks. Someone has to cook meals when he comes in from the field, battered and weary.

He can't do it alone.

Not that Iain is anything more than a silent shadow at the moment.

Iain had vanished for a day and a night after their conversation in the stables. Then he had simply and suddenly reappeared in the hall at the end of supper one evening, dirty, bramble-scratched, and with leaves in his hair. He'd sat with Kit and Jed and not said a word.

Harry isn't sure Iain has uttered a word to anyone since then. He does his chores with his usual skill, and shows up to meals, but it's like a light has gone out. The body still moves, but the spirit – that indomitable, shining spirit, bright and clever – it's gone.

Now Harry stands in the entrance to the stables and tells Iain what to pack for the journey, while Iain brushes Numbles down. They'll need the cart; Numbles can pull it. Harry will ride Libby, and Nomad will walk behind the cart. There's the tent and a cooking pot and tripod to go in; Harry's old squire's mail and Sir Simon's newer armour. The plate. The repair kit. Swords and helmets and the practice jackets and blades. The good shield and the practice shield. Clothes, including one set of court clothes for Harry. Provisions. Soap. The four lances Harry has, plus coin to buy more. His banner. The travelling pallet, the one that rolls up small and is waxed against the ground's dampness. The iron pegs, for tethering. Good oats for the horses. A snare for hunting. Rope.

Iain's back is to Harry but every so often he makes a curt nod to show he's listening. His eyes never leave the horse he's working on.

'Oh, and have Ralf down to check their shoes, especially Nomad's,' Harry adds. He notices that the dagger he gave Iain for Christmas is hanging from his belt, and the sight makes his heart constrict painfully.

Iain nods again, to show he understands about the black-smith.

Harry sighs, and leans against the lintel. 'You don't have to come with me,' he says.

Iain gives him a look that would scorch battlefields. His knuckles are white around the curry comb.

'Fine, then,' Harry says, retreating back into the courtyard.

They leave on 4 January for practice at Ordlington, and the tournaments thereafter. The whole estate comes out to see them off, all Harry's loved ones hugging him and wishing him good luck, asking him to make them proud.

Iain gets a surprising number of hugs too, from Annie and the kitchen girls, a punch in the shoulder from Piers, a near-crushing embrace from Ralf. Jed approaches him and Harry expects them to embrace as well, but instead Iain smiles and presses a hand to his own chest, bowing. Jed's face splits into a grin and he repeats the gesture, saying a short sentence in a language Harry doesn't recognise.

Kit hugs Iain, slaps himself on the forehead, runs into the hall, and comes running back with a compact hunting bow which he thrusts into Iain's hands with a quiver of arrows. Iain also smacks Kit on the head, then collars him with an arm and hugs him again.

Once they're far enough from Dartington that the children and younger servants have stopped jogging alongside the cart, Harry exhales.

He presses his outside leg against Libby, angling her in so she walks close to the cart. 'I know this is obvious,' he says, 'but Ordlington won't be any fun for you.'

Iain gives him his best *no shit* look. He's dressed defiantly, in his Scottish-style blue shirt, no breeches, barefoot, and his cloak slung over his shoulder in the Highland manner. His dagger sits at his hip.

Harry prays inwardly for patience. 'You'll practise against the other squires in the afternoons, when we're done. Mostly swordplay, but usually we'll get you all up on horses for a turn at jousting,' he says.

Iain stares ahead at the road.

'I want you to lose your practice bouts,' Harry says.

That gets Iain's attention. His brow furrows.

'Look,' Harry explains. 'This isn't just practice. This is the beginning of the season, and you have to think of it as such. *Lose.* Lose now, when it doesn't matter, while learning the weaknesses of the squires you're fighting. A knight is never so sloppy as when he thinks he's got an easy win.'

The annoyance in Iain's expression fades, replaced with a cold calculation.

'It's up to you,' Harry continues. 'I haven't even asked if you want to fight in the *bohort*, the squires' competition. Do you?'

Iain nods.

'Mm,' Harry says. 'Then lead the other squires to believe you're not a threat. They'll look down on you anyway, because you're Scottish, so use their bias against them. And don't rise to their bait.'

The horses' hooves clop against the packed dirt and stone of the road, and the cart's wheels creak.

'If you find you're not getting enough real practice, let me know,' Harry says. 'We can go out before dawn and I'll beat you up a bit.'

Iain glares at him.

Harry smirks. 'I've been holding back.'

It's true. In their occasional sparring at Dartington, Iain's technique has improved immeasurably from the vicious, fast mess it had been in October. But Harry has years of practice on him, and the sort of quiet calculation in the midst of clashing steel that wins out over Iain's hot passion every time.

They cross the moor in silence and arrive at Ordlington as the sun is setting. The party there turns out to be six knights plus their squires. Rabbie and Harry, plus Sir Morien and Sir Malachi, brothers of Moorish descent from Cornwall; a wiry Dorset knight named Sir Hugh who had been a close friend of Sir Simon; and another Devon knight, Sir Gervase. Ordlington is far bigger than Harry's estate, the hall itself rich with tapestries and teeming with well-ordered servants. Rabbie welcomes them and waves Harry in for supper while Iain and one of Rabbie's stable-boys put the horses away for the night.

Harry is at Rabbie's table at supper with the rest of the knights. Iain, when he comes in from the stables, is directed to the next table down, with the squires. The other squires greet him in a friendly enough way, and Harry sees Iain introduce himself with a quiet murmur. Then Mark, Rabbie's squire, nudges one of the others and whispers in his ear. The boy's eyes widen, and he looks over at Iain. Mark snickers.

Iain appears not to notice, but at this point Harry knows Iain's body language as well as his own. So he catches the almost imperceptible tension in Iain's shoulders. There's another whisper from Mark, a look of surprise and disgust from Sir Hugh's squire Rolly. Iain sighs, and shifts away from the group, isolating himself. It makes Harry irrationally angry. Iain is better than the lot of them. Smarter, funnier, probably a more skilled fighter, certainly more learned. He shouldn't be treated like a stray dog, to be mocked.

'I can't believe you really brought him,' Rabbie says, elbowing Harry and gazing over at Iain.

'Lord Montagu said make him my squire, so I made him my squire,' Harry mumbles.

'Harry,' Rabbie snorts. 'That was code for *lock him up and toss the key down the nearest well.*'

'Well, nobody told *me* that,' Harry grumbles, crossing his arms.

'You have,' Sir Gervase says from across the table with a bemused grin, 'a Scottish squire.'

'Yes,' Harry sighs, reaching for a leg of chicken.

'What a novelty,' the man gasps. 'Is he any good? Can he speak French? Does he speak at all? How did you acquire him?'

Harry stuffs some chicken in his mouth. 'Yes; yes, also English, Gaelic and Latin; he only speaks to people he likes; and he came in a box.'

'A box!' Sir Gervase guffaws. He seems a good sort; not the sharpest of blades but there's no real malice to him. 'A *box*. Did you get him for Christmas?'

Harry shakes his head. 'No. Midsummer.'

Rabbie clears his throat, pointedly. *That's enough.*

Sir Hugh refills Harry's glass with wine. 'I am sorry about Sir Simon,' he says quietly.

'I am too,' says Harry. 'He was a great teacher, and a good man.'

'Hear, hear,' says Sir Hugh. 'There aren't enough of those.'

Harry glances over to check on Iain. The other five squires

are thick in conversation already. Harry can hear them working through mutual acquaintances and past competitions. To one side, Iain eats silently, hunched over his food. One of the Cornish brothers' squires, a slim black man with curious white patches to his skin, says something to Iain, attempts to draw him in. But Iain just shakes his head and returns to his food. He has nobody in common with them.

He has, indeed, nobody but Harry.

The next morning, they're awake at Lauds to draw the carts up to a large, flat pasture that will serve as the training field. There's a temporary fence around the mêlée area and, a short distance away, servants are marking off the tilting field. The squires are already by their carts, unpacking armour and weapons. A few older knights and men-at-arms, too elderly or too maimed to fight, have shown up to watch the young men play their games. They'll shout pointers, Harry thinks. They always do.

Iain looks a little lost, glancing out under his lashes at the other squires, trying to figure out what to do

And Harry realises he's been so busy teaching Iain how to be a knight, he forgot to teach him how to be a squire.

Iain looks down helplessly at the three-piece suit of mail, and the pile of plate armour to protect Harry's joints. Then he looks up at Harry, and over to the other knights, their squires fitting them into their plate with quick, practised motions. A few squires look over, sensing his distress like sharks sense blood in the water.

Harry brushes his fingers against Iain's shoulder and whispers, 'It's fine, Iain, I'll do it.'

Iain flinches away, and hisses, 'No.'

He glares down at the pile of armour like it's personally offended him. Then he picks up a mail chausse, squinting at it.

'There's a wool understocking that goes on first,' Harry murmurs out of the side of his mouth. 'The leather straps at the top of both attach to the belt of my braies.'

Iain snorts and gets down on one knee, tapping Harry's leg like he's a horse with a hoof that wants cleaning. Harry lifts his foot off the ground and he holds onto the side of the cart for support. Iain's hands are rough, yanking the wool up and the mail over it, then pulling at Harry's belt to slip the leather straps underneath and around it. He buckles them and looks up at Harry. Harry nods, and Iain moves on to the other leg. While he's buckling that, Harry whispers, 'Now the padded jacket, and the hauberk atop it.'

Harry holds his arms out as Iain pulls the jacket on him and laces up the front with quick, harsh motions. Harry himself did this for Sir Simon countless times, but this is the first time anyone's done it for him and he feels like a doll, naked and vulnerable under Iain's touch despite the fact that the squire is covering him in armour.

Iain glances at him as he arranges the mail hood around Harry's neck, and Harry shivers. One look from Iain's pale eyes can still strip everything away, reduce him from being a knight in a field of other knights, squires and servants to a man who can sense nothing else in the world but the other man in front of him. Who can feel the very volume of air between them. He closes his eyes and whispers, 'Now the plate. Spaulder, couter, poleyn and greaves. Work your way from the top to the bottom. It's important they be tight. Don't go by the existing wear on the straps; these were Sir Simon's and this is the first time I've used them.'

Iain nods and moves to stand behind Harry. He looks out over the field as Iain fits the first spaulder. Everyone else is finished, waiting around, watching them. He wills his body to behave, as Iain braces his hand against Harry's shoulder and tightens the first set of buckles. It's a strange, erotic torture, having Iain's hands on him like this, moving slowly down his body, making sure he's protected.

He looks up at the heavens, rather than at Iain kneeling down to attach the plate to his knees and shins. He watches wispy clouds that don't even have the good grace to form shapes against the grey sky as they scudder past.

Iain taps his right greave twice, to show he's finished, and stands up. He looks at Harry expectantly.

'Gauntlets. Then practice shield, blunt sword and helmet,' Harry sighs. 'Buckle the sword belt around me.'

Iain's face twists in annoyance at himself and he whirls to get the weapons. Harry curses his lack of foresight. Iain hates being made to feel stupid, and Harry's just caused him to look the fool in front of all the other knights and squires. He wants to apologise, but he knows that will just make Iain angrier.

Iain's arms are around him briefly, to attach his knight's belt, and it takes everything Harry has not to step back into that, to make it an embrace. 'You've done well,' he says, letting out the breath he's been holding for what seems like forever.

'Lyon, are you finished doing your hair yet?' yells Rabbie.

'I'm ready,' Harry calls back, pulling out his sword and swinging it, loosening up his wrist and shoulder. 'Iain, where's my charger?'

'Uh,' Iain says, then looks over to the horse lines, where all the other destriers wait, saddled and bridled, spaced out at distances of twenty feet so they can't harm each other. '*Fuck*,' he says.

They've always sparred on foot, Harry thinks. Iain wouldn't know that the real practices are on horseback. 'Go,' he says, giving Iain a shove towards the stables. Then he turns to the other knights. 'Sorry! Beginning of season. Shall we warm up on foot?'

Rabbie rolls his eyes but walks towards the mêlée area, ducking underneath the fence and swinging his mace. The other knights follow.

Iain reappears ten minutes later on Nomad's back, at a fast canter. Nomad still has straw in his mane and his tail isn't bobbed up like it should be, but he's saddled and bridled and his feet are wrapped. Nomad arches his neck in annoyance and bucks as they pass the other destriers. It's not in the nature of a war-horse to like other chargers, and a bunch of stallions in one place is always asking for trouble. Iain stays on nimbly, although his feet aren't in the stirrups – he's crossed the irons over the pommel. As they reach the end hitching post, he slides off the huge war-horse and ties him up. Then he pulls a comb out of his belt and starts attacking the knotted mess that Nomad manages to transform his mane into every night.

We'll cut it tonight, Harry thinks. Down to a length of a couple of inches, so it sticks up like a crest and won't tangle in anything. Nomad's mane hasn't been battle-short since last summer, but it's time once again.

The Cornish squire, the one with the white patches on his skin, Ibrahim, saunters over to Nomad with a few spare pieces of ribbon. While Iain combs Nomad's mane, the other squire starts to braid his tail. Iain stops working and walks over to watch. The other squire doesn't say anything, just slows his braiding down enough so Iain can understand. He demonstrates to Iain how to loop and wrap the braid up to create a blunt bob that will protect the delicate cartilage of the horse's tail, making it less likely to snag or be broken in battle. Then, before Iain can thank him or become embarrassed, the other squire turns and leaves.

Iain sits on the cart for the rest of the morning, his eyes never leaving Harry as he fights a mock mêlée. Then Harry moves up the field and Iain waits in position by the list as the knights break a few slow, warmup lances on each other. Well, everyone else is taking warmup runs. Harry is hitting at close to his tournament pace. He knows that his advice to Iain applies just as much to himself: play it slow, don't let them know your real skill or speed. But he can feel Iain's gaze burning into him as he jousts, and he wants to be worthy of it.

He wants Iain to be impressed with him above all other knights.

He shakes his head, and fights the urge to put it in the way of Rabbie's mace. He'll be riding up and asking for Iain's favour next, to wear into battle. What a concept. His squire's favour.

(It would be something pale blue, he thinks. A scrap of ribbon he could wear around his wrist, where nobody would know.)

He growls at his own folly and grabs a lance, turning Nomad to square up against Sir Malachi. He shuts everything out of his head but the feel of the horse beneath him, the thunder of the hooves, the jarring impact of the other knight's lance on his shield. He prays the force of the blow is enough to knock the stupid out of him.

Both their lances shatter, and both of them manage to stay on their horses. There's a light applause from the watching knights, the claps ringing like small bells as mailed hands are brought together.

When the knights finish and the squires remove their armour, Rabbie's servants bring them small beer and bread and cold meats to eat, and the knights lean against the fence to watch their squires fight. They have the boys fight on foot the first day, in mail shirts and padded jackets and helmets, to make sure they're safe. Most range in age from sixteen through to Rolly's nineteen, but Sir Gervase's squire is only fourteen and, though he's come up like Harry from paging at a young age, nobody wants to see the lad hurt.

Rabbie throws a blue banner over the fence at one end of the mêlée enclosure and a red banner at the other, and sorts the squires into teams of three. The first team to seize the other team's banner wins.

Iain's team is Sir Gervase's boy and Sir Malachi's squire Ibrahim, and they're against Rabbie's squire Mark, Sir Hugh's squire Rolly (who will be made knight this year, most likely) and Sir Morien's squire Tristan.

Harry scratches the stubble on his cheek. It's not a good matchup. The other team are all older, stronger, and have years more experience. Rolly, a big, strawberry-blond lad with a broken nose and freckles all over his face and arms, was Harry's nemesis in the squire contests of past years. And Mark's a sadistic, ruthless bastard. Iain's the only one with any size and force on his team, and Harry had instructed him to lose. He knows how he'd turn the stakes and win using Iain's team, but he's not allowed to coach Iain. The squires have to learn on their own.

Harry feels Iain's eyes on him. Harry very deliberately looks to Gervase's little squire, who is all legs and arms like a young colt, and then to the red banner that is their team's goal, then back to Iain.

Iain makes an infinitesimal nod of his head, and turns away.

'We betting?' says Rabbie.

'Yes,' says Harry.

'Not going to enjoy taking your money, Harry, seeing as you're already in hock to the Baron.' Rabbie snorts. 'But I'm going to do it anyway.'

As the teams of squires assemble at opposite ends of the enclosure, in front of the banners they are guarding, the knights and onlookers engage in a spirited exchange of odds.

Mark's team is the favourite, three to one.

'Make ready!' yells Rabbie.

The squires shoulder their shields and raise their swords.

'Go!'

Iain howls something blood-curdling in Gaelic and runs directly at his opponents, sword too high to parry, shield too low to block. Twelve stone of disorganised, suicidal Scottish fury, who thinks he can barrel through the other team straight to the red banner.

The knights leaning against the fence snort and shake their heads.

'Oh, your Scotsman's going to go down so *hard*,' Sir Gervase gasps. 'Odsbodkins, and then Eddie's going to get *walloped*.'

Eddie, Sir Gervase's little squire, follows Iain, as does Ibrahim. Their team looks a mess. Ibrahim comes in on the side, wanting to help Iain, but Eddie hangs back, fearful of getting involved in the messy encounter he can see playing out in front of him.

Rolly and Mark look at each other, grinning with bloodlust, and break into their own run, converging on Iain. Tristan looks to edge around the side, but is blocked by Ibrahim. They know each other well, and they close on each other cautiously, looking for an opening, the way knights *should* approach each other.

Mark plants himself in Iain's path, raising his sword for a hell of a blow to the side of Iain's helmet. Rolly crouches behind his own shield slightly in front of Mark and to his left, hoping to make Iain swing early, while denying him space to use his sword arm. The setup is fast, well co-ordinated, and comes together with all the elegance of a steel trap at the exact moment Iain can no longer dodge it.

Harry's not breathing. Any moment now there'll be the most horrific clash of steel.

'No wonder Halidon Hill was a slaughter,' mutters Sir Morien.

But they'd all assumed Iain was trying to hit Mark with his sword, like a normal person. Harry sees the shift just before it happens and he grabs the fence so hard he feels splinters jab into his fingers.

Iain is *insane*. It's beautiful.

Iain leaps and twists, slamming into Mark at full speed like a battering ram, and almost casually back-handing Rolly in the neck with his blunt sword as he smashes his shield into Mark's face. They go down in a heap, the three of them, and then it descends into a tavern brawl. Iain's holding Mark down and punching him, and Rolly is thumping Iain, trying to make him let go, to make them separate enough that their swords will be useful. And then Iain starts *laughing*.

Because there, standing over them and shifting nervously from foot to foot, is little Eddie, with a wad of balled-up red cloth in his hands.

Tristan curses and throws his sword at Ibrahim, who smiles and shrugs, and goes to help Iain up. Iain's face is bloody but he's grinning with a savage glee.

Rabbie's jaw drops open. 'That cunning little bastard,' he growls.

'Pay up,' says Harry.

The next morning, Iain is waiting at the field when Harry and the knights arrive. Nomad is brushed, bobbed and tacked up at his post, and Harry's armour is laid out neatly on top of the cart. Harry's chest feels too small to contain his heart at the sight, and he falls behind Sir Gervase for a moment, to twist his fingers around his sword belt and collect himself.

Iain's hands are still rough when he puts the armour on Harry, but his touch is sure and efficient. Harry mutters a few instructions – the chausses a hole tighter; the greaves a little looser – but mostly leaves him to it.

Then Harry flips over both the shields and shows Iain how to look for damage. 'You do this every night, after cleaning and polishing the armour,' he explains. 'The shields will wear over time, and if you see any of the cracks changing or increasing, it's time to replace the shield. If you're not sure, mark them with a bit of charcoal. It will all seem pointless until you see a shield fail at a tournament. The knight usually dies.' He peers at the back of the practice shield he'd used yesterday, fingering a join in the wood. 'This crack bothers me,' he mutters. 'I'd swear it's bigger than it was before.'

Iain stands there, silent, his bright eyes taking it all in.

The knights fight a mounted mêlée that morning, three on three. Harry feels he does well. Sir Hugh is his favourite opponent. The older knight is slow but cunning, with a great tactical mind. The jousts after dinner are more intense, faster, more violent than the easy warmup of the day before. He gets knocked off his horse by Sir Morien, the other knight's lance-tip swinging inwards at the last moment and catching on the edge of Harry's shield where he is less able to absorb the blow. One moment he's focused on his own lance and then *bang*, darkness, and he's on the ground. Iain's by his side in a moment, Nomad's reins looped over his arm, pulling Harry up to his feet.

Sir Morien trots his horse up. 'Sorry about that. Felt off target to me.'

'No,' says Harry, rubbing his backside. 'It was a fair lance. I just didn't catch it very well.'

He's sharply pulled away from Sir Morien by Iain's hands, which roam over him, checking for injuries. 'Iain,' he mutters, his throat suddenly thick. 'We have to clear the field. I didn't break anything, trust me.' He doesn't move, though, doesn't push Iain's hands away.

In the afternoon, the squires fight one on one, rotating around in short bouts with each of the others. Mark is sporting a black eye and a split cheek, and he clearly has it in for Iain. Iain loses his bout with Mark deliberately, slowly retreating and letting Mark show his bad habits, his favourite attacks. Harry isn't sure whether the loss to Rolly is deliberate or not; Rolly is good, probably the best of the squires, and even though Iain is fast, Rolly doesn't have to consciously think through tactics the way Iain still does. Ibrahim gives him a surprising amount of trouble, too – there's not much power in him, but there's a lot of speed, and Iain as always relies too much on his offence. Ibrahim's a perfect opponent for Iain to have this early on; through sparring with the Cornish squire, Iain learns all the raggedy holes in his own technique. He simply out-reaches Eddie, who's all defence, and runs over Tristan, who is more interested in making swords clash than in hitting his man.

Harry and the other knights applaud their squires, and Rabbie announces that the squires will fight mounted the next afternoon, so to have a horse ready.

Harry sits with Iain for a while as he cleans armour and tack, and checks the shield and everything else for signs of wear. He's not sure Iain is listening – the man is still barely speaking, to him or anyone else – but he goes through Iain's bouts, talking quietly about his opponents' strengths and weaknesses, what Iain did well, what he needs to work on. He discusses his own fights as well, marking out clever moves by his opponents that he wants to copy in future, and admitting his frustration with how he has to change tactics against Rabbie's mace, a bone-crushing weapon from which his mail offers scant protection. It must be blocked with a shield.

Iain continues his work, silent.

Harry sighs. 'You're doing well, Iain. I want you to know

that.' He hops off the cart and heads towards the hall for supper. 'Be here at Lauds with both Nomad and Numbles ready to go. I'll teach you how to fight on horseback.'

Harry isn't sure, but he thinks he hears Iain grunt his assent as he walks away.

Iain arrives at the makeshift tiltyard, squinty and sleep-rumpled, as the last bell of Lauds rings across the frost-limned fields.

Harry has never wanted so badly to kiss someone in his life.

For that's how Iain *should* be woken up, pressed against the trunk of an apple tree, kissed and felt up until he begins to smile, until he squirms and grumbles *Lyon, no, that spot is ticklish*, until his fingers weave into Harry's hair to kiss him back.

Instead Harry puts a practice sword in his hand and tells him to get on his horse.

'In the middle of a mêlée you're a lot less mobile than you think on horseback,' Harry says. 'On the one hand, that's good for you, because your fighting style doesn't really encompass retreat. On the other, the lack of mobility means that you can't pull the sort of stunt you did the first day. It's solid technical fundamentals that will make you win on horseback, and your ability to cope with the horse, who is going to do things you don't expect.'

Iain nods. He looks much more awake now, and Harry realises that Iain isn't just humouring him out of some perverse sense of duty. He wants this; he enjoys it.

They don't have a lot of time before breakfast, but there in the half-light of dawn Harry shows Iain the basics of mounted combat: left to left encounters, when shields clash and you swing across your horse to hit your opponent (or, why bad knights' war-horses are often missing their left ear), and right to right, where it's sword against sword. Then there's how tactics change based on the distance between the horses. Harry talks him through other sorts of weapons: spears, crushing weapons like maces and axes. And last, he shows him some quick argybargy with the horses, how to shove or turn an opponent's horse with your horse's shoulder.

As they walk back to the hall afterwards, Harry claps Iain on the shoulder without thinking.

Iain puts his hand on Harry's shoulder too, and squeezes once, before releasing it. It's their first real touch since Christmas.

Iain doesn't do well at his first mounted mêlée. He doesn't do badly, but his score is at the bottom end of the squires' group. He's furious with himself, hissing in Gaelic like a wet cat as he slides off Numbles and strips off his shield and mail next to the cart.

'Hey,' Harry says.

Iain ignores him.

'Hey!' Harry repeats, more sharply. He grabs Iain's shoulders and slams him against the cart. 'No,' he says.

Iain's eyes are wild, and Harry braces himself, half-convinced Iain is going to swing at him.

'Do better tomorrow,' Harry says, stepping back.

And Iain does.

Both of them get through the week, improving every day, not in a straight line but there is forward progress. Iain survives his first afternoon jousting, which ends up being more of a lesson in how to fall off a horse. His second, he and Rolly break lances on each other and the two of them grin and whoop like they've just inherited the world. Harry spends a lot of time with Sir Hugh and Sir Morien, the three of them drilling hard on combinations that have Rabbie rolling his eyes with boredom and Iain watching every move they make.

Harry still reviews the lessons of each day's combat as Iain attends to his chores, and Iain still doesn't say a word. There's a discomfort between them yet, as they learn to navigate around each other all over again, but Harry is incredibly grateful for Iain's presence. It's easier. Less lonely. Even though Iain talks little, he's *there*, loving the thing that Harry loves, next to him, with him.

Then, four days after Epiphany, they start the journey to the great tournament at Dunstable.

Where he and Iain will live in a small tent together, sharing a travelling pallet at night, for a whole week.

Harry shuts his eyes and prays to Agnes, patron saint of chastity.

The road to Dunstable is packed with knights and nobles, peasants and gawkers and merchants, all streaming towards the week-long festival celebrating the victory over the Scots the summer before. Harry is glad he travelled up with the other knights from Ordlington, not just because of the way people move aside when they see six armed knights moving along the road in formation. No. Iain's still wearing his Scottish clothes, and he's getting more than a few sharp looks from passers-by. And, memorably, an apple core flung at his head.

They reach the festival lands after six long days on the road. Servants in the King's colours direct them around a copse towards a pasture adjacent to the tourney field, where they're to put up their tents.

As their party rounds the stand of oaks, Harry gasps.

There are over a hundred knights already encamped, their multicoloured banners glistening in the breeze above bright pavilions so densely packed it's like a field of canvas flowers.

The biggest tournament Harry had competed in before this was London, three years ago, and had numbered maybe eighty knights. He slides off Libby, in shock, and just stands, looking over the vast array of tents.

He'd had delusions of winning this tournament, his first as a full, belted knight. But with a list this crowded? Not a chance. He's not even going to scratch the top five.

Harry sags against Libby's shoulder. So much for making Dartington proud.

He feels more than sees Iain next to him, also gazing out over the sea of gaily striped tents. Iain leans in, bumping Harry's shoulder with his own. 'Lot of knights,' Iain says.

Harry looks over, shocked. That's more words than Iain's said the entire journey. Iain catches his eye and smirks, bumping his shoulder again. 'You're better,' he says.

'I— I'm not—' Harry stutters, but Iain just shoves past him.

'Tent's not going to set up itself,' Iain mutters, beginning to unload the cart.

Harry grabs the pole and braces it as Iain hammers the iron pegs that will hold it in place. 'This isn't a tournament, it's a *party*,' Iain comments. 'Most of these idiots are only here to be *seen* to be here.'

He stands up. 'C'mon, Harry, how many do you recognise as serious competition? Which ones do you think practised all last week?'

Harry furrows his brow and looks out over the field again. The Bohuns, they can have good days and bad days. Arundel doesn't joust, not really. Montagu doesn't either. If that's Henry de Beaumont's flag he can see near the end, he's fierce, but getting older. Morley's there, and he's a perennial champion, probably the best knight in the land. Some of Montagu's Galloway gang is there: Colin Crocker and Billy Lang are solid but not great. Lord Waldegrave's a joke, cruel and cretinous. Thomas Howland can impress—

A memory of Galloway flashes up in Harry's mind: Howland cleaving a serving-maid's head in. How she fell slowly to her knees on the flagstones as if in prayer, the wet grey mass of her brain shining with blood and fragments of skull in the torchlight. Harry shivers, and has to swallow down the bile that rises in his throat.

He turns his gaze towards other parts of the field, away from Montagu's archipelago of sycophants, and focuses on cataloguing the heraldic devices of the knights attending.

Iain is right. Out of the whole field, there are maybe a dozen knights who are serious competition.

'It's still going to be tough,' Harry says, the tension bleeding out of his shoulders.

Iain's watching him, and smiles when he sees Harry relax. 'Everything worth doing is tough.'

'Thank you,' Harry mutters.

Iain shrugs and turns back to his work. 'Some Sassenach idiot's been giving me pep talks. Apparently they're contagious.'

Harry snickers, and bumps his shoulder. 'We should go and present our *bona fides* and see who's actually signed up to compete.'

They finish with the tent and amble over to the check-in area set up at one end of the field, joining a queue of knights and squires in front of a long table, at which sit a trio of elderly men in the King's scarlet-and-lions uniform. As they wait, Harry explains the process to Iain: these are the heraldry clerks, the Three Fates of knightly combat. The first writes down the name, lineage and coat of arms of the knight on a piece of paper; the second checks it against a large book listing the legitimate knights of England and stamps it good or denied; the third copies the name of the approved entrant onto the lists and tells the knight his schedule. Harry thinks sometimes that the book is just for show; the old clerks know every English knight on sight, and every single one knows them.

When Harry reaches the front, he gives his name, coat of arms and the date of his knighthood. The first clerk squints at him. 'Ah, Sir Simon's squire, got your belt young! Good lad you were, nice manners,' he says. 'And *this* is a new face,' he continues, waving the feather end of his quill at Iain. 'Scottish,' he frowns. 'Don't get many of those.' He turns to the second clerk. 'Magnus, we have a listing for the Scottish quality?'

'Michael, there *is* no Scottish quality,' the second clerk grumbles.

Harry squeezes Iain's arm and says, 'Well, I assure you he is. Seonaidh mac Maíl Coluim, and I'd like him put down for the *bohort*.'

'If we dealt on assurances, m'boy, I'd be assuring everyone I'm the Queen of Bohemia,' mutters Magnus.

The third clerk leans over. 'Seonaidh mac Maíl Coluim, of . . . ? You know the rules, Harry, if we wanted to see peasants fight, we'd hold our tournaments outside taverns. Speak up, boy. Who are your parents?'

Iain goes very still, and speaks quietly. 'Maíl Coluim mac Lochlann, Laird of Galloway Forest. Of Castle Doon. Although I'm laird, now, technically.'

'No mother?' says Michael. 'We can't take him if he's a bastard, Sir Harry.'

'Perhaps the boy was born like Athena, right out of his father's headache. But I doubt it,' sighs Magnus. 'Still, quite a sight, if he was.'

'I'm not a bastard,' Iain growls. 'My mother was French, and is not in your book.'

'Isn't Lord of Galloway Forest enough?' Harry groans.

The third clerk hums. 'Balliol's Lord of Galloway Forest now,' says the man. 'He won't shut up about it. Personally I think the Scots'll throw him out before the year's done, just for the peace and quiet. Sign the boy up, Michael.'

Aside from being the final arbiters of England's knightly worth, the clerks could also be the most wicked gossips in the land.

The third clerk hands them their stamped *bona fides* and says, 'Sir Harry, you're in the opening mêlée the day after tomorrow, on the outside, against the King's Insiders. Congratulations. Is your coat of arms on your banner, and your banner on your pavilion?'

'Yes, Lord Morris,' Harry says, his heart loud in his chest. That's far better positioning than he'd dare dream.

'Good. There'll be a man by in the morning with your

jacket. Best of luck to you and the new squire,' the clerk says, already turning to the next knight in line.

Rather than go back to the tent, Harry drags Iain to the market area outside the knights' enclosure, babbling excitedly to him about how this draw means that he'll be fighting against extremely prestigious but not very skilled opponents, and that with luck he can place very high off his first day.

Iain just smiles at him, fondly.

They buy two new shields and put an order in for lances, and then get huge plates of roast beef and bread and gravy, and tankards of ale, at an open-air tavern set up right in the middle of the market field. They're both happy and exhausted and a little drunk, and Harry thinks, gazing at Iain across the table from him, that everything might just turn out well.

Then he hears his name called, from the edge of the tavern enclosure.

It's Lady Alys de Morton, elegant in a long lavender over-tunic with the teal-blue sleeves of her dress underneath showing. She's walking with two other courtly ladies.

Harry stands up immediately and strides over. The two ladies, a blonde and a redhead, giggle to each other behind their hands.

'Alys,' he says. 'I'd hoped you'd be here.'

'Harry,' she admonishes. '*Everyone* is here.'

'And you manage to look more elegant in the middle of a field than most ladies do at court,' Harry says, then hastily corrects himself. 'You *all* look elegant.'

This causes more giggling from Alys's friends.

'We're late to supper, but I'd love to catch up,' Alys says. 'When are you competing?'

Harry smiles, bashful. 'I'm in the opening mêlée. Fighting against the King, but one can't have everything.'

'Ooh,' Alys says, placing a small, pale hand to her chest. 'Are you very good?'

'Just look at him,' Alys's blonde friend simpers.

Harry shrugs. 'I try.'

'I think I shall place the most enormous bet on you. Don't lose,' Alys grins, waving as she and her friends depart with perfect, unhurried footsteps.

Harry turns around to go back to his seat, but Iain and the two new shields are gone.

When Harry gets back to the pavilion and can't find Iain there either, he begins to panic.

But then he sees the new shields resting against the cart. He looks in the cart, and Iain's curled up on its rough wood boards, snuggled under his cloak.

He pokes his squire. 'Don't be an idiot, Iain.'

Iain glares at him. 'Leave me alone.'

Harry rolls his eyes. 'It's cold out here, there's a pallet in the tent, and I'm getting you up at Lauds to spar so I suggest you pick the option that allows you decent sleep, rather than spending a miserable night playing martyr in the bottom of a cart. Besides, imagine your devotional pictures. A palm leaf in one hand and the splinter that pierced your bottom in the other.'

Iain sits up, still cocooned in his cloak. 'I hate you,' he says.

'Well,' Harry mutters, holding open the flap of the pavilion, 'we're not here to be nice. We're here to *win*. Also, it looks like rain.'

Iain stalks in and throws himself on the small pallet, putting himself as far over to one edge as he possibly can.

Harry sighs and settles down on the other edge.

The rain begins sometime in the middle of the night.

By early dawn, it's a downpour, the steady drumbeat of rain on the tent canvas; puddles of water encroaching under the edges. And Iain and Harry are tangled up together in the middle of the pallet.

Harry doesn't know when they both admit to being awake but he's pretty sure Iain's been faking sleep for the past half-hour. Of course Harry only knows that because he's been faking sleep too. He's spooning Iain, arms around him, leg thrown over him, morning erection slotted against his bottom.

'Well, then,' Harry says, rolling away from Iain and sitting up. 'Let's get out there and hit each other.'

'You have got to be fucking kidding,' Iain says.

'It's *England*,' Harry replies. 'Fighting in the rain is an important skill.'

'So is hiding the dead bodies of Sassenach idiots,' Iain growls.

Harry flicks the back of Iain's head with his hand. 'Come on. Practice swords and the new shields, and the horses. Helmets only. We'll go bareback and without mail because mud's a bitch to clean out of the armour.'

Iain looks at him and shakes his head. 'Only a crazy person makes friends with a boy in a cage,' he says, as if realising something profound. 'I should have seen it. Only a crazy person.'

Harry grins. He's become aware over the past two weeks just how silent Iain is with everyone else. Everyone except him.

And it feels like a gift, to have that intelligence, that quiet, sly wit, as his and only his.

He still kicks Iain out into the rain, though.

They strip their shirts down to the waist and grab weapons from where they hang in the tent before riding the horses over to the practice areas. Iain sees that they're the only ones out there practising and glares at Harry, muttering *crazy person*.

Harry laughs and knocks him off his horse into a puddle.

Iain clambers back up onto Numbles, muddy and furious, and is about to ride hellbent at Harry when Harry shakes his head. Iain, to his credit, calms himself, and circles Harry, looking for an opening. Then the sparring *really* starts.

They keep at it until well after the bells toll Prime. The downpour never lets up, but somewhere around halfway through their session both of them forget about the rain and reach the zone where there's nothing else but the weapon in your hand and the opponent in front of you. By the end of it, they're both soaked to the bone, Iain's mêlée skills are passable, and Harry's ground down on mistakes in his own form until they're almost gone.

Harry calls things to a halt, sheathing his sword, when a bolt of lightning cracks through the sky. He reaches over, pulls Iain's helmet off, and ruffles his hair. Iain grins at him, then grabs his wrist and yanks him off Nomad and into the mud.

Harry laughs, and they walk back to the pavilion, their mud-splattered bodies getting not a few stares from squires and knights huddled at the entrances to their tents. By the time they've tied up the horses, the heat of sparring has worn off and a chill has begun to set into their bones. Nobody has dry wood. No fires are lit, except possibly in the grand marquees of the nobility.

Both boys strip down in front of their tent. They hang their shirts off the guy-ropes so the rain washes the mud off, and they do the best to rub the dirt off their skin. Harry has to avert his eyes, because Iain's body glistening with rain, his muscles heaving from their workout, is more than he can bear. He notes from the corner of his eyes that Iain looks away too, and feels a petty thrill of victory at that.

But there's nowhere to hide once they're in the tent.

And there's nothing to do but sit and wait out the rain. They finish off the last of the food from the journey, old bread and hard cheese, and then swaddle themselves up in their cloaks for a snooze. It's still early morning; the call of sleep is strong.

Harry wakes up a short while later to another rhythm underneath the beating of the rain on the tent canvas. He and Iain have homed in on each other in sleep again, and are lying back to back, sharing warmth.

And Iain is pleasuring himself, as silently as he can.

Harry grips the waxed canvas of the pallet, and squeezes his eyes shut. It's all he can hear now, the soft sound of Iain's hand over his cock. And he wants, God how he *wants*, to turn around and bracket Iain's hips with his thighs, and say *no, let me*, and pull Iain's broad back into his chest and reach down between his legs, and kiss his neck and run the fingers of his other hand over Iain's nipples, already hard in the cold air, and Iain would arch against him, making those pretty sounds that he only makes for Harry—

He swears under his breath and sticks his hand down his front. His own cock is thick, twitching, demanding attention.

Iain stills at the motion. Then, as Harry starts moving his own hand, the tension bleeds out of Iain's back and he resumes his own attentions. It feels as if there's nothing else in existence but them, their little pavilion with its jolly white and blue stripes marking the entirety of the world; the warm, solid weight of Iain against his back is his Adam, promised to him in Eden.

And if, as they both reach their climax, the fingers of their free hands entwine, that's nobody's business but their own.

Sir Morien sticks his head in later, around noon, and asks if they play chess. When the answer comes in the affirmative, he invites them to his and Sir Malachi's tent, where Sir Hugh is apparently engaged in fleecing them of their worldly possessions one game at a time. They pass a pleasant afternoon lounging in the Cornish brothers' pavilion with the other knights and squires of the West Country, playing games and telling stories. Iain and Harry prove to be a formidable team at the chessboard, the squire's daring balanced by the knight's careful strategising.

The rain tails off by supper, and the morning of the tournament's opening dawns sunny and clear. The ground is still soft but there's little other evidence of the previous day's downpour. Iain dresses Harry in his armour and the new, green-and-gold aketon that marks his mêlée team, then leads him out on Nomad to the main enclosure. As well as the destrier's reins, Iain carries an extra sword, shield and helmet. Though the mêlée is fought with blunted weapons, swords still break or get knocked out of hands. The stamped *bona fides* are tucked in Iain's belt, next to his dagger. Like Harry, Iain is in a mail hauberk. Over it, he wears Harry's old surcoat. It marks him out as Harry's squire. The sight of Iain, in his coat of arms – the Lyon star and hawks – thrills Harry more than it should.

They both halt, awestruck, as they reach the enclosure. Hastily constructed benches, their wood still green, have been built up all around the competition area. On and around them, over a thousand people are assembled to watch, with more streaming in by the moment. The far benches, across from the entrance, are the purview of the nobility. Harry can see Alys and her friends seated near Queen Philippa. Arundel and Montagu are nowhere to be seen among the spectators, which suggests they must be competing. Sir Gervase waves from a nearby bench and Harry grins, returning his salute. Sir Morien calls out too, wishing Harry *bon courage et bonne chance.*

Iain shows Harry's *bona fides* to the steward at the entrance – it's ceremonial, of course, but still required – and then Harry rides to the end of the enclosure where the other eleven Outsiders, in green, await him. Iain lines up behind him, along the fence with the other squires.

Harry squints against the morning sun. He can see the King, tall and fair and bearded, at the other end, with the Insiders. The short knight must be Arundel; he can hear Montagu and Rabbie; and there's Waldegrave, old Burstbelly himself. The Bohun brothers will be trouble, though.

On his side they have Sir Hugh and Sir Malachi, and their captain is Sir Robert Morley, who Harry remembers as the champion of the great tournament in Stepney. Harry gains an immediate respect for the Norfolk knight, who minces no words, giving them each an opponent according to their ability. Morley himself will encounter the King; they are the oldest of friends and sparring partners, so he can put on a good show without actually risking injury to the monarch.

The herald steps out and announces each knight, which is the knight's cue to ride out and salute the Queen before returning to their lines. A few knights then approach wives or lovers, receiving a scarf or ribbon to wear as a favour.

When the applause dies down, swords are drawn, stirrups are tested, and knees are tightened against their mounts.

Then, with a scream of trumpets and a crash of kettledrums, it begins.

Harry unhorses Arundel quickly. Once a knight is unhorsed, he is allowed to continue fighting on foot, but few do. The risk of being kicked or trodden by a couple of tons of war-horse is far too high. Arundel throws up his hands melodramatically and exits the enclosure, accepting a cup of beer from his squire. He doesn't look very upset. There is no clear goal to the mêlée, other than stay on your horse until the kettledrums crash again and the time is up, but it's a lot easier to do if your team has more knights left in the field than the other team.

Harry's next target is Waldegrave, but before he can make his way to the stout Yorkshire knight, he is caught up by Rabbie and his damned mace. The mêlée prohibits attacks with the point of the sword. That puts him at a disadvantage against a mace, where the best response is to block with the shield and then thrust with the sword. Sir Hugh rides to his aid, distracting Rabbie with a hard blow across his lower back.

Harry peels off to pursue Waldegrave, who is hanging around the outside of combat, shouting and waving his sword and trying to look busy. He doesn't even bother fighting Waldegrave; he just rams into the man, and unhorses him with a hard blow of his shield.

Then there's a flash out of the corner of his eye. Waldegrave's squire has ducked the fence and is running out into the field, not towards his master, but directly towards Harry. The boy grabs Harry's stirrup and shield and tries to yank him off his horse. Harry frowns and clouts the boy on his head with the pommel of his sword, and the squire goes down. He's yelling over his shoulder to Iain, *Drag the boy out before he's trampled*, when Rabbie's mace connects with his helmet.

Harry stays on his horse, barely. Nomad has the sense to get clear, biting Rabbie's destrier then taking Harry to the edge of the battle where he can regain his balance. Arundel's squire is dragging Waldegrave's boy out, so he's safe. Iain is glaring murderously at Rabbie, and being physically restrained by Tristan and Rolly. Harry shakes his head a last time to clear it, and turns Nomad back to the fray. He's going to knock Ufford on his arse if it's the last thing he does.

And, a split second before the trumpets sound, Harry succeeds.

The Outsiders are announced as the winners and take their bows before the Queen. Then Morley and the King ride out of the enclosure arm in arm and laughing, showing there's no hard feelings. Past them, the fools and gymnasts are already dancing onto the pitch, to distract the audience before the following mêlée. Some of the knights scheduled next are heading around the edge of the pitch, towards their ends of the enclosure. They nod to Harry as he passes on his way to the exit gate.

Tomorrow, Harry's group will begin jousting, and he will tilt individually against each member of the opposing team over the course of two days. Then, if he places highly enough, there's a final day of jousting against the top knights from the other mêlées.

Iain meets Harry at the enclosure's exit, his body tense and jaw tight as he reaches for Nomad's reins. The first words out of his mouth are, 'Why did that squire attack you?'

Harry looks down at him. There's a feral anger in Iain's pale eyes, and Harry worries his unspoken second question is *And can I kill him for it?*

Harry sighs. 'There's a rule, Iain. A squire can run into the mêlée. If he unseats a knight, he can keep their horse. But nobody actually *does* it. You have to go in unarmed and without a shield, at most in a mail shirt and a helmet.'

'Oh,' Iain says, a grin playing at the edges of his lips.

'Iain, *no*,' Harry says.

Harry comes second in the tournament overall, behind Morley. It's a far better result than he'd dreamed of when he glimpsed the hundreds of tents in the competitors' field.

Iain does well in the squires' competition. Rolly wins, which surprises nobody, but Iain makes it a close-run thing.

There's a celebratory dinner on the last day at a nearby castle, hosted by the King. Harry is startled to be invited, and even more taken aback when he begins to be known around the camp. Knights he's never met nod and smile to him as he goes by, and seek him out for conversation.

He manages to sit next to Alys at the dinner. She is like no other woman he has ever met: beautiful, yet down to earth. Courtly and appropriate, yet not simpering like so many of the other women. Harry begins to wonder what it would be like to have Alys in his life more permanently. If she'd ever be satisfied with his shabby little estate in an unfashionable corner of England.

He feels no pressure with Alys. There's not the panic, the feeling of drowning in a lake of bright fire, that he gets around Iain. He and Alys talk, and they dance and joke, and that's it. And this, in its own way, is right.

He asks her as the dancing begins why she spends so much time with him, and her brown eyes crinkle at the sides with merriment. 'You don't think I'm the envy of all the other ladies, having the attention of the tournament's young champion?'

'But Morley won,' Harry says.

'Morley always wins,' Alys groans. 'And he's *old*. And married.' Her eyes sidle to the edge of the hall, where Rabbie is kissing Alys's silly blonde friend up against a wall, his hands roaming up her front. 'Besides,' Alys says quietly, 'you respect me.'

'I would never do anything to besmirch your honour,' Harry says, his stomach churning at Rabbie's display.

Alys smiles a private little smile and takes his hands for another dance.

The next tournament is at Woodstock, with barely enough time to travel the fifty miles west from Dunstable. Harry is again with the Outsiders against the King, but this time Morley fights on the King's side and they have Waldegrave. It's a bad trade, and the mêlée is a brutal, uphill fight.

Iain climbs the enclosure fence and leaps from it onto Rabbie's back.

Harry swears, too engaged with Morley and Montagu to

save his squire from the inevitable pummelling into the dirt he'll receive.

Rabbie howls in fury, but Iain is silent, fighting hard and dirty, twisting Rabbie's right arm behind him until he is forced to drop his mace. It clatters to the ground. Rabbie fights dirty too, bashing his shield against Iain's left leg, trying to re-break it, but Iain just keeps hitting him, nasty low punches in the kidneys and head with a mailed fist, until Rabbie is unhorsed, slipping to the ground in a daze.

Iain gathers up the destrier's reins and cries something in Gaelic, whirling the horse and riding straight for Montagu.

Shit, Harry thinks. He breaks off from his fight and rides at Iain, using Nomad to barge Iain's horse and turn him.

'Now you leave,' Harry growls at Iain.

'No,' Iain says. 'I want to—'

'*Now you leave*,' Harry repeats, his tone hard and final. 'You unhorse someone, you capture the horse, you leave with it. *Rules*. Now get out of here while we can still profit from your distraction.'

'I could have taken Montagu,' Iain hisses as he reins the skittish horse.

'No you couldn't,' Harry hisses back.

When the trumpets sound, it's judged a tie between the two teams. Morley smiles warmly at Harry, nodding to him in appreciation of his fighting. The King claps him on the back, and tells him with a grin that his squire's flying attack is the best thing he's seen in ages.

'God's teeth, don't encourage him, Your Majesty,' Harry sighs, and the King roars with laughter.

Rabbie ransoms his horse back that afternoon via his squire,

Mark. Iain presses the money into Harry's hands, mumbling about Star's death.

That evening, Iain stays behind at the open-air tavern to pay their bill, and on the way back to the pavilion he's jumped by Mark and some of the other squires.

When Iain doesn't join Harry at the pavilion in good time, Harry comes looking for him.

When he hears the sounds of a beating being administered behind Montagu's marquee, Harry guesses exactly what is going on.

'Hey!' he cries, striding up to them, rattling his sword in its scabbard. There are six squires, four of them holding Iain down while Mark kicks the daylights out of him. Harry recognises Montagu's two squires, and Waldegrave's, and he thinks the red-haired boy might belong to Colin Crocker. They leap off Iain at the sound of Harry's sword, and he sits up, unsteady, blood dripping from his mouth.

'Coming to rescue your dog?' Mark spits.

'No,' Harry smiles. He clasps Iain's forearm and helps his squire up. 'Just bringing him his dagger. He left it in the pavilion.' Harry pulls the weapon from his belt and presses its hilt into Iain's hand.

Iain draws the dagger. A few of the squires step back, hearing the metal rasp of the blade leaving its sheath.

Harry turns to leave. 'After all,' he calls back, 'what's one dead Sassenach?'

'A good start,' Iain hisses, and leaps on Mark.

Iain limps back to the pavilion not long after, bloody but triumphant.

'Please tell me you didn't actually kill any of them?' Harry says, as Iain wipes the blade of his dagger.

'Nah,' Iain says. 'But Mark won't be walking much for a few months.' He grins, wild and free. 'Fucked up his left leg but good.'

Harry leans back against the central tent pole. 'Let's pretend I've given you a stern lecture about the morality of maiming other squires in back alleys.'

Iain salutes him, then flops back on the pallet. 'Let's pretend I'm very contrite.'

Harry snorts, and nudges him with his foot.

He thinks that's it for the night, but an hour later, Iain's voice cuts through the darkness. 'Harry?' he whispers.

'Mm?'

'Mark said Rabbie gets Dartington if I die.'

Harry exhales. 'That's not entirely true. Dartington has a lot of debts, and Montagu bought them up after you were captured, as a surety that I'd keep you prisoner. Montagu wants you alive, and both Rabbie and Mark know that.'

'Of course Montagu bloody does,' Iain mutters.

'You know you're with me in spite of Montagu, right?' Harry whispers. 'I'll do anything to keep Dartington together, but . . . if Montagu didn't have me under threat, there's not a single thing I would have done differently. Not one thing.'

'I know,' Iain says, reaching over to squeeze Harry's hand. 'I know.'

Harry's relentless practice jousting with Iain pays off, and he wins at Woodstock. Iain's injuries from Mark's beating slow him down in the *bohort*, and he places fifth, furious with himself. Rabbie appears at the joust with one of Montagu's squires, and Harry hears that Rabbie dismissed Mark because he has no use for a squire on crutches.

Arundel hosts the celebratory supper. Montagu scowls when he sees Harry seated on Arundel's left, between the Earl and Alys, but he can't reasonably object. Arundel senses the tension in the air, and keeps his voice big and his talk small.

At the end of the evening, Arundel passes a purse filled with coin under the table to Harry, whispering, 'Alys convinced me to make a sizeable wager on you. Thought you should have a share in it.'

Harry blinks at him in shock, at the weight of the purse, and tries to push it back.

Arundel shakes his head minutely in refusal and says, 'Keep winning, lad, it pisses the bastards off.' His eyes flick to Montagu and Ufford as he says it.

The next day, as they pack up, Harry gives the purse to Montagu. It pays off about a third of Dartington's debts. Montagu takes it, his eyes narrowing.

They narrow still further when Harry asks for a receipt of debts paid.

The final tourney of winter is in Newmarket, hard on the heels of Woodstock. It's a hundred miles back east, past Dunstable, past Cambridge. Montagu hosts it; he has a castle nearby. The contest takes place over Rabbie's birthday, and there is much ado among that faction of the King's intimates.

Iain has developed a teasing camaraderie with the three elderly heraldry clerks, mostly based on their ability to insult each other in Latin, so he gives Harry's *bona fides* for him.

Harry is painting his star-and-hawk coat of arms on a blank shield when Iain comes running back to the pavilion, waving the stamped paper and grinning ear to ear.

'Harry, you're on the King's team!' he gasps, breathless.

Harry drops the paintbrush. 'What?!'

Iain nods. 'Lord Morris said!' He counts off on his fingers. 'Apparently it's you and Rabbie and Morley and Sir Hugh and the King, of course, and the Bohuns, and Montagu, and Crocker, and Malachi and Morien, and somebody else. And Arundel's captaining the other team. Percy is the only name I recognise there.'

Harry sighs. 'Montagu is setting this up. He wants a win.'

'Fuck,' Iain groans, his smile disappearing as he understands what's been done. He sits down next to Harry. 'He wants someone to win other than you. He's put you on a weighted team so you can't shine.'

So much for a good end to the winter season, Harry thinks.

Newmarket makes Harry uncomfortable. Everybody seems to be his friend now, calling out 'Sir Harry!' as he passes. It's nice, of course, being in the orbit of the King. But he can't help feeling that none of this is real, that it will vanish as easily and suddenly as it's appeared. In a camp of thousands calling his name, there is only one person he trusts.

And Alys.

Maybe Alys too.

The mêlée is dull. Arundel's team fights valiantly, but they're no match for the power and experience of the King's men. Rabbie is ruthless, picking off easy targets one after another, and to nobody's surprise he comes out of the group battle with the highest score.

Harry is so wound up afterwards that he drags Iain off to the practice field. They spar all afternoon, until the two of them can barely stand. When they hear the Vespers bells, he sends Iain back with his armour to clean it for the next day's jousts. Before following his squire home, he stops to dunk his head in the nearest horse trough. It's mid-February, but God seems to have blessed the Newmarket tournament with unseasonably warm weather. And Iain is an increasingly strenuous challenge to his swordfighting abilities.

Harry shuts his eyes and leans against the fence for a moment. *Iain.* His frustration, he admits to himself, isn't just about the shoddy mêlée. It's Iain. It's always Iain. The distance between them makes Harry's skin feel the wrong size for his body. He feels misshapen, out of sorts, and nothing can put him right again except his squire's arms around him.

Harry shakes his head. The rational part of his brain screams that they can't do this. That he has *duties*. But his heart whispers, *find a way*.

Sir Colin Crocker falls into step next to him on the way back to the pavilions, starting up some idle chatter about the weather. All the tension Harry had worked out of his body sparring with Iain seeps right back in again. He doesn't like Crocker; he's second of Montagu's bullies behind Rabbie. Nothing good can come of his attention.

His instincts prove right as they reach a bend in the path, secluded by a few trees. 'Word to the wise,' Crocker whispers. 'Rabbie's going to win this tournament.'

'He'll have to get a lot better at jousting first,' says Harry.

'Nah,' sneers Crocker. 'He'll do just fine as he is. What will happen is, you're going to get a lot worse, or else Rabbie's cousin the Bishop will hear about what you get up to with that squire of yours. Be a shame, to see a decorated knight hanging in Exeter Market like a common criminal.'

Harry is sure he's gone completely pale, but he digs his nails into his palms and tries to remain as emotionless as possible.

Crocker pats him condescendingly on the shoulder. 'You haven't been with Montagu long enough, pup. You think the base of his power is money? No. It's spies.'

When Crocker leaves, Harry waits five minutes, then throws up behind a tree.

In the end, Harry doesn't have to make a choice. It's taken out of his hands.

For two days he jousts through the twelve members of the Outsiders, and his insomnia and moral agonies manifest themselves in little more than dark circles under his eyes and monosyllabic replies.

He doesn't tell Iain.

There's no point. Iain would do something stupid, like try to kill Rabbie in his sleep.

(It's tempting to tell Iain.)

The third day of jousting, it's the top six knights riding against each other. Harry's up against Crocker first. And Crocker cheats.

Harry feels the illegal iron tip of the lance slide off his shield and pierce his chest, feels his rib snap, and then he's on the ground.

Somebody's screaming.

He jerks back into consciousness to see, not grey Newmarket sky, but the jolly blue-and-white striped canvas of his pavilion. Iain's hands are on his cheeks and Iain's face is above his and Harry hears, '—don't die, you son of a whore, you can't die, God's blood, stay with me—' and outside a herald is shouting, 'Can he continue to compete, yes or no?' and Harry's shaking his head no and Iain's yelling, 'Will you please shut up so I can find out,' and then Harry mumbles, 'Don't talk about my mother like that,' and then darkness closes in on him once more.

When Harry next wakes up, his armour is off, his arms and legs are tied, and he's gagged. He tries to sit up but the pain in his ribs nearly makes him black out again.

He's still in his pavilion, though. And his chest wound has been carefully bandaged.

Iain isn't there.

It's . . . very strange.

Then it gets stranger.

Harry sees himself walk into the tent. His armour, his shield, his helmet, his sword.

He wonders briefly if this is what death is.

And then he thinks, not of his family, or of Dartington, but that he didn't do a very good job painting the star on his shield. It's lopsided. He's going to greet Saint Peter with a badly painted shield. That's embarrassing.

The shield is dumped unceremoniously on the ground.

The knight that's him but not him takes his helmet off.

Dark hair falls over pale eyes.

Iain.

'Please, Harry, tell me you can stand up,' he says.

Harry grumbles against his gag.

'Shit, that, yes,' Iain says, shedding armour and crouching

down to untie Harry's gag. 'Look, I hate to say this, but you have to get all this nonsense on right now and present yourself in front of the King.'

Harry frowns. 'Iain,' he says, a feeling of dread rising in his stomach. 'What did you do?'

'Um,' Iain grins, sitting back on his haunches and blushing. 'I won you the tournament, Harry. Knocked Rabbie clean off his mount. He landed in a pile of horseshit, too. It was *glorious*. Morley got me, but you were enough lances ahead that we still won.'

'Oh, Iain, *no*,' Harry groans, shaking his hands free of the ropes. 'Do you have any idea how against the rules that is?'

'Quite,' growls Iain, opening his hand. 'As is *this*.'

In his palm is a bloody lance-point of sharpened iron. There are bits of the plaster used to disguise it still stuck around the join between it and the splintered wood of the lance-shaft.

The sight of it makes Harry furious. All the fear and pain of the past three days is replaced by pure, burning anger. 'Well, come on,' Harry says. 'Get my armour on me. The King's waiting.'

Iain grins his savage grin.

The crowd erupts when Harry is led out on Nomad by Iain. The herald makes much of him, overcoming grave injury to ride to victory, and so forth. They don't notice that he can barely stay on his horse, or perhaps they do, and it sells the heroic legend a little bit more. So does the surcoat Iain is wearing, its white stained red with Harry's blood.

Harry looks over the benches, at all the people on their feet applauding and shouting his name, and feels nothing. At the other knights, some cheering him, some sullen and envious.

Nothing. He bows as best he can to the Queen, wincing in pain, and shifts his helmet to his shield arm so he can accept the King's kiss on his cheeks.

When the King puts his arm out to steady him, Harry tucks the broken lance-point into Edward's hand. The King feels it, and his eyes widen minutely in shock, his jaw tightening in anger.

He returns it to Harry's hand, under the guise of a friendly clasp of arms.

Harry inclines his head in deference, and then signals to Iain to lead him back to the pavilion.

The King and Queen leave Newmarket unexpectedly, before Montagu's celebratory supper. It's passed off as *important state business, so sorry*, but Harry knows it for what it is: a deliberate slight.

If it gets back to Montagu how and why that slight occurred, Harry will be in a worse situation than he already is. He needs allies. So in the scrum at the beginning of the meal, as each knight and noble looks for their table, he brushes past the Earl of Arundel and whispers, 'I have developed an interest in French politics.'

He doesn't look at the Earl, or turn around, as he walks by. He has learned the hard way that there are spies everywhere.

When Alys dances with him later, she mentions how she has heard that the bridle paths in Newmarket are delightful.

Second only, apparently, to the ones outside Paris.

Harry proposes a picnic.

She accepts, then suggests he dance with some of the other

ladies of court, as it's not fair of her to monopolise the attentions of their handsome young champion.

Eventually, the men of Montagu's retinue retire to the Baron's bedchamber to drink. Harry wants to refuse, but knows he cannot. He must continue his act as the simple provincial knight a little longer: their pawn; their fool.

Openly opposing Montagu at this time would mean death for him and ruin for Dartington. And God only knows what would happen to Iain. *He would be free*, something within Harry whispers, even as another part of him pictures Iain starving to death in some grim tower of Montagu's, subject to the beatings at will of men like Rabbie Ufford and Colin Crocker.

Speaking of Rabbie: he's drunk.

He is deep in his cups and furious, and Harry overhears him whining like a spoilt child to Montagu out by the privies about how it was his birthday and he should have won the tournament.

There's the unmistakeable sound of a slap, and Montagu's voice, low: 'The King, unfortunately, has decided he likes Lyon, so we're stuck with him. Focus on the goal, Rabbie. What is one inconsequential tournament when we can have *France*? The dukedoms of Burgundy. Normandy. Untold wealth. The French barons hate Philip of Valois. They'll side with us, and we have the pivot point to drive Edward across the Channel. Don't cause trouble now, Rabbie.'

Rabbie mutters again about fairness, and Harry hears another slap. Harry wonders idly if it was Rabbie's other cheek this time, or the same one.

'And don't drink so much. Go home,' Montagu says.

Harry ducks behind a buttress as the two of them pass back into the hall.

When Harry returns to Montagu's bedchamber, the crowd of knights and nobles is even more raucous than when he left. There are no more tournaments until May, so tonight they can let themselves go to the twin vices of drink and dice games.

Waldegrave looks up and opens his mouth as Harry makes his way over. Thomas Howland tries to shush him, but Waldegrave bats him away and says in his high, screeching voice, 'What I want to know is if Lyon is fucking that squire of his because, God's breath, that boy's pretty.'

'No,' Harry splutters, angry and incredulous.

'Pity,' Waldegrave shrugs. 'That's what they're there for. Of course, pages are even better, but I'd make an exception for that boy of Lyon's.'

Harry thinks of Waldegrave's squire running out into the mêlée, of the boy's blind affection for such a repulsive man, and feels sick.

'*That* savage?' one of the other knights says, snatching the jug of brandy out of Waldegrave's hand. He was one of the twelve who rode to Scotland, Guy d'Audley, a big olive-skinned man with a scarred cheek. 'You know he's the one we captured, right? Be worried he'd slit my throat in my sleep. Somewhat surprised he hasn't cut Harry's.'

Montagu watches them all with hooded eyes, over a cup of small beer.

'Oh no,' Waldegrave says, leaning back and patting his expansive stomach. 'I bet he's the kind that would beg for it. Those tough-acting ones always are. Spreading his cheeks, crying out to be filled up . . . with that long hair and fine features, he's halfway to being a woman anyway.'

Colin Crocker shakes his head and snickers. 'If that's how your Yorkshire women are built, Waldegrave, no wonder you go for the pages.'

Waldegrave gestures with one of his little hands. 'Still. Imagine bending that over a table . . . How tight he'd be. Bet he's *loud* too.' He turns to Harry and licks his lips. 'What's *fuck me harder* in Scots?'

Harry stands up so sharply that the bench he's sitting on clatters onto its side. His wound sends hot bolts of pain throughout his body but he clenches his jaw, not letting it show in his face. He's learned from the best.

'Yes?' Montagu says, raising an eyebrow.

'If you touch my squire,' Harry says to Waldegrave, low and threatening, 'the only moaning and crying to be heard will be your own, as he rips your guts out of your belly with his bare hands and then chokes you to death with them.' He throws his cup onto the ground. 'Good night, *gentlemen*,' he says as he leaves.

Harry hears Colin Crocker's mocking kissing noises and the laughter and whistles of Montagu's men as he storms off, but he doesn't care. He stalks out of the castle into the night, not caring where he ends up, until he finds himself quite alone in the middle of a copse, as far as he can tell in the opposite direction from the tournament fields.

He sinks down against a birch tree and lets the tears come, an ugly tangle of rage and frustration and fear.

And then he reaches down and presses against his shame.

Because that was the worst part of listening to Waldegrave's filth.

It made him hard.

Images of Iain come into his mind, unbidden and unwelcome. Iain in the rain, bare-chested, swinging the practice broadsword. Iain in Harry's armour, the knight's belt low on his hips. Iain in the tack room at Dartington, leaning against the saddle, legs spread in invitation. Iain on his knees, attaching the straps of Harry's chausses before a tournament, looking up at him, those plush lips parted in question.

Harry pulls his straining dick out of his breeches and strokes himself, imagining Iain's hands moving from the leather straps at his thigh to his cock, freeing it from the linen folds of his braies and tilting his head as he gazes up at Harry the same way he does when attaching Harry's armour, *Is this right? Is this what I do next?* And then taking Harry in his mouth, those bowed lips that could go from savage to spoilt over the course of a breath now stretched over Harry's cock, taking it in all the way, fast and sloppy as Iain comes off him and moans and begs Harry to fuck him, and Harry says they can't, they're in the pavilion and due out in a few minutes, and anyone could hear, but he fucks his release into Iain's mouth and Iain's so eager, letting himself be used, savage for everyone except his Harry, Harry who loves him—

He comes shatteringly hard, so hard he gasps as pain floods his chest from the lance wound, so hard he's dizzy with it. And then he sits there and lets the hot tears run down his cheeks as his dick softens and the seed on his hands cools into an unpleasant, sticky mess.

Because *he loves Iain.*

His strong, brave, wild Iain, who charms the bitchy old heraldry clerks with Latin insults and has Annie wrapped around his little finger and who knocked Rabbie Ufford into a pile of horseshit because winning a tournament mattered to Harry.

He knows now the word for the soaring feeling he gets in his chest every time he looks at his squire. He knows now the name of the song his body sings when he touches his friend.

It is love.

And it is impossible.

He is brought back to the present by a rustle of leaves. For a lucky man, it would be a fieldmouse or a squirrel, going about its nocturnal business.

But Harry is not a lucky man.

Montagu steps out of the shadows in front of him. 'Well,' says the Baron, cocking an eyebrow at Harry's disarray, 'I see he managed to seduce you.'

Harry shoves his dick back in his breeches and stands, wiping his hand on the tree trunk. 'I like to think it was mutual,' he says.

Montagu snorts in amusement. '*Harry*. He's from a family that have been playing games with the fates of nations since both our forefathers were simple Norman spear-chuckers. Honestly, my only regret in this whole endeavour is I'll never get to match up directly against him, see what he could do if given some power.' He folds his arms. 'So no, Harry. You were seduced. And the sooner you realise how vastly outclassed you are and how the only way out is to keep your head down and do what you're told, the better it will go for you.'

Harry's mouth splits into an emotionless grin. 'See, you

overstepped there. I know you're lying now. Because, because you don't know him. You just think you do.'

'And how often do you lie, Harry? To your priest? To the boy? To the de Morton girl, who thinks she has your love? What a pretty web of deceit you are spinning,' Montagu smiles. His tone drops, growing serious. 'Here's the thing, Harry. I don't lie. There's no point in it. I just present the truth from the right angle. And now I'll give it to you: to ally yourself with that boy is to put yourself on the wrong side of history. There is no power in Europe that can save him from his fate, and when he goes down, everyone he touches will go down with him. Think on that, *Sir Harry*, and good night.'

Montagu salutes him, and strides off into the darkness.

Harry trudges back to the tourney fields in devastated silence. Iain is already asleep, sprawled on his back over half of the pallet. Harry looks at him and thinks of the energy he has left, and what fights he must conserve it for. And he snuggles into Iain, his head on the man's shoulder, his arm across Iain's chest.

Iain mumbles sleepily and opens an eye.

'I'll tell you tomorrow,' Harry snuffles, pulling him closer.

Iain opens his other eye and tips Harry's chin up with his fingers, examining his puffy, red eyes, the tracks of dried tears. 'Mm,' he says. 'But you have to sleep on your back, or you'll open that wound up again.'

'As you wish,' Harry says, as Iain's arms come around him.

Harry meets Alys and her chaperone after breakfast the next morning, all of them mounted up on their palfreys. Alys is on a chestnut horse, while her chaperone, an elegant dark-skinned girl in a yellow dress, follows on a fine black mare.

'This is the Lady Fatima,' Alys says. 'Her father is an Egyptian nobleman who is very interested in selling his cotton to the English, and Lord Arundel is keen to help. So he sent his youngest daughter to build ties with us barbarians.'

'And how do you find us?' Harry asks.

'It's too wet, too cold, you don't bathe enough and your food is horribly bland,' the woman smiles. 'Yet I consider myself lucky. My older sister went to Moscow.'

'The poor thing, I still think we should mount a rescue,' Alys says. Then she winks at Harry. 'Come along, I've picked out the perfect route.'

They ride in silence along winding, elm-lined cinder trails away from the tourney grounds and into swathes of flat farmland separated by the occasional copse of oak and ash. Fatima lags close enough behind to keep an eye on them, but far enough that she is plausibly out of earshot.

'So,' Alys says eventually, 'I hear you have a sudden interest in international affairs. What's brought that on?'

Harry rubs the rough leather of Libby's reins with his thumbs. 'I made rather an enemy of Rabbie Ufford this week. It made me realise that I can't win, the way I'm going about this.' He looks over at Alys, suddenly nervous. 'Give me a broadsword and I have all the confidence in the world. But this sort of fighting . . . spies and influence and secrets . . . I'm at sea, Alys. Completely at sea.' He shuts his eyes. 'Rabbie wanted me to throw the tournament.'

'But you didn't,' Alys says.

'We didn't,' Harry corrects.

Alys arches one of her immaculate dark eyebrows. '*We.*'

Harry exhales. 'I was . . . more injured than anyone knew

when I fell during the joust. Crocker used a tipped lance, covered in plaster and painted to look legal. My squire . . . took matters into his own hands. That wasn't me, in the final tilts. It was *him*.'

'Hm,' Alys says, her lips turning down in mild surprise. 'He's . . . an impressive specimen.'

'He is,' Harry says, a small, private smile threatening to overtake his carefully schooled expression. 'I'm afraid for him.'

Alys snorts. 'Rabbie Ufford is so stupid, you don't need to defeat him, Harry. You just need to wait patiently for him to defeat himself.'

'If Rabbie were our only problem, we would indeed be fortunate,' Harry whispers.

'I think we should ride this way,' Alys says, turning down a side trail that winds, serpentine, to the top of a low ridge overlooking a lovely, small castle.

Harry follows. And as he watches Alys sway gently with the motion of her horse, he knows that his epiphany last night remains true in the harsh light of day. It wasn't, as some tiny shred of him had hoped, a product of drink and exhaustion and fevered late-night desperation.

He adores Alys. She's beautiful. She dresses immaculately. She's witty, she rides as bold as a man, she's smart, and she's both confident and modest. She is everything he should want physically.

And yet . . . he does not.

If he takes his fantasy by the birch tree and tries to imagine it with Alys, it's *wrong* somehow. There's nothing but wet ash inside him, whereas with Iain, there is a wildfire.

He still wants to laugh with Alys at dinner, and climb trees with her, and dance, and watch her raise children, and she can take care of all the damn politics and he can manage the estate and fight . . .

. . . and love Iain.

'Ready for your first lesson?' Alys asks, shaking him out of his reverie as they approach a copse at the top of the ridge.

'Of course, but I warn you, I'm a bad student,' Harry says.

'Oh, this one is easy,' Alys replies, sphinx-like. 'You already know all the answers.' Then she stops her horse and points down at the tidy little castle below them. 'Do you see the woman there, by the camellias? Do you know who she is?'

Harry looks. In a walled garden, a middle-aged woman stands at a bush heavy with pink flowers. She is fair-haired and curvy, and richly dressed. Two handmaidens wait behind her. The woman isn't familiar, Harry thinks. But then his eyes go up to the banner flying from the castle: lilies and lions, quartered.

Lilies for France, and lions for England.

He sucks in a breath. 'Isabella,' he says. 'The Queen Mother.'

Alys says nothing else, and Harry watches the woman, the queen who invaded her adopted country and toppled her own husband before she herself was brought low by her son, as she dodders about in rural exile. She clips an early flower. It falls to her feet, and a handmaiden scrambles to pick it up and place it in her basket. As she progresses to the next clump of bushes, a scarf slips from her hand, and one of her attendants snatches it up before it touches the ground. The maid then runs around in front of the Queen Mother and kneels, proffering its return. When the maid stands, her skirts are stained from the dewy ground.

Not once does Isabella look at the women, or address them.

They are simply the furniture of her life, like a bench, or a tapestry.

'I am fond of her, in a way,' sighs Alys. 'She was a very ambitious woman, daughter of a strong king and married off to a weak one, who ignored her. With a better match, and a little more art to her ways, she could have united her two countries.' She darts a mischievous look at Harry, through her lashes. 'Do you want to hear my favourite story about her?'

'I always want to hear your stories,' Harry says warmly.

'Flatterer,' Alys snorts. 'This one might change your mind. It takes place when Isabella was seventeen. Already married to Edward of Carnarvon for five years. And she had a son. An heir, potentially to two kingdoms.'

'Our Edward,' Harry supplies. 'Edward of Windsor. The King.'

'Indeed,' Alys continues. 'And one day fate handed her an easy way to undermine her own dynasty back in France, the Capets. It started when she made her sisters-in-law, the wives of two of her younger brothers, some needlework purses one Christmas. She was surprised to see those purses again in the spring, carried by two handsome young Norman knights. So she waited, and organised her spies, until she learned that the sisters and the knights were planning to meet in secret at the Tour de Nesle, a discreet little keep across the Seine from Paris's royal palace. Isabella's men swooped in and had them all revealed as adulteresses. See, Isabella wanted both France and England for her son, so she needed to remove the competition. The women were cast out and those two brothers, Kings of France one after the other, produced no viable heirs.'

'That . . .' Harry begins. He hasn't the words. 'That is the most vicious, cold-blooded thing I've ever heard. To her own *family*.'

'Ah, but that's not the best of it,' Alys continues, as they watch Dowager Queen Isabella potter about her flower garden. 'Her sisters-in-law were not even the point of her scheme. They were merely collateral damage.'

'Who was Isabella's target?' Harry asks.

'Her older sister, Philip's first child,' Alys says. 'The favourite. Betrothed to the Holy Roman Emperor, but in love, they say, with a Scottish lord. He was also at the Tour de Nesle that fateful night. The scandal was enough for His Imperial Majesty to break off the betrothal. Philip was *furious*. He did everything but disinherit her. Within the letter of the law, she was still legally a princess of France, but in spirit? She was cut off. Financially. Socially. She had been as headstrong and wilful as her father, and he ruined her for it.'

'My God,' Harry mutters. 'What a father to have.'

'I'm not sure it's possible to be a good father and a great king at the same time,' Alys says, nudging her horse into a walk. The chestnut palfrey follows the trail as it loops downwards, away from the little castle, towards Newmarket again. 'Philip chose greatness. For himself; for France.' She looks up at Harry, her keenly intelligent eyes searching out his blue ones. 'My own father was ambassador to the French court for a while, you know, and met Philip the Fair. He was aptly nicknamed. Tall, dark hair, pale eyes. Cleft chin. Ridiculously handsome. A sort of fairy-tale image of a king.' Alys tilts her head, as if making a very important point. 'And his eldest daughter took after him.'

Harry has a horrible, sinking feeling in his stomach. He manages to choke out, 'What happened to her?'

Alys smiles. 'She vanished. Probably for the best. Think what would have happened if she had married and produced an heir. The boy would have a stronger claim to the throne of France than either King Edward or Philip of Valois. Imagine the trouble, my God.'

'What was her name, Alys?' Harry says. He feels nauseous, his entire body wracked with pins and needles.

'Hm?' Alys says, all innocence.

'The daughter,' Harry grits out. 'The favourite.'

'Didn't think you were interested in French royal politics,' Alys hums, patting her horse.

'*Alys*,' Harry growls.

'You know her name, Harry,' Alys admonishes.

He closes his eyes and breathes the name that a scared boy with a broken leg whispered to him on a dark night months ago: 'Marguerite.'

'Yes. See? You *do* know the answers. Most people presume her dead by now, of course,' Alys says.

'She is. Dead,' Harry stutters. 'She died. Last year.'

'What a shame,' Alys says. 'I would have liked to meet her. She lived life on her terms and hers alone. Few have the courage to do that.'

'I . . . I have to go, Alys,' Harry says.

By the time Harry reaches the tournament fields, he's managed to calm himself, slowing from the heedless gallop with which he'd abandoned Alys and Lady Fatima to a safer, more appropriate walk. He slips off Libby's back and leads her through the camping area. With the winter jousting season over and the King gone, some knights are taking down their pavilions, eager to start the ride home. Others are resting, sleeping off hangovers, taking pleasure in *not* having to be hustling on to the next town, the next tourney. Harry barely responds to all the new friends calling his name as he ties up Libby by his pavilion. Their shouted bonhomie is just so much background noise to the beating of his heart, the rhythm of *it can't be true, it can't be true* that overwhelms all else.

Iain is shovelling horse manure.

His shirt's down at his hips and he's dirty, barefoot and stunningly beautiful. He's singing softly to himself in French as he fills up a large bucket and prepares to carry it to the waste pile at the corner of the field.

Harry pictures Isabella, and how her servant lunged to pick up the Queen's scarf before it could touch the unclean ground.

Before he can think about it, he has a hand on Iain's arm and is relieving him of the stinking bucket.

'I'll do that for you,' Harry says. 'You don't have to.'

Iain's brow furrows. 'Why? It's my job.' He reaches for the bucket, taking it back. 'Besides, you're wearing your nice clothes and it's *also* my job to wash them.'

'No. It's— you shouldn't,' Harry stutters. 'I'll wash them from now on.' He grabs for the bucket again. 'Give me that. It's beneath—'

Iain's eyes widen in realisation, then a look of misery comes over his face. 'Harry . . .' he sighs, putting down the bucket.

'I'm sorry,' Harry says.

Iain looks up, his eyes icy. 'Who?'

Harry groans. 'Alys. I think Arundel worked it out. They didn't tell me, so much as they gave me the ability to work it out for myself. God's blood, Iain, I . . .' He starts to sink down on one knee.

Iain looks around, panicked, and grabs Harry's arm, pulling him up. 'No, Harry. Get up. Harry, *please*. People are staring.' He hauls Harry back on his feet then pulls him close, whispering in his ear. 'You've stuck your dick in me. The only reason you should be on your knees in front of me is if we're having sex. Just . . . ignore it, I beg you. Nothing's changed. *Nothing*.'

'But . . . why are you my squire?' Harry says. 'You could have run away, at Plymouth. Got a boat across the Channel. You're cleaning horseshit, when you could . . .' Harry gestures to the southeast, towards France.

Iain tilts his head and looks at Harry in profound annoyance. Then he sighs and gives Harry a shove. 'If you're too stupid to understand why, there's no point in my telling you.' Then he picks up the bucket again. 'I'm going to dump our horseshit on the big manure mountain now, and when I come back, please have made up your mind whether you want to leave this afternoon, or tomorrow morning.'

He stomps off, muttering to himself in Gaelic.

'Iain—' Harry says.

He just grunts and makes a rude gesture at Harry, shit-pail clanging against his leg as he walks.

There's such a press of people on the roads leaving the tournament that Harry decides to postpone their departure until the following day. The once vast and prosperous pavilion city is now a much diminished settlement, with only a score of tents left up. Iain disappears with Kit's hunting bow and returns, bathed and bearing two fat trout, which they cook over a campfire.

Harry says little, and Iain as ever is content in silence.

Internally, though, Harry is overwhelmed by an avalanche of worry. As soon as he finds his footing on one subject, the floor is yanked from under him and there is suddenly further to fall, more to figure out. It was bad enough realising he is in love with his squire. In deciding that, amidst this world of murder, deceit and betrayal, he would no longer flagellate himself for a sin based in love.

But no. It can get worse.

He's in love with a *prince*, a person who, when the natural order of things snaps back into place (which it will, it always does), will be so far above his station he might as well exist on the moon.

If Harry doesn't foil Montagu's plan, something terrible will happen to Iain, he's sure of it. If he *does* foil Montagu's plan, Iain will ascend back to his royal status. Whatever choice Harry makes, he'll lose Iain. As much as he wants to believe the heartfelt words of the boy who got on one knee and pledged himself to Harry at Christmas, he knows that boy will grow up, and inherit a world that is so much bigger than Dartington.

Harry is twitchy and restless that night. About an hour after they've supposedly settled down to sleep, Iain decides he's had enough. He sighs operatically and climbs on top of Harry, pinning him down everywhere but his chest, where he carefully avoids putting weight on Harry's wounded ribs.

'Stop it,' Iain grumbles.

'I can't,' Harry says. 'God's teeth, you're a *prince*.'

Iain groans and flops down next to him. 'Yes. Isabella's my aunt, Edward's my cousin. No, none of them have ever met me; if the French allowed the monarchy to pass down the female side I'd be first in line to be king, but they don't, so I'm not. Instead I'm penniless, landless and the squire to a great Sassenach idiot who pays too much attention to heraldic bullshit.'

Then Iain gasps and sticks his face in Harry's, grinning. 'Harry. Can you imagine? Lord Morris would brick himself. I show up and give him my full lineage; find *that* in your book, Lord Magnus. The poor old bat would keel over.'

Harry snorts. 'Iain, don't abuse the heraldry clerks. Without them, English knighthood would fall apart.'

'The first step in my war of vengeance,' Iain hisses. 'Actually, no,' he adds, in a normal tone of voice. 'They're exempt from vengeance, for reasons of decent Latin.'

'His wrath was mighty, but swerved for epigrams,' Harry snorts.

'Exactly,' Iain says.

Harry shakes his head and fidgets.

'What *now*?' Iain groans.

'I . . . have had a lot of sex with a member of the French royal family,' Harry says.

'I wouldn't say a *lot* of sex,' grumbles Iain. 'More like *not enough*.' He grins, pressing his groin into Harry's. 'This member likes your member awfully much.'

'I love you,' Harry says.

Iain freezes at that, his eyes widening.

Harry begins to sob. 'I loved you before and I love you now and I'm going to lose you.'

'Wait, what?' Iain says. 'Where did that come from? I'm not going anywhere, Harry.' He sits back on Harry's thighs and starts rubbing his hands up and down Harry's sides, as if calming a spooked horse.

Harry presses into the touch, desperate. 'I should have told you earlier. I was so scared. Montagu . . . Montagu knows about us.' Harry sighs. 'I feel like the world is constantly stacking odds against us.'

'I don't care. We'll beat them,' Iain says, pressing his lips to Harry's forehead, at the furrows of stress there. 'I *choose* to be here with you, Harry. If it comes out publicly who I am, then I will have to go away for a while to take care of some things, but *listen to me*.' He takes Harry's face in his hands and holds him there, gazing into his eyes, deadly serious. 'I will always come back to you. *Always*. Even if I have to drag myself out of the grave to do it.'

Harry squeezes his eyes shut. 'Don't joke about that.'

'I know,' Iain breathes, as he leans his forehead against Harry's. 'Ssh. Next month I'll be eighteen. And after that we'll start planting the bean fields, and worrying about the lambing. Then there's the tournament in Burstwick. I'll be with you, if you'll have me.'

Harry shakes his head. 'You're ridiculous. Of course I'll have you. You're all I want. But you could have so much *more*, Iain.'

'You stood by me when I had nothing,' Iain says. Then he smirks. 'Besides, my side of the family has a glorious tradition of doing stupid things for love.'

'Only a prince would have the gall to throw everything away for another man,' Harry says.

'Or a pig-boy,' Iain replies. 'Wat nearly threw down his life for Peter.'

'But those in the middle,' Harry says, feeling tears begin to prick at his eyes again, 'we *can't*. We're stuck with halls and responsibilities, and the need for heirs . . .'

Iain rolls onto his back and snuggles in close to Harry. 'I don't have an answer. I don't know what to do.' His voice, when he next speaks, is rough with emotion. 'I never wanted to assert my claim to France, but I'd do it, if it meant we could be together.' He snorts. 'King of a country I don't even remember. What a joke.'

'You're already king of a country,' Harry says, tracing his finger down Iain's face, those glorious cheekbones, that strong jaw. 'A very small one, comprising a simple country knight, and his sword, and his heart.'

'Mm,' Iain says, leaning forwards to kiss Harry. 'My lands are of surpassing beauty,' he murmurs, running his fingers appreciatively down Harry's body. His nails scratch through Harry's pubic hair. 'The fields golden, and the monuments—' his hand circles Harry's soft cock, which begins to plump under his touch— 'impressive.'

Harry presses his eyes shut, and whispers, '*Please*.'

'And when I am away from my country, which I love with all my heart,' Iain says, throwing his leg over Harry so he can straddle him, 'I am diminished, and sour, and must content myself with the work of mine own hands, which are cold comfort, compared to the warm embrace of my home.'

NINE

February–July 1334: Empire of the Senses

Harry shivers as Iain runs strong, rough hands up his chest. He shuts his eyes, giving in to the sensation. The night is silent but for the occasional low call of an owl, and the crackle-and-pop of campfires by the few remaining pavilions. But for Harry there is no world outside the striped canvas of their little tent, nobody exists except him and the man above him, straddling his thighs.

Iain's lips ghost along his jaw, from chin to earlobe, and then he whispers, 'Don't suppose you brought that oil?'

Harry shakes his head. 'I wasn't . . . I thought I could . . .' Then he opens his eyes and looks up at Iain. 'I was an idiot who thought ignoring love could make it go away.'

Iain bites his neck, sending a jolt of pleasure straight down to Harry's groin. '*My* idiot,' Iain growls. 'Crazy person befriending boys in cages.'

Then Iain's weight is off Harry's legs. Harry can hear him rustling in one of their travelling bags, hung from the tent's wooden frame to keep dry. He wishes it were daylight, or they still had more than the small night-lamp lit, as even what he can see in the dark of Iain's back and thighs is breathtaking.

Iain makes a small, happy noise in his throat and then suddenly he's straddling Harry again, reaching for his right hand. 'Luckily, I am a well-prepared squire and stable-hand, and brought oil for the tack.' There's the quiet pop of a cork unstoppered, and then Harry feels a cool wetness on his fingers, and the sharp, neutral smell of the liquid. He can hear the smile in Iain's voice. 'Among other things.'

Harry shudders, his desire vibrating through him like a plucked lute string. His fingers ghost up Iain's inner thigh, over his balls, soft and heavy, and then around his cock, feeling it twitch and stiffen in his grip. Iain gasps, pushing his hips forwards slightly, trying to get Harry to begin fingering him. But Harry ignores him, and continues stroking him to hardness. He doesn't even need to touch himself. The quiet noises coming out of Iain's mouth, half impatient grumbles and half involuntary little whimpers and moans, already have Harry hard and leaking.

Finally Iain grabs Harry's hand and places it where he wants it: considerably further back.

Harry huffs out a fond, amused laugh and takes the oil bottle out of Iain's hand. He slicks his fingers up more. And then he holds them there. Close enough so Iain can feel the warmth, the proximity of them against his hole. But not quite touching. Not yet.

When Iain's breath becomes a desperate little whine, when his leg muscles start to quiver, Harry finally touches him. Iain arches back, his body going taut. It's as if a dam has been broken. A tide of whispered profanity and adoration tumbles out of his mouth as his body thrusts down on Harry's fingers, still teasingly circling his hole.

'You're only prolonging the wait for yourself, too,' Iain hisses, as Harry presses the tip of a finger in, then withdraws it again.

Then something in Iain changes, that savage dark thing uncoiling in a subtle shift of body posture and a smirk that Harry can't see but would bet his life is there. It's matched by something primal that sparks low in Harry's stomach whenever he's around Iain.

With everyone else, he exists behind the heavy armour of the good knight, the good protector. But Iain can shatter his defences with a glance. Iain has seen his worst, and loves him anyway. And that . . . that makes Harry want to possess him, keep him from the world's harm with a ferocity that he never suspected lay within him.

He hears Iain suck two of his own fingers, and he shivers, his curiosity building about what the boy has planned.

His shiver turns to a gasp of surprise as Iain traces the pads of his fingers ever so lightly down Harry's cock. 'Turnabout is, after all, fair play,' Iain breathes, leaning down to kiss Harry, honey-sweet.

Then those fingers move again, up the sides, swiping under Harry's foreskin.

Harry thrusts up, both hips and fingers, grunting out his need. The animal is coming out in him. He starts moving his fingers in and out of Iain, fast and deep, and when he hits the right spot Iain throws his head backwards and bites his own fist to keep from crying out in pleasure.

And Harry looks up at him from where he lies on his back, at the arch of Iain's muscled chest outlined in the lamplight, at his cock already hard and dripping, and he loves him so much in that moment he thinks he could just fall apart, just let go of his carefully held composure, and everything would be well. Iain would hold him together.

'Are you ready?' Harry whispers.

'God, yes,' Iain breathes, leaning down to kiss Harry again as he pulls his fingers out.

Harry rubs a hand up and down the hard lines of Iain's thigh, feeling subtle shifts in the muscle under his fingers as Iain melts into the kiss. Then Iain reaches behind him and takes Harry's cock in hand, lining himself up. He breaks the kiss then, and sits back slowly, exhaling as he goes.

Harry shuts his eyes. It's *heaven*.

And if this is the act that will send him to Hell, then he is willing to burn.

Iain's heavy weight finally settles on him as the boy takes all of him in. His hand reaches down, fingers tangling in Harry's, and they spend a moment there, just breathing, in the night.

Then Iain begins to move. Despite the fire burning hot in both of them, it's not the frantic, desperate pace of their previous encounters, because the fear is gone. Every kiss is no longer a prelude to goodbye. This won't be their last time.

It is, if anything, a first time.

As lovers. As partners. As *themselves*.

Iain rolls his hips, riding Harry slowly and sweetly, as their hands remain tangled together. Harry rubs his thumb over Iain's palm, feeling the swordsman's callouses there. Then he presses them to his lips. Iain hums, above him, and traces Harry's smile with his fingers.

Then he moves Harry's hand to his cock.

'Yes, Your Highness,' Harry murmurs, earning a growl from Iain as the boy contracts his body hard around Harry.

'That's— that's not the way to get me to stop saying that,' Harry moans, beginning to move his fist over Iain's dick.

Then Iain picks up the pace until Harry isn't able to say anything at all. Harry bends his knees, flattening his feet against the tent floor and thrusting up to meet Iain. They don't last long, like that. It's too good. Harry can feel Iain coming first, his cock jerking and spurting under Harry's hand and his body tensing around Harry like a hot, velvet vice. Harry isn't far behind, as he grabs Iain's hips and fucks up into him, hard, sloppy and unco-ordinated, until his own orgasm begins to crash through him. He sits up, ignoring the spark of pain from his ribs, and pulls Iain forwards onto him as he comes, needing to feel as much of the boy's body against his as possible, wrapping his arms around him, tucking his face into Iain's neck and gasping his name as he shudders through his release. Iain holds him just as tightly, arms like steel bars around him, as they come together, in a field far from either of their lands, finding their only true home in each other.

They hold each other until Harry softens and slips out, and then for a bit longer still. Then Iain pulls Harry down to the pallet, shivering slightly, and drags their pile of cloaks on top of them. Iain fits, just so, against Harry's side, like a matching puzzle piece long thought lost. And Harry can't help breathing out his adoration and his wonder as he strokes Iain's hair. 'I love you, my prince,' he whispers, pressing a kiss against Iain's neck.

'Don't say that, Harry. Don't get used to saying it,' Iain mumbles, fidgeting uncomfortably against him. 'It's not safe to say aloud, even between us. I am nothing more than your Scottish squire.' He smirks. 'Whom you may love.'

Harry twists one of those dark locks around his index finger and then feels it uncurl. 'But Montagu knows. And Arundel has guessed,' he says, reaching for another lock to twirl.

Iain shifts, pulling away from his grasp. 'Harry,' he says, his voice serious. 'If it gets out who I am and Edward goes to war against France, they have to kill me. I *have* to die for Edward's claim to be valid. They'll probably kill me anyway even if we keep quiet, but . . .' He sighs. 'I don't know. Montagu didn't kill me when he found me, so he must have some use for me alive.'

'I think Arundel wants to help us, Iain,' Harry says, reaching out to pull him back into his arms. 'I think he wants for there not to be a war. He has the money and power to protect us.' Harry wants to say more, explain the situation with Alys, but he can't figure out how to put it into words.

Iain groans, cutting through his still-muddled thoughts.

'I think Arundel wants to fox Montagu, and we are awfully tempting pawns,' he says. 'Look, Harry, the best way for Arundel to discredit Montagu is to bring me publicly to Edward's attention. Montagu looks terrible, Arundel steps into the void by the King's side that Montagu leaves, and boom, I still have to die if England rises against France. And if I run to France . . .' He shakes his head. 'Why would Philip of Valois take me in? I'm a threat. I even *look* like my grandfather. The French barons could use me to pressure Philip into almost anything. *Be nice, or we'll go back to a proper Capet king*.'

'Are people really that awful?' Harry whispers.

'Trust me,' Iain says, tracing his finger up Harry's ribs, along his collarbones. 'I grew up having the secret history of my family drummed into me until I could recite it from memory. Three hundred and fifty years of vicious dynastic politics.' He glances up at Harry, eyes ice-pale under their curtain of dark lashes. 'A family doesn't hold onto the crown that long by being nice people, Harry. Or by not learning from their predecessors' mistakes.' His voice drops away to almost nothing. Harry can't tell in the darkness, but he suspects Iain is blushing. 'My mother never recovered from her shame at being outmanoeuvred by Isabella. She wanted to make sure that fate would never happen to me.'

'Would that you had been born with any other name,' Harry sighs, brushing his lips over his lover's cheekbone.

'Mm,' Iain hums. 'But then I would not be me, and perhaps I would never have met you.'

'Perhaps you would have been happy, though,' Harry says, drowsily, for Iain is warm and the night is cold.

'I'm happy now,' Iain answers, snuggling against him.

The trip back to Dartington is leisurely; spring is showing herself in the buds of trees and the low, early flowers of the season. Harry feels too as if he is sprouting anew, something green in him pressing upwards through frost-stiff earth towards the sun.

He thinks perhaps the whole world can see how in love he is, but nobody seems to notice, too caught up in their own concerns. They spend their evenings at campsites and inns, hot, silent kisses on strange beds in unfamiliar towns. In public they are still the respectable knight and his scruffy, brooding squire. They're stared at no more nor less than any other pair of travellers, even with Iain's Scottish clothes. The only difference is that Iain has to smack Harry's hands away from trying to help too much.

Harry never lets a hint of Iain's true title pass his lips again, but he still thinks it. He still looks at Iain with wonder when they're alone. It's a cataloguing of little details that he had either missed or misinterpreted before: the way he holds himself. His pride, which isn't the insecure bravado of someone like Ufford, but a wry, quiet superiority. His education.

Part of Harry wishes they could be on the road forever, in this liminal space between destinations, without responsibilities. But as Harry's little corner of Devon draws ever closer, they both unconsciously begin to hurry. In their last tavern of the journey, just over the Devonshire border, they rise in wordless agreement and depart before dawn, so they can be home in Dartington in time for dinner.

They don't make it.

It's entirely Iain's fault.

As they turn onto the lane that leads in one direction to the manor, and in the other to Harry's pond, Iain just raises an eyebrow. 'Perhaps we should go for a swim before arriving home,' he says, voice low with promise. 'Clean up.'

Harry knows Iain's plans are anything but clean, and he turns Libby towards the forest anyway, anticipation rising in him like a cloud of suddenly awakened fireflies. They tie up the three horses and the cart at the edge of the forest and climb down the wooded slope to the pond.

'So,' Harry smiles, unhooking his belt and sword and hanging them over a tree branch. 'Swimming?'

'Mm, maybe in a minute,' Iain says, walking out onto their rock and kneeling down. He doffs his shirt and tosses it onto the leaf-strewn bank, before smirking up at Harry. His belt comes next, but he doesn't toss it aside. Instead he lays the dagger and sheath on the bank end of the rock and wraps the leather of the strap around one of his hands. 'I was wondering something first,' he purrs, glancing up at Harry from under his lashes.

And *that look*.

That look means *trouble*.

Harry slips off his boots and breeches and tunic and walks out to Iain, completely naked. 'And what were you wondering, *squire*?' Harry says, looking down at the man. He's already getting hard, just from Iain's submissive posture below him.

Iain leans forwards and rests his chin on Harry's leg, like a good pet, as he looks up at him, his eyes darkening with lust. He blinks those long lashes, as if innocent. Harry knows better. 'I want to see if I can make you come just from playing with your chest and talking dirty to you,' Iain says. Then he brushes a kiss into the crease of Harry's groin.

Harry's brain whites out, and when he can think again he kneels down so fast it elicits a snort of amusement from Iain. Iain kisses him, gently manipulating his hands backwards and guiding him to grasp his own ankles. Then Iain moves behind him, and Harry feels the old, soft leather of Iain's belt wrap around his wrists and ankles, binding him there. His body is bowed backwards, chest and cock on display for his lover.

'Is this acceptable?' Iain asks. He runs his hands up Harry's arms from behind, soothing, questioning. Harry presses back into him, reaching out the fingers of his bound hands. Iain sees the motion and links his fingers with Harry's, leaning in to kiss down his neck. It's startling, the coldness of the air against his naked body, compared with Iain's fiery touch and wet, hot mouth. The kisses turn to bites as his mouth reaches Harry's shoulder. Iain groans, pulling his hands away from Harry's and using them to drag down Harry's chest, over his hips and around to his rear. Iain's grasp turns possessive, almost harsh, and his bites send sharp jolts of pain through Harry's body, each bite soothed with a kiss afterwards.

Iain spreads Harry's arse and runs two fingers down between his cheeks, to his balls and back again. He's pressed against Harry's bound arms, straddling Harry's feet with his knees, and Harry can feel his arousal heavy and hot against his forearms.

Then Iain growls and pulls away. 'No,' he says, his voice thick with lust. 'I have a plan.'

'No plan survives a contact,' murmurs Harry, flexing his body and clenching the muscles of his arse. He glances over his shoulder. Iain is staring at him, a wild look in his eyes as he holds his own cock, already hard and purple.

'Stop it, Harry,' Iain says.

'Make me,' he replies.

Then Iain's straddling him from behind again. As his lips claim Harry's mouth, his hands reach around to find Harry's nipples. He rolls the two pink nubs between his fingers, hard, and Harry's entire body lights up. He loses his ability to continue the kiss, can't do anything more than gasp into Iain's mouth.

And Iain is rutting against his bound wrists, smearing his arousal all up and down Harry's arms, as he digs his hands into Harry's pectorals. Harry's head lolls forwards, because it's *so* good. Iain hasn't even touched his dick and Harry is already so aroused he can't think.

Iain kisses his way back to Harry's earlobe, and then takes it gently between his teeth, nibbling, as his hands abuse Harry's chest. 'Look at this,' he whispers, twisting Harry's nipples again, before grabbing two handfuls of chest. 'This is all mine. Your fucking body, Harry . . . the things it does to me. The things I want to do to you . . .' he murmurs, kissing and biting the soft flesh under Harry's ear. One of Iain's hands dips lower, tracing down the trail of blond hair at Harry's abs, but stops short just above his cock. Harry groans in frustration and pushes back against him.

'No, *a sheòid*,' Iain says, moving around so he's in front of Harry. He braces his knees outside Harry's and frames Harry's hips with his hands. He leans down and sucks on Harry's left tit, briefly assuaging some of the punishment he's given it. The heat of Iain's mouth burns wet on his chest, while Iain's fingers continue to manipulate his other nipple. Then Iain starts alternately biting Harry's nipples and flicking them ever so gently with his tongue. Harry has to grit his teeth to keep from shouting. He writhes against his bonds. He wants to push into Iain and move away from him at the same time, make it stop, but have more. Tears are streaming down his face, and his cock is so hard it *aches*. Every so often Iain gets close enough that Harry can feel the warmth of the boy's body near his groin, and he arches further, trying to push up to get some friction against his aching dick.

'Ah-ah,' Iain smiles, around a mouthful of Harry. He pulls away.

The worst part is Harry can see how hard Iain is too, and he wants to do something about that. 'Untie my arms,' Harry says, and Iain complies, moving back around behind him and leaning down to slip the knot in the belt. Harry immediately reaches back and drags Iain's hips towards him, until he can feel Iain's cock nestling between his cheeks, and as Iain abuses his chest with one hand and fists his cock with the other, he grinds back on his lover, feeling him gasp and hiss, feeling his hips start to thrust upwards.

Harry reaches down and drags Iain's hand away from his cock, placing it back on his chest. 'Harder,' he gasps. 'More. I'm so close.'

Iain makes a low, feral noise in his throat, and yanks Harry back against him, thrusting up along the cleft of his arse. He assaults Harry's neck with his mouth, kissing hard and sloppy, using teeth. Then he rakes his fingernails up Harry's chest, and grabs his nipples, pulling them and twisting them. The pain is ferocious, and so is the pleasure.

'Fuck,' Iain growls, emphasising each word with a thrust, with a twist. 'You. Are. Mine.'

And Harry thinks, *Yes, yes I am*, as he comes, his body shaking, tears slipping out of the corners of his eyes as his aching cock finally releases. Iain grabs him then, and having his strong, calloused hand around his cock after coming practically untouched is almost too much, the stimulation too intense, and he curls forwards, trying to hold onto this earth, to not come apart from it as his orgasm continues.

Iain lets him, slowing his strokes on Harry's cock, his touch turning kinder, more soothing, as he uses his free hand to rub up and down Harry's flank. Harry ends up on elbows and knees, still shaking, still coming down. His chest and nipples burn with a remembered fire, but now it's mixing with the cold of the air and that is a sort of pleasure too, and he shivers again, his body barely able to contain all that he feels.

After a moment, Iain collects him up, turning Harry towards him and embracing him. Harry relaxes, boneless, sinking into his warmth. They don't say anything, just holding each other, until Harry feels something against his hip and realises that

Iain is still hard. He slides down his lover's thickly muscled body, down to where the dark hair begins to grow.

'Harry, you don't have to—' Iain starts, but is silenced when Harry takes him in his mouth. Harry can feel how Iain's entire body tenses as he starts to bob his head, starts to suck up and down Iain's shaft, and he hums his pleasure at the power he has over Iain. He feels Iain's hands bury themselves in his hair. Iain's hips start to thrust shallowly, almost unconsciously, and he can taste the warm, salty precome leaking into his mouth.

Harry glances up at Iain. He's looking down at him with a sort of amazed wonder, as if Harry is his own personal miracle.

Iain covers one of Harry's hands with his own, and the other hand continues to caress the back of Harry's head, petting him, combing through his hair. Harry sucks harder, running his tongue up and down Iain's cock, and is rewarded by the hand in his hair tightening. The rhythm of Iain's hips begins to stutter, and all too soon he is pulling Harry off him. He wraps his hand around his own cock and thrusts, once, twice, and then he's coming over Harry's face.

Iain all but collapses onto his back on the mossy rock. He pulls Harry down on top of him, throwing a leg over him to keep him there. 'I think we missed dinner,' Harry murmurs, snuggling his face into Iain's neck.

'All your fault,' Iain mumbles back. 'You're distracting—'

A loud, echoing *krak* sounds across the pond, like ice breaking, or branches shattering.

Then it repeats, again and again.

It's *applause*. Someone is clapping.

Harry pulls away from Iain, terror coursing through him, and looks up.

'Bravo!' a voice calls from the top of the bank. 'Looks like we've found someone to hang after all.'

It's Rabbie.

Rabbie's grinning, and saying something about Alys de Morton, but Harry is distracted by a swift movement at his side. Iain is already moving forwards, blind fury on his face and dagger in his hand.

'Iain, no!' Harry yells, lunging for him, but Iain just tears out of his grasp and flings the dagger.

It embeds in a tree trunk, inches to the left of Rabbie's ear.

'You missed,' Rabbie snarls.

'It was a warning,' Iain seethes. 'If you try anything towards us, say a word to anyone, I will kill you and everyone you hold dear.'

Rabbie holds his hands up, a taunting smile on his face. 'I'm the King's Sheriff! I could ride in tomorrow and drag you out of Dartington by your hair and there is nothing any of you could do to stop me.'

'But you won't,' Harry says, doing his best to project an authority he doesn't feel. 'Because Montagu holds your leash and he isn't quite ready to let you slip yet. So run home to your master, you ugly dog, and bark at someone who cares.'

Iain grins evilly then, and barks at Ufford, a series of terrifying, barely human noises. When he finishes, he turns his back on Rabbie, dismissing him.

Ufford is crimson with anger, shaking with it, and he snatches Iain's dagger out of the birch tree and flings it back at him. There's a brief, heartstopping moment as the weapon flashes through the air, but then Iain sidesteps, neatly catching it as it flies past his shoulder.

Rabbie is pointing, jabbing his index finger at them as he tries to formulate a comeback. His lips twist in hatred. 'There will be a reckoning,' is all he manages to hiss before stomping off back towards his own lands.

Harry remains on guard until the crunch of Rabbie's departing footsteps fades into silence, body tensed against attack, then once the birds begin to sing again he all but collapses against Iain.

'I will kill him one day,' Iain whispers into Harry's hair.

Harry just shakes his head. Iain feels more than sees the motion. 'Let's go home,' he says. 'I'm tired.'

They put on a happy façade for the people of the manor. Over supper, Harry and Iain take turns describing their adventures at the tournaments. But Harry excuses them both as soon as is polite, claiming exhaustion.

He wants to tell Annie about Rabbie, about Montagu having a spy in the hall, but he doesn't know how to do it. Annie will want to know *why* Rabbie threatened them. While Annie is probably aware what Iain means to Harry, he fears what might happen if he confirms to her that they are lovers. At least now, if Rabbie tries to spread rumours, Annie can deny them and it's not lying.

He and Iain hold each other that night, up in the solar, and every night afterwards for two weeks, waiting for the hammer to fall.

But no bishop arrives. No mob, no men-at-arms darken their gates.

They almost come to believe that the incident with Rabbie will pass, when late into the night on the eve of Iain's birthday, the screaming begins.

Their home is on fire.

It's fitting, in a way. You burn a pig-boy for loving his friend by piling up hawthorn around him and throwing torches into it. You burn a lord for loving his friend by setting his manor alight.

Dartington is an old hall, thatch and wattle and daub, not the elegant stone of newer, more prosperous manors. It's hard to light thatch, harder than people expect, to get the densely packed reed to burn. But once ablaze, it's nigh impossible to put out.

Harry rouses at the first scream. As soon as he comes to his senses he can smell the smoke. Everything is too bright for this depth of night. Iain bolts awake too, rolling out of bed and grabbing for his shirt. 'Fuck,' he growls.

The ceiling is glowing at the edges, from the side adjacent to the great hall. Iain sees it and his eyes grow wider. '*Fuck*,' he repeats.

Harry yanks his shirt on and grabs his sword belt, already heading for the stairs. 'Iain!' he shouts over his shoulder. Iain is standing in the middle of the room, tying his own belt, looking around the room, eyes sharp and panicked.

'Come on!' Harry yells.

'You go,' Iain says. 'Get everyone out of the hall. I'll follow.'

'What are you doing?' Harry says, pausing as he reaches for the door.

Iain waves his arm towards Sir Simon's books, towards his mother's mirror. 'Your things,' he says.

'Forget them,' Harry says, throwing the door open. A hot wind slams into him, singeing his hair and eyebrows, and he backs into the room, coughing. The hall is an inferno.

Judging by the panicked shouts outside, it seems like a goodly proportion of the hall's residents made it into the courtyard. Harry runs to a window and shouts down for Annie, for Kit, for *anyone*.

It's Kit who responds. '*Get out!*' the man yells. '*The roof's already going in over the kitchens!*'

Iain pushes past him and shoves a bundle in a knotted cloak out the window. '*Kit! Catch!*' Then he turns to Harry. 'What else?' he asks.

There's the sound of a horse screaming. Harry looks out. The fire hasn't reached the home barn or the stables yet, but the wind is sending sparks that way and the animals are beginning to panic. 'Forget the things,' he says. 'Get the horses.'

Iain nods, and throws a leg over the window sill. It's a tight squeeze; the windows are small so they can be covered easily in colder weather, and Iain is broad. He jumps, and Harry watches him as he lands and dashes towards the stables.

Harry looks back over his shoulder one last time at his family's big bed with its heavy wool curtains, now starting to smoulder. At the carved chest that was made for his grandmother's marriage. At the little room that had been his home for his entire life, and is now blazing into ashes.

Then he, too, jumps.

Iain comes out of the stables on Numbles, bareback, leading the other horses by ropes. All are panicky, high-stepping and tossing their heads. Even if the fire never gets to the stables, there's too much chance of the horses bolting or injuring themselves to let them stay this close to the blaze. Horses instinctually know the evil that fire does, even if they've never experienced it.

Harry yells, 'Take them to the north barn, and stay with them all night,' and Iain nods. The north barn is where they store straw, and it's three pastures away. Ironically, it was built distant from the house in case the straw ever caught fire.

As Iain leads off the little group of horses, Harry can see both his dagger and Harry's old sword at his belt, and a hunting bow slung over his shoulder. Harry grunts, pleased that Iain thought to raid the weapons they keep in the stables, but wishing he'd grabbed a hauberk too.

Harry strides out into the courtyard, the heat from the fire hammering at his back, as he mentally counts the people gathered there. Everyone is huddled together, watching the hall go up in flames. It's hard to tell who's who in the mass of cloak-wrapped bodies, faces obscured by smoke, hands clutching whatever paltry belongings they could salvage.

Harry identifies Annie. Piers. Katie. Kit. With lambing so close, Jed would be out with the livestock, so him being missing isn't a worry, yet. Two of the three kitchen girls. Six other servants.

'*Annie*,' Harry says, pushing through the terrified crowd towards his steward. '*Who's missing? Did everyone make it out?*'

Annie nods. She's crying, her eyes wide and wet, as she clutches an iron cook-pot in her arms. It's filled with the kitchen knives Iain used to try to steal. '*We're all here. Cecily's off visiting her family, her ma had another baby and needed the help, and Adam's helping Jed with the lambing.*' Then Annie flinches as a terrible crack sounds through the air.

All eyes turn to the immolation of their home, the unspoken terror of *what now, what next?* running through everyone like a fever. The hall's roof slowly collapses. It's as if the house is bowing to them, knowing this is its final performance and apologising for the state in which it's leaving.

'*I double-checked everything in the kitchen tonight, Harry,*' Annie gasps through her sobs. '*You know I always do. All the lamps and candles were out, the fire was down to embers behind the screen . . .*'

'*I know you're careful,*' Harry says. He brings his arms around her, cook-pot and all. '*It wasn't any of us. I'm sure of it.*'

Annie looks up at him then, her eyes red from smoke and tears.

'*It was Rabbie,*' Harry whispers. '*I should have told you to keep an eye out. He's angry about losing the Newmarket tournament, and we met him again on the road back. Iain had . . . a confrontation with him.*'

He realises it's not enough, that Annie deserves the full truth. He sucks in a breath, hot and bitter with ash. '*Annie, Iain and I are . . .*'

Annie pinches his arm. '*I know,*' she whispers. '*Would that we all could find someone who looks at us the way you two look at each other.*' She shifts too, her manner heavy with guilt. '*There were some young 'uns helping us out over Christmas in the kitchens. One asked a lot of questions about Iain. I sent the little rat packing with a whack on the head from my ladle for the trouble, but I think somehow he'd seen you two.*'

Harry squeezes her again and looks over her shoulder as the walls of the solar fold in on themselves, sending sparks high into the sky, poor, gaudy imitators of the stars looking down on them. As he releases her, he says, '*We need to get everyone to a safer place.*'

Annie nods, and sends Katie to the home barn, just beyond the stables, to let the chickens and geese out. They may not come back, but it's better than them being burned alive if the wind shifts any further round. It's too late to move the ploughs and scythes and farming implements stored there, or the grain.

Harry raises his voice, calling his displaced people to him. '*If you have family homes on our lands, go back to them for the night. We'll meet again here tomorrow to salvage what we can. If you have nowhere to sleep or your homes are too far, follow me to the north barn.*'

He ends up leading a little party of eight, including Annie and Katie and Kit, who still clutches the bundle of books Iain had thrown him. The normally short walk to the big old barn seems to take an eternity, as they all keep turning to stare at the glow on the hillside behind them. At the death of their home.

It's as if each of them hopes they'll look back and God will say, *just kidding*, and Dartington will be there as old and solid as it always was. And they could put down their burdens and their fears and just go home.

But the light never goes out.

And there is no longer a home to go back to.

Iain meets them at the entrance to the barn, bow drawn and eyes narrowed. When he recognises Harry, he lowers the weapon. When he recognises Annie, he drops it.

The humans all go through the motions of sleep. They lie down on the straw-strewn floor, huddled together in a group. They pull what cloaks they've brought over themselves, and shut their eyes. The horses shift anxiously from foot to foot and snort from where they're tied not far away, but the humans pretend to rest.

And Iain holds Harry close against the coming dawn, and whispers in his ear, 'You will survive this.'

When the sun does light the horizon, their little group are soot-smeared, hungry and sore. Yet it all seems unreal, a collective nightmare, until they stumble back down to the smouldering ruins of Dartington Manor. The house, once squat and welcoming if never grand, is now a blackened, smoking skeleton, jagged walls reaching up to scratch at the sky, roof open to the heavens' pitiless glare.

Harry has no idea what to do. He's four months shy of his twentieth birthday, lord of a heavily indebted manor, without a penny to rebuild. He can feel his face redden in shame and fear.

The logical thing would be to ask the neighbouring lord to house them until he could beg or borrow the money to construct a new hall.

But the neighbouring lord is Rabbie.

Harry bitterly misses his mother in that moment. She'd know what to do. He thinks how she never flinched, was never scared, even as a horrible thought floats to the surface of his mind, like a corpse in slack water: *what if she was?* What if his mother was faking it too, as confused and terrified as he was about what would become of them, of how long their small, unprofitable estate could hold together against bad luck and worse harvests before the inevitable end?

Iain puts his hand on Harry's shoulder and squeezes. '*Guess we're going to be living in a barn for a while*,' he says in

English, gesturing with his chin at the home barn. It's untouched, as are the stables, thankfully. The chickens and geese scold them for their doubts from atop manure piles and ploughs.

'*Guess so*,' says Harry. He pinches the bridge of his nose, the small pain of digging his fingers into the corners of his eyes helping to focus him. Then he inhales, long and deep. Everything smells of ash and burned earth. *One step at a time*, he thinks. Get everyone settled, then figure out how to rebuild.

It takes all day to clear out the farm implements from the home barn, move them to the north barn, and then cart straw back down. Ralf shows up early to help, as do Adam and Jed and a number of the vassals. The horses go back in the stables, and the chicken coop gets moved to the southern end of the building, where it's best protected from the weather.

The chickens are the only creatures to venture back into the hall. A fat red hen sits on a half-collapsed wall and watches them, her yellow eyes impassive. For everyone else, it's too much, too soon. The embers of the fire haven't yet burned down, and nobody has the heart to start looking for anything not destroyed in the fire. Not yet.

Throughout the day, more people from the village and the vassal farms show up, bringing food. It touches Harry's heart beyond belief. Nobody has extra to give, but they find *something*, even if it's just a small loaf of bread.

And everyone is surviving. They're all moving as if in a daze, but they're moving. Perhaps, Harry thinks, because if any of them stop and really consider how bad their situation is, they'll never move again. Harry glances over at Iain, deep in conversation with Annie. He's worried the man will try for revenge against Rabbie, but for now, it seems, there's too much to do simply to put their lives back together.

On Annie's instructions, Iain and the other young men start clearing the debris from the kitchens. The big stone hearth and ovens didn't take much damage, but the rest of the room is a shell. Harry and Ralf retrieve the timber laid aside for repairing barns, and work on creating a basic roof over it. Kit carries the rescued books one last time, to Father Gilbert for safekeeping. Harry knows they'll need to be sold, but not yet. He can't face that yet.

Slowly, over the next fortnight, the abnormal becomes normal: sleeping in a barn; cooking in a makeshift kitchen still half-open to the elements. Turning a couple of spare stalls in the stables into a buttery. Working a rotating watch, so at night someone is always awake, in case the arsonist comes back.

It'll be survivable for the spring and summer, but come winter, they'll need a real home.

And there's the problem.

Harry could go to Montagu for the money. But then Montagu would own him completely, even more than he already does. Or, worse, Montagu would refuse, and give Dartington to Rabbie, forcing Harry to become a vassal knight of the House of Ufford.

He *can't* go to Montagu.

Arundel has the money to spare, too, but Harry doesn't want to switch being beholden to one great lord for being beholden to another. Especially one who also gains from using Iain as his pawn.

There's a third way. Harry keeps shoving it to the back of his mind, because as much as it solves the majority of his problems, it causes as many more. But as the weeks stretch towards May and the tournament at Burstwick draws closer, it seems like the only choice left to him.

A dowry.

A marriage to Alys.

And he does love Alys. Just . . . not the way he loves Iain.

Iain, who is looking at him across the makeshift dinner table in the barn, and who nudges his ankle with his foot. 'What's wrong?' Iain mouths.

Harry shakes his head. 'Nothing. Burstwick's coming up. We should start training again.'

Iain nods and grabs another piece of chicken. 'Tomorrow?'

'Yes,' Harry says. Luckily, most of their tourneying equipment and weapons had been in the stables, spared consumption by the fire.

'Should we ask Sir Hugh up? And the Cornish brothers?' Iain says.

'Iain,' Harry groans, motioning to their ramshackle accommodation. 'We can't host anyone. Not like *this*.'

Iain shrugs. 'They have their tents. And I don't think they'll care.'

Harry shakes his head. Sometimes it's hard to make Iain understand exactly how rigid their social codes are. That just because Iain knows what rock bottom is, has been there and climbed back up from it, does not mean others will be as forgiving of any slip in status. Those who have travelled great distances on the class scale often forget how much those who have not measure every inch above and below them as if it were a league.

Harry rationalises his shame by telling himself that it's not necessary to invite others, that Iain is getting to the skill level where he's a real challenge for Harry. He says as much. 'You and me. Every morning. On the horses. We can set up a tiltyard in the fallow bean field.'

Iain nods. 'I'll get on it.'

Harry hopes that their practices don't become a spectator sport for the entire manor, because the change in living arrangements since the fire has meant that the two of them have no privacy. Sure, they sleep in each other's arms in the barn every night when one of them isn't on watch, but they're a few feet away from two dozen other people. Not that those people themselves don't have sex, quietly, in the dark – and sometimes less quietly. But he and Iain can't.

They snatch their time where they're able: in the north barn, Harry pushing Iain down onto the winter straw. Behind a tree, deep in a copse, desperate mouths seeking each other out, fast hands reaching under shirts, unlacing breeches. But there's always the risk of discovery.

Harry misses being able to take his time with Iain. He misses the time he wasted, believing he could somehow turn off his feelings for the boy.

Hitting each other with broadswords and lances is an adequate, if ultimately unsatisfying, way of working out his frustrations. He dreams of fucking Iain in the field, in armour; of dragging him into a nearby copse and pushing the boy onto his knees, having Iain take him in his mouth. But, as he feared, their sparring sessions become popular events, with a dozen vassals and friends cheering them on. He knows it takes everyone's minds off the perilous state of their lands. He's not sorry to provide the distraction. He just wishes he were allowed his own distraction now and then.

They leave for Burstwick shortly after May Day celebrations. Harry hugs Annie and quietly promises her that he has a solution. That one of the reasons he's tromping the entire length of England to faraway East Yorkshire is to get the money to rebuild the hall, bigger and better than ever. And she nods, and smiles, even if something in her eyes doesn't quite believe him. After all, last summer he'd promised her Scotland would make his fortune.

The trip takes ten days, moving quickly, staying in crowded inns along the Great North Road before they break east at Doncaster, towards Hull. Harry becomes increasingly restless as the trip goes on. He's so close to Iain, with the boy every minute of the day, but not *with* him. Not in the way he wants. Not even at night, in an inn bed often shared with other travellers.

Iain merely retreats into silence, growing quieter and yet wilder the further north they go.

They arrive in Burstwick the afternoon of 14 May, two days before the tournament is set to begin. Two days Harry thought they could have to themselves. But the problem with being the standout of the winter tournament season is that everyone recognises them. The other attending knights see the star-and-hawk banner and drop by to invite him to dine with them. To practise. To drink and gossip. To do everything except the thing he wants to do (pin Iain down and fuck him until he screams), and the thing he *has* to do (find the red-and-gold lion rampant banner of Arundel).

So Harry smiles and waves and exchanges pleasantries, and Iain finds Lords Michael, Magnus and Morris, and gives

Harry's *bona fides*. Harry is with the King's Insiders for the mêlée, while Rabbie and Montagu are with the Outsiders. And something petty in Harry is deeply pleased he'll have the chance to knock Ufford around the head a few times.

Finally, night falls, and for the first time in what feels like months, he and Iain are alone. Or, they have the illusion of being alone, in the late-spring evening, thin walls of striped canvas keeping the rest of the world at bay for a few short hours. There's a moment where they just look at each other, almost in disbelief, as the crickets begin to sing in the night. Then the moment breaks, and they come together.

The sex, the *first* sex, is hard and fast, nothing more than two people satisfying a burning need as quickly and as silently as they can. Harry wants to shout as he comes inside Iain, shooting into him, filling him, but instead he muffles his cry of pleasure into the soft skin of Iain's neck.

The second time is slower, waking up after a post-coital doze to kiss and feel and stroke, to relearn each other's bodies. Harry moves Iain's hand down between his legs, asking a silent question. Iain just groans, soft and quiet, as he feels Harry's hole beneath his fingers. He leans down and kisses Harry, and begins to open him up. And later, when Harry is almost bent in two, gasping, so full of Iain it hurts, Iain fucks him so calmly, so completely and methodically, continually pulling him back from orgasm, that it takes him an hour before Iain finally lets him come.

Harry can still feel it the next day, as he pours a bucket of water over himself and then dresses in his court clothes to see the Earl of Arundel and his ward. Alys isn't in, but the Earl invites him to dinner. 'And bring that squire of yours as well,' the Earl says with a wink.

'Alas, he'll be too busy preparing for tomorrow,' Harry demurs. He hasn't told Iain about his plans, or about his fondness for Alys. He should, and he will eventually, but not now. He has a pretty good guess how Iain will react.

Harry has to win this tournament. And he can't keep the focus he needs to win, if Iain is the throes of furious jealousy.

Harry knows it's not a good thing that he does, to either Alys or Iain. But ultimately it's not about them. It's about survival for the people of Dartington. He will be truthful with both of them, but later. After the tournament.

Harry realises the Earl has asked him a question. 'Hm?' he says. 'Sorry.'

'He competing, your Scottish boy?' the Earl says.

'Yes,' answers Harry.

'Is he going to win the squires'?'

Harry smirks. 'We're both going to win.' And then another plan, on the fly, forms in his head. 'If you're a betting man, I'd take note of that.'

The Earl grins. 'I am, and I will. Half the profit to you if the pair of you pull it off. Never heard of a knight and his squire both topping the lists.'

Harry bows. 'There's a first time for everything,' he says as he leaves.

Iain is polishing armour when he returns to their pavilion. The boy looks up and grins lasciviously at Harry's court clothes. 'I like you in hose,' he says, and Harry can feel the blush rise to his cheeks.

'I did something,' Harry says. Iain raises an eyebrow at him. 'You have to win the *bohort*,' he continues. 'At any cost. I've asked the Earl of Arundel to bet on us. If we both win, we'll have enough to start rebuilding the manor.'

'Harry,' Iain breathes, warily. Burstwick is a smaller tournament than the southern ones of the winter, with many of the fashionable Home Counties knights not willing to make the trip. But in their place are tough Northern knights, experienced in real border warfare against the Scots and the Welsh.

'We can do this, Iain,' Harry says, with a confidence he doesn't entirely feel. 'I, I have a back-up plan too, but we can do this.'

Iain smiles up at him and runs a hand up his leg, appreciating the way the thin woollen knit clings to his muscles. Harry's eyes flutter closed, but then he steps away as he feels a spark of interest in his groin.

'Iain, no, I have to go to dinner with Arundel, I can't,' he stutters. 'I'm sorry,' he says, leaning down to brush a kiss over Iain's lips. As he does, his long-tailed liripipe comes unwrapped from around his shoulders and the soft wool falls across Iain's face.

Iain wrinkles his nose and snorts in amusement as Harry flails. 'Oh, fuck this,' Harry grumbles, trying to right the ridiculous garment. 'Fuck these clothes.'

'I was trying,' Iain mumbles, faux-grumpy, 'but you stopped me.' He flows to his feet with that easy grace of his, and with a few gestures manages to arrange the hood properly. Then he takes Harry by the shoulders and presses his lips to Harry's, in a kiss that's more than half smile. 'Go and charm the Earl, Harry, and don't do anything I wouldn't.'

Harry snorts in mock derision. 'He wanted you to come too, by the way.'

'No thank you,' Iain says, his tone decisive.

Harry kisses the line of tension that's appeared on Iain's forehead. 'I already sent him your regrets.'

Arundel's supper is an awkward meeting of the two great factions at court, and they all react to it by drinking too much. Bar the King, still to arrive, nearly all the major nobles at the tournament are there: Percy, Morley, the Bohuns, John of Eltham, even Montagu. And goddamn Rabbie Ufford, who grins at Harry and lifts his glass to him in a mocking toast. Harry's cheeks burn with fury but he doesn't react, beyond a slight incline of the head and a bone-dry comment about how much he's looking forward to the morning's mêlée.

Harry is placed far from Arundel, which he had expected, and next to Alys, for which he had prayed. On Alys's other side is Rabbie, and Harry half-hopes she'll make good on her earlier promise to impale his wandering hand on her eating knife. Harry looks around. It's all the great, fashionable barons, and him, and a year ago Harry would have given all he had for this seat, at this gathering. Now he sighs in relief when he sees Sir Hugh take the empty place across from him. The older knight smiles ruefully, as unenthusiastic about the company as Harry, and mentions that Sirs Malachi and Morien haven't made the long journey.

The men around them talk of everything and nothing, trying to score social points against one another. Harry finds it tedious, and a glance up the table suggests the Earl isn't having much fun either. Arundel is famous for lavish parties where a cup isn't emptied before it is refilled again. And yet the Earl's smile is fixed as he urges his friends to greater heights of drunkenness, while sipping at a cup that never seems to go down and is never refilled.

Harry gives up even pretending to sip from his. A hangover is the last thing he needs in the mêlée tomorrow. He's pleased to see Rabbie drinking heavily, and less pleased at the way he nestles in closer and closer to Alys.

Alys shifts uncomfortably next to Rabbie, trying to move away from the man's increasingly drunken attentions. But, Harry notices, she doesn't seem to wish to shift closer to Harry either. He coughs, and shuffles further over to his left, giving her more room to manoeuvre.

Alys shoots him a grateful glance and moves away from Rabbie's grasping hand.

Harry catches Montagu's eye and nods towards Rabbie, raising an eyebrow at the man's inebriated state. Montagu just shrugs, opening his hands as if powerless. Harry wants to pick Rabbie up by the scruff of his neck and throw him in the nearest horse trough, but this is no time to antagonise the man further. Montagu is surely aware of the fire at Dartington, but Harry would prefer it if Alys and the Earl don't find out just yet.

Unfortunately, Rabbie has other ideas. He grabs at Alys, trying to haul her into his lap. She flinches violently at his touch, and Harry loses the will to hold back. He bangs his cup on the table. 'Rabbie! Stop it,' he says, loud enough to cause heads to turn. 'Lady de Morton clearly isn't interested in what you have to offer.'

Rabbie stands up then, a thick accusatory finger jabbing towards Harry. 'Least I offer it to *women*, Lyon,' he snarls, before looming down over Alys. 'Pretty thing like you all alone in the world,' he slurs, licking his lips. 'There's so much I can give you. An' all you have to do is give me a little—'

Alys's fist crashes squarely into Rabbie's face.

The man stumbles backwards, trips over the bench leg, and lands on his rear. He looks utterly confused. 'Bai dose,' he whines, touching his fingers to the torrent of blood starting to flow from his nostrils.

'I think this might be a good time for us to go for a walk,' Harry says, offering his arm to Alys. 'Perhaps get some fresh air?'

'I agree,' says Alys. She's a pale English rose at the best of times, but right now she is white, and Harry can't tell if it's with terror or rage. She puts her small, strong hand on his sleeve as he bows to the Earl.

'With your permission, my lord,' Harry says.

Arundel waves his hand. 'Her handmaiden, Rohesia, will go with you,' he says.

'Of course,' Harry agrees. An unmarried noblewoman is never taken out by an unmarried man without a chaperone. A slim, strawberry-blonde girl, quiet but with an intelligent look to her eye, rises from one of the side benches and walks after them, head bowed.

Harry and Alys pace three circuits of the pavilion field before either of them can speak. Alys quickly withdraws her hand from his arm as soon as they are out of the tent. His mind spirals with dire interpretations of her reluctance to touch him.

Perhaps he was wrong. Perhaps she doesn't like him at all.

'Alys,' he begins, searching for a way to put his tangle of thoughts into words.

'Don't ask me to marry you,' Alys says softly. 'I don't need saving.'

'I, I saw that,' says Harry. 'In fact, my admiration for you has only increased. Anyone who punches Rabbie Ufford in the face becomes one of my favourite people instantly.' Harry trips over a slight divot in the turf, but catches himself. 'Uh, not that you weren't my favourite woman anyway.' He stops, and smacks his palm to his forehead. He's screwing this up so badly. 'What I'm saying is, you're not the one who needs saving. I am.'

Alys is looking at him, hands clasped modestly over her stomach, the slightest of smirks tugging at the corners of her lips. 'Oh, please,' she says. 'I can't believe that. You do have the most almighty attraction for trouble, but a knight like you? What could possibly vanquish you?'

A dark-haired Scottish boy, Harry thinks.

But what he finally says is, 'A single torch.'

Alys's brows arch in confusion.

'My manor burned down in March,' Harry whispers. 'We have no proof, but we think Rabbie did it.'

'Couldn't you go to the King's Sheriff?' Alys asks.

'Rabbie *is* the Sheriff of Devonshire,' Harry sighs. 'And our neighbour. If I don't find money to rebuild, he will get my lands, and our people.'

'Oh,' Alys says. She begins to walk again, and Harry hurries to catch up. 'Ask the Earl, he'll give you the money,' she tells him.

'I don't want to go from being beholden to Montagu, to being beholden to Arundel,' Harry confesses.

'So you'd rather make me beholden to you?' Alys asks.

'Alys,' Harry groans. This woman. She mixes him up so badly. Then he sags. 'You're right. It isn't fair.'

'I will think about it. There are considerations,' she says, her chin high. Then, more quietly, she adds, 'On both our sides, I'd hazard.'

She pats Harry's arm. 'I enjoyed our chat. Good luck tomorrow,' she says. Then she beckons to her handmaiden, and they walk back towards Arundel's tent, leaving a perplexed Harry in their wake.

The tournament begins well. Half the knights in the mêlée are sporting ferocious hangovers, courtesy of the Earl of Arundel, and Harry manages to hit Rabbie so hard he is unhorsed in the first moments. He's carried out, unconscious, by his new squire. Harry is also ahead by several lances at the end of the initial day of jousting.

That afternoon, Iain destroys the competition in the *bohort*, making it to the finals. What he still lacks in technical finesse, he makes up for with speed and an absolute, unhesitating ferocity. It's thrilling to watch, and Harry secretly thinks the squires' foot-combats are more exciting than the knights' mounted ones.

That opinion isn't shared. The *bohort* is usually attended only by the knights whose squires compete, but Iain's final match against Sir Hugh's squire Rolly attracts a real crowd. Both squires are tired; both have been fighting in nearly constant bouts for the past three hours, and Harry knows exactly how heavy a broadsword feels at that point.

Harry also knows that this, in the finals, is when the fighting gets extremely tactical. You can't waste strength because you don't have it left to waste. If you overextend yourself early in a futile chase for a quick win, you're then too tired to defend properly. This is the habit Harry fears Iain will lapse back into, and as the match begins, it's exactly what Iain does. It's a bad tactic, and it only works against bad fighters.

Rolly's not a bad fighter. Harry has lost to Rolly in the past.

Harry's heart is in his throat as he watches Iain rush Rolly, driving him back with a flurry of hard hits. Rolly parries them all, losing ground with it, and Harry shakes his head. Iain's using too much force. He's going for the kill with every hit, even the ones he knows Rolly will parry. He's going to exhaust himself and all Rolly has to do is wait for him to slow. Iain still fails to see the point in tactical retreats, so when Rolly does strike, Iain has only his parry to save him.

Harry wants to glare at Iain, but he knows it's useless at best and match-losingly distracting at worst.

Three body or head hits, that's what they have to get. First to three wins.

'Eesh,' breathes a voice next to him, where there wasn't one before. Harry glances over. The Earl of Arundel is leaning on the fence, his shoulder touching Harry's, watching the match. 'Protecting my investment,' the Earl mutters. 'Your boy going to pull through? And which one is he, again? The pants-shittingly terrifying one, or the one that—'

'Hit,' cries out the steward judging the match.

'The terrifying one,' Harry sighs.

'The one that just got a strike against him,' the Earl says.

'He'll come back from it,' Harry says, but fear begins to eat at his stomach.

Iain doesn't change his tactics in the next round. Harry

wants to punch something, very possibly Iain. He can see the fatigue starting to sap Iain's speed and strength. Rolly's tiring too, but not as quickly as Iain. *God damn it, Iain*, Harry thinks. *You're better than this. I taught you better than this.*

Iain disengages from one of Rolly's parries and tries to trap Rolly's blade, running up the inside of it. But Rolly must sense a weakness as he just smashes Iain's blade down and, before Iain can get up his guard again, he scores a hard hit against the side of Iain's helmet.

Iain staggers backwards.

After calling the hit, the steward asks Iain if he's able to continue. Iain's wavering on his feet, looking like he's barely able to keep standing. He doesn't respond. The steward repeats the question.

'This isn't good, Lyon,' the Earl mumbles.

Iain puts his hand up, and nods. He will continue. He raises his sword, shakily.

There's a collective exhale from the crowd and a smattering of applause.

Rolly shrugs and raises his sword. He knows it's over. Everyone knows it's over.

Everyone except Iain.

Rolly strides forwards, using Iain's own tactics against him: rushing him, driving him back with hard blows that give him no time to recover. Iain, to his credit, actually retreats. Then Rolly brings his sword down in a high, overhead chop, and Harry can tell he's put all his strength and momentum into it. It's the kind of hit that breaks swords. And people.

But it doesn't land.

There's the thunderous crash of steel on steel, and then Rolly is stepping backwards, stumbling. Iain had not only parried the overhead hit with some unforeseen reserve of strength, he'd kicked Rolly in the stomach at the same time. Then, snake-quick, he steps forwards and thwacks Rolly hard on the right elbow with the flat of his sword. Rolly's sword falls out of his grasp onto the ground at the same time as Iain's first hit lands on his body.

The steward marks the hit. It's customary to separate if both parties are armed, but if one has lost his weapon, the other squire is free to press his advantage. It's not polite, it's not chivalrous, but it's also not against the rules. Somewhat like booting your opponent in the stomach.

Iain kicks Rolly's sword away and keeps advancing. And Harry sees the moment Rolly realises he's lost. To the squire's credit, he doesn't draw it out, or pretend he can make a comeback. He just sinks down on one knee in front of Iain and bows his head.

Iain gently touches his sword to Rolly's right shoulder, twice. The steward calls the hits, and announces, 'The winner, Seonaidh mac Maíl Coluim, squire of Sir Harry Lyon of Dartington.' Iain briefly acknowledges the win, raising a hand but not removing his helmet, and then reaches down to help Rolly up. Rolly wraps him immediately in a hug, and Iain smacks the back of Rolly's helmet affectionately.

Harry feels something dark and nasty twist in him. He's suddenly, irrationally furious at Rolly, a kind boy and a conscientious squire, because he's walking off the grounds with Iain, arms slung round each other's shoulders in simple, brotherly affection.

'Hm,' Arundel says by his side. 'Is he always that dramatic?'

'You have no idea,' says Harry.

'Well,' the Earl says quietly, 'thank the good Lord and all His angels and saints that fate kept that boy off his grandfather's throne. I'd fear for England, I truly would.' He pushes away from the fence. 'Now if you'll excuse me, I have some winnings to collect.'

Iain ambles over then, his helmet off, his hair sweaty and a grin spreading across his handsome face.

Harry looks down at his own hands, knuckles white against the fence. 'What the hell do you think you were doing?' he hisses.

Harry watches the happy, exhausted twinkle in Iain's eyes harden, and suddenly he feels like the worst person on earth. 'What you wanted,' Iain growls back. 'Winning.' He bashes his shoulder into Harry as he passes him, stomping back towards their pavilion.

Harry trudges back more slowly, rehearsing the apology he knows Iain deserves. The journey is made worse by the various knights along the way congratulating Harry for his squire's victory, saying they'd heard it was one hell of a final bout. And Harry had to admit it had been a stunning bit of tactics by Iain, getting the normally cautious, controlled Rolly to become over-confident.

It just wasn't one of *Harry's* tactics.

And there's the problem, laid bare: Iain no longer needs Harry. Harry was used to Iain being completely dependent on him. Iain in chains. Then Iain with a broken leg. Then Harry teaching him to ride, to fight, to squire. To speak English.

But now Iain strides tall and proud through the tournament grounds, his own man. A lord of Scotland and a prince of

France, a formidable opponent, a witty and charming friend. A man who, somewhere over the past year, Harry has come to need desperately. Iain has filled the lonely void of Harry's life with more warmth than he ever thought possible. He can't lose him. He *can't*.

Iain is rinsing the sweat off himself next to the horses when Harry reaches their pavilion. He stands there, shifting awkwardly from foot to foot, as Iain finishes cleaning. 'I'm sorry,' he mumbles, gesturing towards the field where the *bohort* had taken place. 'That was uncalled-for.'

Iain glares at Harry as he pulls his dark hair back, and then heads into their pavilion.

Harry stumbles in after him. 'Please,' he says.

Iain turns, slow and savage. 'Can you, for once, just say I did something well?'

Harry stops. His mouth opens, but no sound comes out. For Harry, his life is duty. No praise is needed or expected. You just do what is required. But Iain stays with him by choice, not duty. A ridiculous, unbelievable choice for someone as high-born as him, hiding out as a squire on a declining West Country estate.

'I'm never good enough,' Iain says. 'It hurts.'

Harry reaches out to him, the words on the tip of his tongue, but Iain pulls away.

The boy grabs his cloak and tosses it around his shoulders. 'I'll be back for supper,' he says, his tone sour. 'Unless you need me?'

Harry shakes his head.

He watches the tent flap until it has stopped swinging from the breeze of Iain's passage. Then he sinks to the ground, not daring to touch anything but the earth, as all he loves falls to pieces in his clumsy grasp.

The final day of jousting is overcast, the skies pregnant with rain. The knights Harry faces now aren't the familiar circuit of the King's close confidantes. They're tough border knights of the North, keen to teach the soft Southerners a hard lesson at lance-point. And they're all gunning for Harry, the nineteen-year-old golden boy of the previous season.

Harry doesn't go down easy.

His lead is chipped away, slowly, but by halfway through the contest he's still ahead by a few lances. He allows himself the hope that he will win nonetheless. That Dartington can be saved.

Then some big Northern knight named Cradoc comes and knocks him off his horse so hard he doesn't wake up for half an hour. When he comes to, it's over, and another knight has won the tournament. Harry stares up at the grey clouds, his head throbbing, the cheers and shouts of someone else's name echoing around him where he lies on the grass. Iain is kneeling next to him, brushing his forehead with a wet cloth.

He feels more than sees Iain stiffen as footsteps approach.

'Is he broken?' says a voice. Harry thinks it's Arundel.

Iain shakes his head. 'Bad fall. He'll survive.'

Then Arundel squats down, to where Harry can see him. He sees a hint of a lady's dress as well. Alys. 'Hard luck, old thing,' Arundel says.

'I'm sorry,' Harry mumbles.

Arundel sighs. He reaches out to pat Harry's shoulder but stops when Iain narrows his eyes and makes a low noise in his throat. 'Fine, no touching, got it,' Arundel says, his face registering mild surprise at Iain's behaviour.

'Iain, no,' Harry slurs, flapping one of his hands to smack him in the leg. 'D'be rude.' But in his heart, Harry is glad of this display of protectiveness. It means things are mendable between them. They haven't talked about yesterday, and supper was full of sharp silences, but Iain is here and protecting him and that means he hasn't broken them irrevocably.

Iain grunts in a vaguely apologetic manner at the Earl.

'It's fine,' Arundel says, standing up and digging around in a pouch at his belt. 'This is yours,' he continues, placing a small bag of coins on the ground. 'I bet on you both to win, but separately.' The Earl grins. 'Your odds were terrible, Harry. His were great. Thirty to one.' He looks at Iain. 'Congratulations, you cleaned up. See you in Nottingham.'

With the winnings and the sale of Sir Simon's books, Harry is able to engage stonemasons to begin building a new hall at Dartington. Stone is expensive and slow, and he'll need to find more money to complete the construction, but Harry never wants to see his hall burn again.

He has just enough time to return home and organise the builders, before heading back up north to the Nottingham tournament in July. It'll be the last tournament before harvest, then the season closes with a pair of tournaments in September near London.

Harry tries not to think about the debts he still owes Montagu. There's nothing he can do about them; rebuilding the manor has to take priority. The joy he sees in his people's faces when they hear the plans for the new stone hall is worth the risk. He's made them feel safe. That's what matters. Future problems will be dealt with in the future.

The future comes in July.

Baron Montagu is waiting for him in the Nottingham pavilion field. He expresses his sadness over the troubles at Dartington, and questions whether it's really big enough for a self-sustaining estate. He talks about how it would be better for Harry to become a vassal knight of Montagu directly, to move into his manor at Salisbury. How it would make more sense to foreclose on Harry's estate and pass it to Rabbie to manage alongside Ordlington. How Montagu understands the heavy burden of duty Harry shoulders, and how Harry can look at this as a chance to enjoy himself, without being beholden to debts and responsibilities. How the Baron has never seen Harry party like the other young knights do, and what a shame it is to miss out on the carefree days of youth.

Montagu doesn't mention Iain at all, and that little omission terrifies Harry.

It's all so gentle, so calm, so rational. Harry wants to kill Montagu. But all he can do is nod. Nod and wonder if, after all, Rabbie had thought up the idea of torching Dartington on his own. Looking back, it seems too cunning a plan for a person as coarse as Ufford.

Montagu smiles, as if expecting to be thanked for this.

'Give me until the end of the tournament,' Harry says. 'And let me go home and say goodbye, before this happens.'

'Of course, of course,' Montagu preens. 'But we so look forward to having you at Salisbury. Why don't you see the harvest in? And then you can move after the September tournaments.'

Or maybe never, Harry thinks.

And his last, most desperate plan begins to form.

That night, Iain can tell something is wrong, but thankfully the boy doesn't say anything. He just holds Harry, letting him take solace in his body, and not commenting how Harry's face is wet with tears as he comes.

All Harry can do is hope Iain will forgive him when everything is over.

At the mêlée the next morning, Harry is again on the King's team, their aketons sky-blue with gold in honour of Isabella, the Queen Mother, who is attending. There has been some sort of rapprochement between Edward and Isabella over the summer, Harry hears, and she has made a few trips to court. Nottingham in general is a bigger tournament than Burstwick, with the double royal attendance meaning that more of the Southern nobles have made an effort to attend. The Marcher Lords, the powerful barons who rule supreme on the border territories between England and Wales, are also there in force, though Nottingham is no small journey from their estates.

Harry grits his teeth and prays for bravery as he rides out into the arena.

He bows to the Queen and Isabella as his name is called, the applause nothing but a hollow noise.

And then, rather than ride to the lines where the rest of his team are assembled, as he has done every tournament before, he rides up to the benches where the flowers of English nobility are arrayed. Arundel is obvious, gaudy in red and gold. Next to him sits Alys. Harry walks Nomad up as close as he can to where she is, takes off his helmet, looks her in the eye, and bows.

His heart is beating so fast he feels like he's going to be sick. He can't breathe. Everything rests on this moment. If she publicly refuses him—

—but she does not.

Alys blushes, and unthreads a red ribbon twisted into her elaborate hairstyle. She leans over, reaching across the balustrade. And offers the ribbon to him.

Harry extends his wrist, and Alys ties the favour around it. He bows again and rides back to the lines to the whistles and applause of the assembled lords and ladies.

He exhales, loosening his blunted sword in its scabbard. Now all he has to do is show he is worthy of Alys's favour by coming first in the mêlée.

And then weather the tempest he'll find in Iain's eyes afterwards.

The mêlée goes well. Harry is waylaid afterwards by a few of the more pleasant knights, including Morley, who invites them all back to his large marquee pavilion for supper. Apparently, Harry is one of their group now, much as he doesn't feel it. So he follows. Harry knows it's cowardice, sliding off Nomad and handing the reins to Iain then disappearing with the other knights, but he needs to save his strength for the larger battle to come: the fight to save his home.

Iain is thankfully silent as he takes Nomad along with Harry's helmet, shield and plate, and heads back to their tent.

Supper is a large affair. The King joins them, as does Isabella, and Arundel, and Montagu. It stretches on for hours: the meal, then music and dancing, and a fool. The fool is small and gnarled, with a tin crown perched cockeye on his head. He capers about on tabletops, proclaiming himself the King of

France. He declares loudly that he's a Capet but he slurs it, instead making it come out as *poupée*, the French word for a child's doll. He manages to slur Valois into *fantoche*, or puppet, too. He jests about how he was found in a hedgerow, and how France misses a real king, but he'll do.

Then of course the fool does something incompetent, like dropping a knife which gets stuck in his thigh, or pouring wine down his face. Harry knows it's a prank to show honour to Isabella, and promote Edward's Capet lineage, but the fool's clumsy japes sour Harry's mood.

The 'real king' is in Harry's pavilion, probably cleaning tack at this very moment.

Harry makes eye contact with Alys, who is not sitting next to him, and glances towards the tent's entrance. Alys stands and whispers to Lord Arundel, who nods, and then she and her inevitable handmaiden approach Harry. He rises and excuses himself, saying he needs some air.

Before he can make it three steps, the fool is dancing in front of him, demanding, 'A knee! A knee! Bend a knee to the King of France and you may pass!'

Harry knows what he must do. He loudly declares, 'Of course,' before turning to Edward, kneeling, and saying, 'Your Majesty, may I pass?'

The fool howls in dismay and the lords and ladies cheer, none more loudly than Isabella. And if Harry in his mind had been kneeling before his dark, brooding prince of a squire, there is no one to know but him.

He rises stiffly, bows, and flees out the door with Alys.

'Court. So much fun,' Alys says, through gritted teeth.

'Indeed,' says Harry. Then, as they leave the noisy tent

behind, he relaxes. 'Thank you for today,' he says, 'and for walking with me.' He glances over Alys's shoulder. The chaperone has drifted about ten feet back. And they have walked far enough towards the edge of the field that there is nobody else around.

Harry takes a deep breath. 'Alys,' he begins, looking into her bright face. 'I think by now you know I hold you above all women—'

Her lips quirk. 'Yes, but that's the problem, isn't it? Above all women. But . . . it is not a woman you think about, in your most private moments, is it?'

Harry's cheeks flame red. 'I . . .' he chokes, his voice high.

Alys places a hand on his bicep, and tilts her head. She's not condemning him. And that's somehow worse. 'Oh, Harry. Your Scotsman, isn't it? When you took my favour, he glared at me like he wanted to kill me.'

'To be fair he, uh, looks at most people like that,' Harry mumbles.

'Mm. Except you,' Alys says. 'And you are inseparable from him.'

Harry wilts. It was a stupid plan, anyway. 'I love him,' he breathes.

'He is your squire,' Alys says. 'Your *servant*. Are you not concerned that he couldn't say no?'

Harry snorts in amusement. 'Oh, he bloody can. He says no every day. He's the worst, most insubordinate servant you've ever met. One time? He stabbed my horse. When I first met him? He bit me. Bit me! I still have the scar.' He looks at Alys again, deadly serious. 'Besides, you and I both know he is no squire. Not really.'

'But a manor cannot be maintained without heirs,' Alys sighs.

'Or money,' Harry replies. 'Montagu is taking Dartington. It's why . . .' He gestures at Alys. Then he brings the back of his hand to his face, brushing away the tears that track hot and silent down his cheeks. He strides over to an old oak tree at the edge of the field and collapses against it. 'He is my entire world, Alys. I loved him as a Scottish orphan; I love him as a prince of France, I love him. *I love him*.'

Harry squeezes his eyes shut. 'What do we do? I fear for his life. I fear Montagu's plan for him. I can't lose him. But I also can't abandon Dartington. I can't let Rabbie loose on my people.' He smiles up at Alys, weakly. 'And I feel terrible for leading you on. You made a good escape, though. All I could have given you is a poor Devon manor, and a lord who loves you never more than in a courtly way.' Harry bows his head. 'You are worth so much more than what I have to offer. I'm sorry, Alys.'

Alys leans her shoulder against the oak tree, and puts a small, cool hand on Harry's cheek. 'What if I do not want more than courtly love?'

Harry blinks at her.

'Don't go assuming you know what is best for other people, Harry,' Alys admonishes. 'You have few faults, but that's first among them.'

As their shadows creep long across the field, she continues. 'I have a proposal for you. You wish a wife, while you love another who you cannot be with publicly. I wish a husband I can trust, and . . . not to be touched.'

Harry opens his mouth to say something, but Alys holds up

a finger. 'I'm not frigid. I don't need to be *warmed up*. I am fine the way that I am. And if I enter an arrangement with you – because it's you or the convent, to be honest – you must understand what I want, which is that our love remain chaste and courtly. And you never make me feel lesser for what I do not desire.'

'Children will be . . . expected,' Harry says.

'I know. There are ways.' Alys pauses, and looks back at the bright glow of the pavilions scattered behind them. 'What's it like, to love like that? The way you love him?'

Harry stutters. How do you put into words something so all-encompassing? 'It's a fire, always burning, threatening to consume me whole. It's terrifying, flying over an abyss, knowing your wings will fail. It's the best feeling in the world.'

'Sounds like a tremendous amount of bother,' Alys sighs.

'It is,' Harry says. 'He's worth it.'

Alys hums, then shifts, so her back is against the tree. 'Here is my proposal, Harry. First, I meet your boy—'

'Iain, he's called Iain,' Harry says.

'I meet Iain. We must explain this to him. If he agrees, and if he and I can get along, then you and I marry. My dowry severs your financial obligation to Montagu. Your boy goes to the King and swears fealty—'

'Ah, that's not likely to happen,' says Harry.

'Would he formally give up all claim to the French throne?' Alys asks.

'Yes, I believe he would,' Harry says. 'He doesn't want to be king.'

'That's good,' Alys breathes. Then she whispers in Harry's ear, and he can hear the smile in her voice. 'He's terrifying.'

Harry melts a little. 'I know,' he says.

'We need to let people know who he is,' Alys says. 'If he's a secret, he's a pawn. If he is known, then he is a considerably more powerful piece in the chessboard. And with me, you get Arundel, and his protection, as he won't let anything happen to his beloved ward.'

'You don't mind if we continue to . . . ?' Harry says.

'Believe me, it would ease my anxieties greatly if you and he go at it like the clappers,' Alys snorts. 'Then I know you're getting what you need from someone safe, who's not me. That you're not going to bring me home and then try to "change my mind" about sex.'

Alys looks at Harry, and raises an eyebrow at the grin on his face. 'What?' she asks.

'It's just . . .' Harry begins. 'When I was a child, I'd go to this pond and lie on a rock and dream of my future, of having a staunch knight as my best friend, and a noble lady to love with all my heart. And now I find myself a man, a warrior I love with all my heart, and a noble lady as my best friend.' He shakes his head. 'This is. Not how I expected my life to go.'

'No. Nor mine,' sighs Alys. 'Yet here we are.'

Harry walks Alys and her handmaiden back to Arundel's tent, with a promise that he will speak to Iain, and arrange a time for them to meet after the next day's jousting.

Except Iain isn't at Harry's pavilion.

Harry strides back to Morley's tent, where the party is still in full force. He looks among the squires and servants milling at its margins for the familiar broad shoulders, the dark mop of hair. But Iain's not there, either.

He tries to calm his rising panic as he criss-crosses the pavilion field, looking for his squire. Iain wouldn't have run, would he? Their horses are still tied up. Nothing is missing from the tent. If Iain were really escaping he would have grabbed Libby, who's fastest, along with provisions and weapons.

Or maybe he slipped away on foot, Harry's terror whispers. He could disappear into the tourney crowds, slipping north for the Scottish border, never to return.

Harry clutches his chest and has to grab a nearby tent's guy rope for support. He can't breathe. Iain's gone. There is no forgiveness. It's like a vice is crushing his chest. He wants to sink to the ground and curl up, but he can't. They can't see him like this: their champion, scared into paralysis by misplacing his squire. Nobody will help him then, if they see how weak he truly is.

Harry pulls himself up by sheer force of will alone, and reaches for the next tent rope. He'll get to his own damn tent and curl up there, even if he has to do it by lurching from rope to rope like a drunk. Drunkenness is, after all, excusable in a knight.

And that's when he hears it: a low moan from the other side of the canvas. From inside the tent whose support he's clinging to for dear life.

Harry's heart turns to lead in his chest.

He knows that moan.

He's *caused* it, so many times, in so many different ways.

Harry lurches towards the tent's entrance and throws it open.

He thought the worst thing that could happen to him was Iain leaving.

He was wrong.

Things can always be worse.

It's Sir Hugh's tent, Sir Hugh who is still at Morley's party. And his squire, Rolly, the big sandy blond, is on his knees, Iain's cock in his mouth. Iain has one hand around a jug of wine, and the other fisted in Rolly's hair as he fucks into the boy's mouth. He's wearing the blue shirt Annie made him. The one that brings out his eyes.

Harry must make some sort of noise, as when his gaze rakes up Iain's body, he finds the boy's pale eyes, half-lidded with lust and debauchery, looking at him in unfocused amusement. Iain thrusts a few more times into Rolly's mouth and then comes, his eyes never leaving Harry's.

Harry is frozen in place, unable to move, hating his own cowardice, hating Iain's stupid pride. Hating how hard he is from watching someone else defile the man he loves.

He watches as Iain reaches down and drags Rolly up, a grotesque parody of his action after their bout in Burstwick. He kisses the other boy, slow and filthy in the way only Iain can kiss, and then he looks over Rolly's shoulder at Harry. 'Go finish your celebrations with Lady de Morton,' Iain slurs. 'And leave me to finish mine.' Rolly tenses, becoming aware of Harry, and Harry watches the muscles of Iain's arms flex, restraining the other boy, reassuring him.

Harry is over there at the speed of thought, grabbing Rolly and shoving him away from Iain. Rolly is drunk too, babbling apologies, then falling inelegantly on his backside. Harry yanks Iain by the hair. 'Fuck you,' he hisses. 'You have no idea what is going on.'

'And whose fault is that?' Iain growls back.

Harry slaps him across the cheek, so hard it makes his hand sting. Words, hateful words, tumble out of his mouth. 'You savage little Scottish cur, you perverted piece of filth—' He doesn't mean it, of course. He picks the most wounding words he can, so he can hurt Iain just as much as it hurt him to see—

To see—

He watches as Iain pales, his luminescent blue eyes widening in horror. That Harry of all people should think this of him.

Harry wants to take the words back, catch them and stuff them into his mouth and swallow them down like a handful of wasps.

But he can't.

He knows he deserves the punch that Iain lands on his stomach, but it doesn't make it hurt any less. He stumbles across the tent, backwards, trying to catch his breath, and his foot connects with something metal that falls over with a *klank*.

Harry glances down. It's Sir Hugh's practice kit, neatly piled. Padded jackets, plain helmets, blunted swords. Out of the corner of his eye he can see Iain advancing on him, fists balled, murder in his eyes.

Harry flings a padded jacket at him. Iain catches it, and the helmet that comes after it.

'Outside. *Now*,' Harry barks, grabbing a helmet of his own. 'We finish this.'

In retrospect, the middle of the pavilion field, in the narrow areas between tents, wasn't the smartest place for them to take out their anger on each other. But both he and Iain are beyond good sense. There is only the bottomless fury that comes from a betrayal of love.

Neither of them holds back. Harry knew it was going to be that sort of fight, from the moment he slapped Iain, from when Iain slammed his fist into Harry's stomach with the full power of his muscular frame. Harry honestly doesn't know what's going to happen when one of them wins, whether it will really settle anything at all. Because part of him still wants to knock Iain's sword out of his hand, shove him down, and grind on him until he comes.

That quickly gets ruled out as a possibility. It's between Vespers and Compline, when everyone is drifting back to their tents for the night, and the sound of clashing blades rings loud in the calm of twilight. They draw a crowd. Two young men in peak physical condition, expert swordsmen, who know each other's every weakness and ruthlessly exploit them. The fighting is savage, fast, and beautiful. Swords move almost swifter than the eye can see, and blows are landed with feet and fists as often as with blunted steel.

Harry hears snatches of talk from the crowd, wondering who they are, what they're fighting about. If this is an entertainment that the King has organised. Then he hears Edward's rich tones in response: 'Nothing to do with us, I'm afraid.'

The King is in the crowd. *Marvellous*, Harry thinks. The King is watching him have a very public, armed spat with his lover. So much for his grand hopes for a triumphant Nottingham tournament.

Harry's momentary distraction is enough for Iain to wind his leg behind Harry's and knock him to the ground. He hits the grass and rolls, kicking out at Iain to keep him away, then springs back to his feet. He's winded, though, and Iain can see it. Iain doesn't let him regain his breath, relentlessly pushing his advantage and landing blows where he can to Harry's chest, repeatedly punching the air out of him.

Somewhere in that assault, Harry loses heart for the fight.

He's tired of everything. The politics. The drama. The way he has lied to and failed the people he loves, Iain foremost among them.

Iain whacks him in the head with his blade, and Harry sinks to his knees, discarding his sword and his helmet. You can kill a man with a blunted sword easily enough, if that man's not wearing a helmet.

He hears the susurration of voices through the crowd as they realise who he is.

Harry bows his head and spreads his arms. If this is the end, let it come.

Whoever follows after him will probably do a better job anyway.

But the blow never comes.

Iain just grunts and shoves the point of his sword into the ground, in front of Harry, then walks away.

Harry watches Iain pace within the circle of onlookers like a wolf in a cage. He's still wearing his helmet. Alys is right, Harry thinks idly. Iain is terrifying when he's like this.

A woman's voice rings out from behind them. 'Who is this knight of England who defeats our young champion?'

Iain whirls, and rips off his helmet. Harry gasps, because he's never seen that much hate on his face. 'I am no knight of England,' Iain hisses.

Harry glances over his shoulder at the plump blonde woman who had asked the question. At the rich embroidery of her azure clothing; at the thin gold circlet she wears. His heart sinks. Things, apparently, are not yet done getting worse.

Another voice from the crowd yells, 'Have some respect for the Dowager Queen Isabella!'

Iain's lips twist into a mocking smile as he strides towards Isabella. 'Never. She is not *my* queen,' he snarls. Harry hears the sound of two dozen swords being drawn out of scabbards as Iain looms over the Queen Mother. 'Do you know who I am, *ma tante?* All your schemes lie in dust, and I am living proof.'

Isabella screams, goes white, and falls backwards in a dead faint.

The crowd dissolves into uproar. Harry is on his feet, making his way to Iain, the instinct in him screaming *protect protect protect*, but others are closer, and they have weapons drawn, weapons that are battlefield-sharp, and Iain raises his blunt sword and—

'Seonaidh mac Maíl Coluim, Lord of Galloway Forest,' comes the Earl of Arundel's voice, cutting loud across the pandemonium. 'Son of Marguerite of France, herself eldest child of King Philip the Fair.'

That shuts almost everyone up. Someone from the crowd yells, 'A pretender!' but the person is quickly shushed.

Arundel continues, pushing his way through the stunned circle of courtiers towards Iain, standing defiant in its centre. 'A full-blooded prince of France, first in line to the Capet dynasty. France could be yours, boy. It technically is. Galloway could be yours, and, knowing Scotland, probably will be before the year is out. And yet you've been hiding yourself away in Devonshire. What do you choose?' Arundel says, spreading his hands open in front of Iain.

'Not to play,' Iain growls, lifting his chin in defiance.

'Ah, but that is not an option for someone of your birth,' Arundel says.

Iain narrows his eyes. 'I can do whatever I want.'

'Well, if there was any doubt you're a prince, you just removed it,' Arundel says, to scattered laughter in the crowd. Harry is close enough to Iain now to see Arundel lean in to Iain's ear, and hear as he whispers, 'The King will either summon you or kill you. Be prepared for both.'

'I've been preparing for this since I could walk,' Iain answers.

'Indeed,' Arundel says, catching Harry's eye as well. 'If you two need safe haven, Arundel Castle is always open to you.'

Iain nods.

A dozen men-at-arms in the King's colours force their way through to them. Two minister to the Queen Mother, lifting her onto a litter and carrying her away towards a knot of anxious handmaidens. The rest circle Iain, and open a path through the crowd.

Harry suddenly sees Montagu in the crowd. They lock eyes, and Montagu smiles, before disappearing. Something terrifies Harry about that smile, but then the King is striding towards them up the path flanked by his soldiers, and there are more important matters to be concerned with.

Harry and Arundel kneel before the King. Iain does not.

Two men-at-arms step forwards, the lead one asking Iain if he will take a knee for the King by choice or by force. Iain says nothing, and remains standing. The soldiers lunge forwards, grabbing for Iain.

Edward raises a hand when he sees the man-at-arms about

to seize Iain's shoulder. 'Stop,' he commands. 'You will not put your hands on someone of royal blood.'

Harry hears the gasps of the crowd, unwilling to believe Iain's identity until the King acknowledged it.

Edward steps up and kisses Iain on both cheeks. 'Cousin,' he says.

Iain inclines his head and replies, 'Cousin.'

Iain quickly doffs his practice jacket and hands it and his borrowed sword back to Harry. 'Please give my apologies to Sir Hugh,' he says.

Harry's loins twist at how damn regal Iain is. Even barefoot in his simple blue shirt, he's twice the man of any of the nobles gathered there in their damask and parti-coloured scarlets.

'We have much to discuss,' the King says, taking Iain's arm. 'Let us return to my chambers. Sir Harry may come with us too.'

Iain glances at Harry, emotionless, then turns back to the King and says, 'No. I'm afraid Sir Harry has business back at his manor, and his impending marriage to plan.'

'Alas,' says the King, 'and congratulations. Let my steward know the details, so we may send a gift.'

Then he steers Iain down the corridor of men-at-arms, and out of Harry's life.

TEN

July–November 1334: Castle of Sand

'Told you he was a lord,' Annie says.

Harry sighs. '*I know*,' he says. He stares dully out at the foundation of his new, larger hall. Progress is slow; they'll be in the barn all winter at this rate. Especially as half the workmen are likely to vanish as soon as harvest starts.

At least they are debt-free now. Arundel caught up with Harry on the second day of the tournament, after Harry informed the heraldry clerks he was dropping out of the joust to go home. The Earl sat himself down on Harry's travelling chest, sighed, and said, 'How bad is it, lad?'

Harry had almost said *it feels like there is a hole in my chest that will never heal*, before he realised that Arundel was tossing a bag of gold from hand to hand. Probably not referring to Iain, then.

So Harry sat down on the ground and named a number. 'That's for Montagu,' he explained. 'Our old debts.'

'And the new ones?' Arundel had asked. 'Alys says you're rebuilding your manor. Oh, here's a tip: garderobes. Also, a lady's chambers. Alys would prefer that. And for the love of all that's holy, glass windows. You wouldn't believe the difference.'

Harry had shaken his head and laughed hollowly to himself. 'We can't afford that, your lordship.'

'Please. I'm about to be your father-in-law. Wait, not father.

You're my ward-in-law. Or something like that. In any case, call me Richard. And, lad?' Arundel said.

Harry raised his head, and Arundel tossed him the bag of gold. 'You can afford it now,' the Earl said.

Harry opened his mouth to protest, but the Earl's frown cut him off. 'Don't argue. Alys is used to a certain standard. I'd be derelict in my duty as her protector if I didn't ensure you can keep her in the manner – or indeed the *manor* – to which she's become accustomed.'

Harry reluctantly pocketed the gold. 'Look out for him, will you?' he had asked, at the end.

Arundel nodded, and patted his shoulder.

And now it is August and Harry is back in Devon, with everything a man of his position could want, and without the one person he needs. His people try to cheer him up. Annie cooks him his favourite foods; Adam and Jed drag him to see calves and piglets and the goose that Jed has taught to perform tricks; Kit serenades him with some of the most tasteless songs he's ever had the misfortune to hear. But Harry sleepwalks through his days, attending to his duties, and then goes to his corner of the barn to pretend to sleep at night.

At least the harvest is starting soon, Harry thinks. He can lose himself in physical labour.

Harry and Alys correspond. They set the wedding for Christmastime, at Arundel Castle, after the final tournaments are over and the new hall is at least partially completed. Iain's approval is no longer an issue. They also agree that while Alys will visit Dartington after the wedding, she will not move down there permanently until the new hall is finished. Harry will not have his wife living in a barn.

There's no word of, or from, Iain.

Harry almost drops out of the September tournaments. He thinks about them with every swing of his sickle in August, with every fistful of wheat he harvests. He's lost his stomach for fighting.

But what other chance will he have to see Iain, beyond tilt-yards and mêlée fields?

Once the wheat and beans are in, he packs up the cart and heads for Guildford. Kit and Piers go with him. Neither can squire worth a damn, and he hadn't been planning on the company, but on the morning of departure Kit gets up in the cart's seat next to Harry and takes Numbles' reins from his hand without a word. Piers unhitches Nomad from the back of the cart and clambers up on the big destrier.

Guildford isn't far. Three days' travel, four if they go slow. And it is *painfully* slow. Post-harvest, the roads of the South are clogged with carts of grain going to mills, markets and ports; villagers returning from helping their families harvest; and travellers heading home for Michaelmas.

With the most important event of England's year over, the mood is one of holiday both on the road and at the tournament. It's another Dunstable, thousands of people crowding the grounds, the field fenced off for the knights' pavilions a gay canvas city in its own right. This tournament is short, a two-day affair, before the entire circus begins all over again in Smithfield, just outside the City of London, in two further days. The Smithfield tournament will last the rest of the month, until Michaelmas.

Harry slumps in his seat and looks over the crowd. So many faces, and yet none are the *right* face. They find a decent spot towards the edge of the field, and Harry leaves Kit and Piers to set up the pavilion while he goes to check in with the heraldry clerks.

Lord Michael sees him approaching and waves him to the head of the queue. Harry smiles awkwardly at the knights and lords in line as he cuts in front of them. 'Checking in, milord,' Harry mumbles, once he reaches the clerks' long oak table.

'Morris already has your paper prepared, young man,' Lord Michael says, his sharp eyes twinkling with amusement. Then he leans forwards and pats Harry's hand, across the table, conspiratorially. 'You could have *told* us, you know,' Lord Michael whispers. 'Poor Magnus almost had an attack of dyscrasia—'

'Did *not*,' grumbles Lord Magnus.

'Yes you did, you liar, don't try to blame it on bad eggs at breakfast—'

'No, Michael, *you're* the only bad egg here—'

'Of course we *knew*,' interjects Lord Morris, waving Harry's paper. 'Always so charming, and held himself so well.'

'Not like *some*,' mutters Lord Magnus, glaring at a minor knight sighing dramatically at the delay in the queue.

'Looks like Lord Franklin is going into the final mêlée again, the one nobody watches,' Lord Morris singsongs under his breath, noting down the name of the impatient knight. 'You'd think he'd figure out why it keeps happening, but *no*.'

Harry edges over to Lord Morris and takes his stamped paper. 'Um, is he competing?'

'Franklin? Alas, yes,' Lord Magnus sighs. 'Overbearing in victory, petulant in defeat. The very model of the modern chevalier.'

'No, Iain,' Harry says. 'Uh. I mean, Lord Iain. My former squire. The prince.'

Lord Magnus's eyes crinkle in delight at Harry's discomfort. 'We shall see,' he says. 'We shall see. *Next!*'

Harry looks at his paper as he wanders the pavilion field. He's not in the main mêlée, and he wonders if Iain is the reason he's fallen out of favour between July and September. If he's not in the opening mêlée, he's not guaranteed a place in the joust – especially in a tournament this short. Once each knight from the Inside team of the main mêlée has jousted through each knight from the Outside team, the top few scorers joust through the top two knights from each of the other mêlées. Which means there's now additional pressure on Harry to score high in his mêlée.

He sighs. At least if he's in a later mêlée, he tells himself, he can sleep in a little tomorrow. (He won't, but it's a nice idea.)

He looks across the field until he spots Arundel's red-and-gold lion banner, and then directs his feet there. The Earl – *Richard* – embraces Harry warmly, and tuts at the dark circles under his eyes. Harry bows to Alys, in periwinkle blue over a scarlet underdress, and presses the back of her hand to his lips.

Then Harry sinks onto a travelling chest with a sigh. He looks up at Arundel, then at Alys.

'Richard knows, Harry,' Alys whispers, coming to perch next to him. 'Everything.'

Harry's shoulders hunch down, as if the wires supporting him have been let go. He's so damn tired of pretending to be fine. He glances around to check if any servants are within earshot, then whispers, 'How is he?'

'He scrubs up well,' says Arundel, pouring them both a cup of wine. 'Those legs in a pair of tight hose? Should be illegal.

And there's rampant speculation at court about whether he stuffs the front of his hose or he simply has the most enormous—'

'Richard!' Alys squawks and smacks Arundel in the arm, spilling his drink. 'That's *not* what Harry wants to hear.'

'Well, he's not sitting there pining for you, I'm sorry to say,' Arundel says, shaking the spilled wine off his hand. 'He's not taken up with anyone that I know of, despite a lot of offers, but he's been . . . quite busy with court politics.'

Harry closes his eyes. A long sigh escapes him, the last ghost of hope leaving his body. 'What is he doing, then?'

'Playing a dangerous game very well,' Arundel says. He pulls over a bench and sits down. And a smile breaks across his face. Harry blinks. He thinks it's the first genuine smile he's ever seen on Arundel.

'Isabella can't even look at him. It's wonderful,' Arundel enthuses. 'She refuses to leave her estate near Newmarket. Added guards, even. That woman's lover executed my father and stole my lands. I feel like a terrible person for saying this, but your Iain putting the fear of God into that scheming harpy?' He salutes Harry with his wine cup. 'Repayment in full for every penny I gave you.'

Harry doesn't have it in him to salute back. All he can think is *he's not my Iain. Not any more.* He stares down at his cup, tilting it back and forth, then asks the question that haunts him at night – that, and the memory of a smile in the Compline shadows. 'And Montagu?'

'Ah, you mean Iain's great saviour?' Arundel snorts. He places his hands on his chest and begins to speak in a fair approximation of the Baron's nasal Home Counties twang. 'My brave knights and I rode far into the enemy's territory to rescue the boy before he starved to death or was killed by Balliol. Your Majesty knows of course that the prince's father was a dangerous Scottish nationalist. Despite our fears over his loyalty, we did all we could to keep the young prince safe in England—' Arundel breaks off and shivers in disgust, then squints at Harry. 'How true is any of that?'

'All of it,' Harry says, remembering the muffled sound of oars and the sharp iron stench of blood. 'And none.'

'Montagu's usual, then,' Arundel says, taking a long slug of his drink.

'Did the King believe him?' Harry asks.

'Montagu has committed no crime,' Arundel sighs. 'And Iain is in fact here because of him. We can't get around that. The King won't remove a baron that powerful just because some people at court don't like him, or disapprove of his methods. If he would, I'd have managed to get Montagu turfed out long ago.'

Harry squeezes his eyes shut, willing down the almost visceral fury he feels. It's *wrong*, what Montagu did. What Rabbie helped him do.

A small, cool hand comes to rest on his forearm. 'Iain is going after Montagu,' Alys says. 'And winning.'

'I thought you said—' Harry begins, looking at Arundel in confusion.

'I said neither the King nor anyone else would go against Montagu directly right now,' Arundel replies. 'Not even me. Too dangerous – lost my lands once, won't go through that again. But Montagu's supporters? Another story. Iain's making life quietly difficult for quite a few of them and, well, that costs

Montagu money.' Arundel sighs and rolls his wine cup between his fingers. 'I fear for him, though, goading the Baron like that. Montagu is extremely dangerous when he's cornered. I want to help Iain, but . . . he avoids us. He won't talk to me.'

Harry gulps down the contents of his own wine cup, long ignored in his hands. The alcohol burns in his throat, cutting sharply through the misery that has clouded him since July. 'Is he here?' Harry says, his voice thick.

'Yes,' the Earl says, squinting out of the tent at the milling crowds of knights and squires. 'I believe he is.'

Harry doesn't sleep. His body, under the striped canvas of the pavilion, aches with the space Iain has left. Not that there is any space on the pallet, not really. Piers is all elbows as he sleeps, and Kit lies on his back like a starfish, snoring.

They all rise shortly after dawn. Piers holds up Harry's court clothes, raising an eyebrow. Harry shakes his head. Not today. Maybe never again. He knows he's going to watch the first mêlée, and he should dress in finery and make an appearance with Alys, but his heart isn't in it. Later. After the fights, for dinner, he'll make himself fancy.

Instead he pulls on his favourite travelling shirt and a pair of old breeches, throwing his knight's belt on over it. The three of them trudge outside to buy breakfast from the vendors at the edge of the field. And Harry would find it hilarious, if it weren't so sad, the way all of them are distracted by any glimpse of dark, shaggy hair or broad shoulders.

It's not *him*, though. It's never him.

His hair wouldn't be shaggy any more, Harry thinks, as they wander over to the mêlée grounds. It will be sleek and styled, and he'll be wearing fine silks and velvets. Too fine for Dartington, but no less than he deserves.

Harry leads Kit and Piers over to the second stand, the one for common knights and squires not in the circle of the King. It's crowded, but they manage to squeeze in about three benches up, on the end. A few of the knights recognise Harry and comment with surprise he's not in the starting group. He shrugs and replies, 'I guess they've decided to spread the talent out a bit more. Besides, I'm looking forward to fighting against different people from the usual lot.'

There's a quick and lively comparing of schedules, and Harry meets a few of the knights he'll be fighting with and against in his mêlée. They're all good knights, highly competent men who are no longer rising stars nor fashionable at court. Sir Brian Cradoc, the knight who'd unhorsed him at Burstwick, is on his team here in Guildford. Harry takes to the wry older Durham knight immediately.

Harry smiles to himself. This is the group Sir Simon would be in, if he were still alive. Harry had wanted to be part of the King's group for so long – and he was, for a brief, turbulent winter. Now he's out, back down where he belongs, and he finds he doesn't mind at all. The fighting will be as good, or better, if not nearly as popular.

Iain is neither in the opening mêlée nor in the stands watching it. And Harry checks many, many times. (He can picture Iain in court clothes, lounging with Queen Philippa in the royal enclosure, pointing out the finer details of the fighting to her. Making her laugh.)

Harry is both at a loss, and pathetically glad for Iain's absence, as he hurries to put on his armour for his own bout.

He doesn't know what he would have done if he had seen Iain. He's pretty sure it would have been something foolish.

It takes a solid whack on his shield-edge from one of the opposing knights for him to stop glancing at the stands during his own mêlée. The fighting is . . . the fighting is *great*, once he gets his head into it. All twenty-four knights on the field are there because they're good, not because of who they know. There's none of the easy unhorsings of the opening mêlée. It's a slow grind against men, veterans, who have done this for real, with sharpened swords, in battles against the Welsh and the Scots, and against each other on Isabella and Mortimer's long ride across England to dethrone Edward's father.

Harry holds his own. He earns the respect of the knights he's fighting with. If he's not doing it for them, but for a pair of pale eyes that he hopes is watching, well . . . the result is the same, in the end.

He rides out of it a respectable second, behind Sir Brian, so he qualifies for the next day's jousting. Which means if he places well in the joust, he'll be invited to the celebratory supper with the King. Iain will be there, if he's anywhere.

There are friendly faces all around him, and invitations to dine – Sir Brian; Sirs Malachi and Morien, up from Cornwall; even jolly Sir Gervase. Sir Hugh hails him from afar, but . . . Harry pretends not to see. Fond as he is of Sir Hugh, he can't be in the same tent as Rolly right now. Or indeed ever again. Harry hands over Nomad to Piers and stands still as Kit fumbles his armour off. Then he nods, leaves them money for dinner, and says he'll be back later. He ignores their concerned looks.

And as he walks out of the stifling, overcrowded pavilion field, he starts to notice who isn't there: Montagu. Rabbie.

Percy. Several of Montagu's lot are in attendance: Colin Crocker and Odo Waldegrave competed in the opening mêlée. Harry has glimpsed a few others, too, from the Galloway Dozen – the knights who rode without honour into Scotland to murder a king's daughter and put her son in a cage.

And for the thousandth time that day, he wonders what Iain is doing. If he's well.

Harry finds a small chapel on the outskirts of town. He doesn't have much to say to God right now, other than *please keep Iain safe from harm*. But the cool solitude and the smell of the candles and incense make him feel better. He stays through None, past Vespers. Then he walks back to his pavilion through the September twilight. He notices absently that he's hungry, but it's not important.

Nothing is important any more.

The next day, Harry rides to the tiltyard. Part of him is looking forward to the thrill; the thundering hooves and jarring impact of the joust. Part of him is afraid that not even breaking lances at a gallop will be able to make him feel anything.

Apparently being completely numb makes him better at jousting. He unhorses both Sir Brian and Robert Morley, and breaks his lance every time against his other half-dozen opponents. There is no joy in victory. He takes no pleasure in the shouts of his name from the thousand onlookers.

There's one opponent left: Colin Crocker. Then he's done. Then he can go back to his pavilion. He readies his lance and waits for the steward's hand to drop.

Rather than starting the first pass, the steward becomes distracted by the sounds of a kerfuffle over by the entrance to the tiltyard, behind Harry. His peripheral vision is limited by his helmet, but he can see the steward nod. The man's hand then closes into a fist, and he bends his elbow, pulling that fist down to chest level.

It's a postponement.

Harry raises his lance. He's confused, and wants to turn Nomad to see what's going on, but once he does he'll have to circle round again to get in position.

'Change in order,' the steward calls. 'Sir Harry Lyon of Dartington, to tilt second.'

Well, Harry has to turn Nomad now, because he needs to go back to the waiting area. He's annoyed, because this is his last run. Why can't he just tilt against Crocker, make his three passes, then go home? Why does he have to delay for some oversleeping nobleman who missed his earlier slot and is demanding the right to catch up? (He knows why: precedence. Because he can win all the tournaments in England, but he's still nothing more than a minor country lord.)

It's hard to communicate a truly effective glare through the narrow eye slits of a helmet, but Harry is making his best effort as he turns to face the newcomer.

The intruder knight is all in new armour, the most modern style, with almost no mail visible under bright, shining plate. His shield is also new, so new it's still blank. The only colour is his lance: red as blood. He's big. And eerily calm as he rides past Harry without a glance. His dark brown destrier is of the finest quality, the horse's coat brushed and oiled to almost a mirror shine, caparisoned in white.

Harry's heart twists within him as he realises who the knight must be. It's too late, though. The knight is already past him.

He'd spent so much time checking out the man's fancy plate armour and horse that he'd never thought to look him in the eyes.

But he *knows* Iain. He knows how Iain moves. He taught Iain how to joust.

And he would bet the entirety of his already-damned soul that this shining knight is the man he loves.

It's a wonderful piece of showmanship, in any case. The crowd above him is abuzz with rumours. Is it the King? Is it a foreign noble? All eyes turn towards the steward, as he offers Crocker the chance to cross lances with the stranger. Or to refuse, as is his right.

'Sir Colin Crocker, will you tilt against the Knight in Silver?' the steward calls.

Crocker hesitates, then looks at the benches. Everyone is on the edge of their seat. In front of a crowd this big, this excited, he'll surely be booed for a coward if he backs down.

Crocker nods his acceptance.

The cheers are thunderous. The Knight in Silver bows to the crowd, and raises his lance hand to his helmet in salute. The shouts grow even louder.

Show-off, Harry thinks to himself.

The two knights level their lances and spur their horses. Harry sends a little prayer up for Iain's victory. Crocker is well trained, and plays as dirty as he can. But Iain's armour looks strong and good, and he's sitting well, lance steady—

Both lances break. Even score. Iain didn't move an inch in his seat when the lance hit his shield; Crocker was forced back a little on impact. The knights slow their horses when they reach the opposite end of the lists, tossing their broken lances away. Stewards' assistants run out onto the grounds of the lists and pick up the splintered remains, so the horses don't injure their feet on the next pass.

Harry watches Iain reach out for a new lance. It's put in his hand, plain scarlet like his first one. He grasps it midway up the lance, then tosses it upwards, catching it just behind the vamplate and tucking it under his arm as he turns for the second pass.

The steward's hand is out flat, like a knife, and high in the air, arm straight. He drops his arm in a fast, chopping motion, and the thunder of hooves fills the air.

Iain's leaning forwards. He's enjoying it, Harry thinks. Crocker's lance wavers, and he reseats it but it's a little too late—

Crocker's lance slips off Iain's shield. Iain's lance shatters against Crocker's. Crocker tosses his unbroken lance aside and raises his arm, acknowledging the point against him.

Now Iain is back on Harry's side. As he slows his horse and takes his final lance, Harry stares at him. He doesn't know what he's hoping for. A glance from silver-grey eyes. Perhaps an acknowledgement.

He doesn't get it. The knight just turns around and makes ready for his final pass.

Harry looks over to Crocker. The man has rejected one lance and is pointing towards another. Fear clutches at Harry's stomach, and the scar on his chest from Crocker's sharpened lance-point in January burns in sympathy. If Crocker is up to his tricks—

The steward's arm slices down. Final pass.

Both knights spur their horses to full gallop. Harry winces.

They're going to come together hard; bone-crushingly hard. And if Crocker's lance-point is sharpened, it will go far deeper than just a shallow chest wound. It could go right through a man.

The Knight in Silver – Iain – twists his torso to the left at the last moment, sending Crocker's lance glancing off his shield, and putting even more power behind his own lance hit. Crocker misses it, too busy trying to adjust his aim as Iain's shield moves.

Unfortunately for Crocker, as he chases his target with his lance-point, he shifts his shield, too.

Iain's lance glances off the edge of Crocker's shield and is knocked upwards, into his helmet.

Through his helmet.

The lance breaks. It's not the shattering of a well-aimed and well-caught lance. It's the wet snap of a spear that's got one end stuck in flesh.

The crowd gasps as one, and then the screaming starts.

Crocker's horse keeps running. The lurching, dead weight of the unresponsive knight on his back terrifies the destrier. It reaches the end of the enclosure and whirls, as squires and stewards' assistants fan out around it, trying to grab its reins without getting kicked in the face.

Harry nudges Nomad with his knees, shouting 'I'll get him' at the terrified squires, and trying not to look at the foot and a half of ash wood sticking out of Colin Crocker's eye. The assistants scatter. Harry yells at the closest onlookers to move back, and manages to close off Crocker's terrified horse against a corner rail with Nomad's body. He leans over and pulls the reins out of Crocker's numb fingers. Then he leads the horse back to Crocker's squire. The horse is still in the grip of panic, rolling its eyes and tossing its head, and Harry knows it needs to be removed from this small, crowded area before it does any damage.

The squire glances up at Crocker, unsure what to do.

'He's dead, lad,' Harry says. 'Don't . . . don't take him off his horse here. Let the crowd think he rode out. Give him that dignity.'

The boy's brow furrows, furious on his master's behalf. 'But we need to look at that knight's lance,' he says.

Harry sighs, and glances at the long, deep scratch in the white paint of the Knight in Silver's shield, the sort of scratch a properly tipped jousting lance could never make. The boy's eyes follow his. Then Harry looks over at the glinting, sharpened metal tip of Crocker's shattered last lance on the ground. At the plaster flaking off the iron point. 'Boy, you don't want to do that,' Harry growls.

The boy gulps, and nods. Crocker's corpse sways in the saddle as the boy leads the horse out, back to the pavilions.

Accidents aren't uncommon in jousting. Nearly every tourney, there's a knight who breaks a bone, or worse. A couple of times a year, someone gets hit so hard they never get up again. The crowd's used to the high stakes. It's part of the fun for them, Harry thinks. But it's one thing to see a man knocked cold off his horse. It's quite another to see a spear through a knight's eye, to see blood leaching out the bottom of his helmet in a sluggish, red tide, staining his surcoat. It's a little too close to real war.

Harry can feel how unsettled the atmosphere is. Nobody knows what to do. The steward is distracted, looking at the sharpened tip of Crocker's lance brought to him by the assistant who was cleaning the detritus off that lane. The Knight in Silver is pacing his horse back and forth at the other end of the tiltyard, waiting to be cleared. And the crowd grows increasingly restless with the lack of information.

So Harry steps in and gives the situation a nudge.

'Steward,' he calls. 'My opponent?'

The steward grips the sharpened lance-point. Harry can see the anger in the man's eyes at Crocker's deception. 'Fair lances,' he cries. 'The winner of the tilt, at three lances to one, is the Knight in Silver.'

There's an audible sigh of relief from the crowd. Order is restored.

The knight presses his lance hand over his heart and bows his head, both in thanks and in honour of the life taken, the solemnity of the accident that occurred. The crowd responds with thunderous applause.

Bloody showman, Harry thinks. But God's breath, he wears armour well.

He shakes his head, before those thoughts can plough any further into the gutter.

The steward turns again to the knight. 'Knight, will you ride another tilt? Against Sir Harry Lyon of Dartington, champion of Woodstock and Newmarket tourneys?'

The knight hesitates. He's two hundred yards away and yet Harry knows that body posture perfectly. It's Iain trying to find a way to say no. But they both know that it's bad to end the day on a death. If Iain doesn't ride against Harry, Crocker's accident will be all the crowds talk about when they look back on Guildford. And it will look suspicious, the knight showing up only to tilt against Crocker.

It will almost look like a grudge match.

The knight nods. He will ride another joust.

Harry manoeuvres Nomad into position and tucks his lance under his arm, the point still at forty-five degrees, as he waits for the knight to be ready; as he waits for the steward. His heart is beating like a terrified bird, even though there is no opponent he knows better than Iain.

The steward's hand falls. And then it's—

Hoofbeats, the huge muscles of the horse under him. The lance coming down across the horse's neck, clamped under his arm, keep the point steady, aim it true, left to left, shield to shield, brace only at the last moment—

Icy silver eyes glint through helmet slits—

Brace—

The lance-point crashes against Harry's shield, his whole body tensed against the blow, and then the lance does what it's built to do, and shatters.

His lance also hits the knight's shield, also shatters.

Nomad slows to a canter, then a trot, as Harry's muscles unclench. Behind him he can hear the steward call, 'One lance to each,' and he doesn't have to look around to know the man is holding two fingers up. Harry walks Nomad around in a circle and beckons for Kit to pass him another lance.

They line up again. Harry inwardly curses himself; it was only by the grace of God his lance broke. It had been badly set. His head was too full of thoughts to concentrate. First he's too numb and now he can't get his brain to shut up.

He bites down on the inside of his cheek until he tastes blood. Then he nods to the steward. Iain is already in position.

The steward's hand drops. The second pass begins.

Harry is there now, more present, not riding with half his attention outside his body. He sets his lance and braces for impact as Nomad thunders towards the knight. Iain shifts his shield slightly and Harry follows it, minutely adjusting the angle of his lance. He clamps down on the butt of it and tenses his legs around Nomad as the point of Iain's lance comes rushing at him and—

Two more shattered lances.

Harry realises, distantly, that the crowd is cheering. He's not sure if it's him they're cheering for, or the knight, or simply for the spectacle of the combat. He and Iain have done this so many times in practice. And somewhere along the line, in fallow bean fields and borrowed tournament tiltyards, they stopped going easy on each other. They just set the war-horses galloping hell for leather and knew that no matter how hard they rode, the other one would always catch the lance. There is no hesitation here.

They line up for the last pass. As Iain gallops towards him, lance perfectly aimed, some cloud in Harry lifts. They can still communicate, in a way. They still are mirrors of each other, so in sync that—

Iain's lance wavers, an instant before the strike—

It glances off Harry's shield, rather than hitting true. Harry feels his own lance hit, and then there is no resistance—

Iain is on the ground, rolling.

Harry slews Nomad around, stopping the big horse, and he throws the butt of his broken lance onto the ground. The lance had shattered against Iain's shield, but he'd also unhorsed Iain, because Iain had missed.

Iain never misses.

Harry dismounts before he can think about it, discarding his helmet and shield on the grass behind him. The knight is already rising to his feet, brushing the dirt off his plain white surcoat. 'Are you hurt?' Harry says, and it is only with an extraordinary act of will he keeps his hands from reaching out.

The knight looks at him, and shakes his head.

It *is* Iain. Harry never doubted, but he knows those eyes anywhere. And they are not the eyes of a man furious with himself for a poor final tilt.

Iain turns away from Harry and strides over to his horse, which has stopped a dozen or so yards away and is nosing around in the grass for clover. He swings up onto the horse easily, armour and all, and raises his mailed hand in salute.

He's going to ride away.

He's just going to leave. Again.

The steward is saying something and everyone is cheering.

Iain is leaving.

Harry moves to follow Iain but feels a hand on his arm. He whirls around, ready to punch the person restraining him.

It's the steward. The steward is raising his arm in the air, and the crowd are on their feet, yelling his name.

Harry looks at the man, bewildered.

'You won the tournament, Sir Harry,' the steward says. 'Don't you realise? You won.'

Harry washes and dresses in his stifling court clothes for the celebratory supper. He still moves like a man asleep, insensate to the smiling faces, the pats on the back. His hands are so clumsy pulling up his hose that he thumbs a hole into them, up near the thigh. Hopefully his coat is long enough to cover it. He throws on his hood and tries to arrange the tail of it in the casually elegant way Iain managed so well, but the damn wool serpent seems put on this earth purely to vex him. Eventually he gives up, rakes his hands through his hair, and trudges to the King's marquee.

The King's tent is a palace of canvas. Three hundred knights, nobles and ladies are assembled inside, a fabric hothouse of English high society in microcosm.

A servant guides Harry towards a table in the top rankings, the third closest to the King's own. It's an honour that would have thrilled his eighteen-year-old self, who would have counted each seat, weighed each courtier in judgement, that remained between him and the King. Back when he thought there was merit in this game.

But Harry is twenty now, and he can't bring himself to care. He's seated next to Alys. For this, he is grateful. They can still place next to each other while they are engaged. Afterwards, custom dictates that they sit separate, a rule for all but kings.

Edward and his retinue are late. It's expected. Kings are always late.

It's a balm to see Alys again, though, and Harry even welcomes Arundel's brash humour, across from him. They chat about everything and nothing, and she even makes Harry snort with laughter over a tale of a very arrogant but illiterate knight she'd witnessed dictating a love letter to a monk.

After a few cups of ale and banter with Alys and the Earl – no, *Richard*, he wants to be called Richard – Harry feels almost human again.

Suddenly the hum of chatter in the canvas hall dies down, save for a few clear voices emanating from the entrance. 'All stand for the King, His Majesty Edward of Windsor and Queen Philippa,' cries a harbinger, and there's the scuff and groan of benches pushed back, the little clatter of cups and eating knives placed on the table.

Harry stands and looks.

Just behind the King is Iain, in cobalt-blue silk, picked out with gold embroidery at the cuffs and neck. His knight's belt is slung tantalisingly low on his hips. A long, simple sword hangs from it on one side; the dagger Harry gave him on the other. His jacket is short, barely to mid-thigh, and his legs are encased in hose of the same vivid blue. His long hair is oiled and sleek, twisted back in a bit of ribbon. He's smiling, joking with the Queen in their soft, Continental French, completely at ease.

Harry can't breathe. He feels Alys's small, cool hand over his, wordlessly offering support.

Iain looks well. He still moves like a predator, but now there's an elegance to it: a sophisticated hunter, rather than a starved, feral dog.

He sees Iain's eyes rake over him in passing, as the man prowls towards the King's table. There is no acknowledgement of Harry in his expression, and there will be none, for Iain sits down with his back to the hall.

Harry has to turn his head to see the King's table, but he finds if he's careful he can look out the corner of his eyes, checking to see if there is still a blue silk coat there, a broad back slouched in lazy elegance, a strong, graceful hand gesturing with an eating knife.

Nearly everyone is rushing off to Smithfield in the morning, as the big London tourney begins in two days' time, so there are no *ludi* or fancy entertainments this night. Yet still the evening seems to drag on. Harry looks at Arundel in despair. 'Please try to speak to him,' Harry says. 'Tell him . . . tell him everything.' He closes his eyes. 'Tell him I can't live without him.'

Arundel considers. 'Tell him yourself,' he decides.

'How?' Harry all but howls. He inclines his head towards the King's table. 'I should march right up there and say excuse me, I'd like to borrow Iain for a minute?'

'You could write him a letter,' Arundel says.

'The things I want to tell him cannot be read by others,' Harry whispers. 'You know that. I cannot even consider putting them on paper.'

Arundel stands up. 'Your Majesty,' he shouts.

Harry turns beet red, cringeing, trying to make his large frame less noticeable. He kicks Arundel under the table.

'My lord of Arundel,' the King calls back. 'What have you on your mind?'

'A petition for Sir Harry here to come back to our team on the opening mêlée, that is all. When he's around I don't get knocked on my arse so much,' Arundel admits, to general laughter.

'Except for that time he knocked you on your arse,' Iain purrs, his grin wicked. And *God*, that goes straight to Harry's groin.

Arundel points at him. 'That's why I said *our* team, Your Highness. Whatever team I'm on. If he's going to be on the other team, he can bloody well stay in the scary mêlée with the veterans.'

There's a laugh from Iain then, rich like smoke and honey, and he and the King exchange a glance. Iain shrugs.

'Done,' says the King, waving a hand. 'If only all such boons were as easy to grant. Oh, and congratulations, Sir Harry. We believe this makes your . . . *third* championship this year?'

Harry stutters. He hasn't been looking at the King, not since midway through His Majesty's second sentence. His eyes had followed the King's glance down to Iain's hand, where three fingers are casually extended.

Now it's Arundel's turn to kick him under the table. 'Yes, this is my third, Your Majesty. Thank you very much,' Harry manages to eke out. Then he sits down.

Harry makes his excuses soon after, forcing himself to leave while the party is in full swing. He doesn't want to be that sad person lurking around miserably to the bitter end, hoping desperately to catch the attention of a prince.

When Harry gets back to his pavilion, Piers gives him a hug, and Kit squeezes his shoulder affectionately.

They don't ask about Iain. They don't need to. The answer is written all over Harry's face.

Iain isn't at the Smithfield tournament.

Rumour has it the King has asked him to go north, to stand by in Carlisle in case an opportunity presents itself to negotiate with the Scots for the safe return of Balliol and de Beaumont. Both are still over the border, badly under duress by the forces of Andrew de Moray.

Harry has never prayed harder for England to hold the North than he does upon hearing that rumour. If they forfeit Scotland, he will lose Iain forever to the wilds of Galloway again, he knows it.

Iain isn't at Smithfield, but Montagu is.

So is Odo Waldegrave, at least until he's found dead in his pavilion on the third day. There's blood on his pallet, and apparently on his wrinkled old cock too. It's not his blood. There isn't a scratch on the man. But he's dead, and his new page is long gone.

With no heirs, and with the disgraceful manner of his death, Waldegrave's lands revert to the King.

Ten, Harry thinks. Ten left of the Galloway Dozen, including him.

Of course, it could be a coincidence, but he doesn't think so.

Harry loses at Smithfield. Well, he comes in a respectable fourth, but it *feels* like a loss. The cramped, close quarters of the city, the dirt and the smells, so many people but none of them the right one, it all pecks away at him, bit by bit. And without Iain there to perform for, there is no reason for him to resist London's thousand tiny cuts.

The English are losing the North.

The rumours are conflicting – Balliol's fled back across the border; no, he's still fighting. Henry de Beaumont, the old fox, will sweep down on them all. Balliol and de Beaumont have split, and the Scots are in open revolt against Balliol. De Beaumont's broken his siege and is riding to Balliol's aid. Dundarg has fallen and de Beaumont is prisoner of Andrew de Moray. Of princes and parleys, there is no news.

Harry returns to Dartington. There is great comfort in the familiar, even as his heart still breaks in his chest to ride through the gates and see, not a house, but a hollow where a home had been.

And foundations. New, larger foundations, of unburnable stone.

There's been quite a bit of progress in the month he was away. Walls are going up. They're not much taller than Harry is, at the moment, but Harry's been told it's the foundations that take the longest. The rest should move almost quickly, now.

They'll still be spending all winter in the barn, but it's hard not to be hopeful when everyone can see the new grey walls reach a little higher every day.

Harry thinks he catches a flash of sorrow on Annie's face when he and Kit and Piers come back by themselves, no dark, lanky fourth at their side. She hides it quickly, though, and everyone at Dartington continues with the conspiracy of Not Talking About Iain.

Harry lasts three weeks before he loses his mind.

He wakes one morning and goes outside to an unseasonably warm early-November day, the leaves on the trees gone to gold. And he realises that a year ago on this day was the first time he showed Iain the pond.

The first time they kissed.

Suddenly the ache inside him of Iain's absence is so great, he nearly drops to his knees, unable to stand the hurt of all that empty space echoing inside him. He lurches against one of those new stone walls they were all so proud of, rebounds off it with minor bruising to his hip, and staggers into the stables. He's going to fall down in Nomad's stall and finally cry: for the fire that consumed his home. For his mother. For Iain.

But Piers and the new stable-boy, Bevis, are already there, mucking out.

Harry mutters something to them about going for a ride. He waves them back to their duties, throws a bridle on Numbles who's tied out while they're cleaning his stall, and clambers up bareback.

He even manages to keep a straight back and high chin for the hour it takes to ride to the pond. There's no one on the lanes this early to witness this stoicism, but he keeps himself together, just in case.

Harry feels made of cracked glass. If the world jostles him, even gently, he will shatter into a million unmendable pieces. And then how will the people of Dartington carry on, if they know he can't?

Harry leads Numbles off into the woods, around the pond. He doesn't want even a chance of anyone seeing the horse and coming looking for him. Nobody should witness him like this, crumbling under the lonely weight of his responsibilities.

He feels very ordered, all of a sudden. Each small task a defined, practical goal that takes him a step closer to . . . what? He doesn't know, until he's kneeling on the mossy rock where Iain first kissed him, first took him in his hand. Until a sob wracks his body so hard that he bends almost double, forehead touching the cold, dewy surface of the moss in supplication.

He is dizzy with grief, lost in the vast, empty wasteland inside himself he never realised was there until Iain left. And he's an idiot, because he's a common country knight, in love with a prince. A prince who now despises him, because Harry doesn't have the benefit of three centuries of dynastic experience at court and when Montagu backed him into a corner he thought he could handle it.

It turns out Harry can't handle anything at all. Especially if it involves love.

He loses an indeterminate amount of time staring at the tear-blurred shapes of dead leaves as they flutter down from the ghostly, skeletal birch trees onto the grey surface of the pond. The worst part is knowing he has to continue. That he'll be expected to be happy at Christmas, and glad for the spring. But this is his season, the dead end of autumn, when the life fades from all things. The season when he began to love, and when he said farewell to it a year later.

Although, if he's honest with himself, he thinks he started to love Iain a lot earlier.

Harry shuts his eyes and feels more fat tears squeeze out. The moss is cool against his forehead and keeps at bay the sharp pain in his head. He wonders what it would be like to die here. To just give up, to surrender to eternal sleep. He doesn't really want to die, he wouldn't want to put Annie or any other of his people through the trouble of finding his body. But the idea of it is a comfort. Vanishing. Dissipating like the low mist on the water. Not having to put on a brave face any more.

He's not really surprised when he looks up and sees a vision of Iain rising up out of the water like a forest god, tiny autumn-gold birch leaves on his shoulders like a mantle of state; in his hair like a crown. Iain is naked, and Harry's traitor mind immediately looks down to his sex soft against his leg, at the drops of water caught in the dark hair there, glinting like jewels.

Maybe he is already dying, and this is what heaven is.

Then Iain touches him – cool, wet fingers tipping up his jaw, a thumb brushing along his cheekbone – and Harry shivers, somewhere between terror and longing.

It isn't a hallucination.

Iain is here.

Unless I've gone completely mad, Harry thinks.

Iain gets down on one knee, all thick, taut muscle, firm from the cold water.

Iain's face is inches from him as he kneels on the stone, his hands framing Harry's cheeks. 'Did someone hurt you?' Iain growls, soft and low. 'Tell me. Tell me and I will kill them.'

Harry makes an ungainly snorting sound and throws his hands over Iain's arms. Feels the heat of his body as it burns through the chill of the water on his skin. Feels the hardness of the muscles that shift slightly under his palms as Iain's thumbs brush his tears away so gently. 'What are you doing here?' Harry stutters out.

A soft smirk tugs at the edges of Iain's mouth. 'Stopped to wash on my way to see you. You don't think I ever ceased loving you, did I? Although I was sure you no longer wanted me. That is, until Arundel had a word with me. Took me quite to task, if we're being honest, and—'

Harry surges forwards, a whimper escaping his lips just before he presses them against Iain's. He feels the hollow wasteland inside him explode into riotous spring as Iain makes a startled noise in return, and slides a hand around the back of his neck.

Iain's lips are so soft. And he's so *good* at this, so confident, tilting his head so they fit together perfectly, nipping at Harry's lips. Kissing him, feeling his tongue slip between them, makes Harry blaze into joy. He wants nothing more than to taste Iain forever, chase these jolts of ecstasy that come from such a simple act – lips moving against each other – for the rest of his life.

Iain moans into his mouth, 'God's breath, Harry, I've missed you so much. I hate court. I *hate* it. There's always someone watching me. I can never relax. I'm still many months away from finishing what I have to do, but all I want is you.' His kiss turns into one of those Iain kisses that's mostly a smile pressed against Harry's lips, and he murmurs, 'So I ditched my guards and sneaked away.'

Harry's eyes rake down Iain's body, hard and strong with muscle, and adorned with scattered leaves as if Nature herself would jewel him. He feels like he is drowning in desire.

'I missed you so much I wanted to die,' Harry says, as he puts his hands along the broad planes of Iain's back and hauls him in close for another kiss, and this is what kissing should be, this is how it is meant to feel, and every kiss Harry has had was just practice for *this*, the real thing. 'I am so sorry. I was going to explain. I didn't think I had any option, and Alys—'

'I like her,' Iain says. 'Arundel tricked both of us into coming to dinner on the same day.' He snorts a laugh into Harry's neck. 'Served finger food. Hid all the sharp objects. We spent an afternoon sniping viciously at each other across the Earl's table.' Iain sighs. 'And then she made me laugh. I see what you love in her.'

'No,' Harry says. 'I love only you. I adore her.'

Iain hums, and tilts his head. 'I can't promise I won't have tantrums,' he says.

'I hear they're a royal prerogative,' Harry replies. He tries to sound witty but it comes out weak, watery.

Iain takes Harry's face in his hands again and looks at him, really looks at him. 'God's blood, Harry.'

Harry flinches, ahead of what Iain will say next. But Iain remains silent. He pulls Harry into his arms, wraps his legs around him, until Harry is surrounded by him. Safe. *Home*.

It's not enough.

Harry presses his lips to Iain's neck, kissing up into his hair, down to his shoulder. Anything he can reach. Iain just holds him tighter and strokes his hair, as hungry for the touch of Harry's skin as Harry is for his.

Iain is naked, gorgeously so, and still damp from his swim. Harry slips out of his clothes quickly – he hadn't even put on his sword belt that morning, just a shirt and an old, loose pair of breeches – and honest-to-God trembles as his body is finally against Iain's with no more barriers between them.

Iain shivers too, and Harry feels his hips twitch in a small thrust. A ball of warmth and wonder expands within him, that he can do this, that such a beautiful man reacts like this to him. He slides a hand down Iain's back to the swell of his rear, and strokes his fingers lightly down the cleft. 'I need—' is all he manages to say, before Iain is arching into him, trying to push his arse back against Harry's hand while also trying to rut his erection against the soft crease of Harry's hip.

'Yes,' Iain gasps. 'Yes.' He fists a hand in the back of Harry's hair and pulls Harry's mouth to his, kissing him slow and filthy. 'There has been no one else,' Iain breathes. 'Beyond the afternoon I used Rolly. Which,' he sighs, 'wasn't my finest moment.'

'Do not ever mention his name again,' Harry growls, digging his fingers into the firm flesh of Iain's backside. 'Don't ever go near him again.'

Iain whimpers, shuddering, and Harry can feel the scratch of stubble on his cheek as the man nods. Then he's readjusting himself in Harry's lap, so both their hard cocks are pressed between their stomachs, and he starts grinding.

Harry kisses him again, gripping his arse to pull him even closer, to get more pressure. He hasn't touched himself in months, not since Iain left, just hasn't felt like it. But now his libido is uncoiling within him in waves of lust so dizzying he can barely decide what he wants to do next with this gorgeous, muscular body in his lap.

He knows what he needs, though. He shoves two fingers into Iain's mouth, grinding harder against his lover as Iain runs his tongue over those fingers, getting them wet. Watching Iain suck on his fingers, eyes lidded in bliss, is enough to push Harry even closer to the edge he's already on, making his hips judder forwards in abortive thrusts.

Harry gently pulls out of Iain's mouth, taking a moment to appreciate the red of his lips, shiny with saliva, before moving his wet fingers down to Iain's hole. He kisses Iain then, invading his mouth with his tongue as he pushes both fingers relentlessly into his lover. Iain is beyond words, arching, pushing down on Harry's fingers, gripping Harry's waist with his strong thighs. Harry sinks his fingers in all the way and then begins to fuck Iain with them, in and out, curling and dragging them along the place inside Iain that makes him shake and moan.

He adds a third finger, and a fourth, slowly, relentlessly opening his lover up and filling him. Iain is clawing at his back, trying to grind forwards and push back at the same time, kissing and biting at any part of Harry his mouth can reach. 'Ssh, be still, Iain, or you won't get my cock,' he whispers, and Iain looks at him then, wild and desperate.

'Ssh,' Harry says again, leaning in to kiss him.

Then he pulls his fingers out and spits on his palm, wetting himself before moving his hands back around to Iain's arse to lift him up, position him.

'I love you,' Iain breathes, as the head of Harry's cock pushes into him. 'Even though I have to be away from you, to finish this, the thought of coming back to you when it's over . . .' Iain makes a sound that's half-moan, half-sigh as Harry feels himself bottom out. 'It keeps me alive. Otherwise . . . I don't know what I'd become. Something terrible,' he says, and Harry realises Iain's eyes are wet.

He wants to ask Iain so many questions. *What do you have to finish? Did you kill Waldegrave? Why do you need guards?* They tickle at the back of his mind, messy, like feathers escaped from a pillow.

And then Iain pushes Harry down and rolls his hips, and Harry forgets everything that isn't the feeling of Iain riding him, the almost painful sight of his beauty in the soft, dappled morning light. Iain's thick cock bobs as the man slowly thrusts himself down on Harry, trails of precome stringing from the hard purple tip to his abdomen.

Harry reaches up and wraps a hand around it. Not to bring him off, more of a *hello, I've missed you*. Neither of them are rushing through this. Iain rides him slow and filthy, while Harry returns the favour by fisting his cock alternatively loose and hard, and removing his hand entirely when Iain looks too close. If Harry could expand this moment to all of eternity, have this and nothing more, he would. Iain is so beautiful, and *his*, still his, impossibly. He tangles the fingers of his free hand through Iain's and sits up, pulling him in for a kiss. In their world of blood and betrayal and struggle, they have *this*, this sweetness and passion, and Harry feels the luckiest man alive for it.

They rock together, cradled in each other's arms in the slow sunshine of the morning, golden pleasure pouring like honey through their veins, sweetening everything around them.

Harry increases the speed of his hand on Iain's cock, marvelling to himself how good it feels in his hand. How right. How perfect Iain feels around him, as if they were made to fit only each other, two outcasts who have fought their way back from the edge of darkness together. Iain begins to stutter and moan against him, and Harry relishes every little noise out of his true love's mouth, every passion-fuelled, uncontrolled shift of muscle under that tanned, freckled skin. He starts pushing his hips up to meet Iain's, pushing so deep into him that Iain cries out, grabbing at Harry.

Iain's fingers twist into Harry's hair and he touches their foreheads together, looking him in the eyes as he thrusts down hard once, twice, and then he's coming, his eyelids fluttering, and Harry is too because Iain's entire body clenches down on him and it's—

Nothing.

Will ever.

Equal.

This.

And he presses his lips into Iain's, and they're not kissing, just shuddering against each other, clutching as wave after wave of pleasure rocks through them, and Iain whispers *always* into his mouth.

They curl up together on the rock and nap in the morning sunshine after that, Iain in Harry's arms, where he belongs.

Harry is going to get up and start getting dressed, before half of Dartington comes looking for him, but Iain's lying there, and he's a little bit hard again. Harry kisses his way down Iain's body, because he can. He bites at Iain's nipples, sucking them, and he hears Iain come awake with a gasp. And so he trails his kisses down faster, brushing his lips along Iain's abs, along the crease of his hip, and down to his cock.

He smiles as his lips wrap over Iain's head, and he takes him into his mouth. Iain arches his neck, moaning and trying to push his hips up further, to make Harry take him deeper. But Harry pushes off him. 'No. Get up. Lean against that tree,' Harry orders.

Iain nods, rising gracefully and walking off the rock onto the shore. He keeps a hand on his cock, pressing it against his belly as he walks. Then when he reaches the oak tree that Harry indicated, he places his back against it, spreading his long legs for balance. His eyes never leave Harry as he stalks towards him.

Harry sinks to his knees and looks up at Iain through his lashes. He knows what he is doing is an exorcism of sorts, but that still doesn't lessen how much he wants to do it. Ever since that morning in the solar, he's known how much he loves taking Iain's dick in his mouth. 'I want you to use me,' Harry breathes, and the spark of lust and fear he sees in Iain's eyes is enough to make him need to put his hand on his own cock. He licks his lips, getting them good and wet. 'Use my mouth.'

Iain whimpers, a hand combing through Harry's hair as his

other hand guides the head of his cock into Harry's mouth. He starts thrusting, shallowly, as Harry wraps his lips around Iain's shaft and sucks.

Iain's being too gentle. Harry glares at him and growls, then sinks all the way down on Iain's cock, choking on it, feeling it hit the back of his throat and then some. He digs his fingers into the hard muscles of Iain's thigh as he pulls all the way off Iain's cock, kissing the head and then going straight back down again.

He hears Iain make a noise of wonder above him, and then finally, Iain's hands go around his head, holding it in place, as he begins to thrust into his mouth. He's still too gentle at first, and Harry has half a mind to lift his lip so he gets a bit of tooth dragged across him for his trouble. Then something snaps in Iain. The only warning Harry has is a tightening of Iain's fingers in his hair, so tight it's almost painful, and then a low, rumbling grunt as Iain thrusts all the way in.

Harry is so damn hard it hurts. Iain is using his mouth, his throat, blind to nothing but his own pleasure, his eyes glassy as he looks down at his cock going in and out of Harry. There's something in Harry that wants to worship Iain, to give himself completely to him but also possess him at the same time, and letting Iain face-fuck him like this hits every facet of Harry's darkest desires and then some.

Iain's thumb moves down to Harry's jaw, feeling how open his mouth is, pressing into Harry's cheek so he can feel himself on the other side, thrusting down Harry's throat. 'Fuck,' Iain moans, thrusting harder, faster, until he pulls Harry so hard against him that Harry's nose is buried in Iain's groin and Harry has a moment to register that Iain's cock is somehow even thicker, even harder, before Iain is coming down his throat with a ragged cry.

Harry feels him soften in his mouth, and slump against the tree. He pulls off Iain, wiping the saliva and come off his mouth with his forearm. 'We're not done,' he says.

Iain looks up at him, a question in his eyes.

Harry glances at the tree. The bark of the oak will be too hard against Iain's front. 'On your hands and knees,' Harry says, holding a hand over his own cock, purple with arousal.

Iain's lips quirk into a dirty grin and he whispers, 'As you command,' and falls to all fours, facing away from Harry. He spreads his legs and then just about screams as Harry grabs his rear, forcing his cheeks apart.

Harry pushes back into Iain, back into the loose, hot mess of his own come and spit from their sex an hour before. He groans as he bottoms out in one long, fluid thrust. And then he pulls almost all the way out, grabs Iain's hips and rams himself home again.

Iain moans, and Harry reaches a hand forwards to pull his long hair. 'That good? That what you want?' he asks.

Iain nods as much as he can with Harry holding onto his hair. 'Oversensitive. Too much,' he breathes. 'But don't stop,' he finishes.

Harry smiles, and drops a kiss between his shoulder blades before ramming home again. He pounds into Iain, using his arse the way Iain had used his mouth, doing nothing but chasing the orgasm that's been building in him since his lips wrapped around Iain's cock. It's brutal, nothing but the slap of flesh and both of them grunting, moaning, until Harry can't stop any more and reaches around to grab Iain's half-hard dick again, forcing one last orgasm out of him even as Iain whimpers *no, no*, forcing that body to clench one last time around him because there's nothing in the world like that feeling, and it's Harry's favourite way to fall over the edge. Iain's so spent he manages only a small bit of come, his dick not even fully hard, but Harry grunts and bangs into the vice-like tightness of Iain's channel, flooding him, filling him up.

They both collapse onto the ground afterwards, finding each other's lips with lazy kisses that are barely more than sharing breath.

'I love you,' Harry says, once he can think again. 'I want to help you, with whatever it is you're planning.' And Harry has a pretty damn good idea what Iain is doing, but he's not going to say it until Iain does.

Iain shakes his head. 'It's too dangerous, Harry. If I lose right now, all that is lost is an inconvenient boy who was never fated to live to adulthood anyway. If you fall, you take down all of Dartington with you. Alys, too, now.'

Harry sinks his fingers into the short hairs around Iain's cock and twists. Over Iain's gasp of surprise and pain, he says, 'You are not alone, you stubborn fool. *I love you*. Everyone at Dartington loves you. You should have seen their faces when I came back from Smithfield without you. They all assumed you'd be coming home, even for a visit. You're not alone, and you need to be careful because if you are lost you will break so many hearts beyond repair. First among them being mine.'

Iain stares at him for a long moment, then nods, and kisses Harry on his forehead. 'I guess I should get dressed and we should go home to Dartington, yes?'

Harry snorts and punches him in the shoulder. 'Yes, we should.'

Iain goes back into the pond and washes himself off, then crosses to the other bank and ducks behind a tree. His things must be there, Harry thinks, as he too eases himself into the pond and rinses off the evidence of their tryst.

Harry grabs his discarded shirt and breeches from the rock and slips them on, then follows the low whistle towards Iain. He climbs up the bank, expecting to find Iain pulling on his old Scottish shirt, or some other simple travelling outfit.

When he gets to the top, he nearly chokes.

Iain is poured into dark, tight riding breeches, and a cote-hardie, also dark, but with ragged, tipped sleeves faced in scarlet. A bright saffron fabric lines the seams and hems of the slim, laced tunic, and a knight's belt in scarlet leather rides low on his hips.

Harry gestures in surprise at Iain's fashionable clothes, and the light coating of road dust on them. 'You sneaked away in *that*?' he says.

Iain smirks. 'I wanted to look good for you.'

'Well,' Harry breathes, 'you succeeded.' He wraps his fingers around Iain's belt. Iain still wears Harry's dagger on his right hip, and that causes a swell of fierce pride in Harry's chest. It's like a favour, a secret admission to the world that he belongs to Harry and no other. 'You were knighted?'

Iain shrugs. 'I think it was more a courtesy, really.'

'It suits you,' Harry says. 'And it's awfully convenient for doing this.' He pulls Iain into him by the belt, parting his lips for a kiss.

Iain smile-kisses him back. 'You have no idea how many times I wanted to do that to you,' he says.

'I think I do,' Harry murmurs back.

It's midday by the time they collect their horses and head back towards Dartington Manor. The lanes are still oddly quiet, nobody in the fields. *Figures*, Harry thinks, just when he wants to show off to the entire estate that Iain is back, and more beautiful than ever.

He assumes it's just because it's November, and days are short, and the farming year is all but done.

But then he rounds a corner and realises how wrong he is.

A dozen men-at-arms spring from behind hedges to block their way, and more behind to cut off their retreat. Most are foreign-looking, short rough men with dark hair and olive skin. Each has a crossbow at the ready. Harry doesn't recognise their leaders, six knights with painted-over shields and cloaks covering their surcoats. They're not Rabbie's men, he's sure they're not Montagu's—

Then the lead knight throws back his cloak to reveal his surcoat.

The lily of France.

'Shit,' Iain hisses.

'Iain, run, I've got them,' Harry says, reaching for his sword—

—which he hadn't put on that morning.

'You are the Capet pretender?' the knight in the disguised surcoat asks, pointing his mace at Iain.

'I am no pretender,' Iain growls, drawing his own blade. 'But I am curious what scum at Windsor dares to have me followed.'

'I'm not of your court. I am a chevalier of France, here at the request of Philip of Valois,' says the knight. Then, to his crossbowmen, 'Kill him.'

'Liar!' Iain yells, raising his sword.

Harry lurches, yanking the reins of his horse to put his body between Iain and the crossbow bolts zinging towards him, but then the French knight's mace is connecting with his shoulder and he's tumbling down, grabbing at the fabric of the knight's surcoat to at least pull him down too, but it tears, and then he's falling, watching in horror as bolts embed in Iain's shield arm, raised to protect his chest.

As a bolt buries itself in his neck, the blood bubbling out pink with the hiss of air from his windpipe.

As Iain's sword falls from his hand as he scrabbles at the arrow in his throat.

As those pale eyes go dim.

Harry hits the hard, packed earth of the lane with a thud, and then everything is black.

Part Four

ELEVEN

November 1334–March 1340: The Bad Sleep Well

Harry awakens in a strange room.

There are men nearby, their voices low but earnest, and someone is brushing his temple with a cool, wet cloth. Whoever they are, they haven't noticed he's awake yet. He closes his eyes again and listens, trying to figure out where he is.

A fire crackles, and a man's voice says, 'I think we're rushing to conclusions.'

Harry thinks dimly, *Arundel. That's the Earl of Arundel.*

'You heard Scrope; he's being obstructive, not belligerent.'

'He wants an excuse to seize the Duchy of Aquitaine, Your Majesty. Leave Scotland alone and come on his preposterous crusade, or else.' It's a voice Harry has heard, but doesn't know well. William Bohun or Henry de Grosmont, perhaps? And he said *Your Majesty*. Wherever Harry is, the King is present.

'Fuck his crusade,' a voice growls, and Harry flinches. It's Rabbie's voice.

'We will not postpone our campaign in Scotland. It is clear to us that Philip is being belligerent. This murder of our cousin proves his ill intent goes beyond idle threats,' the King says. Harry stirs at that: murder of our cousin. *Iain.*

Iain's dead—

'No proof,' Arundel is saying.

'*This* is your proof,' Rabbie yells, and Harry opens his eyes.

'He's awake,' says the unfamiliar voice. It's William Bohun.

'Harry,' Arundel sighs, hurrying over. 'Are you able to tell us who attacked you?'

Harry tries to sit up but he's hit with a wave of nausea so severe it forces him to lie back down. The pain in his head is crippling. He contents himself with turning slightly to face the room.

They're in Rabbie's bedchamber at Ordlington, and he's in Rabbie's bed. In front of him is an *ad hoc* council of war: the King, and England's most martial peers. John of Eltham. Ufford. Arundel. Bohun. De Grosmont. Morley.

And in the corner sits William Montagu, smiling.

'What happened, Harry?' the King asks, his voice kind.

'Iain, uh, Lord Iain was visiting from court. He, he used to live at Dartington,' Harry says. 'I'd met him a few miles off the Exeter road at the edge of our estate and we were riding home, around midday. A score of men jumped us. Not locals. Six knights, and the rest men-at-arms with crossbows. They were foreign-looking.'

'Genoese mercenaries,' Arundel supplies.

'The leader asked if Iain was the Pretender, and then identified himself as a knight of Philip of Valois and ordered Iain to be killed. I tried to stop them, but—' Shame fills Harry like a rush of freezing water. Sir Harry Lyon, tournament champion, great knight of England, and the one time he needed to defend what he loved most in the world, his sword was in his bedchamber, forgotten in haste. '—I failed,' he whispers.

'Harry,' Arundel says, 'we found this in your hand.' He gestures to Rabbie, who holds up a navy-and-gold piece of fabric: the surcoat Harry grabbed as he fell. 'Do you believe the knights who attacked you were agents of the French king?'

Harry's head throbs with pain. He knows there's something off, but he can't think what. Iain had said something, as the men had attacked. He shuts his eyes and tries to remember, and all he can picture is the frothing pink of blood coming out of the strong column of Iain's neck and he has to clench his jaw so he doesn't throw up. 'I believe so,' he says at last.

Arundel squeezes his shoulder. 'I'm so sorry for your loss,' he says.

'He's dead, then,' Harry says.

'There was no body, Harry,' says Rabbie, and the man sounds downright sympathetic. Harry vaguely remembers that they were almost friends once, when Harry was younger and thought he wanted what Rabbie had. 'There was so much blood.' Rabbie sighs and sits down. 'Look. I hated the man. You know that. Ever since this,' he says, touching the ragged top of his right ear, where Iain had bitten part of it off a lifetime ago. 'But that was our issue to settle. Foreigners coming onto our lands and murdering our people? That's something else entirely.'

Harry whimpers, and turns his head away. He has to swallow down bile.

He hears someone stand, behind him. 'We leave for Scotland tomorrow. Retake the North, then we prepare for war with France.'

'Yes, Your Majesty,' Montagu says.

'My lord of Arundel, you will stay behind in the South. Raise us a fleet,' the King continues.

'But,' Arundel splutters. 'What do I know of boats?'

'More than any of us,' William Bohun shrugs.

'All of you, leave us,' says the King. 'We would have a moment alone in conference with Sir Harry.'

Harry can hear the scraping of benches and the rustling of fabric, the subtle clink of a scabbard shifting against a belt, as the assembled barons rise and depart the room. The heavy door shuts, and soon there is only the occasional hiss from the embers in the hearth.

'He knew this would happen,' Harry said quietly. 'He truly had no desire to be king.'

'I know,' Edward replies. 'He reminded me of my father, in some ways. My father didn't want to be king either. He was a good man, though I fear history will not remember him as such.'

'Born with the wrong name,' Harry mutters. He wants to break, to grieve, but he won't, not here in front of the King.

'Indeed,' says Edward.

Edward shifts, his blond beard glinting in the firelight. Harry is struck by the youth of the King. In the two years Edward has on him, has he learned not to be afraid in his quiet moments, as Harry is? Is he no longer terrified of being outmanoeuvred, of letting everyone down? At twenty-two, does he walk proudly now down the corridors of power, sure of his righteousness? Does it get easier?

The dark shadows under the King's eyes suggest not. 'I wish I had known him longer,' Edward sighs.

'Me too,' Harry says.

'Montagu says last year he took Iain from Scotland to keep him safe from things like this happening. Is that true?' the King asks.

Harry thinks it over. 'It is one facet of the truth,' he says at last.

The King exhales as he stands. 'As always with Montagu,' he says softly. Then, more loudly: 'We ride north the day after tomorrow, against the Scots. If you are well enough, will you join us?'

Harry doesn't even have to think it over. He knows with Iain gone, he isn't living any more. He's merely existing. And fighting makes the time pass.

'Yes, Your Majesty,' Harry says.

In the end, it takes Harry a fortnight to follow in the King's footsteps. Harry had barely thought before agreeing to go to war, only afterwards realising how much it would impact. How much still needed to be done before he could leave. Luckily, Arundel had brought Alys with him to Ordlington, and the three of them strategise as they ride to Dartington the next morning.

Alys falls in love with Dartington on first sight – half-finished walls and all – and Dartington falls in love with her. She agrees to give up the Christmas wedding at Arundel Castle and instead they are married, swiftly, by Father Gilbert in Dartington Church. Alys and Arundel will take turns managing the rebuilding of the hall while Harry is at war in the North.

Arundel complains the entire time about the navy he must raise, until Harry loses his patience and drags the man down to Plymouth, seeking the *Halygast* in port there. Jed tags along, hoping to see his cousin and hear news of home. They're told by the harbourmaster that Captain Wekesa's ship will be in from its usual run to France within the week, and they settle down at the dock's least disgusting tavern to wait.

Five days later, the *Halygast* sees Harry before Harry sees the *Halygast*. There's a shriek of joy from high up in the rigging of an anchoring ship, and then a short time later, a skiff bumps against the docks and Harry is nearly bowled over by two slim, tanned, tattooed forms.

Once he disentangles himself from the two sailors, he realises they are none other than Peter and Wat. Harry steps back to look at them, as Jed calls out cheerfully to Captain Wekesa in their native language.

Wat will always be scarred from his attempted burning. Little hair grows on his head; instead, tattoos of sea creatures and waves cover the area, ameliorating the rough appearance of the mangled skin. His body, too, is adorned with mermaids and monsters. Peter sports a flight of sparrows inked onto his forearms, and both boys are sun-brown, fit, and clearly happy. Harry finds himself smiling at the couple's infectious enthusiasm for life.

And then Peter peers over Harry's shoulder and says, '*Where's Iain?*'

The spirit goes out of Harry so fast he has to support himself against a wharf post.

Peter steps back, aghast at Harry's pale face. '*No*,' the boy says, his own face scrunching up in stubborn refusal.

'What's wrong?' Captain Wekesa asks in his soft, Continental French, striding up, looking between Peter and Harry. His French—

Harry clutches at his stomach in horror as everything falls into place. He turns to Arundel, who hangs back, both confused and fascinated by the sailors being disgorged by the skiff. 'Richard,' Harry says. 'The knights. They. I was wrong.' He swallows, his throat dry. 'They weren't French.'

'What?' Arundel says.

Harry closes his eyes. 'Iain said "Liar" when the knights

attacked. I didn't understand then. Everything happened so fast.' He opens his eyes and looks at Captain Wekesa, and then at Arundel. 'But I know now. What he meant was they were not knights of France. A knight close to Philip of Valois would speak like Iain, or like Captain Wekesa. You, you know how Iain speaks. *Spoke*.' Harry takes a shuddering breath. 'The knights who attacked us, their accent was common Norman French like you and me.'

'The French king's men speak High Court French,' Captain Wekesa says. 'As did your friend. Once you hear it, you never forget it. And it's an accent almost impossible to replicate unless you grew up in a French palace.' Then he looks at Harry. 'What happened? Is Iain wounded?'

Jed turns to his cousin and rattles out something complicated in their native language, and all Harry can think is that the captain looks a lot more affected than he should about a man he met once, and only briefly.

'We saw them,' Captain Wekesa says.

Harry stands up so fast his head spins, and he has to lean onto Arundel for support. 'Are you sure you should be going to war?' Arundel whispers.

'Shut up,' Harry says. Then, to Wekesa: 'When?'

'Two weeks ago, at twilight,' Captain Wekesa says. 'They loaded a body onto a French ship, docked a few piers down from us.'

Harry feels a desperate hope lurch in his chest. 'Is it still—'

'Long gone,' Captain Wekesa says. 'Whoever the men who brought the body were, they didn't board the ship, and there was a lot of angry negotiation with the captain.' He sighs. 'We keep an eye out round here, most of the captains do. Sometimes folks get the bright idea to sell unfortunates into slavery. So any prisoner or body going onto a ship attracts some quiet notice, if you know what I mean.'

'Are you sure it was him?' Harry asks. 'Was he alive?'

Captain Wekesa indicates Peter. 'You'll have to ask our little sparrow in the rigging. He's the one who saw.'

Peter's mouth opens and closes, as he thinks. And Harry realises that while at sea, Peter has learned to speak French. 'I couldn't see much. It was a big man, limp and bloody. There was dark hair, like Iain, but he was bigger, broader,' Peter says, a note of sadness in his voice. 'His clothes were fine; that's what caught my notice most of all.'

Harry struggles to breathe. 'He got bigger over last winter,' he gasps, through new tears. 'Grew up. And he . . . he is the King's cousin.'

'Which one?' asks Wekesa.

'Both of them,' sighs Arundel.

'*Jesus' bones*,' Peter says, covering his mouth in horror as he switches to his more familiar English. '*If I had recognised Iain we would have* known *something was wrong, we would have gone down there. I owe Wat's life to him and you.*'

'*Peter*,' Harry says as calmly as he can, '*was he alive?*'

'*He was mostly wrapped in a cloak. Two people were carrying him. I couldn't tell. I don't know*,' Peter says. Then, more haltingly, '*Why would you bother carrying a dead body anywhere?*'

'*Well, if you want to start a war, killing a prince and telling the English that the French did it, and then shipping the body to France to prove English culpability . . .*' Arundel begins, gesturing.

Harry switches back to French. 'We have no proof,' he says. He almost doesn't care any more. If Iain is dead, then the world can burn itself to the ground for all he cares.

'*A man came, to look at the body as they were loading it,*' Peter adds. '*He paid off the captain and the men who brought the body. He looked at the face, then nodded, and pulled out his purse.*'

'*Can you describe this man?*' Arundel asks, and there's a razor edge to his voice, under the politeness.

Peter shrugs. '*Not well. He was in a hooded cloak. Medium height. Taller than me but shorter than Sir Harry.*'

Arundel turns to Harry. 'There's your proof,' he says. 'Montagu.'

'And nobody will believe us,' Harry says, forcing down the lump in his throat, gritting his teeth against the voice that says this is his fault, for forcing Iain out into the open. For making him into a target.

Arundel introduces himself to Captain Wekesa, and asks him to speak to the French captain next time the two of them are in port. A casual enquiry from a fellow ship's captain, they both reckon, will go down better than a landlubber coming in with an interrogation. 'See if you can find out what happened to the lad, if he was really dead,' Arundel asks. 'And if there is any cost involved . . . ?'

He reaches towards his purse but Captain Wekesa shakes his head. 'Harry's friend was a good man,' Wekesa says. 'And I will look out for news of him.'

Everyone falls silent for a moment, listening to the incoming tide slop against the wharf pilings, at gulls cawing and the wet smack of halyards against masts in the light breeze. The air stinks of seaweed and tar. Harry's mother used to say that when a conversation falls quiet, it's because an angel is passing overhead. All Harry can think is *please don't let it be Iain.*

Arundel shifts nervously. 'There is another thing,' he says.

Captain Wekesa raises an eyebrow.

'The King has asked me to raise a fleet. Possibly build one, too. I know nothing about boats. This is a boat, yes?' Arundel says, pointing towards the *Halygast* as it bobs at anchor in the bay.

Captain Wekesa laughs, long and rich. 'It is indeed a boat, my lord. Specifically, it's a cog. We must unload our cargo before the tide goes out, but if you come back in a fortnight and you can stand my men their meals, we will teach you everything you need to know, and introduce you to all the wrong people.'

'Sounds like a deal,' Arundel smiles.

'You haven't seen how much a sailor can eat. And drink,' Jed warns. 'You may regret this.'

'It's fine,' Arundel says. Then he turns to Harry. 'I'll look in on Alys, too.'

On the ride back to Dartington, Harry and Arundel agree that they should say nothing to the King, nor should they move against Montagu, not yet.

Harry is miserable that night. Montagu played them all, and got exactly the result he wanted. The boy he brought home in a cage to use as a pawn had been let loose on the chessboard, made it all the way to the end where he was promoted into a prince, and then had been knocked over, dramatically, at the very climax of the game. It had all gone perfectly to plan.

All this time they thought they were escaping Montagu,

fighting back, maybe even winning, and instead they were dancing the steps he wanted, to music orchestrated solely by him.

Harry is glad he is riding to war. He badly wants to harm a lot of things.

They cross into Scotland at Roxburgh. Edward's army is not as large as Harry had expected, certainly smaller than the huge force of Halidon Hill eighteen months and a lifetime ago. They face bitter opposition the entire way, from December through to February. There are no winners, no decisive victories. Just a grinding, exhausting attempt at survival. Knights die one by one, picked off by bowmen hidden in the high heather of Scotland's dramatic terrain. There had been hope of driving north to relieve Henry de Beaumont up in Aberdeenshire, but by Christmas that hope has flown. De Beaumont is captured by the Scots and the King is forced to ransom him.

Come the hardest part of winter, most of the men-at-arms decide not to renew their contracts, and slip back across the border to England, and safety.

Edward and his household knights are forced to follow.

The great Scottish campaign of winter 1334/1335 ends with lives lost on both sides for nothing. A truce is declared, and Montagu begins to whisper in Edward's ear, of the great army he will raise, of how they can go back in the summer and burn their way across the Highlands, torch these Scots out once and for all, and then they can cast their eyes to the real prize: France.

Harry is invited to stay in York with the King's household but he begs off, riding back to Devon. Iain is right. Court is terrible.

At Dartington, the new hall is almost done, and thanks to Arundel's money and Alys's oversight, it's far more luxurious than the old one. Harry marvels at the glass in the windows; the holes for the garderobes; the enlarged solar with its two chambers.

Arundel visits, and shares news that he and Captain Wekesa had found the French captain. The man absolutely refused to talk, holding his tongue against both offers of gold and threats of violence. Captain Wekesa says the man was terrified, the sort of terror that comes from being accidentally complicit in a great crime.

As winter eases into spring, Harry vacillates between believing Iain will appear at any moment, all brooding pale eyes and quicksilver grin, and knowing in his heart that Iain will never return. Eventually, for his sanity, he has to let go of his hope. Even though it feels like he is killing something inside him.

The roof is on in time for the May Day celebrations. They have a grand party, all the vassals for miles around, and all the knights he and Alys have befriended, coming to inaugurate the new hall with a feast and good cheer. Harry's body smiles and chats and goes through all the motions of the great lord and the good host, while inside he feels nothing.

He counts the days until he can go back north, to meet the King's army in Newcastle for the new Scottish campaign. He only feels anything, any more, when he's at war. It terrifies him a little, but not enough to change. War is simple.

Harry thinks back to Halidon Hill often, to the naïve boy who rode to war like it was another game, with stewards and rules and clear winners. Now he knows it's just a tangled, horrid mess with no law except that of the winners. He wonders if he, now, would have wetted his sword at Loch Doon.

He shudders. He's not that man. Not yet.

'So when will Dartington have an heir?' Sir Gervase calls from down the table. Harry's cheeks flame red as he's brought back to the present, to the celebratory dinner for their new stone hall. He glances at Alys, panicked. They haven't talked about this. He's been in *mourning*. It's not been—

'Well, now that I know the baby won't be born in a *barn*,' Alys tosses back at Sir Gervase.

Harry rises to the occasion, crossing his arms and pantomiming displeasure. They can joke their way out of this. 'I don't know what you're objecting to, Alys. It's a very nice barn.'

Alys winks at him, and he feels a genuine smile cross his face. 'We missed our chance at a tournament pavilion,' he jests.

'Alas,' Alys groans in mock horror, then pats his arm. 'No more tournaments for you.'

'No,' Harry whispers, sober again. 'Only the real thing, now.' He looks at Alys, how her new gorget and wimple hide her dark hair but frame her delicate face and warm brown eyes. 'You don't have to stay here, you know,' he says. 'If you don't like it.'

'Odsbodkins, my entire life seems to be spent wanting to stab idiot boys from Devonshire with my eating knife,' Alys says. 'Have you ever considered that I will have my family's own estates returned to me in a few years, and I jolly well need to know how to run them?'

'Uh,' Harry says.

'Quite,' Alys replies, reaching for a plate of honey cakes that Annie is placing on the table. 'Now if you'd stop trying to decide what's best for me and instead focus on not dying in Scotland, I'd appreciate it.'

Harry survives the dinner. He also survives, barely, Alys informing him that they will try for an heir when he returns from the war, because Annie (who is also present for the conversation, up in the new solar) says that any competent midwife can help a woman conceive without penetration. It's by far the most embarrassing conversation Harry's ever had.

He breaks down when Alys suggests they call the child Iain, if it's a boy.

Through his sobs, he apologises to her for the man he's become. Alys just hugs him and tells him it will stop hurting one day. Harry doesn't admit to her that is what he fears most.

The hurt is all he has left. Once it's gone, he won't feel anything at all.

Harry departs one gentle, drizzly May morning for the North. He rides alone. The idea of taking another squire with him is nauseating. He'll make do. War is, after all, not nearly as complicated as a tournament.

The army meets at Newcastle in June of 1335. They march north across the Scottish border shortly thereafter. Montagu has, damn him, delivered what he promised: a huge force. The King favours him with a new crest in the form of an eagle, and a fine horse with that eagle crest embroidered on all the tack and clothing.

Arundel is still in the South, messing about with boats.

Their new, larger army burns through Scotland from west to east, and Harry hears tell of an equally large force under Balliol riding to meet them from Galloway. Of all places, Balliol had to choose Galloway.

It's not even fighting this time. It's just punishment. They encounter small Scottish forces, they slay them, they burn their towns. Harry volunteers to ride ahead with the scouts, so at least when he faces bands of Scottish patriots it feels more like a fair fight.

He sees Iain in them sometimes. In their dress. Their ferocity. Even when they scream at him in Gaelic, it's familiar, a fond memory. He still does his duty and kills them.

The two English armies meet in Perth in August, and King Edward instals himself in the city with only occasional punitive forays out into the countryside. As the bulk of the English army streams home to harvest, a fragile truce is negotiated.

Harry heads back to his manor too, away from the ash and the blood and the stink of burning hair and gut-stained steel.

The international politics he shunned so long now follow him, the talk of taverns and travellers, a mocking shadow of his past ignorance. Threats fly between the French and English kings. Edward accuses Philip of harbouring David II, last of the House of Bruce, the king the Scots actually tolerate. Philip accuses Edward of protecting Robert d'Artois, a rebellious French noble. Nobody speaks of Iain, but he's there, in a way, hanging over everything. There's no point talking about the dead, but they haunt the living still – in a simmering mistrust between royal second cousins, each thinking the other would stoop to assassination to get his way.

Harry misses the harvest, but gets home in time for Michaelmas. Alys becomes pregnant. It's awkward, and involves several more cringe-making conversations plus having to spill his seed into a glass vial, but it's managed without Alys having to endure the act she has no interest in. Harry doesn't ask the specifics after he hands over his part. The rest is women's matters.

Alys takes to being pregnant with her usual fierce good spirit, though it's clear to Harry in their private moments that she veers between terror and frustration at the changes in her body.

The Scottish truce falls apart on St Andrews Day, when a small force under Andrew de Moray kills the foolhardy young Earl of Atholl, an English ally. There is brave talk of a vengeance mission, but it's too late – the great English army has long since disbanded.

Harry leaves again for war with Scotland in the spring. It's 1336 now, the fourth year in a row Harry has ridden north to fight. It feels to him like the world is unravelling. Everything seemed simple after Halidon Hill. Scotland was solved; England relaxed into a summer of play and a winter of tournaments. France slumbered, content with its own problems.

And now, a scant few years later, France and England are at each other's throats, and the French king is threatening a full-scale invasion of England from the North to support David II as Scotland's king. The French fleet, mustered at Marseilles in the spring for Philip's crusade, is in Normandy by summer, ready to leap across the Channel at any provocation.

That summer's Scottish campaign is as bad as last summer's. They ride and burn, ride and kill. The army rescues the widowed Countess of Atholl, de Beaumont's daughter, besieged for a year by Andrew de Moray. Then they torch the East Coast of Scotland, destroying Aberdeen harbour and anywhere else that might give succour to a French fleet.

Harry returns in October 1336 to Dartington, to find he has a daughter named Joan, and so he and Alys try again. He watches Alys and Annie chatter, and Jed and Kit joke, and remembers a time when the laughter came from him, when he and Iain would bring merriment and roughhousing wherever they went.

Now he barely speaks. He just waits for the next summons to war.

Home doesn't make sense to him any more, the way the campaign field does. At war, he always knows what he has to do. Break camp, march, fight, kill, pitch tents, take care of the horses, post sentries. Eat when you remember. Sleep when you can. Here, at Dartington, there is nothing of real importance to fill his days. He can't go to the pond; there is no solace there. And God . . . Harry doesn't want God's contemplative silence any more. He wants orders.

When he thinks of tournaments now, they seem like nothing more than cruel jokes. It sickens him to think he was once proud of winning those charades.

Christmas approaches, and they travel to visit Arundel. The Earl seems noticeably older, his beard and temples peppered with grey. All Harry says as he sits down at dinner the first day is, 'When are we going against France?'

'Next summer,' Richard says. 'I'm up to Nottingham for a King's Council as soon as the holidays are finished. It's a council of war.'

Harry nods. Good. A nice long campaign. That's what he needs. Then he looks up, and realises Arundel is staring at him.

'You're losing yourself,' the Earl says.

'I know,' Harry replies. 'I know.' He just can't find it in him to care.

With 1337 comes the elevation of Montagu to the status of Earl of Salisbury, and Rabbie to Earl of Suffolk. Harry isn't even surprised by the reward given to evil men any more. Then in the late spring, Philip confiscates the Duchy of Aquitaine, King Edward's last possession in France.

They don't actually go to war until the following year. The King tries to create an alliance with Flanders, with members of his wife Philippa's family. Nothing comes of it but wasted months and wasted money.

Early in 1338, Alys has a son, whom they name Iain, though he inherits Harry's fair hair. Harry loves them all, Alys and little Joan and Iain in her arms, but in a distant way, as if there's a fog between them and him. He can only take their company for a short time before he has to excuse himself and seek out the quiet of the solar, or take a long ride across the moors.

In March, the French fleet attacks and burns Portsmouth. Harry fidgets, waiting for the call to arms.

Alys reaches her limit over Easter, when Dartington emerges green and fresh into springtime, delighting in soft fields of bluebells and new lambs, yet Harry remains tangled in the winter of his memories. When she sits down one night by the fireplace in the solar, after the children are in bed, he can tell it's the end. The only surprise is that she's borne with him this long.

'Harry,' she begins.

'I'm sorry,' Harry says. He slumps onto her bridal chest, which rests at the bottom of the new oak bed.

Alys waves a hand. 'I'm not interested in apologies, Harry. I think we're past that,' she says. Her voice is ineffably sad, and all Harry can think is how he's failed her. How he's failed everyone he's loved. 'I miss my friend. I thought . . .' Her sentence trails off as she stares into the fire, its orange shadows dancing on her pale cheeks. 'I thought perhaps if I stayed cheerful, enough for both of us, you'd . . . you'd come back. I now see that was naïve.'

Harry catches himself before he says *I'm sorry* again. He can't think of anything else to say.

'It's very tiring,' Alys says, her soft words barely audible over the crackling of the fire. 'There is an old well in the gardens of Arundel Castle. I was fascinated by it as a child. My ladies' maids warned me it was terribly dangerous and I was absolutely never to go near it, so of course I ran to it every chance I could. If you prise up the boards and toss a rock down it, it's so deep you don't even hear the stone hit the bottom. Everything you throw into it just vanishes into the darkness.' She folds her hands in her lap, staring at them. 'That's what loving you is like.'

'I'll try—' Harry starts.

Alys shakes her head. 'Don't. Just *don't*. We both know you're off to France as soon as the King snaps his fingers.' She gets up, smoothing the skirts of her pale green wool dress. 'Bury your ghosts, Harry, by the time you return. He would hate you like this.' She looks at him then, as she departs for her bedchamber. 'It means they've won.'

The muster to war comes barely a month later, in May 1338. Harry tells Alys and the children he loves them, and that he's sorry, and he has to go. Alys hugs him, her small hands digging painfully into his back, and all she says is, 'Fight.' Harry knows she's not talking about the French.

The army assembles at Dover in June. They cross the Channel in a motley collection of cogs and other commandeered merchant ships organised by Arundel. Harry looks for the *Halygast* in the flotilla of cogs, but it turns out one boat does in fact look much like another to his untrained eye and he can't pick her out, if indeed she's part of the fleet.

They arrive in Antwerp in July. It's their designated base for the coming war. Antwerp is a flat, tidy trading town and it takes less than a week for the English army to turn the surrounding fields into a mud pit. By the middle of August, there isn't a blade of grass for miles. *We are locusts*, Harry thinks.

The politics of allegiances drag onwards. The army sits idle. The knights grow bored, and the younger ones start making raids into France, chasing glory, attacking small castles, trying to provoke Philip into action.

Because that's the rub: for all his threats and ultimatums, his strategically placed fleet, the King of France does not actually go to war. He doesn't even invade Gascony, the main holding of the Duchy of Aquitaine in the southwest. He just waits and watches as King Edward and twelve hundred of his best men spend England's gold sitting in Flanders through September, arguing with potential allies. It's an amazing non-tactic. Philip of Valois is either a dithering fool or the greatest military strategist of his age, and nobody in the English camp is quite sure which.

Harry is bored too, but it's an acceptable kind of bored. The boredom of a military camp is different from the boredom of a home. Sooner or later an earl will come and tell them to break camp and march, or to prepare for attack. The fact that Harry has nothing to do but train and stay ready is not his fault.

He trains all the time now.

He's very aware of the things that *are* his fault: his all but abandonment of Dartington and his family. He thinks of his son, of how little Iain risks growing up as Harry did, with no memories of his father. With him dead in a foreign field before the boy can walk.

Harry knows Alys is right. He's been holding onto this hurt for too long. He knew Iain a mere eighteen months, and four years later he still can't let him go. He promises himself he'll finish this campaign and then hang up his sword. He'll be a father, and a husband. He'll cut the first sheaf of wheat at the harvest again, a duty he's missed the past few years, cutting down lives in the North.

He wants to feel warm inside again. He just doesn't remember how.

He'll try, though. After this campaign. There's something about setting foot in Iain's birth country that he thinks will finally allow him to heal.

He starts going on the knights' raids into France as the summer draws to a close. At first it's just to keep an eye on the young knights, the hot-headed ones who had stayed south for the Scottish campaigns and missed out, as they put it, on *all the fun*.

And then some of Montagu's men get involved, Sir Guy d'Audley and Sir Thomas Howland, and Harry goes because he knows these men, he saw the slaughter they were capable of in Galloway, and he wants to make sure their knightly raids don't turn into rape and murder sprees.

The young knights idolise Sir Guy and Sir Thomas: important men, friends with Montagu, Earl of Salisbury. Harry, on the other hand, is a stuffy rural knight who won some tournaments once. They call him 'Auntie Harry' when he makes them ransom a local lord rather than killing him; when he demands they don't touch the women. They're just foreigners, the young knights say. It's not like they matter.

Chivalry doesn't exist on the battlefield, Harry decides. It's something invented afterwards, in the war they describe in letters home. *Met with an unfortunate accident* is code for *slain while unarmed and begging by an opposing knight*. *Succumbed to grief after her lord's passing* usually means *raped and left for dead*. Unfortunately the written word is stronger than memory, so the myth of glorious knighthood lingers onwards in the minds of boys and patient wives. Otherwise no mother would let her child ride to war.

The French start fighting back. They still won't cross the border, but English raiding parties begin to disappear, or limp back to Antwerp beaten and bloody.

It's three days' ride from the English camp outside Antwerp to the French border, then there's usually a week spent raiding, and three days' back. So it takes a fortnight and a dozen English lives before they realise something has changed.

The survivors talk of organised patrols waiting for them. Of foreign sell-swords, and a mercenary leader in beeswax-blackened armour who goes by the name of the Chevalier de la Mort. Harry wakes a few mornings later to find that Guy d'Audley has left in the pre-dawn darkness, taking a force of thirty knights and men-at-arms, riding for Amiens to teach this Lord Death a lesson. They clearly hadn't wanted 'Auntie Harry' along.

Harry trudges heavily across camp until he finds a familiar pavilion. Sir Hugh and Rolly, now Sir Roland, are at their breakfast in front of their tent, and when Sir Hugh sees Harry he beckons him to join them. Harry sighs and eases himself down onto an upturned bucket, still leaving a goodly distance between himself and Rolly.

Harry looks up at Sir Hugh, at the grey dirtying his light brown hair, the spider's webs of care at the corners of his grey eyes. Sir Hugh is an old man in a young man's profession, and Harry both respects and fears him for that. 'What would Sir Simon do?' Harry asks, as Sir Hugh proffers him a bit of bacon.

'About what?' Sir Hugh asks in his thick West Country accent. 'If we're talking about breakfast, he'd take the bacon.'

Harry grins, despite himself, and pulls the strip of meat off the proffered knife. 'One of Montagu's bully boys and a bunch of young knights have gone off to raid the French. You've heard there are mercenaries on the border now?'

Sir Hugh nods. 'Rolly saw the party come back a few days ago. One of his friends was severely wounded.'

'I have a bad feeling,' Harry says. 'I think they're going to get themselves killed. Sir Guy is experienced enough that I'm not going to stop him riding to Hell if he wants to . . . but,' he sighs, 'some of the boys with him are no better than squires.' He glances up at Rolly. 'No offence.'

'I've been a knight for three years,' Rolly smiles. 'None taken.'

'And now you're wondering if you should ride after them and try to save their foolish hides,' Sir Hugh mumbles, around a mouthful of egg.

'I'm wondering if Sir Simon would. I'm not sure my moral map is working any more. Think I lost my way, in Scotland,' Harry says.

'If you're worried about it, you're still on the path,' Sir Hugh says, poking at their campfire. He sighs then, and looks every hour of his nearly fifty years. 'They made their choice, Harry. You can't . . . you can't save *all* the young fools, even the ones you look at and think, there but for God's grace was me.' He smiles. 'Besides, they might win. And if they don't, the next ones will be more careful.'

They don't win.

Out of thirty knights and men-at-arms, only four ride home. They are the youngest knights, raised from squires in the mud of Antwerp, and they have the pale, pinched look of boys who have seen their nightmares made real. Half the camp sees them limp in, a bloody, fly-blown sack hanging from the last one's saddlebag.

They go directly to Montagu's tent. Harry follows them.

He's just stepping into the Earl's marquee when one of the returned knights upends the bloody bag. Sir Guy's severed head tumbles out of it.

'We were ambushed,' the young knight stutters. 'They said the Black Knight and his men were camped outside Esplechin . . . as we rode through a village their bowmen cut us down.'

Montagu kneels to look at Sir Guy's mottled, bloated visage. 'Who killed him?' the Earl asks.

'The knight in black, he killed Sir Guy in single combat, and then they said we could go, and to take his head to you and tell you that this is the fate of raiders.'

'This Black Knight,' Montagu snarls, standing up. 'What *exactly* did he say?'

The knights look at each other, warily. One of the others, his sword arm bandaged, speaks up. 'He never said a single word. His men spoke for him.'

Montagu grunts, and nudges the severed head with his foot. It rolls over. On the left cheek is carved a strange, curled wound, like a loose, badly joined-up circle. 'And what is this?' he asks.

'I, I don't know,' the young knight says.

But Harry knows.

It's not a circle.

It's the number nine.

Nine knights left. Nine of the Galloway Dozen, the men who murdered Marguerite of France. Crocker, Waldegrave, and now d'Audley dead.

It's impossible, Harry thinks. It must be some freakish coincidence; his foolish heart leaping at the thinnest wisp of hope and constructing an entire castle on it.

But why else would the mercenaries specify Montagu by name? Why not the King?

'I need to speak to His Majesty,' mutters Montagu, pacing. He points at the head. 'Take this thing away and bury it. You, come with me,' he commands, his index finger rising to indicate the young knight who had spoken first. 'You'll give a full report in front of the King. Number of troops. Weapons. Likely nationalities. Tactics. If the King approves, we'll raise a larger force and destroy this resistance and all who support them the same way we took care of it in Scotland.'

'I'd like to go,' says Harry, stepping forwards before he even realises it. 'I've been on several raids across the border. I know some of the land.' Harry inhales, and plays his final card. 'Sir Thomas Howland, too, he is the most experienced raider of us all.'

Montagu smiles at him, his hooded eyes as dead as a December garden. 'Good old Sir Harry. We can always count on you.'

The King prevaricates. Sending enough men to end the border resistance once and for all would mean sending an earl, and if they send an earl, they might as well just invade France. The King doesn't want to invade until the Holy Roman Empire and the Low Countries get off the fence. Plus, their army at Antwerp is not large. A hundred and twenty knights, plus about a thousand men-at-arms.

Then in October 1338 France again unleashes its fleet on English port towns. Southampton is burned. Guernsey is seized. The news reaches Antwerp at the same time as a letter from Oliver Ingham, the English seneschal in Gascony, begging for help against a French invasion.

Edward sends messengers to England to begin raising a real army.

And, as soon as the frosts of winter are over, he sends an earl over the border.

In April 1339 Montagu takes a quarter of their men-at-arms and twenty knights, including Harry and Sir Thomas. They follow the Scheldt river southwest to Ghent and then towards Tournai, just across the line into France. Once they reach Tournai, they will turn north and travel along that border, killing and burning their way towards Calais. It's a cumbersome force, ill-suited to fast raiding in enemy territory. Instead, Montagu plans to intimidate the locals into giving up the mercenaries: each village will be asked for information, and if they don't respond, the town and everyone in it will be destroyed.

The monotonous, flat fields of Flanders are finally relieved by low hills as they approach the border. Sparse stands of trees thicken into forest and Harry is grateful for the cover, glad to be out of the stark, endless visibility of the farmlands. The docile-looking barns and quiet farmsteads of the plains are not friendly to the English cause. Any of them could harbour enemy combatants ready to slip out under the cover of night and devastate an English camp. But at least it looks like enemy territory. The hilly lands they ride through now remind Harry heartbreakingly of home. He spends a day in turmoil, imagining men like them riding through Devonshire, burning and killing.

They cross the Scheldt at a little stone bridge late on their third afternoon, and then the small army makes camp at the edge of the elm forest just on the Flanders side of the border. Tomorrow, they ride into France. Tonight, their last night on neutral soil, they eat cold rations of cheese and hard bread and sausage, and turn in without fires. Harry sleeps in his mail. He learned that lesson in Scotland.

Their first mistake is assuming they are safe in Flanders.

Their second is assuming the mercenaries would fight like Englishmen.

The raiders slay the sentries with knife and bolt in the deepest pits of the night, when the moon has already begun her decline. Harry jolts awake to the sounds of screaming and the creak and twang of crossbows. He slams on his helmet, grabs his shield and sword, and unlaces his tent flap. His first instinct is to head for Montagu, because he has a feeling that is where the Black Knight, this Chevalier de la Mort, will be. But as he looks cautiously outside his tent, his military instincts take over. First, he has to secure the horses.

The camp is pandemonium. Montagu brought with him a score of longbowmen but their ranged weapons are useless in a packed, close-range night fight in a forest. Harry keeps his shield up and his head down and yells, '*To the horses! To the horses!*' as he runs through the camp towards the lines. He speaks in English, hoping none of the raiders understand his language.

He ducks under a crossbow bolt and whirls, his sword coming up low and under the bowman's short hauberk. Harry feels the wet suck of the blade hitting the man's thigh bone and yanks hard, pulling it out. He runs on. There's no point making sure the man is dead. If he can't stand, he's as good as gone, and with luck one of his friends will stop to aid him. Then Harry will have halted two raiders rather than just one.

A few men-at-arms from their camp stagger towards him, clutching weapons and shields, most still in their nightshirts. By the time they get to the horse lines there are two dozen of them, knights and spearmen and a few longbowmen, massed together. It's enough to make them a hard target in a camp full of easy ones, and but for a few opportunistic shots from passing raiders with crossbows, they're left alone.

Harry doesn't hear the sound of hooves anywhere but from their own horses, fearful and restless in their lines. Inside, he's panicking, because he knows the raiders' mounted force is out there somewhere. But where? It makes his skin crawl, knowing that the main part of the attack hasn't even happened yet, that any moment now will come the thunder of heavy armour riding them all down. The forest will slow them, but it's an old forest, with tall trees and little undergrowth. Nothing to stop a mounted knight.

Harry throws a bridle on Nomad then jumps up on him, bareback, and once again yells, '*To me! Rally to the horse lines!*' He orders the younger knights, all with fresh memories of squiring, to grab the remaining destriers and take the men-at-arms and head as a body back over the Scheldt bridge, deeper into Flanders. All Harry can do is send a quick prayer heavenwards that he's not sending them to their death. It's strange that the raiders hadn't already cut loose the horses, or stolen them . . . unless they *want* the English to run.

Unless the bridge is a trap.

'*Ride back along the river!*' Harry calls, his guts twisting in panic as he remembers the little copse of trees on the Antwerp side of the bridge, and what perfect cover it would be to turn the crossing into a killing ground. '*Don't take the first bridge you come to. Take the second.*'

The men call out their understanding.

Harry whistles to some of the men-at-arms he's worked with before: Walter and Ranulf and Welsh John and old Conrad. He has just enough time to point out the horses of the Earl and his household knights, before the raiders – who hadn't been avoiding them, they'd been organising – are on them. It's a dozen enemy against the six of them, but Harry is on horseback and Welsh John has his bow. John can shoot six arrows for every one from the more cumbersome Genoese crossbows, and they soon even the odds. Ranulf's hit, they can't tell how badly, but Walter and Conrad get him over a horse and they'll worry about it later, when they have the luxury of time.

They push through the camp towards Montagu's tent. Part

of Harry wants to abandon Montagu to a fate he more than deserves. But it wouldn't be just the Earl who would suffer. There's a score of loyal men-at-arms and knights of quality bunched around Montagu, pressed hard by enemy raiders. They don't deserve to die for their master's sins.

Montagu is furious, screaming at the raiders from behind the cordon of knights defending him. 'French scum! Brigands! Your leader calls himself a knight, then why won't he come out and fight like one?'

There's a soft, harsh sound then, somehow audible under the clash of steel and the thud of arrows into shields. It's a crackling, gasping wheeze, and Harry realises after a moment that it's *laughter*.

A chill runs down his spine as he looks to its source. There, deep in the shadows of the trees, is a pool of even greater darkness: a knight, huge and broad in black plate, his shield plain but for a bend sinister, on a large black war-horse. And he's *laughing* at them.

Harry hears the muted chink of the horse's tack as the knight shakes his head in amusement and turns his steed, disappearing into the forest. And that's somehow the most terrifying thing of all: that the Black Knight didn't feel he had to engage them. That they weren't worth his time.

The little, delicate sprout of hope in the arid desert of Harry's heart withers and dies. That monster, that cold beast on horseback casually observing a slaughter . . . that could never be Iain.

Harry hears a scream and a thud, and watches as a knight falls, his skull and helmet cleaved with a raider's axe. The Black Knight's men may not fight like gentlemen, but they're winning.

'*My lord!*' Harry calls. '*Your horse!*'

Montagu sees Harry and his lips shape the words *Thank God*. The knights widen their cordon and one by one they mount up and peel off towards the Antwerp road. Out of the thirty knights that rode out, maybe half are left. Five went with the horses, and Harry can see himself, Montagu, Sir Thomas, Sir Sebastian Sharp (another of the Galloway Dozen) and maybe six more, some badly wounded and doing little more than holding their shields up. The full moon both hides and reveals, turning skin white and blood black, and Harry feels as if he is fighting in the midst of a nightmare. That perhaps he will wake up and find himself at Dartington, Iain's arms around him, the smell of fresh honey cakes wafting up from the kitchens.

But there will be no waking up. There will only be enduring, barefoot and badly armed, against the men whose villages and families they'd been burning for months.

A crossbow bolt buzzes past Harry's ear like an angry wasp. He belatedly raises his shield. It's swiftly followed by another bolt, and he realises that none of them might make it out of this forest alive. Then movement in front of him catches his eye: Sir Sebastian Sharp's horse is going down, shot high in the neck. There's an arrow sticking out of Sharp's leg, too, just below his hauberk, where it ends at bare flesh. It's pinning him to the saddle. He can't get free as the horse falls, he's screaming as the destrier lands on him, snapping his good leg, and they're right in front of Harry, and Nomad can't stop, not that fast. Sharp's horse jerks and kicks its death throes on the ground. Harry digs his heels into Nomad's sides and raises his weight up as he hurtles towards them. Nomad gathers himself and leaps the fallen horse and rider.

Harry reins Nomad around, so he can try to pull Sharp out, because the man's still alive, but then his courage wavers as a fresh barrage of crossbow bolts whizz past them.

'Leave him!' Montagu yells. 'Lyon, leave him! Cover our retreat!'

'No, God, help me, I can't move my leg!' Sharp gasps, hoarse with pain. 'Lyon!'

Harry dithers for a moment longer, but there are a dozen raiders massing to charge them on foot and the Devil knows how many French knights on horseback still waiting in the shadows. He shakes his head and spurs Nomad on towards the river.

As they ride out of the woods, keeping their heads down to avoid low branches, Harry can hear Sharp calling for Montagu, swearing at him. Sharp's voice climbs higher, and he's begging for his life, saying he has money, he can be ransomed, and then there's nothing at all.

When they reach the second crossing over the Scheldt, the grey haze of pre-dawn is just starting to light the eastern horizon. The river itself is covered in a low fog; its tendrils even reach up to the little stone bridge. And Harry hopes, *prays* the night is done, and that over the bridge lies safety.

But nobody is listening to English prayers this night.

When he hears the clop-clop of shod horses walking across the bridge towards them, he allows himself to hope for the briefest of moments it's the knights of their company that had gone on before. But there is no friendly greeting, no comrade's halloo. Harry pushes himself to the front past Montagu and Sir Thomas and the others, his shield high. He hisses to Montagu, '*Get back off the bridge. Ride along the river to the next crossing. Now.*'

Montagu hesitates, until the mist clears and they all see the massive dark form of the Black Knight on his war-horse. The sight of that silent, terrible silhouette advancing would send shivers down the back of the bravest of men on a good day. And it's far from a good day. Two other knights in plain armour ride on his quarter, the trio blocking the bridge.

Harry draws his sword. 'Fight me, O Death,' he says.

The knight shakes his head. Harry notices he's not holding a sword, but a small recurved hunting bow. His shield is slung across his back.

Harry hears more than he sees old Conrad and the other men-at-arms move to support him. Welsh John is out of arrows, but he's fought alongside these men, and he knows they could bring down a mounted knight together. But three mounted knights . . . that will take a miracle.

Montagu turns his horse to escape, swearing at Sir Thomas and the others to give him room. The bridge is narrow, though, and Montagu isn't the only one who wants to turn tail.

'*Go*,' hisses Harry to Conrad and his men. Conrad glances up at him, clearly uncomfortable with the order, so Harry repeats it. '*Guard the Earl*,' he says.

Then he looks again to the French knight. 'Why won't you fight?' Harry yells.

The Black Knight shifts, and before Harry can react, a pair of arrows fly from his bow, one after the other. They pass terrifyingly close to his left; he feels the wind of their passage and then there's the slick wet tap of them hitting a body. Someone screams; Nomad half-rears at the sound, striking sparks on the stones of the bridge with his front hooves.

Harry risks a glance over his shoulder. Sir Thomas is leaning strangely on his horse, his weight too far to the rear. Two arrows stick out of his back. The horse itself is trotting in a confused serpentine at the entrance to the bridge, effectively covering the retreat of the Earl's group with its body.

Harry turns back to the Black Knight. He doesn't understand any of this: the knight's strange stillness; his choice of targets—

Harry's eyes widen and his skin prickles with goosebumps.

His choice of targets.

Sharp and Howland. Two more of the Galloway Dozen.

But not him. The knight has not lifted a hand in battle to Harry, and neither have the rest of the raiders.

'Who are you?' Harry says. His voice shakes.

And in front of him Harry doesn't see a knight, but a starving little ball of Scottish fury in a cage, hissing that his name is Lord Death. Threatening to kill every one of his captors, despite being too weak to stand.

But the Black Knight only raises his hand to his helmet in salute, and spins his big destrier around in a showy pirouette before riding away. His two vassal knights follow him.

A lump rises in Harry's throat. He wants to ride after him. He wants to shout the name that's never left his heart, but he's too aware how voices carry in the morning stillness.

Montagu would hear.

Harry sheaths his sword. He turns back, wearily collecting Sir Thomas's horse and binding the dead man over his saddle. They walk up the river to the next crossing, and over, as dawn paints Flanders' farmlands in hues of rose and gold. All is peaceful, all is calm. As if the terror and death of the night before had never happened.

A rabbit flashes across the road. Nomad, usually rock-solid, shies, and Harry feels his heart beat faster. He hates this deadly inaction, this strange halfway existence between waiting and war.

He hates not knowing who his enemies are.

Harry catches up with Montagu and the rest of their once-proud force outside Ghent. He's glad to discover that most of the men-at-arms and young knights made it out of the forest, with nearly all the horses.

Montagu's proud army of three hundred limps back into the Antwerp camp only fifty strong. They never made it into France.

Harry spends the next month going out for long rides alone, each time angling Nomad southwards towards France. It's ridiculous. He doesn't even go beyond Ghent. There's no way French knights would be this far into Flanders. But he *hopes*. His eyes bore into the shadows of barns, looking for blackened armour, dark hooves.

But there is nothing. Just bored, fly-bitten cows and wary milkmaids.

After the rides, deep into sleepless nights, Harry's mind fills with plans, each of them more ridiculous than the last. He'll find the King, alone. Tell him that he thinks Iain is still alive. He'll ride to France and surrender himself and ask for the Black Knight. In the strict light of morning, all these fantasies wither away, their mad nature exposed. But he feels he must do *something*. If only to prove to himself that he hasn't gone insane.

Harry is summoned by Montagu on a brilliant sunny day in late May.

He steps into Montagu's tent to find the usual crew of bully boys, plus one extra: a priest, ferret-faced and richly robed.

Montagu smiles at Harry without any warmth at all and indicates he should take a seat. 'We are here to solve a mystery,' Montagu says to the assembled group. 'My friend Père Auguste has come to help. He is a regular at the French court.'

The priest fidgets, clearly displeased to be in the English camp. Harry wonders idly if the man is being bribed or blackmailed. Or perhaps a little of each, knowing Montagu.

'Now, let's begin,' Montagu says, leaning back in his chair and gesturing lazily at the priest. 'This Black Knight. Tell me about him. I want to know everything.'

'He appeared a couple of years ago,' the priest says, his Parisian French shaded with an unpleasant, nasal twang. 'Nobody knows anything. His men are mercenaries: redshanks, Genoese, Germans. Desperate sorts of men, but he pays well and he has their unquestioning loyalty.'

'Have you—' Rabbie says, before the priest interrupts.

'Both with gold and with threats.' The priest looks down his large, hooked nose at Ufford. 'The ones that will speak don't know, and the ones that know won't speak.'

'Who commands him?' Harry asks.

'We think he takes his orders directly from the King, but he has never been seen at court,' says the priest.

'Dammit. There must be a man behind that helmet, who has a life, who has friends,' Montagu snarls. 'Family. *Weaknesses*.' He runs his hands over the arms of his chair, to the eagle heads carved at their ends. Only Montagu, Harry thinks, would bring a throne to an army camp. Well, Montagu and the King.

Montagu steeples his fingers and continues. 'Who arrived at court around the time the Black Knight first appeared?'

The priest sighs and gives a great shrug. 'You don't understand. Philip has been consolidating his barons and planning for war since your king murdered the Capet boy. We have had so many country knights joining the court, it could be any of them.'

'We did not mur—' one of the younger knights, Billy Shayler, begins, but swallows his words at a gesture from Montagu. Montagu never looks at him, just makes a sharp, palm-down cutting motion: *silence*.

Montagu's smile grows strained. 'Well, which of them are not at court right now?' Montagu asks, as if talking to a child. He indicates Harry. 'It would be someone his size, good with a sword and a bow. There cannot be many.'

The poor, hapless courtier gestures. 'We are invading Gascony, milord. Half of them are there. How can we know if one knight rides north instead of south?'

'You will know.' Montagu's eyes narrow. 'Because I *pay* you to know. Unless you no longer wish to be paid?'

The priest frowns, and shifts uncomfortably. He indicates Harry with his chin. 'The only man at court his size is the Comte de Marche, but the Comte is a fop. I don't even think he owns armour. He throws parties and drinks, that is all. I saw him, passed out drunk in the royal stables, as I was leaving. You must understand—'

'I understand you are failing me,' Montagu cuts in, barely above a whisper. 'That is not a recipe for a long life.'

Harry looks around as the assembled knights cackle at Montagu's threat. There are seven knights from the Galloway raid left, and all are in the tent at that moment: Montagu, Rabbie,

Brendan le Rous, the two Billies (Sir William Shayler and Sir William Lang), Sir Roderick Griffith. And him. They are all enjoying the priest's discomfort, whispering back and forth what likely punishment Montagu will find for the man if he disappoints. All but Harry.

Harry decides then and there who his enemies are. He is standing in the presence of the man who ordered Iain's murder. Who gave the order to burn Dartington. A man who bent the fortunes of an entire country towards war because he wanted the lands and profit that come from fighting it. A man so powerful that Harry will never be able to raise his hand openly against him and survive.

But he can mess with Montagu's mind.

He half-sits, half-falls onto a bench, and puts his head in his hands.

Montagu glares at him. 'What's wrong, Lyon?'

'What if he is Death?' Harry whispers. He doesn't even have to fake looking pale. He's barely eaten or slept since the attack in the forest. 'What if there is nothing under that armour?'

'Don't be ridiculous,' says Rabbie.

'No. We were cursed,' Harry says, tugging at his own hair. 'She cursed us, you know.'

'Who?' says Sir Roderick.

Harry glances up, his eyes red with exhaustion. 'Marguerite. When we killed her.' His lips twitch into something that could be a smile, but isn't. 'I wonder . . . with the Templars' Curse so heavy on the Capets . . . perhaps she was able to throw some of it on us.' He shakes his head. 'I don't know. It's just . . . we're *dying*, one by one. We of Galloway. Once we were twelve, and now we are seven.'

'Nonsense,' grumps Brendan le Rous, a stocky, no-nonsense lord from Chester. 'That was five years ago. A few of us dying off here and there is to be expected.'

But some of the others look shaken.

Harry stands. 'I'm going to church to ask forgiveness of my sins. The Devil himself rides after us for the evil we have done.' He sighs as he goes out the door. 'Thank God the Capet boy's murder isn't also on our souls.'

Then he exits, his little play-act finished, his lines delivered.

The King secures his allies and over the summer their camp swells from a thousand men to nearly twelve times that. Harry can't help but wonder which ones are French spies. He supposes they'll find out soon enough.

They ride out in September and lay siege to the bishopric of Cambrai on the Flanders border, hoping to force the French king to come to the aid of his ally. But Philip does not. There is no sign of the French army, even as the English surround the town. No challenge, even as for a fortnight they burn everything within a ten-mile radius. No relief.

Yet also no English victory. The town holds fast behind its walls.

On the morning of the tenth day, Brendan le Rous is found dead in his tent, his throat cut. In his hand are six white feathers. The redheaded camp-follower he had taken to his bed that night has vanished into thin air.

Six feathers. Six knights left.

Even Rabbie looks shaken now. He pulls Harry aside the next night at supper in the King's tent and says, 'Look, Harry, you need to stop talking about this. Curses don't exist. It's coincidence. Just coincidence.'

Harry says, 'Sure, Rabbie,' and pours both of them another drink.

King Edward crosses into France on the Feast of Saint Denis. It's a deliberate provocation, invading a country on its patron saint's feast day, a calculated insult to both Philip's legitimacy and his war strategy. But, frustrated with the French king's evasiveness and running out of funds to pay his vast army, the English monarch is left with little other choice.

Harry realises on the march that he's been away from England for more than a year. Both his children will be walking now, and another harvest has passed without him cutting the first wheat. And, rather than finally laying Iain's memory to rest in France, Harry feels increasingly haunted by him. It's as if at any time Harry will open his eyes and find Iain standing there, ghostly pale, asking if Harry really believed a grave could keep him down.

Philip of Valois raises an army while Cambrai is under siege, but for another stultifying fortnight the two armies move parallel to each other, as if shadow-boxing, neither willing to make the first move. They drift south, towards the Somme, and finally near the town of Péronne the distance between them is narrowed to fifteen miles. Yet still Philip doesn't repel the invaders. He sits. He waits, either for his courage to appear, or Edward's money to disappear. Nobody is sure.

War is as boring in France as it was in Flanders. The knights ride out on raids. Edward has raised more than sixty squires to knighthood and the boys are keen to show what they're made of. Harry can hear them bragging to each other as he sits around the campfire with Sir Hugh their first night near Péronne. One with a light, high voice swears he'll take a French life within a mile of their army, *so help him God.*

Sir Hugh shakes his head.

But then Harry gets an idea. He spends another night sleepless, but this time with excitement, and in the morning strides to Montagu's tent. Both Montagu and Rabbie are out, probably in attendance on the King, but a couple of his boys are there. And that's exactly what Harry was hoping.

'You look like shit, Lyon,' mutters Billy Shayler, looking up from his breakfast.

Harry puts a hand to his face. His hair is still cropped fairly short, but he's let his beard grow. Hasn't mended the holes in his surcoat. Can't remember the last time he washed. He looks down at his arms, at the webs of scars from sword and armour that cross them like silver bands, and sighs. It's too late now. 'Haven't been sleeping,' he says. 'Bored and restless.'

'Mm,' Shayler nods in agreement.

'Thought I'd take some of the young ones out raiding. Wondered if any of you wanted to come.' Harry tries to smile, tries to pretend he's excited for the reasons they would be excited. Not for a different reason. Not because he's in love with Death, and keen to chase him across the French countryside. 'Wanted to get the good stuff before anyone else had a chance.'

Sir Roderick Griffith stretches, rising. 'Amen to that. I'm going mad with boredom. I'll come.'

Billy Lang shakes his head.

The other Billy, Shayler, jabs him. 'Don't tell me you're afraid of that curse malarkey,' he says.

Lang fidgets, and when he speaks, his voice is a near-whisper. 'I had a nightmare about him. The Black Knight.'

Shayler jabs him again. 'You've just been doing nothing too long. We all have. Inactivity makes us cowards. C'mon, Billy.'

But the man doesn't get up from his seat.

Roderick Griffith and Billy Shayler do, and they grab four of the new knights and set out for a small keep they've heard mention of, a little west of Péronne. It's a poor thing, a single tower surrounded by mud huts, defended by a few men-at-arms with spears and swords. But it's close enough to the French lines to be an insult to Philip of Valois and a provocation to his deadly enforcer.

Harry's stomach turns as the knights ride in and kill everything in their path: the poorly armed, terrified soldiers; the merchant whose cart is in the wrong place at the wrong time; an old man who just doesn't get out of the way fast enough.

Harry curses to himself. Of course the Black Knight isn't going to magically appear, just by the force of Harry's desire. France is vast. The territory between the two armies is huge. Even if the Black Knight is with the French army, the chances of him being *here*, in this little town, are minimal. Harry knows it's just a paranoid delusion that the Black Knight has spies watching over him, but the idea stubbornly remains. As does the hope that a man he watched die is somehow, miraculously, still alive and causing all the trouble he possibly can.

Harry looks around and signals to the other knights, *time to go*. One of the young ones looks a little green, taking off his helmet to get some air. He must be no more than eighteen. His brown eyes are wide and frightened against his olive skin and short brown-black hair.

Harry rides up to him. 'You well?'

The boy shakes his head.

'You're from the South,' Harry says. It's not a question. The campaigns in Scotland over the past few years have meant that there have been no tournaments since Smithfield. But it was only Northern knights, after a while, who rode to fight in Scotland. The Southerners stayed home. Boys like this who were squiring for Southern knights, Harry knows, would have spent the last few years with not even the play warfare of tournaments to ease them into battle.

'Near Colchester,' the boy says, his French almost incomprehensible through a strong Essex accent. 'My name's Nicky. I mean, Sir Nicholas.'

Harry places a hand on the boy's mailed shoulder and switches to English. God's teeth, these boys were so green they didn't even speak French properly yet. '*Welcome to knighthood, lad. I'm sorry.*'

'*It doesn't get better?*' the boy asks, his voice cracking.

Harry shakes his head and rides to the keep's gate. '*No. It does not.*'

Then he realises: Sir William Shayler is missing. He turns to Sir Roderick. 'Where's Billy?' Harry asks, switching back to French. 'It's afternoon, we have to head back now.' They both know it's all very well to ride out towards the French lines, but another thing entirely to be stuck a skirmisher's distance from them at the Vespers bell.

Sir Roderick gestures inside the keep, where Harry sees a

flurry of movement on the second floor. 'He went after a woman,' the reedy East Anglian knight says.

'Shit,' Harry says under his breath. Then he yells, '*Billy! Get out here now, or we're leaving you!*'

A nervous minute or two passes. Something's wrong. Harry can feel it in his guts. '*That's it*,' he says, hauling Nomad around. '*We're leaving*. Now.'

'*No*,' says Sir Roderick, preparing to dismount. '*We have to get Billy—*'

The rest of his sentence is cut off by a high, piercing whistle from the keep. There's the clatter of doors being opened in the vassal houses dotted around it, hovels they'd ignored as too poor to be worth plundering. And the long hiss of swords leaving scabbards.

'*Billy's dead*,' growls Harry, and sets his heels into Nomad.

He rides out of the keep at a gallop, not even checking to see who follows. They follow or they die. It's that simple. The boy, Sir Nicholas, is on his left quarter, barely in control of his steed. Horse and boy have wide, terrified whale eyes. The other young knights are behind, and Sir Roderick – wrong-footed when Harry took off – brings up the rear.

Harry allows himself a moment to get his own heart under control when they pass a copse, and a shadow detaches itself from the darker shadows of the oaks to ride down and intercept them. '*Keep riding straight back to our lines*,' hisses Harry, slowing Nomad so the boys gallop past him. '*Don't try to fight him. You're not good enough*.'

'*How would you know, Lyon?*' asks Sir Roderick, loosening his sword in its scabbard.

Because I think I taught him, Harry says to himself.

The Black Knight's horse is fast, and much fresher than their own mounts, who have been under saddle all day. He pulls ahead of them, galloping along the edge of a wheat field, then angles his horse over the low earthen bank to the road, turning to charge them as soon as the destrier's hooves hit its hard-packed dirt. He does not slow. Sword out, shield up, he gallops straight at them.

Harry prays the young knights scatter, and they do. One tries to get his sword up, get in a blow at the infamous Chevalier de la Mort, and receives a savage cut on his forearm for his trouble. The boy drops his own sword and howls, gibbering at the white flash of bone amidst the blood pouring from his arm.

And then the Black Knight is upon them. He barges Harry aside, sword high, their shields cracking against each other, and then he swings low, leaning out of his saddle and flicking his blade under Sir Roderick's shield. Harry gasps as he sees the strike, a nasty cross-body thrust that has all the power of the knight's shoulders and torso in it. The blade's point slips through the mail as if it were butter, burying itself about six inches in Sir Roderick's stomach. It doesn't seem like much, but then a man is barely ten inches deep.

The knight pulls his sword out as he gallops past, the suction of the blade worsening the cut and forcing Sir Roderick to twist around. The knight flicks the blood off the point of his sword and sheaths it, galloping back towards the keep. He doesn't look back. Harry knows, because he watches him until he's out of sight.

Sir Roderick takes three days to die in screaming agony, the gut wound infecting his entire body.

And thus is the Galloway Dozen reduced to a quartet.

The morning after they return, Harry wakes with an erection. He can't remember the last time he'd woken up with the normal morning arousal, and he looks down in confusion at his body and its traitorous moods.

He touches himself, of course. His mind fills with old images of Iain, fading now, blurry and indistinct. But as he writhes and arches off his pallet, he also sees the Black Knight, imagines the man riding him down in the woods where Harry first saw him, pulling him off his horse and taking him right there on the forest floor, not removing a single piece of his black armour, a gauntleted hand on the back of his neck and another hooked round the flesh of his hip under his hauberk, the heavy weight of a muscled, armoured body thrusting into him.

He comes so hard he almost passes out.

From then on he's hard every morning, like he used to be. It's as if his libido has just strolled back into his life after a long holiday and taken up residence again. As if nothing had changed in all the intervening years.

Harry takes to riding out alone again. He dawdles in copses and behind hedgerows, looking for shadows within shadows. He never finds them. It's after one such trip in mid October, a couple of weeks into the English army's residence in France, that Sir Hugh finds him at his campfire. The older knight carries a jug of something strong, bought or stolen from a nearby French village. Harry doesn't bother to ask which.

Sir Hugh sits down and passes him the jug. Harry uncorks it and takes a long swig. Whatever it is burns like a stripe of fire down his throat, and leaves an aftertaste of apples.

They sit in silence for a while, watching the sputter of green wood burn in Harry's fire. Watching the sun set. 'You're cracking up,' Sir Hugh says at last. 'You should go home.'

'I'm fine,' Harry says, passing the jug back.

Harry can see the flash of white in Sir Hugh's eyes as the older knight glares at him. Sir Hugh takes a drink and then says, 'This damned non-campaign is getting to us all, Harry. No shame in it. England won't lose the war if you have to take a break.'

'No,' Harry says, an edge creeping into his voice. 'Hugh, thank you for your concern, but I can't leave.' He sighs, raking a hand through his hair. It needs cutting now. He glances down at his nails, dark with dirt. 'I know it seems like I'm going mad. I wonder it myself, in the deep hours of the night. But the only way for me to know is if I stay.' He wants so desperately to unburden himself to the other knight, to tell him his hopes and fears. But these are not things that can be spoken aloud, to anyone.

'Do you see them? In your dreams? The people you've killed?' asks Sir Hugh quietly. There's a pause as a chunk of wood in the fire splits with a loud pop. Both knights flinch. Then Sir Hugh exhales, long and ragged. 'Because I do.'

'It's not that,' says Harry, though the dead visit his dreams as well. 'My ghost walks in daylight.'

Harry watches Sir Hugh's brow crease in confusion, and then smooth, as the old knight's eyes widen slightly. He had always been a perceptive man.

Sir Hugh nods. 'I'll fetch another jug, then.'

'Good idea,' Harry says.

It's a terrific idea. They get astoundingly drunk, to the point where Harry almost pitches forwards into the embers as he tries to stand. The ground is surprisingly . . . unsteady. He ends up having to crawl into his tent, collapsing face-down on his pallet. It's the most relaxed Harry's felt in years.

He pays for it the next morning. The taste of small beer at breakfast has him scurrying off to a waste pit, jaw clenched around the vomit rising in his throat. Kneeling over the stinking pit, he throws up until there's nothing left in his stomach. As he wipes his mouth on the back of his forearm, he notices how filthy his hands are.

He feels like he's sweating alcohol, on a stiflingly warm day for late October.

Harry grabs the bar of lye soap and a brush from his tent and staggers down to the river. He discards his clothes on the bank and wades in. A few other knights and men-at-arms are bathing, and some camp-followers and squires are doing laundry on the bank, over buckets. The cold water feels heavenly on his abused body.

Harry scrubs himself until he's pink, then climbs out, wraps himself in his cloak, and heads back to his tent. He digs out the small silver mirror he hasn't used in months, and his whetstone. Knife sharpened, he shaves. He has great plans to go out riding later that day, but for now, he goes back to sleep again. It's a luxurious feeling, being clean. He used to be so meticulous about such matters. He'd forgotten what it was like.

When he wakes again, the sun is low in the sky, but there's still a couple of hours of riding time left. Harry staggers to his feet and pulls on his clothes and mail, trying to ignore his half-hard dick. He decides he won't bother with the plate. He's not going far. And besides, he never sees anybody on his rides.

Until he does, of course.

Until the sun is skimming the horizon and he's still an hour away from the English lines. Until a raiding party of French knights, well armed and well armoured, sweeps out from around the side of a stone farmhouse. Half a dozen men; maybe more. They come at him from the west, so the low sun is in his eyes, blinding him. Their shadows reach him long before they do.

And Harry doesn't have a death wish – not any more, at least – so he raises his hands in surrender. He glances down at his old, battle-worn clothing, hoping he can somehow appear worth ransoming rather than putting to the sword then and there. Not that anyone on the English side would raise a purse for him. But his captors don't need to know that.

A sudden, desperate thought occurs to him: if he is taken behind French lines, maybe he will see the Black Knight. Maybe he will find out if the man under the helmet has pale eyes and an off-kilter, roguish smile.

'I surrender,' Harry says. 'I am Sir Harry Lyon of Dartington, friend of—' He hesitates— 'friend of the Earl of Arundel, who would ransom me.'

A small but broad knight with a dark beard visible under his helmet looks Harry up and down. Then the man turns his head and spits on the ground. 'We have no room to ransom common knights. In a few minutes, Englishman, you will meet the Devil. Ask him to write to your Earl of Arundel. He probably knows the address.'

The knights laugh.

Harry shifts uncomfortably. He still has his hands in the air. There are eight knights, all mounted, and they surround him.

Two have light war lances. One mace. The rest have swords drawn.

His mind races through tactics; angles. Drop off Nomad and roll under one of their horses . . . and then get run down on foot. Any plan that allows him to escape the circle doesn't let him outrun the knights; any plan to outrun the knights won't succeed in breaking the circle without grievous injury to him and Nomad. He can't get out of this.

The bearded knight raises his sword, and Harry can see the mace rising too, out of the corner of his eye.

'Wait,' Harry says. 'I need to speak to the Black Knight. To the Chevalier de la Mort. I know him.' He suddenly realises he's crying, tears running down his cheeks under his helmet. '*Please*. I know him.'

One of the knights with the lances speaks up again. He moves the lance-point so it hovers just beneath Harry's helmet, at the soft flesh below his jaw. It's no tournament lance, built to shatter, with a blunt end meant for catching shields. It's a war lance, light and strong and tipped with sharpened steel. 'What is your name, again?' he says.

'Harry Lyon, of Dartington,' he says, his voice shaking. He reaches his left hand down to his right wrist, slowly, so it's not a threat, reaching under his gauntlet to the mail of his hauberk. He pushes up his sleeve until the little half-moon scar on his forearm is visible among straighter, newer souvenirs of war. 'Believe it or not, he bit me once.'

Harry watches as the lancer's eyes flick down to his forearm, then back up to what little of his face is visible. The man looks over to the bearded knight. 'Louis,' the man hisses.

The bearded knight puts his sword in his scabbard and pulls

off his helmet. He stuffs two fingers in his mouth and lets out a whistle so piercing that Harry flinches involuntarily. Then the man turns to Harry. 'Take off your helmet,' he says.

Harry does.

He thinks he sees a sliver of darkness shift, in the long shadow of the farmhouse. In the dusk it could be a man in black armour, on a black horse. Or it could be a trick of the half-light.

Harry's heart starts battering in his chest like a caged bird against its bars.

The bearded knight says, 'You should be more careful, Sir Harry, coming out by yourself so close to our army,' and then gestures. He and the other knights fade away, heading back towards the French lines, just . . . leaving Harry there, alone, without another word.

He drops his hands. Nomad whickers, the skin over his shoulder twitching. He can feel Harry's unease through the saddle and his ears flick back, testament to his own nerves. Harry pats his neck and makes shushing noises.

He squints at the shadowed wall of the farmhouse. Nothing moves.

'Iain?' he calls softly.

He suddenly feels ridiculous, sitting there on his horse in the middle of the road at twilight, talking to what is probably an old, upturned cart, or a restless farm cat. '*I just want you to know I still think of you*,' Harry says, his voice cracking. '*Every goddamn day*.'

He waits.

Nothing happens. Nothing moves.

Then he sighs, shoulders slumping in defeat. He turns Nomad around.

Maybe Sir Hugh is right. Maybe he is cracking up.

He gets back to the English camp as a hunter's moon begins to rise.

Two days later, the English and French armies finally line up to do battle. The French army dwarfs England's twelve thousand, yet rather than trying to run right over them, Philip of Valois draws up his troops in a defensive formation. The lines glare at each other all day. Edward and his earls assume the French will attack their invaders. The French wait for Edward to make the first move.

The day ends without a battle being fought.

Each king claims a victory, of course. Philip of Valois returns with his court to Paris, bragging that the English hadn't made it more than fifty miles over the border before they turned tail and went home.

The English march slowly back across the border to Flanders, with no plans to return. It is money, in the end, that curtails the French campaign, not force of arms. Technically, the English remain undefeated, and that is the narrative the King spins. Just after Epiphany, Edward stops in Ghent on the way to Antwerp and officially decrees himself King of England and France. He invaded France without opposition; clearly, he must be the country's true ruler.

(Harry looks at the ground, schooling his expression.)

The bulk of the army continues onwards to the coast of Flanders, towards the Channel and home. King Edward is bound for England, too, frustrated and out of funds. The army is eating through his treasury at an alarming rate, and the crown's Italian lenders have been reticent to extend more money to England without a distinct victory in hand. The King plans new taxes, but those take time to levy.

Four earls remain in Flanders as spring of 1340 approaches: Ufford, Montagu, de Grosmont and Bohun.

And Harry.

He jots a quick letter to Alys apologising for his long absence, and asking for news of the children and of Dartington. He entrusts it to Sir Hugh, who is crossing the Channel with the King. 'Is there anything I should add?' Sir Hugh asks, tucking the letter into his saddlebags.

'Just tell her I think I've seen a ghost,' Harry says.

Sir Hugh nods. Then he puts his hand on Harry's shoulder. 'Be well,' he says. 'I hope you find him.'

There's little to do in Antwerp while they wait for the King's return. Rumours spread that Philip is massing another navy to keep the King and the bulk of his army from coming back to France, and strange men go back and forth from Montagu's tent at all hours of the day. Harry knows they are spies. Much as he despises Montagu, he's grateful for the Earl's web of informants if they keep the King alive.

But Harry is bored. Tired of weeks of inactivity; sick of the damp cold. The declining temperatures cause the mud all around his tent to grow a thin crust of ice, perfect for slicing bare ankles, or turning incautious feet. The vastly reduced camp means that he can't slip over to France to chase his ghost without raising suspicion. And they are no longer raiding. They're just sitting and waiting.

Perhaps, Harry thinks, he should have gone back to England. Perhaps they all should have. But then a foolish hope will bloom in Harry, and he dreams that maybe a camp-follower will slip him a note, telling him to be at a certain place at a certain time. Or that he'll wake up in the night to a ghost's warm, thick arms around him.

Harry rounds up some of the other equally bored knights and they start training again. They spar for hours, until their muscles feel like jelly and their bodies ache. It helps them sleep, if nothing else.

Rabbie is unbearable. He's not a patient man at the best of times, and the endless grind of the French campaign is wearing on him. He badgers Montagu and de Grosmont to let him attack this town, that castle. Their refusals are taken as personal insults; the whole camp can hear him rage afterwards.

Finally, one morning in early March, Montagu strides out of his tent and pulls Rabbie aside. Their heads are bent close together as Montagu whispers something Harry can't overhear. But then Rabbie straightens, his eyes bright, and the message is clear.

They're going on the attack.

The target turns out to be Lille, a good-sized city just over the border into the Walloon part of Flanders, which had thrown its chips in with France rather than England. It wasn't technically an act of war against France, but it might distract the French king from his naval preparations. It would, of course, bestow great honour on Montagu and Ufford if they take the city.

Harry cleans his armour, washes and repairs his surcoat. Checks his shield for cracks or warping. And waits for Montagu or Ufford to summon him.

They never do.

The two earls ride for Lille a week later with a thousand men-at-arms, leaving only a skeleton camp behind. When Harry confronts Montagu on the eve of departure to ask why he's not invited, Montagu smiles genially at him. 'You're trouble,' is all the Earl says. 'Things go wrong when you're along on a raid, yet you never seem to get hurt. It's curious.' Montagu flicks his fingers towards the door, dismissing Harry, as his attention returns to the map spread before him. 'And I don't have time for curiosity right now. You'll stay and help de Grosmont manage the camp until I return.'

Except they don't return.

Nine hundred and fifty men of the thousand do. Harry rushes to Henry de Grosmont's tent to hear the captains of the men-at-arms – exhausted, road-dirty, but unhurt – give their report. It seems Montagu took Ufford, Billy Lang and about forty other knights and men-at-arms to reconnoitre the approach to the city. They had ridden in close to its walls, assuming they were hidden from the Walloon forces' view by the great defensive earthworks set up around the town. But the earthworks also hid them from their own army's eyes.

The men-at-arms talk of their panic, watching the low sun descend in the sky, hearing the distant bells for Sext, then None, watching for a sign of their leaders' return. It was as if the city's earthen bulwarks had just swallowed them whole. Finally, as dusk approached, the main force abandoned position and fled back across the border, leaving only a small party of scouts behind. The scouts caught up with them two days later and confirmed their greatest fear: capture.

The two earls were French prisoners.

The others, including Billy Lang, had been put to the sword.

Henry de Grosmont sends for Harry again early the next morning. He stumbles into the Earl's tent to find William Bohun there, as well as the Bishop of Lincoln and the King's lawyer, a rumpled Yorkshireman named Geoffrey Scrope. Two other knights are just leaving, men Harry recognises from around the camp but doesn't know well. They're still wearing travelling clothes.

De Grosmont sighs, and sits heavily on a wooden travelling chest. 'The Earls of Suffolk and Salisbury have been taken by the French,' he says to the newcomers. 'You, you and you will leave in the morning for Paris to negotiate their ransom.'

It takes Harry a moment to realise de Grosmont has indicated him as the third, to accompany the Bishop and Geoffrey Scrope. The priest and the lawyer immediately excuse themselves to begin preparations for the journey.

Harry points to himself, confused. 'Me?' he says, his voice going high. It's more than he dared wish for. If Iain really is alive – if this isn't some fantasy constructed by Harry's grief-maddened mind – he will be in Paris, near to the French king. Then paranoia slams down on his hopes like a steel hunting trap. 'Why me?' he stutters. 'I'm not very important.'

De Grosmont sips from his cup of wine. 'You have the reputation of an honest man,' he explains. Then his brow furrows. 'And didn't you take care of that Capet boy? Try to save his life?'

Harry blanches, then nods. 'Yes, my lord. He was my squire. And . . . a close friend.'

De Grosmont smiles. 'That gives you an advantage,' he says, as if it explains everything.

'An advantage,' Harry repeats, his voice flat. He tucks his hands behind his back to hide how white his knuckles are.

'Yes,' de Grosmont yawns. 'Some of the more traditional barons were very loyal to the Capets. Your being the boy's protector may gain you some powerful friends. Or at least it's an interesting conversation starter.' De Grosmont flexes his fingers, cracking them one by one. 'I trust you'll use it to best result.'

Harry's lips twist into a grim little smile; he nods. It's either that or completely lose his temper. He's digging his newly-clean nails into his palms so hard he's close to drawing blood.

'Go. Get them back,' de Grosmont says. Then he shifts, a heavy hand rubbing at the bridge of his nose. And Harry realises then that de Grosmont is just as bored and fed up as the rest of them. The circles under his eyes attest to just how God-damned tired he is of being in a foreign country, in a campaign that's been grinding on for a year and a half yet has gone absolutely nowhere.

'I heard they are being taken in a cage to Paris,' de Grosmont says, staring absently towards the lead wine cup in front of him. 'Like common criminals. Nasty business, an earl in a cage. Who would do such a thing?'

Harry's heart does something funny then. Shifts and swells as if, after a long silence, it remembers a time when it would sing. 'I couldn't imagine, sir.'

De Grosmont dismisses him with a wave of his hand.

Harry hurries to his tent to pack for Paris.

Twelve

March–April 1340: Sword of the Beast

Harry and the lawyer and the Bishop ride to Paris in the company of a dozen loyal men-at-arms and a courtesy escort of French knights. He recognises one of them, the knight with the dark beard from his misadventure near Péronne. Harry wants to talk to the man further, but it's impossible. The French knights keep their distance socially, even as they guard the caravan physically.

It's slow progress. The heavy military ox-carts bearing their own belongings and the prisoners' requirements crawl along at no more than a walking pace. From the Flanders border it's five days to Paris. Harry reckons on Nomad, alone, he could make it in three. He almost suggests riding on ahead, but he can't come up with any viable reason to excuse it. And he'd still need a courtesy escort.

In the end, he's happy to have the Bishop and Geoffrey Scrope to share his awe with him when the French capital comes into view. Harry hasn't been to London often, but compared to Paris, the English capital comes off as no more than a middling county seat. There are three times as many people, spread out over about four times as much space. London is, after all, little more than a square mile. The French king's palace and administrative buildings, on an island in the middle of the Seine, are a square mile *on their own*. Paris's streets are still narrow and crooked like London's, but there are just so many more of them. Everything about Paris is *more* than London. Bigger, higher, busier, fancier. Older.

As they cross the broad wooden bridge to the Île de la Cité, Harry can see rooftops and spires lining the river all the way to the horizon. There's a fortress on the right bank, and a tall, elegant tower on the left. When one of their French escorts casually identifies it as the Tour de Nesle, Harry has to stop his horse right there in the middle of the Grand Pont as a wave of dizziness hits him.

He's reminded that Iain's family built this city, this whole *country*, from a mere stronghold that was originally little more than the island in front of them. And then held it, for three hundred and fifty years.

Harry is overwhelmed by one thought as he enters the vast ceremonial courtyard of the Palais de la Cité: this, *all* of this, is Iain's birthright.

Their party is met by palace officials, who send the men-at-arms down to the Salle des Gardes and show Harry, Geoffrey and the Bishop to their room in a gallery of guest chambers, along the southern bailey wall.

Harry dumps his saddlebags and strips off his shirt, immediately gravitating towards the washing bowl so he can clean the dust off himself from travelling. The palace servants are immaculate, and in comparison Harry feels a rough, dirty beast, slouched in from the provinces. He can hear the other two men also getting settled, sorting through their small bags while they wait for the servants to bring the rest of their personal luggage off the carts. 'When do you think we'll see the French king?' Harry asks.

Geoffrey sighs and sits on the edge of the large bed they will all share. 'Last time I only saw him once, at the end.' The lawyer reaches up and stretches, his back cracking. 'I warn you, Harry. Negotiating with French administrators is going to frustrate you immensely. Please don't speak without checking with me first. They can be . . . touchy. There are hierarchies to be respected, protocols to be obeyed.'

Harry bristles at being treated like a child, but files it away as a fight to have at another time. 'Noted,' he says. He pulls on clean clothes, his good court outfit, and turns to Geoffrey. 'Do you think it would be allowed for me to take a walk?' Harry asks.

The lawyer nods. 'I don't mean to be harsh, Harry. They're just . . . different here. More formal. I'd counsel staying quiet and learning the way things are done in this court, before saying something you might regret.' He smiles, shyly. He's a rumpled fellow, grey curls and lined face, deep circles under his eyes like bruises. 'I'm only giving you the advice I wish someone had given me my first time here.'

'I understand,' says Harry, somewhat mollified.

'There's a fine garden on the western side of the Palace. Ask anyone; they'll point you in the right direction.'

Harry nods his thanks and heads out. The garden isn't hard to find, and it is indeed beautiful, its beds and bowers arranged in formal geometries. Harry settles himself on a bench near a wall of roses and relaxes in the spring sunshine, watching the Parisian courtiers go by.

Even cleaned up and in his good clothes, he feels frumpy next to them. It's not that rich damasks, velvets and silks don't make it to England, but so few people have them. Here in the Palais, *everyone* is wearing them, in every dazzling colour of the rainbow. And every cuff, every collar, is picked out with gold or silver embroidery. The fashions on the men are cut differently from the English court, too. It's all so tight here. And so *short.*

Harry shifts uncomfortably as a young courtier walks by. He can see half the boy's arse under his jacket, with thin hose that leave nothing to the imagination.

The boy sees him looking, and *winks.*

Harry hurries back to the chamber provided for him, blushing furiously, as the bells ring for supper.

The first few days of negotiation are, as Geoffrey promises, incredibly tedious. Their opposite numbers are a pair of French priests and the Chief Justice of the royal law courts. All they do at first is name an incredibly high ransom for Montagu and Ufford and then refuse to discuss it. The number is so huge as to be meaningless to Harry. The Bishop of Lincoln tries to put it into context, telling Harry what the French want is equal to what Edward has already spent on the war to date. It's a crippling amount of money. When Geoffrey Scrope tries to name a lower number, or ask for the reasoning behind the French figure, the Chief Justice merely shakes his head and intones, 'It has been decided.'

Harry wants to ask *decided by whom*, but he bites his tongue, for now.

The English can't storm out of the negotiation, but they can prevaricate. So they ask to see the two earls, and on their third full day in Paris they are taken to the prison where Montagu and Ufford languish.

Harry is struck by how terrible both the earls look when they're brought into the receiving room. Some of the English men-at-arms accompanying them actually gasp: Montagu and Ufford are filthy, with cracked lips and sores on their wrists and ankles from ropes. Montagu seems to have aged ten years in the past few weeks, and one eye is badly infected from a wound sustained during capture. Ufford is angry, yelling at everyone, telling them he's an earl and needs to be treated as such. Montagu is no less furious, but he's unwell and clearly conserving his energy. Other than Montagu's bad eye, their bruises and cuts from capture outside Lille seem to be healing, though it's hard to tell under the prison dirt.

Their men-at-arms give them beer, decent food and clean clothes.

The whole time, Montagu is watching Harry, his eyes malevolent.

'What?' Harry says finally.

'The French have the Devil himself fighting with them. And yet you keep escaping his grasp,' Montagu says, digging hungrily into the bread and cheese they have brought. 'If I didn't know better, I'd say you had switched sides.' It's said lightly, like a joke, and the Bishop even laughs.

But Montagu doesn't joke about things like that.

'Well, my lord, you see,' Harry smiles back, 'I know the Devil of old. Helped him out once.'

Rabbie glares. 'You know who he is.'

'Who *who* is?' Harry asks, innocently, reaching for a piece of cheese off Montagu's plate. 'I've been at war for England for seven straight years, my lord. I was bound to meet the Devil sooner or later.'

Montagu snorts, and bats Harry's hand away from his food. 'When can we go home? Are their terms reasonable?'

'We're working on it,' sighs Geoffrey, 'and no.'

'God damn it!' Rabbie howls, slamming his fist onto the table. 'They put me in a *cage*. Paraded us through the Paris streets like dogs. Peasants threw night soil at us!'

Harry holds up his hands, palms towards Rabbie, with a calm expression on his face. 'I remember Lord Montagu once telling me that a cage was the safest way to transport a prisoner. Perhaps we have more in common with our French cousins than we thought.'

Rabbie stands up and throws the stool he was sitting on against the stone wall, his face choleric with fury.

As prison guards rush in to investigate the noise, Geoffrey Scrope rises. 'I'm sorry, milords, we must leave now to attend our afternoon negotiating session.'

They make arrangements for men-at-arms from the English party to visit the two earls daily with better provisions, and then they depart.

Montagu's eyes never leave Harry. Harry shivers, despite himself.

The English party eats in a lower hall than the King's great hall with its vast black marble table. It's not an insult, for their lesser hall is also the dining place of the French knights and senior household officials. But it isn't an honour either. Harry itches to catch a glimpse of Philip and his retinue, but the royal family remains entirely separate from them.

Every corner of the palace blooms with the possibility of Iain. In the soft Parisian French of the courtiers' speech, which reminds Harry so achingly of Iain's wry turn of phrase. In a pair of broad shoulders seen amidst a distant knot of courtiers;

in a dark head thrown back and laughing. Iain always had so much *life* in him, so much passion. Harry sees tantalising hints of it among the courtiers of the palace, but upon closer examination they all fade into shadows, dim and insubstantial, against his memory of Iain's fire.

The aides that guide them around the palace have to chivvy Harry along multiple times when his eyes grow unfocused, looking across a courtyard or down a hallway at groups of young, bright noblemen.

And then he's denied the use of the garden for a few days. King Philip is back from checking on construction work at Vincennes. The already not-inconsiderable population of the Palais de la Cité doubles overnight, the royal party overflowing across courtyards and parterres. For Harry, it means there are even more people to look at who could be Iain, but on second glance are not.

It's driving Harry mad. It's *all* driving Harry mad: being in the middle of this massive city. Being followed everywhere by well-meaning but stifling aides. The rigorous stratification of the great French palace. The formal negotiation process, which drags on and on without visible movement.

After ten days, he snaps. When the priests once again say they cannot lower the ransom because of 'considerations', Harry slaps his hand on the table between them and demands to know *what* considerations exactly, especially given that both earls are wallowing in filth in a common prison after a gruelling and humiliating journey across the country.

'If you don't know, then perhaps you are not the right people to negotiate with,' the younger priest responds stiffly, looking down his Roman nose at Harry.

Harry glances at Geoffrey, who surprisingly doesn't lay a cautioning hand on him. The lawyer must be as tired as Harry of the French obfuscation. 'Well, you're not actually negotiating, so perhaps we should petition King Philip for other representatives,' Harry growls.

The older priest points at Harry. 'Ah-ah, young man. This is not the time to be pushy. We could send these men to the law courts and they would be tried and hung for murder. If you want them back, you pay not the cost of their ransom, but of their crimes. And believe me, you are getting them cheaply.'

The Bishop of Lincoln leans forwards, brow furrowed. 'Pardon. I got lost along the way somewhere. What are their crimes?'

The younger priest spreads his hands and looks heavenwards. The judge, however, shuffles the papers in front of him and begins to read. 'William Montagu and Robert Ufford did plot to murder Queen Marguerite of France, eldest child of Philip the Fair, and her son, Seonaidh mac Maíl Coluim, called Prince Iain of Galloway, in order to instigate war with France.'

'Hogwash,' says the Bishop of Lincoln. 'You lot sent a squad of knights and mercenaries over to kill the boy.' He turns to Harry. 'Didn't they?'

'We have a witness,' says the judge, steepling his fingers.

'I would like to speak to this witness,' Harry says, before he can even think about it.

'Alas,' says the older priest.

The younger priest leans forwards and jabs his finger in Geoffrey's direction. 'These men have royal blood on their hands. They must pay our full ransom, from their own lands and purses, or we will hang, draw and quarter them for their crimes against France.'

The older priest pats the young one on the arm, in a ham-fisted attempt to calm him, as if he were one of the little lap-dogs that are in fashion with the French court ladies. 'Beh,' the old priest says. 'This sort of machination is to be expected, but the trouble is, they have been caught, no? So now they pay.'

'Oh, and once released they must never return to France, on pain of arrest and death,' says the judge.

'We will retire for the day,' says Geoffrey. 'We must discuss this.'

The three of them go back to their chamber, bidding their aides goodbye until they are fetched for supper. '*English*,' Geoffrey orders. '*And stay away from the windows and doors.*'

'*This is*,' whispers the Bishop of Lincoln, '*a farce.*'

Harry sighs, perching on a chest and leaning his head back against a bedpost. '*It's all true. I witnessed it too.*'

Geoffrey and the Bishop fall silent and turn slowly towards Harry, their eyes full of questions.

'*I rode with Montagu and Ufford into Scotland after Halidon Hill. I was there when they killed Marguerite and everyone else in her castle except Iain. That's how he ended up as my squire.*' Harry scrubs his hands through his hair. '*I also overheard Montagu and Ufford talking about pushing for war with France so they could gain lands over here. I don't think that's much of a secret, though.*'

Geoffrey pulls a bench over in front of Harry, the wood scraping across the stone floor. He sits on it, putting himself in Harry's field of view. '*Harry, do you have any proof that Montagu killed Suo—, uh, Sine—, ah, the Scottish boy?*'

'*I don't think Iain is dead,*' Harry whispers. '*As to who paid for him to be attacked, I have a former vassal who now sails out of Plymouth harbour. He saw a man of Montagu's description checking Iain's body and paying off the boat that took him to France.*'

'Hmm,' says Geoffrey.

Harry waves his hand, as if shooing away a fly. '*So no, I don't have any real proof of any of this. That's why I've never acted on it.*'

'*Christ's blood,*' sighs Geoffrey. Then, to the Bishop, '*Sorry, Your Excellency.*'

'*Find the boy,*' says the Bishop. '*Find him and we can make a real case for them having to pay that ransom. We can't leave them here, although a silk rope might be kinder in the end than the way the French are planning to bankrupt them.*'

'*But we're at a stalemate until we find the boy,*' Geoffrey agrees. '*I need a drink.*'

Harry doesn't move; just keeps staring up at the ceiling. '*The boy is a man now. And I don't think he wants to be found.*'

'*For England's sake,* try,' hisses the usually mild-tempered Bishop.

'*I have been,*' Harry growls back. '*I* have *been.*'

'*What can we do to help?*' Geoffrey asks. '*What do you need?*'

Harry throws up his hands. '*A miracle. Or for us to get close to King Philip and his retinue. If Iain is anywhere, it's with them.*'

They all agree it would be wise to take a day's break from the negotiations. Harry nearly falls apart when the Bishop takes him aside and says, '*I only met the boy briefly, with the King, but he was the full measure of what a knight should be. As are you.'* Then the man winks. *'I can't promise miracles on command, but Geoffrey and I have been known to do the impossible before.'*

Then they both vanish to the depths of the palace, leaving Harry alone – or as alone as he can ever be, with a French courtier hovering outside his door.

Having nothing else to do, Harry wanders outside for a walk in the afternoon sunshine, trailed by the inevitable aide. To his delight, he finds the palace gardens have reopened, and he goes inside.

The aide waits a polite distance away as Harry finds his favourite bench. The rose hedge behind the bench is fully in flower, and the rich perfume of its crimson-and-white *rosa mundi* sends Harry tumbling into memory. First of his mother, who loved roses and kept beautiful lemony-white ones lining the kitchen gardens. And then of Iain, bright and passionate like the vermilion in the rose.

He feels his eyes grow wet and he asks the aide for a few minutes alone to pray. The man nods and backs off further, to the end of the garden path. It's an excuse, just something to get a moment of privacy, but as Harry sits there he finds he really does want to pray.

He pulls a rose down to him, careful to leave it on its stem so it may continue to grow, and he breathes in the heady scent. 'Iain,' he says softly. '*If you're in heaven, I cannot let you go. I keep seeing you, trying to put you back in the world by sheer force of desire. I saw you in the Black Knight, and I feel like every step I make in this palace I am walking in your footprints. If you really* are *here, please know that I still love you more than anything in the world, and would make any sacrifice to have you with me again.*' He shuts his eyes. '*And if you are but a spirit, protecting me, thank you for that. I have needed it. I have always needed you.*'

Tears are coursing down his cheeks, hot and wet, and Harry wipes them away, fearful of who might see.

There's a rustle in the rose bush behind him.

He freezes. The sound he heard was too loud, too wrong to be a bird.

Harry whirls to his feet and sticks his hand into the hedge. He had expected there to be a wall behind it, but no, the rose hedge *is* the wall.

The aide comes running back down the path towards Harry. 'Sir Harry! You mustn't do that! It is forbidden,' the man admonishes, his voice sharp with second-hand shame.

Harry yanks his hand out of the hedge. He notices idly that it has several deep scratches from thorns. Bright red pearls of blood begin to well up as he stares. 'I— I'm sorry,' he says. 'I heard a noise and it surprised me.' He smiles weakly. 'Battle reflexes,' he says by way of explanation. 'What lies behind the hedge?'

The aide scrunches his face in discomfort. 'Those are the private royal gardens, Sir Harry. We do not look towards them nor do we reach into them, unless we have a very great desire to lose our hand.'

Harry's face reddens in embarrassment as he is led away from the bench, probably never to be allowed near it again.

'Are you worried the King overheard your prayer?' the aide asks.

'No. I prayed in English,' Harry says.

'Pfft,' the aide snorts. 'Then God did not hear it either, for He does not speak the vulgar tongue.'

'So that was the King or Queen,' Harry says, 'on the other side of the roses.'

The aide shrugs, relaxing considerably as they leave the area without further incident. 'The Comte de Marche also has use of the royal gardens, but you would have heard him,' the aide says. 'Where he goes, a party always follows.'

Harry forces a smile. 'A party sounds wonderful. Any chance of wrangling an invitation?' He says it half in jest, but still.

The aide purses his lips. 'Undoubtedly one will be thrown to celebrate your departure,' the man says.

Geoffrey Scrope comes through, however.

There is a royal banquet at Fontainebleau the next day, and the English are invited.

They stop on the way out of Paris to check on Ufford and Montagu. Both look much better. Clean clothes, water for washing and decent food have done wonders to bring them back to themselves. Geoffrey gives them hope, saying the negotiations are almost finished. He mentions the invitation to Fontainebleau as an example of how well they are doing.

Rabbie is overjoyed, and pesters them for more details. But Montagu remains reserved. Something about that nags at Harry.

Their little party arrives at Fontainebleau shortly before supper is to begin, and they rush to clean themselves and change. Harry is struck by the beauty of the ancient edifice as they ride into its oval courtyard. Fontainebleau is a pleasure palace, built without thought of fortification. No such thing exists in turbulent young England; indeed, the very concept unsettles Harry.

'Philip the Fair's favourite palace,' Geoffrey says, a smile playing across his lips as he watches Harry take in the sprawling yet harmonious building. It's a wonder to look at, its architecture a song of elegance and sophistication.

'I can see why,' Harry whispers.

The hall is crowded. Three hundred knights and nobles are in attendance, and there is a full schedule of games, music and amusements. Harry idly wonders if their fool will pretend to be the English king. He smirks. Probably not. That would just be rude.

They take their seats towards the middle of the hall, joining a small company of French knights who all stop what they're doing when Harry sits down. It's brief, but Harry sees the flicker of tension and recognition that passes across the men before they resume their conversations. The knight next to Harry shakes his head, a small private smile on his face, as he reaches for the wine jug at the middle of the table.

There are also a few clergymen at the table, old friends of the Bishop who embrace him enthusiastically, and an elegantly dressed countess who winks at Geoffrey Scrope and kisses him on both cheeks.

Harry's mind is still turning over the actions of the French knights when the man next to him elbows him and offers him wine.

Harry nods. Then his brow furrows. 'Do we know each other?'

The knight chuckles to himself. After pouring Harry's wine and more for himself, he puts down the jug and places his hands in front of his face, cutting off all view except a small slit for his eyes. 'Perhaps I am more familiar like this,' the knight says.

Harry can't help the snort of laughter that escapes him. 'You had a lance. Near Péronne, when I was being a fool.'

'Ah, you have a good memory,' the man smiles. 'Charles de Rochefort, at your service.'

'Where's your friend?' Harry asks, motioning towards his chin with the international symbol for *the one with the beard*.

'Having a baby,' the Chevalier de Rochefort sighs. 'Louis has five daughters. He thinks his wife is spiting him because he's never home for the births. So this time, he returns to his estates.'

Harry raises his cup. 'Good luck to him.'

'Indeed,' says the Chevalier. 'Santé.'

A bell rings, a steward calls, and they stand for King Philip and Queen Joan. The King is small and slight, but good-looking in a dark way. Harry can see a slight family resemblance in his cleft chin and blue eyes, but he has none of the height of the main branch of the Capets, nor the breadth that apparently comes from intermarrying it with Scottish lords.

The King and Queen sit down. A flute sounds, and musicians file out as servants unroll a large tapestry of the hunt along one wall.

Twelve men step in front of it, costumed as rare birds in feathered tunics and elaborate masks that cover their entire heads. As the music begins, they flow into an elaborate dance, posing at certain intervals into clever and picturesque tableaux.

'Who are they?' whispers Harry to the Chevalier de Rochefort.

'The young quality,' Rochefort whispers back. 'Mostly the sons of France's great dukes and counts, plus some relatives of the King.'

It's hard to see anything specific about the dancers. The feather tunics are split down the sides, but reach at the front to each dancer's knees. The headdresses cleverly obscure the actual height and physique of the wearer.

Harry points to what appears to be the tallest dancer, who wears the mask of the black swan and dances with an easy elegance. 'And who is that one?'

'Ssh,' Rochefort says, pulling away. 'They introduce all the participants when the game is over.'

Harry finds his eyes can't leave the black-clad dancer. Something in the way he moves is achingly familiar. He wonders, if after all these years, it will really be this easy. That Iain is here, at the French court, warm and safe and alive, participating in the *ludi* like any proper young nobleman of his class.

The dance ends and, after the applause, the dancers reveal themselves. The black swan takes off his headdress to reveal dark, Moorish skin and brown eyes.

Harry briefly lets his heart grieve for its little fantasy, before turning to Rochefort and asking for more wine.

At that moment, Harry hears the great hall door opening. The King looks up, a broad smile crossing his face. 'Cousin, you are late as usual,' King Philip calls out fondly. There's the answering laughter and calls of a group of bright people, high on their own youth and the possibilities before them.

Rochefort whispers in his ear, 'The Comte de Marche, and sober for once, it appears.'

Harry turns in his seat to look at the group, but in the end he doesn't notice them, the young lords and fashionable ladies preening their way down the main aisle like a muster of peacocks.

Because there, in the middle of them all, is Iain.

Iain is in brown and scarlet, his jacket belted low and a little longer and looser than the skintight styles of his friends. His hose are scarlet silk, so fine they are almost transparent, and his long hair falls in waves to his shoulders.

Harry starts shaking, his breath too shallow, not enough.

He watches Iain as he struts towards the King, that rolling limp-strut he's had since Ufford broke his leg so many years ago, when Harry was innocent but thought himself wise.

Iain has lost the fullness of youth in his face and it's now all angles and shadows, framed by his jacket's high neck. He is so beautiful it's painful. Harry watches him kiss King Philip's cheek, watches how Iain's scarlet hood slips as he bends over. His body is not the body of an idle, drunken court fop, Harry thinks to himself, despite the clever drape of his clothes to hide the breadth and strength in his shoulders, the slight fullness in the sleeves to disguise the thickness of arms used to wielding a broadsword. His knight's belt accentuates the slimness of his hips, and his long jacket disguises the power in his thighs.

Harry presses a hand to his chest, willing his heart to slow its gallop. He is drawn like a magnet to Iain. Everything in him tells him to stand up, to go to his love, but he can't. They are separated by a gulf of a hundred yards and five social classes. Harry deliberately looks down, fixing his gaze on his splayed hands on the table, trying to calm himself.

'Harry?' says Geoffrey, quietly.

'Uh,' Harry replies, glancing up at the lawyer and switching to English. '*That's him, in the brown and scarlet. With the King.*'

Geoffrey merely smiles at him, his gaze travelling slightly above Harry's eyes.

And Harry suddenly knows that Iain is right behind him. He can feel the warmth of another person at his back, and it could be anyone. But he knows it isn't. When a gentle hand falls on his shoulder it's all he can do not to jump right out of his skin. Instead he turns and looks up, his eyes meeting pale-silver ones. There are lines at the corners of them that weren't there before, Harry thinks.

They both stare at each other for a long moment, speechless. Iain's friends call to him, 'Jean, come here, leave the Roastbeefs alone.' They're eager to bring him back to their little party, and Iain acknowledges them with a wave. As he reaches over Harry for their wine jug, he whispers, '*Later.*'

Iain snags the wine jug, then struts back to his group, calling out in a rough, low rasp, 'I wanted to see the English.'

'And steal their wine,' calls back one of the girls.

Iain shrugs and smiles. 'It's wasted on them. I hear they only love beer.'

Iain's voice disturbs Harry. It's not the same; he should have a beautiful, soft baritone, not this sandpaper, this scrape of rusty hinges.

Harry couldn't say how the rest of the dinner passes. He makes appropriate noises at appropriate times, and tries not to stare at the young, fashionable group surrounding Iain. Though, at one point, the Bishop has to rap him over the knuckles with his eating knife, after Harry's mind (and eye) wanders too long.

The Chevalier de Rochefort, to his right, seems amused by all of it, and steadfastly dodges Harry's questions about the Comte de Marche. 'Oh, we see him at court. He's very popular.

No, he doesn't fight, unless you count his ongoing war against his own liver.'

After supper they are shown to their chamber by an aide. Fontainebleau is far enough outside Paris that they will return in the morning; in order to arrive in time for the supper they had left the Palais de la Cité before dawn. The room is far larger and more luxurious than their cramped box in the Palais, but as Harry goes to put his bags down the courtier stops him. 'Ah, you are to come with me, Sir Harry,' the man says.

Harry follows the aide through the corridors of the palace, across a courtyard and to an upper level significantly fancier than the guest quarters they'd been assigned.

The aide leads him through a small antechamber then stops in front of a carved door, bright with gilding. 'You will stay here tonight, if you wish,' the man says, a certain note of disapproval in his voice. He opens the door slighrly, not enough to see inside, but enough to check that it isn't locked.

Harry nods. 'Thank you,' he replies.

The aide sniffs and then leaves him there, disappearing down the lamp-lit hall.

Harry takes a deep breath and goes in, shutting the door behind him as quietly as he can. He looks up at the warm glitter of candlelight off gilded ornamentation.

Part of his mind registers that it's the most beautiful room he's ever seen, rich with tapestries and carved decorations on the wall, and cobalt-blue velvet curtains around the bed.

The other part can only see Iain, lounging on that bed with a nervous look on his face.

Once Harry locks the door behind him, Iain rasps, 'Hello, Harry.'

Harry's saddlebags reach the ground at the same time he reaches Iain. He can't figure out what to do, because Iain's real and alive and still wants to see him, but he settles on throwing his arms around him and hugging him as hard as he can.

Iain's body is thick and strong under Harry's arms and Harry shakes, years of terror and grief and exhaustion falling off him like a cocoon of ashes.

'How?' he says, his own voice cracking into nothingness, unable to hold all the emotion behind that single word.

Iain doesn't answer, but his eyes are deadly sombre as he slowly slips off his hood and unbuttons his jacket. He discards those garments casually, onto the floor, as if they were dirty work clothes rather than the finest scarlets Harry has ever seen.

Then he takes off his linen shirt. He extends his arms out, displaying himself, displaying what became of the perfect, handsome boy Harry loved.

His body is a mass of scars. There is a particularly horrible one low on his neck, hollowed and twisting the flesh around it, and more on his arms and his chest. The old, silvered scars of the crossbow bolts that nearly killed him are overlapped by newer, pinker scars, from sword and lance.

'I—' Iain starts, then he coughs and touches the scar on his throat. 'I'm sorry,' he says, barely above a whisper. 'When they shot me, it destroyed my voice.'

'I'll sit closer,' Harry says, slipping out of his own jacket and hood and laying them neatly to the side of the bed. He sits down next to Iain, close but not touching, unsure how they relate to each other now. He wants so badly to slip back into their easy physical familiarity, but while so much is the same with Iain, there is much that is different too. He's become a stranger whom Harry must relearn.

He looks up through his lashes and sees those pale eyes on him, staring at him.

'I want to explain,' Iain says.

'I don't care, Iain. You're *here*. It's like a miracle. You're here and Montagu is in prison and we both survived,' Harry breathes. 'We won. *You* won, because let's face it, I didn't do anything.'

'God's breath, five years later and you're still the biggest idiot who ever lived,' Iain rasps. Then he shivers, and Harry can see the blush of goosebumps on his skin, how erect his nipples are in the cold. 'Hold me,' Iain whispers, almost silently, head bowed. 'Nobody ever held me like you did.'

Harry throws his arms around Iain and pulls him down to the bed, and even though they're both older now, scarred and hardened to the cruelty of the world, they still fit perfectly together. Iain curls up into Harry, tucking his head in the crook of Harry's neck and throwing a leg over his hip. Harry buries his nose in Iain's hair. Underneath the expensive perfumes, the lime and sandalwood, he smells as he always did: iron and musk and a certain sweetness, the smell of home.

'That was you, the Black Knight, wasn't it?' Harry whispers. 'My furious Lord Death.'

Iain hums and presses a kiss into the side of Harry's neck. 'The King knows, and four of my knights. Nobody else,' he whispers.

'Oh, look at you, you have *knights* now,' Harry says, unable to help falling into their old banter.

'Shut up,' Iain grumbles. Then his eyes brighten. 'How is Dartington? Alys and Annie and everyone?'

'Not pleased with me,' Harry admits, shame creeping into his voice. 'I didn't know what to do after you vanished. I thought you were dead. So I went to war. And stayed there.' He scratches at the stubble on his chin, which is most of the way to being a beard again. 'You don't have to think in war, the way you do in peace.'

Iain smiles and reaches out two fingers, touching Harry's short beard. 'I like this,' he rasps. 'You look tired.'

'I am. I think I've been tired for years,' Harry sighs. 'Oh,' he says, sitting up. 'Peter and Wat are well. Still at sea. Peter witnessed the mercenaries loading your body onto the ship to France. He saw Montagu pay off the captain. But he didn't know it was you until Arundel and I came looking.' Harry gazes at his love, the pale eyes and the scars and the muscles and the will, above everything else the *will* to keep going, not in the empty way Harry had, but ablaze, a spirit of vengeance. 'How did you survive? Other than out of sheer spite?'

Iain shakes his head and grins. 'It was mostly spite,' he confesses, in the sandpaper whisper that remains of his voice. 'That ship was supposed to deliver my corpse to Philip of Valois. They assumed I wouldn't live out the day.' Iain smirks, a bitter little twist of his lips. 'But I did.'

He reaches out and laces his fingers in between Harry's then, and Harry squeezes gently. It's either that or tackle him to the bed and hold him and never let go.

'I was unconscious for a long time. I was later told the ship's captain was horrified to find he might have royal blood on his hands. He patched me up as best he could at sea, and then ditched me at a monastery outside Regnéville-sur-Mer. My recovery took almost a year. Perhaps my voice might have healed if I were elsewhere, but the monks had vows of silence.'

Iain brushes at his cheek and Harry is surprised to see wetness there. 'I couldn't come back,' he says, the words barely understandable, his ruined voice even rougher than usual. 'Aside from the danger to me, Montagu would have killed you. He wouldn't have stopped, Harry. Believe me. Even though it destroyed my heart, I had to stay away.'

'I know,' Harry says, and on impulse he leans in to kiss the wetness off Iain's cheekbone. It's chaste and quick, no more than the touch of a butterfly's wing, and Iain doesn't flinch away.

'Eventually I was well enough to travel. I rode to Paris and presented myself to King Philip.' His smile is bashful now. 'I became his rural cousin from a minor branch of the family, who nobody takes seriously: the Comte de Marche, a lush and an idle sybarite. Although,' he adds, indicating the luxurious chamber around them, 'Philip was kind enough to give me my mother's rooms.'

Harry lets go of Iain's hand and traces up his forearm, to the strong, corded muscles of his upper arm and shoulders. 'This is not the body of an idle man.'

'I invented a sickly relative,' Iain explains. 'I have to run back and attend this uncle on a regular and unexpected basis. My court friends can imagine nothing more *boring* than a backwater castle and a sick old man, so none come with me.' He pauses, and looks down at his hands, at the callouses from sword and shield on them. 'I practised for war, and I waited for my enemies to come to France. It was all I had. If I could destroy them, if I could avenge my mother and ruin Montagu forever, and if you could just manage not to get yourself killed, then perhaps one day we would be free.'

Harry surges over Iain's body and places a hand either side of him, boxing him in. 'That day is now,' Harry says, his voice thick with emotion. 'The ransom will bankrupt them. And England will agree to this ransom, if we can prove they're guilty of trying to kill you. Tomorrow, Iain. Come with us back to Paris. It's over. It's all over. It's all finally over.'

Iain whines and arches on his elbows, pushing himself up to kiss Harry. When they break the kiss, Iain breathes, 'Will you still have me, Harry? Scars and all?'

'Now who's the idiot?' Harry growls and lays the full weight of his body on Iain, pressing the hot stripe of his erection into Iain's abdomen. 'God's blood, Iain, do you even *know* how beautiful you are?'

'Show me,' Iain whispers, trailing his fingers down Harry's back. 'Show me.'

'This,' Harry says, twisting his hips so he can cup Iain's cock through that thin hose of his, 'you can't dress like this in front of me. Because I'll never be able to keep my hands off you. And if anyone else tries to touch you, I will hurt them.'

Iain is arching up into his touch, rubbing himself to hardness against Harry's palm, the thin membrane of the hose slipping between them somehow making it more erotic than if Iain were naked.

Harry moans, and rolls away from him, standing up to quickly strip himself of his remaining clothes. They fall on the floor next to Iain's. Then he leans over Iain and hooks his fingers into the tops of Iain's hose. Iain lifts his hips off the bed and Harry carefully rolls the hose down his legs as if he's unwrapping a present, which he is. He is.

Harry shakes his head, taking in Iain's hardening cock, his half-lidded expression, the tongue that wets his lips. 'It feels like I left you yesterday,' Harry says. 'As if the years apart existed only as a terrible dream.'

Then he climbs back up over Iain. 'I had fantasies about you,' he breathes, kissing his way up Iain's body, 'in that black armour.'

Iain's eyes are wild now, and he twists his fingers in Harry's hair. 'It's the only time I am myself,' he says. 'Here, I am surrounded by idiots, and have to pretend to be the biggest idiot of them all. By all that's holy, Harry, fuck me. Fuck me until I remember who I am.'

'I presume the court lush has . . . ?' Harry asks, raising an eyebrow.

Iain reaches down the side of the bed with one of his thick arms and pulls a small vial off the shelf of wood created by the mattress frame. 'The court lush has a terrible habit of not being able to get it up when drunk, but he's very good with his fingers and he begs the ladies not to reveal his shame,' Iain confesses. 'He does what is needed to maintain his image, and makes sure nobody gets any bright ideas about him being a good candidate for marriage.'

'So you haven't . . . ?' Harry says.

Iain shakes his head. 'The last person to make me come was you. I've pleasured myself, of course, but there's been nobody else.'

'I lost all interest, for years,' Harry mumbles. 'Barely did that, until I got stupidly hard the morning after a narrow escape from the Black Knight.'

Iain snorts. 'Oh, Harry, you're giving me all sorts of ideas—'

Then Harry presses two oiled fingers against Iain's hole and his eyes flutter shut, a breathless moan escaping his lips. And God, it's so easy with Iain, laughing and fighting and fucking and somehow doing all three at once, here in a queen's bed-chamber in France, after they've both lived more lives than any one person has a right to hope for.

Iain is so tight, tighter than Harry remembers, and Harry is reduced to babbling nonsense at him, how gorgeous he is, how much he loves him, as he fingers Iain open and kisses every scar that's been laid on him. Iain's face is transformed by ecstasy, beautiful in the way angels are, perfect and terrible. Harry decides he's waited too long already, years too long, and throws Iain's legs over his shoulders as he presses his oiled cock against Iain's hole.

'Are you ready?' he says, breathless with the need to be inside Iain.

Iain just nods, licking his lips.

And Harry presses inside him, achingly slowly, gazing into his eyes the entire time. Iain starts to shake, little involuntary shivers, as Harry pushes deep inside. Harry shuts his eyes for a moment and just lets himself be. He feels like he's cracking apart inside, the already overwhelming stimulation of Iain under him, around him, stripping him of all his dead years.

Then Iain grabs Harry's backside, digging his hands in so hard it hurts, and he *snarls*. In his ruined voice it's a truly otherworldly sound, and Harry pulls out and punches back into his lover.

Iain tries to yell, but nothing comes out. 'Again,' he mouths.

And Harry leans down to bite at Iain's lips, at the cleft in his chin, as he fucks into him as hard as he can. He'd thought so much of what it would be like to find him again, what they would do, and in his head it was slow and gentle but it's not; now that Iain is really there all he wants is to take him as hard and fast as possible, mark him, reclaim him.

Harry reaches a hand down between them and grabs Iain's cock, not so much stroking him as holding steady as he ploughs into him, rocking him so hard that the motion caused by his thrusts makes Iain's cock slide forwards in his palm. Iain's hands have fallen away from his arse and are fisting the bedsheets now, halfway to tearing them, as he bites his bottom lip and thrusts back against Harry. Harry can feel Iain's orgasm building in him, the way his cock jerks, the stream of precome flowing from it, and Harry urges him on, moving his hand at last, stroking Iain relentlessly in time to the snapping of his hips.

Iain clenches around him and comes with a soundless shout, and Harry follows a few thrusts later, flooding Iain's hole, shuddering with an ecstasy so sharp and overwhelming it's almost like pain.

They slump onto the bed afterwards, entwined, still breathing each other in. And though the sex was amazing, and even more so when they wake up in the middle of the night and do it all again, slower, Harry lying on his side and rocking into Iain from behind, the greatest gift of all is waking up with Iain in his arms. Iain with his squinty sleep face and messy hair and stubble, still as grumbly as ever about mornings, for Harry to kiss awake slowly but surely. The scar on his neck. The cleft on his chin. The little divot where his shoulder muscle meets his collarbone. His nipples, perking into erectness under Harry's tongue. His broad, scarred chest, the flat, solid muscle of his abdomen, and the dark trail of hair that leads lower from there. His arse. Harry wants to get Iain on his knees and eat his arse for days.

There is a knock at the door and the sound of a tray being left in the antechamber outside. Iain whistles his thanks to the servant as he rolls out of bed. He stretches, flexing his muscles like a big cat, and then puts his hand on his lower back. He smirks at Harry. 'Going to be feeling you all day,' he rasps.

And doesn't that make Harry's cock twitch with interest.

Harry bites his lip. 'Stop it, or we'll never leave this room.'

Iain laughs, mostly silently, then begins washing himself in the basin. He changes the water from the pitcher and then pulls Harry towards him, dipping the cloth in cool water and wiping the come and sweat off Harry's stomach. The cloth travels lower, and Iain gently and lovingly cleans Harry's cock and balls, and between his legs. Harry has to lean in and kiss Iain, his heart swelling at the tender expression on his love's face.

'Will you come with us back to Paris?' Harry asks. 'Geoffrey Scrope and the Bishop of Lincoln want to meet you.'

Iain nods. 'Go out once you're dressed,' he says. 'Find an aide. Make it seem as if I've had a tumble with you then discarded you. I'll meet you in my own clothes on the Paris road in an hour.'

Harry's brow furrows, but Iain places his thumb on the little line and rubs it until Harry relaxes. 'I spent a long time building up the Comte de Marche,' Iain explains softly. 'I don't think it's wise to discard him just yet.'

Harry acquiesces, and kisses Iain one last time before pulling on his clothes and leaving.

He manages to blush when stopped by a servant. It's easy enough; the man is aghast at finding an Englishman so far into the royal quarters. He manages to blush again when he is taken back to the guest chambers, surprising Geoffrey and the Bishop at their breakfast.

'*Where have you been?*' the Bishop gasps.

'*Finding the boy,*' Harry says, trying to sound as nonchalant as possible, and not like a man who's just been reunited with the love of his life and then ploughed him senseless several times during the night.

He obviously fails, because the Bishop raises his eyebrows, lets off a prim little, '*I see,*' and returns to his eggs.

Geoffrey opens his mouth to say something, but Harry interrupts. '*He's meeting us, outside Fontainebleau, and he's willing to come back to Paris with us.*'

'*Marvellous,*' says Geoffrey, pushing his plate away. '*We should get going anyhow. If we stop at the prison on the way back and get Montagu to confess, then there is no recourse. We agree to the ransom and return them to Flanders in time for the King's arrival.*'

Harry smiles as he grabs his things. '*If you let me take the lead today, I think we'll be able to surprise Montagu quite a bit,*' he says.

At first, the surprise is on Geoffrey, the Bishop, and their English men-at-arms, as they reach the Fontainebleau gatehouse.

As they pass outside the gates, a mass of darkness, huge and terrifying, silently detaches itself from the shadow of the outside wall. It's the Black Knight, on his ebony war-horse, shield with its bend sinister slung over his back, sword and dagger at his hips. And Harry remembers Iain's words: *I'll meet you in my own clothes*. Harry shifts in his saddle to quell the low spark in his groin and he thinks, *yes*, this is his Iain. Not the Comte de Marche with his showy fashions. This is what the Scottish boy was meant to become.

The Black Knight approaches them. Harry notes absently that the horse's tack is also black, and has been padded so it barely makes a sound. The men-at-arms who saw action on the Flanders border draw their weapons, crying out about an ambush. Even the French courtiers glance uneasily at each other, unsettled by the warlike apparition riding silently towards them.

Harry holds up a hand, and spurs his palfrey between the Black Knight and the jittery, panicking men-at-arms. 'Stop,' he says. 'The Chevalier de la Mort comes in peace, to help us with the negotiations to ransom our two earls.'

The men aren't mollified, or happy about the situation, but they do sheath their arms. The French aides peek out the corners of their eyes at their war hero, so out of place against the delicate façade of the pleasure palace.

The ride to Paris passes in relative quiet, with the Bishop's few attempts to speak to the Black Knight met with silence or simple nods or shakes of the head. Harry rides next to Geoffrey, working out a plan as they approach the city.

They reach the prison in mid-afternoon, the sun already low in the sky. The warden begrudges letting them in this late, but a handful of gold gains them an hour with the prisoners.

As the earls are escorted into the meeting room, Harry notes that Montagu and Ufford look almost good. Their clothes are clean, their wounds more healed (though Montagu's left eye remains milky and sunken), and their bodies show the result of the English contingent's daily food deliveries.

Montagu's good eye sweeps over the English men-at-arms lining the sides of the room, then go to the French guards outside the doorway. 'Did you make progress at Fontainebleau?' the Earl asks.

'Eh,' Geoffrey grimaces. 'Not as much as we'd hoped.'

'Why is everything taking so long?' Rabbie snarls at the little, rumpled lawyer.

'France,' Geoffrey sighs. 'Everything is taking so long because of France.' He pulls up a bench and sits down. 'We hoped to petition the King directly last night at Fontainebleau, but we were without luck. My lord, they won't budge on this accusation that you killed both Marguerite and her son.'

Montagu's face wrinkles in disgust. 'It's lies. They're just trying to extort money from us, Geoffrey. I didn't kill Marguerite—'

Technically true, Harry thinks. It wasn't Montagu's sword, but it was his orders.

'—and I have no idea who killed the Scottish boy,' Montagu declares.

Also technically true, Harry admits. But still. For a moment, he allows himself to admire Geoffrey and Montagu facing off against each other, neither man lying, but each of them occluding the truth to their own advantage.

Montagu looks at Harry. 'You saw who killed the boy, didn't you? Haven't you given your testimony? I thought you told us they were French.'

'They were wearing fleur-de-lis surcoats,' Harry says. 'But

alas, they spoke French as Englishmen do. So I have not, in fact, given my testimony.'

Montagu slaps his hands on the wooden table; the manacles round his wrists rattle. 'Dammit, then, make them show their proof! Because they can't have any. There is no proof.'

'How do you know?' asks Geoffrey, his tone mild, curious.

But Montagu's response is cut off by a strange, rasping, spectral laugh from the doorway. The room falls silent, all eyes turning to the Black Knight as he steps into the room.

'And what the hell is *he* doing here?' Ufford says.

Montagu glares at Rabbie and shushes him, making a sharp, dismissive gesture with his hands.

'You want proof?' the Black Knight rasps, removing his helmet and mail hood in one go. 'I am your proof.'

Montagu turns white. Words tumble out of him before he can stop them. 'You're dead! I had you killed! I saw your body,' he shouts. 'You are *dead*!'

Ufford immediately flushes with terror and covers his face, looking at Montagu through his fingers. 'Shut up! Shut up, shut up,' he whimpers.

'Please identify yourself,' says Geoffrey, turning to the knight.

'I am Iain mac Maíl Coluim, Prince of Galloway, son of Marguerite of France, cousin to King Edward of England and King Philip of France. The French charges against Montagu and Ufford are true; I say so as witness to one murder and intended victim of the other.'

'Well, milord,' Geoffrey says to Montagu, drily, 'this is a bit of a conundrum. I do wish you hadn't admitted to regicide. Makes negotiations ever so awkward.'

'It's not regicide! He's not a king,' Ufford complains.

'Considering the very reason we're all in this Godforsaken country – other than allowing me the chance to take a side trip down to Avignon and visit His Holiness – is because our king is claiming the French throne via descent down the female line, and Iain here has the senior claim, it very much *is* regicide, I'm afraid,' says the Bishop.

Montagu pushes himself to his feet. His face is contorted in fury. 'I did what I had to, to preserve England. Everything I have done is for the good of King Edward. He *understands* that. He knows that this is also politics. So you can take your morals and your fair play and you can go to hell, because you certainly won't last very long in this world with them.'

'Be that as it may,' Geoffrey says, dusting off his tunic as he stands, 'I'm afraid we must go and speak to our French opposite numbers.'

But then Montagu glares at the chief of the English men-at-arms, a broad fellow with cauliflower ears, a scarred scalp and a big mace, and says, '*Slay them. Slay them all and I'll knight you and give you an estate in Devon, and I'll set the rest of you up with gold for life.*' The Earl then grins at Geoffrey. 'Better luck with the next negotiators.'

There's a moment where everyone glances at each other – *Montagu can't really be doing this, can he?* And Harry thinks, *of course he can*. These men-at-arms have been visiting the prisoner earls daily. They've had every chance for Montagu to drip his poison in their ears.

Harry's right. The nearest man-at-arms to the door kicks it shut and bars it, then they all slide their swords out of their scabbards. Other than the dozen soldiers Montagu has turned, only he and Iain carry weapons. Twelve on two.

Just like old times.

Iain and Harry draw their swords together, and the first man-at-arms hasn't even started moving forwards before he's got Iain's steel in his throat. Iain kicks the man's body off his sword, sending the dying soldier reeling into two of his compatriots.

Harry ducks under another soldier's thrust and stabs him in the forearm, nearly severing his hand. He doesn't have time to think before he has to block a wild slash from another man and then there is nothing but parry and cut and thrust, shoulder to shoulder with Iain, who is fighting with a dagger in one hand and his sword in the other.

The French guards are hammering on the door. Montagu, the coward, has backed against the far wall, but Rabbie flips over the table they were sitting at, kicking it at Iain, trying to knock him off balance. He succeeds, briefly enough that Iain takes a bad hit in the shoulder from the chief's mace and staggers. Harry manages to dispatch the man with the mace, with a sword through his mangled ear, *you'll get Dartington over my cold dead body*, but he can't stop Rabbie from throwing the chain of his wrist manacles around Iain. Rabbie tightens the chain around Iain's throat, trying to choke him.

There are too many men-at-arms, and Harry has Geoffrey and the Bishop of Lincoln behind him, unarmed. He can't leave them open to attack. Harry thrusts and parries and swears as a blade gets him in the thigh and something else punches him in the gut and knocks the air out of him. Then out of the corner of his eye he sees Rabbie fly over Iain's head and land on his back on the floor with a sickening *krak*.

Iain is across the room in a matter of moments, his dagger-point pressing into the sagging flesh under Montagu's chin. '*Stop!*' Iain hisses in his rough whisper. '*Put down your weapons.*'

'*He'll kill Montagu, you fools! Stop fighting! You've lost!*' Geoffrey calls out.

Harry sidesteps in the confusion and unbars the door, letting in the French guards and a very furious warden.

'What's gone on here?' screams the warden.

'Minor inter-English disagreement, my apologies,' Geoffrey says, gently righting the table that Rabbie had kicked over. 'All sorted now.'

'Yes, we'll just be going,' huffs the Bishop.

Iain merely smiles down at Montagu and, very gently, traces the point of his dagger along Montagu's throat, up his cheek and over his bad eye. It leaves a long red thread of welling blood. '*Something to remember me by*,' Harry thinks he hears Iain whisper. Then he sheaths his weapons and strides to where his discarded helmet lies on the floor.

'*My work has brought England from desolation to near greatness*,' Montagu hisses. '*Without me, the country will fall to pieces again. You are all* fools.'

'*Perhaps*,' Harry says as they leave Montagu and Ufford and the traitorous men-at-arms in the hands of the warden. '*But I'd rather be a fool than a felon.*'

They reach terms with the French the very next day. Crippling, bankrupting terms, but terms nonetheless.

News comes that Edward has returned to Antwerp, defeating the French fleet en route. The Bishop heads south, to Avignon, but Harry's party swells by four as they travel northeast to Flanders: Iain joins them. He rides as the Black Knight, and brings with him three of his loyal knights. (The fourth, the Chevalier Louis Ney, is spending time with his newborn son.)

They reach Antwerp after a lazy four-day ride across France and then another three days through Flanders. Iain rides in a daze, confessing to Harry one night that he's lived so long for vengeance, he's finding it strange to figure out what's next, what there is other than the hunt. 'It will take me a while to believe it's really over,' Iain whispers, in the darkness.

'It is,' Harry says, stroking his fingers along Iain's back. 'You won.'

'Mm,' Iain mumbles. 'Just . . . I feel odd. I don't know what to do, now that I'm not angry any more.'

Harry's fingers move down to the cleft in Iain's bottom.

They find something to do.

The party of travellers arrive into the English camp with Iain under a white flag of parley, and Geoffrey immediately obtains an audience with the King. He stays long enough to see the look on Edward's face when Iain takes off his helmet. Then the lawyer bows, smiling, out of the King's bedchamber to leave them in privacy.

As always, Harry kneels in the presence of his king, but Iain remains standing. Edward strides up and embraces Iain.

'Cousin,' Iain rasps. 'Please excuse my voice. Crossbow bolts make terrible surgical implements.'

Edward grins, and indicates that Harry may stand. 'We see the years haven't tamed you any.' Then his brows draw together. 'Out of curiosity, do you kneel for Philip of Valois?'

Iain shakes his head. 'Fret not. I only kneel for one man, and it is neither of you, my cousins.'

Harry ducks his head as he stands, hoping nobody notices either his blush or the twitching of his loins.

Edward laughs. 'Please don't tell us it's the King of Scotland. Our pride couldn't take it.'

'Not him,' Iain smiles.

And the King, damn him, glances directly at Harry. Harry's cheeks burn with the heat of fresh embarrassment. It's not made any better when the King continues to stare right at him and says, 'Whoever this man is, he is incredibly lucky, having you at his command.'

'He knows,' Iain says, a fond expression on his face. Then he fidgets, and paces away. 'I wanted to tell you I've formally abdicated any claim to the throne of France, legally, in front of Philip of Valois, in exchange for recognition, and my mother's titles and lands. I don't want to be a king,' he says in his broken whisper.

'We don't blame you,' Edward says, though his eyebrows are halfway up his forehead in surprise. 'What will you do after this? Are you staying on in France?'

'It depends on whether my business here is finished,' Iain replies.

'And what is that?' Edward asks.

'The destruction of William Montagu, Robert Ufford and the nine other knights who rode with him to Galloway to kill my mother and kidnap me,' Iain says. 'The knights are dead, mostly by my hand. Only the earls remain.'

The King tilts his head. 'You wish . . . Montagu's life?'

'No,' says Iain. 'I intend to do much worse than kill him.' He turns to Harry.

'There were actually twelve men with Montagu,' Harry explains. 'I was the twelfth. I asked Montagu afterwards why he had done this, and who Iain was. He said to me that this is what happens when power moves on and leaves people behind. That every hundred years Europe loses a third of its noble houses. That most don't fall very far, but some, like Iain's, fall very far indeed.'

'It is true,' Edward says softly. 'The turbulent reigns, like our father's, don't help with that. We are doing what we can to win back the loyalty of the people that Despenser and Mortimer ruined, but we can't fix all of it, much as we'd like to.' The King sighs. 'And we had hoped, during our reign, to avoid the sorts of men that destroyed our father's years as king. The men who claim to be for England, but in fact think only of themselves.'

Harry smiles, and finds himself a seat on a bench. He rifles in his saddlebags for the papers the French sent over. 'We did our best at the negotiation. However, the French could not overlook his and Rabbie's abuse of, and attempts to kill, a full-blood Capet heir. Montagu, through his own machinations, has put you deeply in debt to the French crown. His ransom is an extortionate amount of money. If you confiscate all of his and Ufford's lands to pay their ransoms, not only would it allow you financially to continue the war, I can pretty much guarantee Iain would be with me in Devon when the battles commence, rather than in black armour, fighting for the French.' Harry shifts, and hands over the parchment with the negotiation terms on it. 'The other condition of the ransom, of course, is that Montagu and Ufford never set foot in France again.'

Edward narrows his eyes, lowering himself carefully to sit at a campaign table. 'Your points are good. We will consider them.' Then he frowns. 'There is something we don't like, however.'

'What is it, Your Majesty?' Harry says.

'Your terms have averted a war and eliminated the enemy's greatest knight. And yet you ask no prize from this, Sir Harry? Are you sure? We badly need a new earl, to replace the two who have just rendered themselves useless.'

Harry shakes his head. 'An earldom is too much for a simple country knight like me.' Then he looks over at Iain, his voice growing thick. 'Besides, he kneels for me. What greater prize is there?'

'Indeed,' the King smiles, bright as a sunny day. Then his nose wrinkles, like a child denied a toy. 'Dammit, we need people like you. Both of you. You are interesting to us because you want nothing of us.'

Harry goes to refuse, but Iain gets there first. 'Yon great Sassenach idiot is too modest to ask to manage Rabbie Ufford's Devon lands for the crown. They border his, and honestly, there's nobody better.'

The King nods. 'So it shall be. We will send a man with the paperwork before the summer begins. And—' he pauses, tucking a lock of his strawberry-blond hair behind his ear— 'do think over our other offers. Not now. You both deserve your rest now.'

'You honour us, but . . .' Iain shakes his head. 'I will not fight against the French or the Scots. Not against my own people. However, if you need diplomats—' Iain glances over at Harry, who smiles his agreement— 'we would happily be of service.'

'Then let us embrace you both one last time, and wish you Godspeed on your journey home,' the King says.

Epilogue

Harry and Iain travel to Sluys to cross the Channel. Both are amazed by the sheer mass of English boats in the harbour. Harry recognises the *Halygast* and shouts for joy, dragging Iain along to see Captain Wekesa, and Peter and Wat.

And, surprisingly, the Earl of Arundel, whose friendship with the captain blossomed to the point that the *Halygast* became one of the lead cogs of the *ad hoc* English navy, and Wekesa's steady hand and wise strategy had helped secure victory against the French fleet.

They load Harry's roan destrier, Nomad, and Iain's black one, who Harry learns is called Nemesis, onto the *Halygast* and spend a pleasant four days pottering down the Channel under blue skies and fair winds to Plymouth.

When they arrive at Dartington at the end of the week, Annie takes one look at Iain, screams, and faints.

Iain jumps off Nemesis and picks her up, rasping at Harry to fetch a cool cloth.

Annie wakes up in Iain's arms, looks at him, and promptly faints again.

Alys comes out with little Joan and Iain clutching at her skirts. They are four and three now, and stare at the man their mother claims is their father with a mix of reverence and fear.

Alys hugs Harry, and pats him on the cheek. 'It's good to have you back,' she whispers in his ear. 'This before me is the man I married.'

'I'll go to war no longer,' Harry whispers back. 'I am yours, and Dartington's, and his, only.'

Alys breaks the embrace then, and looks over his shoulder at Iain. Harry turns too, and sees Iain's face, transformed, as he squats on the ground and beckons to the children.

Eventually, little Joan, the braver of the two, walks over to him.

'*Hello,*' Iain says. '*I'm your Uncle Iain. I can't speak very loudly so we have to whisper, like we're telling secrets. I'm going to teach you all sorts of terrible things to say in Gaelic. Would you like that?*'

Joan beams and grabs Iain's sleeve, before turning back to Alys and saying, '*Mummy! We have so much family now!*'

Harry's heart feels like it's going to swell straight out of his chest, with the way Iain is looking at his children, and Alys is looking at everyone.

Iain catches Harry's glance and ducks his head, embarrassed. 'I've taken lives for so long,' he rasps, his eyes wet. 'I forgot it's possible to make life, too.'

Iain refuses to let Piers and Bevis take the horses to the stables. He settles Nomad and Nemesis in their stalls himself. Harry goes to check on him ten minutes later, but quietly backs out again upon finding Iain, cheeks wet with tears, hugging Numbles while the old beast whickers happily and smears hay-slime all over his back.

Alys takes them both on a tour of the new hall, finished (finally) two years ago, soon after Harry had left for Antwerp.

Harry is frantic with embarrassment the entire time, and finally drags Alys aside, whispering to her that Iain has quarters at Fontainebleau Palace, so he's not going to be interested in Dartington's poky little improvements.

'But this is my home,' Iain says, coming up behind them silently. 'And I care greatly how it's been rebuilt during my long absence.'

Alys smiles and shows them the new, larger solar, with a lady's chambers and its own separate staircase. 'And I'm very glad I planned this, because I need my own space. Especially,' Alys says, indicating the cart overflowing with travelling chests in the courtyard, 'since it appears *someone* has more scarlets and silk hose than I have dresses.'

'Oh!' Iain says. 'Actually, most of that is for you and Annie and the children.'

Alys raises an eyebrow.

'After all, why be cousin to the King of France if you can't make use of his tailors?' Iain smiles.

'We're keeping him,' Alys says to Harry, her voice low and serious.

They all dash down to the cart then, unloading and breaking open chests. Harry hasn't felt this light in so very long, watching Iain and Alys argue with sharp good nature over whether a length of velvet would make a better dress or doublet.

Then Alys finds the chest containing the scarves and ribbons. Her brow furrows. 'Iain, why on earth do any of us need so much haberdashery? I, for one, have no intention of ever going to court again.'

'Well,' Iain whispers, in his rough, ruined voice, 'you're going to go through a lot of ribbons, because every time that great Sassenach idiot rides into a tournament he's going to need a favour.'

'Oh lord,' Harry groans. 'You're teaming up on me.'

And two bright, mischievous brunets look at him and grin. 'Who, us?' says Alys, her face innocent.

'We'd never,' purrs Iain.